The Stingray Shuffle

Also by Tim Dorsey

Florida Roadkill
Hammerhead Ranch Motel
Orange Crush
Triggerfish Twist

The
Stingray
Shuffle

A N O V E L

Tim Dorsey

wm

WILLIAM MORROW

An Imprint of HarperCollinsPublishers

HarperCollins books may be purchased for educational, business, or sales promotional use. For information please write: Special Markets Department, HarperCollins Publishers Inc., 10 East 53rd Street, New York, NY 10022.

FIRST EDITION

Designed by Richard Oriolo

Printed on acid-free paper

LIBRARY OF CONGRESS CATALOGING-IN-PUBLICATION DATA

Dorsey, Tim.
    The stingray shuffle : a novel / Tim Dorsey.—1st ed.
    p. cm.
    ISBN 0-06-052045-0 (hc.)
    1. Florida—Fiction.   2. New York (N.Y.)—Fiction.
I. Title.

PS3554.O719 S87   2003
813'.54—dc21

2002026431

03 04 05 06 07 WBC/RRD 10 9 8 7 6 5 4 3 2 1

For Kerry, Chris and Dinah

The only reason for time is so
that everything doesn't happen at once.
—ALBERT EINSTEIN

Either he's dead or my watch has stopped.
—GROUCHO MARX

Acknowledgments

Gratitude is due once again to my agent, Nat Sobel, and my editor, Henry Ferris, for throwing friendship in with the bargain.

The Stingray Shuffle

Prologue

*U*h-oh. *Lenny slipped me LSD.*
That can be the only explanation.

It's been nonstop hallucinations. Which normally I don't mind, but you wouldn't believe how it complicates trying to cross U.S. 1 against heavy traffic. I must have stepped off the curb and headed back about fifty times now. I think I'm in the Florida Keys.

I keep slapping the side of my head to make the visions stop, but it only changes the picture, like a slide projector.

Slap!

Carjackings, exploitation of the elderly, cigarette boats running from the Coast Guard, melanoma, tar balls, deed restrictions, beefy mosquitoes that crack windshields, Colombian shoot-outs, Cuban boycotts, Mexican standoffs, rampant-growth speculators, offshore-drilling lobbyists, cheap rum, cheaper motels, crack vials, condoms, mouse ears, Patrick Kennedy Smith, Phillip Michael Thomas, chicken wing restaurants featuring women's breasts . . .

Slap!

Shark attacks in two feet of water, barracuda jumping into boats and biting people, alligators roaming backyards and eating poodles named Muffins, college boys named Bo funneling beers on the beach and trampling sand castles and making children cry, broken-down cruise ships with decks full of irritable people from Michigan in puffy orange life preservers, the lottery won by a pool of 23 office workers who quit their jobs to become down-and-out junkies, trained seals playing *In-A-Gadda-Da-Vida* on bicycle horns . . .

Slap!

There. The hallucinations have stopped. I'm in the dark, now. I'm weightless, too. That's much better.

Whoops. Spoke too soon. The weightlessness is giving way. I'm starting to drop. Faster and faster. Free-falling toward a pinpoint of light. The light grows bigger, spinning off bright curved red swirls as I hurtle down this spiral chute like some hokey special effect from *The Twilight Zone*, or Jimmy Stewart in *Vertigo*; I'm helpless, this little black silhouette of a man, arms and legs flailing in a blizzard of chads, plummeting toward a haunting psychedelic pinwheel with the floating head of Jeb Bush in the middle . . .

The spinning has stopped. I'm coming out of the tunnel now. The LSD feels like it's wearing off, but the sky is still ten different colors and the clouds are whispering about me. Just ignore them or you'll end up doing something odd that will attract attention. Are we hungry? My skin is unusually sheen and agreeable. I want to raise my voice and croon the opus of life! . . . I can't think with all the people in my head talking at once! I need to call the room to order. . . . That's better. Next item of business? Yes, you in the back with your hand raised. . . . Why are we wandering in the middle of busy traffic? . . . Good question. How *did* we get out here? I thought we were still on the sidewalk . . . Well, what's done is done. Cars are whizzing by, so work with it . . . Try to get to the opposite curb. So what if that truck is coming? He'll stop because I will it. I am the master of time, space and dimension. Here we go: to the curb . . . See? The truck stopped. He hit that car when he swerved around me, but I've made my point . . . Where's that music coming from? It's The Doors, "People Are Strange." No kidding. The sound . . . it's coming from the sun. God's playing it on his personal hydrogen jukebox, the Big Puff Daddy-G layin' down the master moral rap and spinnin' the eternal hits, *If there's a rock 'n' roll heaven, you know they got a hulluva band!* . . . Oh, no, that horrible song is now stuck in my head. I must kill myself immediately. Damn that Lenny! . . . Wait. Who's Lenny? For that matter, who am I? Why can't I remember my name? And what the heck is this strange outfit I'm wearing? A royal blue jumpsuit with a NASA patch on the shoulder. Am I an astronaut? . . . Now I'm getting a shooting pain. It's coming from my forehead. What's this I feel up here? That's some huge knot you got on your dome—better have a doctor look at it. Maybe that's why I can't remember who I am . . . When in doubt, check your license. Let's see, is your wallet in this pocket? No, not there, but . . . what's this? A prescription bottle? Empty. Wow, that's some serious medication on the label; the guy who's taking this is one real sick-o. . . . Hold a sec. Could this be yours? The first name on the label is "Serge," but the last name has worn off. And the refill date was over a month ago. . . . Now it's starting to add up. This isn't LSD after all. It's not even a drug experience. That's the whole problem—you haven't *taken* your drugs. . . . Uh-oh, hallucinations again; the ground is starting to move. The road is rumbling and rising up. This is no ordinary street. It's a bridge. A drawbridge. Only one thing to do: hurry up and get to the lip of the span and hang on by hooking your arms through the grating. That way, when the span rises, you'll be way up at the top, above the hubbub, alone with some space to think and a clear view of the situation. . . . Here we go, up, up, getting pretty high now, nice panorama. Wish I had my camera. Why are all those people down there pointing at me? And who called the cops? Here they come again, drawing their guns as usual. Now I'll have to dive in the water for my getaway. All this stress can't be good . . .

Two weeks later.

An unconscious man in a blue astronaut jumpsuit lies facedown on the shore of a breezy mangrove island in the Gulf Stream. He's coming

around, talking in his sleep. *Jeannie! Come out of that bottle right now!*
His eyelids flutter in the sand, squinting at the bright sunlight. He
raises his head and sees hundreds of eyes staring back at him.

They're still here. What do they want from me?

Serge stands up.

"I told you. I'm having memory problems. I can only recall textbook
history, plus some stuff about a briefcase and a recent trip I took, but I
can't piece it all together yet."

The eyes silently stay on him. Some blink.

"Okay, okay. One more lesson."

Serge steps forward in the sand and spreads his arms in an encom-
passing gesture:

"Railroads had a seismic impact on the development of Florida,
beginning with the fabled East Coast line slashing its way through the
swamps a hundred years ago, opening up the bottom half of the state,
an unforgiving no-man's-land of eccentric pioneers, cranky Indians and
alcoholic hermits . . ."

Serge. Serge A. Storms. Wiry, intense, unhinged, standing on a
beach in the lower Florida Keys, leaves rustling in the salt wind, surrounded by his students, hundreds of small attentive monkeys.

". . . Then the railroads unveiled the fancy deco streamliners of the
1930s, introducing the northerners to frost-free vacations and society-
page beach sex in Palm Beach . . ."

Serge stops speaking. One of the monkeys in back is chattering.

"Buttons, please, I'm trying to talk up here."

The monkey stops chattering.

"Thank you. . . . As I was saying, the histories of the railroads and
Florida are inextricably entwined. By the end of the twentieth century,
Amtrak had unveiled its latest high-speed express train, *The Silver
Stingray,* for its New York-to-Miami route. The train didn't have the
same seminal influence on the state as its predecessors, but it played a
crucial role in one of the most infamous mysteries in the annals of
Florida crime. The missing briefcase with five million dollars. Remem-
ber? The one with the curse I was telling you about?"

The monkeys stare.

"It was a Wednesday. *The Silver Stingray* clacked down the tracks

on its regular afternoon run. The train entered a tunnel near a phos-
phate mine, and everything went dark. The train came out of the tunnel. Someone screamed! A body lay in the aisle of the dining car!"

Serge lies down in front of the monkeys for effect.

"The victim wore a blue velvet tuxedo and ruffled shirt, one of the
lounge reptiles entertaining the tourists on the trip south. It was murder! All the passengers eyed each other suspiciously. Who was the
killer? Was it one of the other performers in velvet tuxedos? The blues
singer from New York? The Russian? The Jamaican? Or perhaps one of
the women in that book club? And why? Did it have something to do
with the five million dollars rumored to be on board? . . ."

Serge stops talking again, his hyperkeen senses twitching. He
jumps up and runs to the edge of a mangrove outcropping, peering out
at the ocean through the branches.

"A boat's coming! Battle formations! . . ."

The race to invent the first mechanical orange harvester was on.

Dreams and designs for a mechanized citrus picker had been bandied about since the 1940s. But back then, it was science fiction stuff. Anyone who seriously thought it could be done was a laughing-stock.

Near the turn of the millennium, Florida's postcard orange groves had exploded into a six-billion-dollar-a-year industry. Meanwhile, technology had marched. Nobody was laughing anymore. A functional harvester seemed just around the corner. The state's top citrus barons were now so rich that they had almost everything they wanted. They were unhappy. They wanted to be as rich as oil people. A mechanical picker would do that.

Research teams from various nations labored at a feverish pace. Work proceeded in secret, along several different lines. The Swedes were considered to have the lead, advancing the spike-and-drum technique. The Germans placed their bets on hundreds of mechanical arms with spring-action picking fingers. The French used a shake-and-catch design with hydraulic trunk-grabber and retractable manganese skirt. The Japanese were working on something called the Centipede, which nobody knew anything about.

All four teams soon had models up and running. That was the easy part. The last big hurdle was efficiency. Every prototype up to now had either left too many oranges on the tree or squashed too much in the process. They had long since mastered the proverbial low-hanging fruit. The real test now was clean canopy penetration. The barons set a tolerance standard of ninety-five percent. The teams redoubled their efforts, improving performance, everyone getting closer. These were exciting times.

In January, the Japanese were rumored to have caught the Swedes. Competition became brutal. Engineers went without sleep, safety steps eliminated. Hammering could be heard from the German lab late into the night. The French argued. It was anyone's ball game.

Then, on a sunny spring day in 1997, word went out like a cannon shot. A prototype was ready. Dozens of limos quietly converged on a remote grove near the center of the state. Nothing but orange trees in all directions. There was a VIP tent, paddle fans, champagne on ice.

Just outside the tent, at the edge of the trees, a huge object sat under a white sheet. The German team approached the podium. Ludwig, head of design, leaned to the microphone.

"Behold! Der Shleimerhocken GroveMaster Z500."

Someone yanked the sheet, which flew off the device and fluttered to the ground.

The audience gasped.

A large, intricate cylinder imbedded with innumerable jointed metal arms and razor claws fanning in all directions, the gene splice of a carnival ride and Edward Scissorhands. A German flag on the side. The anticipation was unbearable. Ludwig walked to the GroveMaster, dramatically throwing a switch on the side, and it fell over, crushing him.

The Germans had a drawing board, and they went back to it. Work continued tirelessly. Various models and upgrades rolled out. Limos driving into the groves every few months, the barons increasingly bitter, the parade of failures reminiscent of newsreel footage from the early days of aviation—the plane with the collapsing stack of eight wings, the bouncing helicopter-car, the man in bat wings jumping off a suspension bridge and flying like an anvil, the guy with ice skates and a rocket pack, who had to be extinguished with snowballs.

Word leaked out, bad press. Testing was moved to Clermont, for historic symbolism. The demonstration site was in the shadow of the world-famous Citrus Tower, built in 1955 in the rich-soiled, rolling grovelands where it had all started. At least they used to be grovelands. Most of it had been bulldozed for sprawling developments of identical homes and screened-in pools built on top of each other. It was enough to make a baron cry. They needed a harvester now!

The French were next. "Gentlemen—I give you zee Terminator."

The sheet flew off.

A *War of the Worlds* contraption stood on spider legs. A man named Jacques picked up a radio control box and pressed a button. Yellow lights that looked like eyes came on. The device began chugging. Smoke puffed out a chimney. Jacques turned a dial. The machine chugged faster, springing on the spider legs. He turned the dial some more. The legs started clomping up and down, slowly at first, then at a brisk, running-in-place clip.

Jacques moved the joystick on his box. The device began running. The wrong way. It ripped up the spectator tent, flattening chairs and upending the punch bowl. Barons and politicians scattered through the groves, the Terminator running amok. It cornered one of the barons against a Cyclone fence and seized him around the waist with the hydraulic trunk-grabber, lifting him off the ground and squeezing until he squirted stuff. Then it shook the limp body a few times before dropping it in the self-cleaning metal skirt.

Talk about a setback. But there were others. A new and improved GroveMaster exploded in the German lab, unpleasant news photos of men fleeing in burning lab coats. A militant migrant group dynamited the Swedish lab. Then the French blew up their own lab with cooking sherry. But so close! Can't stop now. Work continued through the winter with smudge pots, icicles on the trees. Toes had to be amputated. Finally, spring again.

The Japanese were ready.

The barons had decided to move to the top of the Citrus Tower and watch through binoculars.

"Gentlemen—the Centipede!"

The sheet came off.

The Centipede ripped down three rows of trees, then left the grove and took off in the direction of town. The barons' binoculars swung around to the west side of the tower, toward the distant screams.

The resulting public outcry got the state into the act.

The foreign labs were closed down and a domestic contractor brought in. The contractor was well connected with state government. It had previously only stamped out interstate highway signs at twenty thousand dollars each but was able to convince officials that the technology was interchangeable. An appointed board quickly approved the no-bid contract. Work resumed.

The accidents stopped but not progress. It went backward. Picking efficiency dropped below sixty percent for the first time since 1980. Everything got behind schedule. Cost overruns, redundant parts, the device mutating into unworkable configurations without apparent design or goal. But political contributions were up, and the Florida Robotic Harvester program was considered a smashing success.

The barons were furious. They called in their own markers, and the state met behind closed doors to strike a compromise. It would offer the contractor an incentive. A harvester would be worth tens of millions of dollars a year to a private inventor. If it was made by a contractor working for the taxpayers, however, those rights reverted to the state. The deal: develop a functional prototype by the fall and keep all proceeds for the first three years. It was a fifty-million-dollar carrot. Everyone agreed.

Roscoe Weege was president and owner of Signs of the Times, the traffic sign company that was busy undeveloping the state's robotic citrus picker.

Roscoe was convinced the project was impossible, and he told the state he had complete faith in his workers. Roscoe's plan was to minimize costs, jack up expenses, and milk the thing as long as he could. What did he care? The quarter million a year in R&D seed money was chump change. Just keep up the appearance of work. He hired the remnants of the German team, ninety-year-old scientists who had come to the country in 1945 after the Americans beat the Russians to Peenemünde and scooped up all the best scientists. The Russians took the next bunch. Those that neither country wanted paid their own way to the States and now worked on the harvester. They gladly accepted Roscoe's fifty percent pay cut because it was that or face war trials at The Hague.

The harvester research was the redheaded stepchild at Roscoe's company. The real money was in his other contract with the Florida department of agriculture—an exclusive arrangement to provide the state with sterile Medflies in the event of another citrus infestation. Roscoe had studied the equation from ten different angles before offering the bribes.

The Medfly—now that was an organism Roscoe could respect. Short for Mediterranean fruit fly, the Medfly was a highly destructive, ambitiously reproducing little life bundle whose sole mission was to inject oranges and grapefruit with its eggs, which hatched and gorged themselves on the host fruit until they broke out and laid their own eggs. The buggers multiplied so fast that discovery of a single fly always set off statewide panic. That's why the groves were saturated with Medfly monitors, essentially the old Shell No-Pest Strip, little boxes with openings and sticky pieces of cardboard inside. In the mid-nineties, three Medflies were found in one of the monitors in western Florida, and the state immediately blanketed ten counties with a cheap insecticide that headed off the outbreak and gave people diarrhea and short tempers.

Roscoe was a visionary. He knew people wouldn't put up with that for long. There was another option to deal with Medflies, and even better, it was expensive. Sterile Medflies. The insects had ultrabrief life spans. Drop, say, a million sterile flies—outnumber the virile guys a hundred to one—and math would take care of the rest. Roscoe invited the key people to lunch, wrote the right checks, and soon he had his exclusive contract. All Roscoe had to do now was wait for the next outbreak and the tide of public opinion to come in.

That was two years ago. Roscoe had grown weary. His contract was set to expire, and others were now interested. Roscoe went to the scariest bar in rural Polk County, The Pit, the kind of place where people hire guys to kill their spouses. Roscoe began drinking with a man named Lucky. Lucky had killed two people, one of each, a husband and a wife. Different couples.

Roscoe said he had a proposition.

"It'll cost ya."

Roscoe said that wasn't a problem—now here's what he wanted done. . . .

"There's got to be a catch," said Lucky. "Where's the risk? The difficulty?"

"That's just it. There is none."

"Something's not right," said Lucky.

"Will a thousand-dollar retainer be enough?"

Lucky wrote his number on a napkin.

Roscoe got up one morning the following week and waited by the mailbox. The truck arrived. "Morning, Mr. Weege."

"Morning, Rex."

The mailman handed Roscoe a stack of letters. Roscoe ran inside and spread them out on his rolltop desk. There it was, an envelope postmarked Venezuela. He slit the flap with a *Wallace in '72* letter opener and removed a single piece of stationery. Three dead Medflies Scotch-taped to the front. He dialed Lucky's number.

Midnight. Lucky sat in the dark cab of his four-by-four pickup, listening to the radio and drinking white lightning. Polk was strange radio country. The most enlightened station was static. Lucky turned the dial through various programs about them queers, them exterterrestials, fishin', shootin', huntin', prayin' in classrooms and can't-miss investin'.

Lucky stubbed out a Winston. "Let's get this over with."

He climbed down from the pickup and headed into a dark orange grove.

Two days later, Roscoe heard what he'd been waiting for on the evening news.

"*. . . State agriculture officials tonight announced the discovery of three Medflies in a Polk County citrus grove. Officials are meeting at this hour at the capitol in Tallahassee to decide on the appropriate response, but a well-placed source tells us aerial spraying is out, and as many as a million sterile flies may be released . . .*"

Roscoe's phone rang before the report was over. It was Tallahassee.

"Yes, sir, I just saw it on the news. . . . No problem. . . . I'll have 'em ready."

Roscoe hung up and poured a drink. "This is the easiest money I'll ever make."

It was more than easy. Breeding Medflies—well, try *not* to breed them. A sealed warehouse, two flies, a bunch of rotten fruit, and you're in business. The expensive step was the sterilization, which was why Roscoe skipped it.

The C-130 transport plane flew over the heart of Florida citrus country at three thousand feet. Roscoe was in the back of the cargo bay, supervising workers with gloves, goggles and gas masks as they released the first flies from special bio tanks. Bright light and a whispering roar filled the plane as the aft cargo door slowly lowered, the insects momentarily swirling around in a dense swarm before taking to the sky.

Roscoe laughed. The state had started with only three flies, and those were already dead. But look out below! A million horny flies on the way!

The copilot came back in the bay and yelled over the engines that someone wanted to talk to Roscoe on the radio. The workers cracked open another tank of flies as Roscoe headed for the cockpit.

It was one of the state agriculture officials: "I just heard the good news."

"Yes, we're releasing the flies now," Roscoe said into the microphone.

"No, I'm not talking about that," said the official. "It's the Germans. They've done it!"

"Done what?"

"The mechanical picker. It works! We tested it this morning. Mr. Weege, you're on your way to becoming an extremely rich man!"

The microphone bounced on the cockpit floor. "Hello? Hello?"

The workers releasing flies looked up when they heard the shouting.

"Stop it! Stop it!" yelled Roscoe, running through the cargo hold, snatching at the air, trying to catch flies with his bare hands, hysterical, still running, right out the back of the plane and into the wild blue.

*I*t *was another perfect chamber* of commerce morning in Miami Beach. The sewage slick had cleared up, and the last of the ninety-two Haitians who swam ashore after the daily capsizing were apprehended in the Clark Gable booth at Wolfie's deli before most people knew what was happening.

The sun was high and strong, beach worshipers covered the sand in European swimsuits, and fashion photographers barked instructions at malnourished girls. "Turn! . . . Pout! . . . Look like you're on heroin!"

An inbound 747 appeared over the Atlantic, its passengers getting their first glimpse of land after the six-hour flight from the Continent. The jumbo jet's shadow crossed the beach and the futuristic lifeguard shacks and the art deco hotels on Collins Avenue.

All up and down Collins, people lounged on sidewalk patios. They shielded their eyes and looked up at the jet. The new café society, drinking espresso, speaking French and German, smoking Turkish cigarettes without guilt. There was a traffic dispute. Frat brothers in a Jeep that said *No Fear!* began shouting profanities at another car. Men in linen suits got out of a Mercedes, dragged one punk from the Jeep and flamenco-danced on his crotch until they heard sirens and fled. Nobody saw anything. Chicness resumed.

Five distinguished women in their late forties sat on the patio in front of the Hotel Nash. Tasteful single-piece bathing suits, sunglasses, wide-brimmed straw hats. A pitcher of mimosas and five cell phones on the table, next to five books. It was the quarterly literary field trip of their reading club, *Books, Booze and Broads.* The name was a whimsical joke on themselves; they were trying to break out of obsessively responsible lives now that all their children had left for college. Two cell phones rang.

The five books on the table were all the same paperback, *The Stingray Shuffle,* by Ralph Krunkleton. The women had been on a Krunkleton kick lately.

"I think this was his best book yet," said the Latino businesswoman, getting off the phone.

"Me, too," said the redheaded commercial artist. "All those crazy orange harvesting machines."

"I loved how Roscoe ran right out the back of the plane with the Medflies," added the attorney with cropped blond hair. "Never saw that coming."

"Wait till you find out what happens to the five million dollars," said the petite veterinarian.

"Shhh! Don't tell me! I'm not there yet!" said the self-assured aerospace engineer, flagging down a waiter for another pitcher.

The club went way back, started quite by accident in 1971. It was a Monday morning in July, an office waiting room filled with crying, screaming children who occasionally broke free and had to be chased. They were in Gainesville, the middle of Florida far from ocean breezes, and the room was muggy with the musk of spent diapers. The air conditioner didn't work, and a single electric fan whirred unevenly atop a crumpled stack of *Southern Bride.*

A clerk slid open the reception window and looked at her clipboard. "Samantha Bridges?"

A tall, young blonde stood up, an infant strapped to her chest and a two-year-old girl by the hand. She capped a bottle of milk and stuck it in a pocket in her demin overalls.

There was a short discussion at the window. The clerk shook her head.

"Sorry? What do you mean you can only send him another letter?" Samantha's voice was beyond loud, but the other women didn't seem to notice, bouncing tots on knees. Another day in paradise at the office of child-support enforcement.

"I waited two hours for you to tell me you can only send another letter? He's ignored all the others!"

The clerk told Sam that if she would have a seat, a supervisor would get to her when he was free.

"In another two hours?"

Samantha went back to her chair and sat down and got out the milk bottle.

"Mommy . . ." said the two-year-old at her side.

"What is it, dear?"

"Mommy . . ." Her mouth was still open, but she had stopped talking.

Samantha patted the infant on her chest, trying to get a burp. "What? What is it, dear? Are you okay?"

The girl threw up in Samantha's lap. Samantha looked down, and the infant regurgitated on her shoulder. A dozen children wailed all around. Her checking account was empty.

Samantha raised her eyes to a blank spot on the concrete wall and tried to imagine an afternoon at the beach.

The other women in the waiting room had all been there. Each had that hardened, dazed, lack-of-sleep look usually only seen on men at the end of extended military campaigns. One of the women had once dated a Navy SEAL, who told her about going through some kind of grueling test called Hell Week. One week, she thought. Big deal. If you really want to toughen them up, have 'em trade places with single moms.

Samantha returned to her apartment on the campus of the University of Florida, where she lived in a wing of married student housing nicknamed "divorced student housing." There were day classes and night waitress shifts and midnight feedings and more trips to the support office. Summer became fall. Samantha began recognizing some of the regulars from the support office at her apartment building. They became a group. Teresa Wellcraft, Rebecca Shoals, Maria Conchita, Paige Turner. And Samantha—everyone called her Sam. She was the tallest, a full six feet, blond hair in a semishort soccer-mom cut. She had also *played* soccer. And lacrosse. And basketball. And batted cleanup on her high school softball team. That's where the self-reliance came from. Sam viewed the world in a resting state of unfairness and it was up to nobody but her to change it. She never let anything pass. Rudeness, bad service, Sam was all over you. She favored sweatpants and sports bras and majored in law enforcement.

Paige was the smallest, and she let everything pass, and Sam was always stepping in and defending her, which only embarrassed Paige all the more.

"Please, let's just go," said Paige. "It's no big deal."

"No! Not until this fucker honors his competitor's coupons!"

Paige had grown up inland, and her Okeechobee twang was mistaken for southern. She was the classic girl next door, big brown eyes and no hint of guile. Her hair was always in a ponytail. She would have been more comfortable never saying a word and not joining the group, except Sam pressured her, and she felt more comfortable acquiescing. She wanted to be a veterinarian.

Maria filled the conversation voids left by Paige and then some. She cared about people and wanted to let every one of them know it. At length. Before the pregnancy, she had volunteered at hospices for the terminally ill, where lonely residents pretended they were asleep when they saw her coming. Her personal passion was clothes, and her fashion sense was that unfortunate combination of wrong and bold. She also had trouble with makeup, rooted in her philosophy that *more* is more. She was big and gangly, almost as tall as Sam. She had flunked out of fashion design and went on to probation in graphic design.

Rebecca had the artistic side that so tragically eluded Maria. She excelled at painting and could pick up a musical instrument for the first time and become competent in an hour. She was the reluctant beauty, the one in the group the men hit on the most. Medium height but curvy, with nice cheekbones, bedroom eyes and the kind of exquisite auburn hair with natural body that caused other women to make up things about her behind her back. It didn't bother Rebecca. Nothing did. She was the flower child of the group, barefoot, daisies in the hair, undeclared major.

Teresa was the brain, Phi Beta Kappa, insanely organized with cross-indexed filing systems and a gravity-well memory. She used big words. *Propinquity. Weltschmerz.* But all that was overshadowed. There was no other way to say it. Teresa was a fatso. She also bit her nails to the skin, yo-yo dieted, checked constantly to see if the stove was off and quit smoking every week. She had a knack for tinkering, which led to her double major in chemical and electrical engineering. For Christmas she installed dimmer switches in everyone's apartment.

The women quickly discovered they had several things in common. Number one, assholes in their pasts. Number two, a surplus of guts. Not man guts, where you charge a pillbox, dive in a raging river or punch a biker outside the Do Drop In. This was woman guts. Quietly enduring when there is no acceptable alternative but to endure.

Third thing in common: They loved to make chili, which they did every Friday, seven sharp. The weekly cook-off was the best thing they could have done. Being a single mom at a major football university was the formula for clinical depression, like being in prison with a view of Bourbon Street. Marking time until the next get-together made it all seem a little less hopeless.

The fourth thing in common, however, that was the primary reason these five particular women bonded so tightly. They agreed never to talk about it. Ever.

After a month of chili Fridays, the book club was born of necessity. They loved reading, but there was no time with the kids, not even for literature classes, which forced them to pool notes.

"Who knows what *Moby-Dick*'s about?"

"Man wants to kill fish. Fish kills man. Lots of details about boats."

"*The Jungle?*"

"The rich are mean."

"*Invisible Man?*"

"White people are mean."

"Clockwork Orange?"

"The British are mean."

"Brave New World?"

"The future is scary and weird."

"Naked Lunch?"

"Junkies are scary and weird."

"The Sun Also Rises?"

"We should be in Paris."

The remaining semesters dragged out like a stretch for robbery, but they all somehow managed to stumble through to graduation, where they hugged and took a hundred snapshots and swore they'd always stay in touch and promptly lost contact for twenty-five years.

The Sunshine State has a mind-bending concentration of "cash-only" businesses. These aren't your shade-tree auto detailers or flea market kiosks selling houseplants and nunchuks. These involve amounts of currency that require luggage.

On a day near the end of 1997, there were two thousand seven hundred and sixty-three cash-crammed briefcases floating around the shallow-grave landscape of Florida. Some were under the seats of limousines, some were underwater in ditched airplanes, some were handcuffed to South American couriers flying up to buy Lotto tickets, some were clutched to the chests of perspiring men in street clothes sprinting down the beach, ducking bullets.

One briefcase was different from the others. Really superstitious people said it was cursed, just because everyone who ever touched it wasn't breathing anymore. Whatever you believed, it was still filled with five million dollars.

The briefcase, a silver Halliburton, now sat between two patio loungers next to a motel pool in Cocoa Beach. A pair of men lay on their backs and sipped drinks from coconuts.

Paul and Jethro had plenty of money in the briefcase but not a valid credit card between them. Which meant no reputable inn would give them a room, so they paid cash through a slot in inch-thick Plexiglas at the Orbit Motel.

The old Honduran night manager had made change without ambition. The motel office contained an empty water cooler and the smell of burnt coffee but no coffeemaker; two molded plastic chairs, one with a puddle of something and the other holding a sleeping man in a plain T-shirt who cursed as he dreamed. On the wall a framed poster of a kitten dangling from a tree branch. "Hang in there."

Paul fidgeted as he waited for his change. He straightened a stack of travel guides with space shuttles on the cover. He fiddled with a display of business cards for taxi companies, Chinese restaurants, bail bondsmen, someone who called himself "The King of Wings," and a fishing guide named Skip.

Paul took his change and leaned toward the slot. "Can we get a wake-up call for eight?"

"I'll get the concierge right on it," said the manager, not looking up from his *Daily Racing Form*.

Paul held one of the travel guides up to the Plexiglas. "Are these free?"

"Knock yourself out."

The Orbit was not rated in any of the travel guides. Not even listed. Just as well. The landscaping was long dead, replaced by broken glass, cigarette butts and dejection. The water in the pool had turned the color of iced tea and occasionally fizzed. The 1960s neon sign out front featured a mechanical space capsule that used to circle Earth, but it had shorted out and caught fire over Katmandu.

Until the previous Thursday, Paul and Jethro had been just like any other law-abiding citizens wandering the state fat and happy. That's when Hurricane Rolando-berto came ashore in Tampa Bay. One of the state's two thousand seven hundred and sixty-three briefcases was in the path of the hurricane, which threw it up for grabs like a tipped basketball.

At the time, Paul and Jethro had been staying at another quality lodge, the Hammerhead Ranch Motel. The night before the big blow, Jethro had seen someone creeping around in the dark behind the inn, constantly looking over his shoulder, hiding something. But so was everyone else, and Jethro didn't give it much thought.

It began to nag at him during the storm. The next morning Paul and Jethro went down to the shore and joined the mob that assembles after every hurricane to collect prehistoric shark teeth and washed-up guns. The pair scanned the ground as they climbed through seaweed-draped power lines and uprooted trees.

"Whatever it was, he wanted to make sure nobody would find it," said Jethro. "I swear it was right around here somewhere. . . . Wait! Look! There's something shiny down there! Help me move these bales of dope."

Paul and Jethro popped the latches on the briefcase and raised the lid. They slammed it quickly. Their hearts raced, eyes glancing around to see if anyone had been watching.

Decision time. This wasn't Girl Scout cookie money. People would come looking for it. They should probably go to the police. Yes, that was the only right thing. How could they even think of doing anything else? They might even be allowed to keep it. Maybe get a reward, too. On the other hand, they'd have to report it to the IRS.

Paul started counting the money as they fled on Interstate 4. They were in a baby-blue '74 Malibu, speeding across Florida to catch a cruise ship for the Bahamas. The law allows someone to take up to fifteen thousand in cash across the border. Paul passed that threshold thumbing through his second pack of hundreds, practically the whole briefcase to go. Inbound Customs was tough. But outbound on a cruise to Nassau was another matter. You didn't even need a passport.

Paul and Jethro ran through the ship terminal at Port Canaveral and up to the ticket window. The next cruise left on Friday. It was Wednesday. Nothing to do but wait and freak out. They decided to keep the briefcase with them wherever they went—walking along the shore, around the pool, down the pier, jumping at every sound. They needed liquor.

The Orbit Motel did not have a bar or restaurant, only a bank of vending machines dispensing Ho-Hos and French ticklers. So Paul and Jethro made a series of trips up the beach to the many conveniently spaced tiki bars that now outnumber pay phones in Florida. They returned to the pool patio and used straws to suck pink froth out of coconuts with paper umbrellas. Six empty coconuts sat beside each lounger. The Orbit Motel was not the kind of place to beat back a panic attack. It had that tropical OK Corral glow, a washed-out dustiness of light and color, the air hot, still and silent, except for occasional gusts that pushed a brown palm frond across the concrete with an unpleasant scratching sound. The ice machine had been dusted for prints. Two men came out of a room carrying a large TV and an unbolted window air-conditioning unit, got in a Firebird with no tag and sped off.

Paul and Jethro were an unusual alliance. Jethro was president of the Hemingway look-alike club in Pensacola. Paul was afraid of people and ran a detective agency. He was Paul, the Passive-Aggressive Private Eye.

"What was that?" said Paul.

"Just a car door."

Paul wiped his forehead. "I'm not gonna make it."

"Courage is the ability to suspend the imagination."

"What?"

"We need to keep our minds occupied. Hand me the travel guide."

Johnny Vegas was a golf pro.

As of Thursday.

Vegas's tanned, six-foot frame rippled in all the right places beneath a tight mercerized-cotton shirt, stretched over broad, firm shoulders and tapered to a trim waist under an alligator belt. He had that squinty Latin thing going that drove women wild. His black hair was longish and currently organized for the Antonio Banderas effect.

Johnny had decided to begin teaching golf when he met his first pupil. Her name was Bianca, a tall Mediterranean model in town shooting a swimsuit photo spread for truck tires. Bianca broke golf etiquette by wearing a bikini to her first lesson. That made them even. Johnny didn't play golf.

Johnny had met Bianca an hour earlier on the beach behind the Orbit

Motel. He was standing near the shore wearing two-hundred-dollar sunglasses, holding a surfboard. Johnny was standing on the beach with the surfboard because he didn't know how to surf. Bianca walked up.

"You surf?" she asked coyly, cocking her hip.

"Of course not," Johnny said with playful sarcasm. "I just stand here with this board."

Johnny didn't have a job. Didn't have to. The scion of an insurance mogul, Johnny had a bulging trust fund and the kind of lifestyle not seen since Joe Namath wore mink on Broadway. He also had a secret. You wouldn't know it to look at him, but Johnny had never gone *all the way*. Oh, he wanted to. So did the women. It had just never worked out. It was always something, some kind of bizarre interruption. Johnny had learned the hard way that if getting a woman in the mood was an art, then keeping her there was a fucking science—the whole fleeting phenomenon more rare, delicate and unstable than suspending a weapons-grade uranium isotope at the implosion point. The least little vibration and everything tumbles. Or detonates.

That was Johnny's love life. Hotel fire, civil unrest, military jet crash, ammonia cloud evacuation, George Clooney sighting. In addition to being a trust-fund playboy, he was Johnny Vegas, the Accidental Virgin.

A few months earlier in Miami, Johnny had picked up a Cuban dreamboat with a perfectly positioned beauty mark that made him swallow his own tongue. They had met at a trendy salsa club in Little Havana and were back at her place within the hour. She grinned naughtily as she gave Johnny a private dance, peeling off her clothes piece by piece, tossing them aside with aplomb. Johnny sat at the foot of the bed, ripping open his trousers like a stubborn bag of potato chips.

She finally flung her panties over her shoulder and sauntered toward Johnny. "You've been a bad boy."

That's when they heard the sirens. Flashing blue and red lights filled the bedroom. The woman ran to the window.

"What is it?" asked Johnny.

"I can't believe it!" she yelled. "It's the feds! They're taking Elián!"

"Who's Elián?"

"This is so unfair!" she sobbed. "I'm sorry, but you'll have to go. I need to be alone tonight."

Seven months later, Johnny was back at the plate. He had landed a drop-dead attorney in a serious pantsuit and glasses, her brunette hair in a no-nonsense bun. She strolled up to him at a political cocktail party, slipped off her glasses and shook down her hair. "What do you say we blow this Popsicle stand?"

A half hour later, Johnny was lying in bed on his back, the woman climbing aboard.

The TV was on. Tom Brokaw. The woman heard something and looked over.

"What?" she yelled. "They're taking Florida away from Gore? They can't do that!"

She jumped out of bed and turned up the volume with the remote.

"What is it?" asked Johnny.

"Shhhhh!"

So when Johnny met Bianca on the beach behind the Orbit Motel, he had just one question.

"Do you read newspapers?"

"Read what?"

They headed for the golf course across A1A from the motel, where Johnny said he was the club pro. That impressed her; she said she had always wanted to learn golf.

On the third hole, the ball was three feet from the cup. Johnny interlaced his fingers on the putter's leather grip. Then he handed her the club. "Now you try."

She pretended to be all thumbs. "I just can't do it. Could you show me again?"

Johnny stepped up from behind and wrapped his taut arms around her, repositioning Bianca's hands on the shaft. She turned toward his biceps. "Wow, you're pretty strong. I'll bet you have lots of girlfriends."

"Just stroke through the ball," said Johnny. "One fluid motion."

Bianca tapped the ball with the putter.

"Darn! It hit the windmill again. I just can't play this game."

"Let's try the dinosaur hole," said Johnny. "That's an easy one."

"It's not golf," said Bianca, pooching out her bottom lip, then staring off.

"What is it?"

"I have this problem. . . . It's medical."

Just my luck, thought Johnny. Probably a week to live. On the other
hand, a week's a week.

"What kind of problem?"

"It's embarrassing. My boyfriend dumped me because of it. . . .
Autagonistophilia."

"Is that like a bunion?"

"It means I can only become sexually aroused if I'm doing it in a
public place near people."

"You do it in public?"

"Not actually *in* public, but where I can see lots of people close by,
and there's a high risk of being discovered, possibly arrested. . . . You
okay? You look pale."

Johnny braced himself on the side of the windmill.

"Wait, there's more," she said. "I've also got chrematistophilia—
that's getting excited if you're blackmailed into sex. And hybristophilia,
sex with convicted criminals, and symphorphilia, sex during natural
disasters, and formicophilia, wanting to have sex on cheap counter-
tops." She held out her left arm. "See? I have a medical alert bracelet."

Two men walked by them on the cart path, sipping coconuts and
reading their Cocoa Beach travel guide. They strolled past the water-
fall, the pink elephant and the airplane crashed into the side of a plastic mountain on the thirteenth hole. They crossed the Japanese
footbridge over the lagoon that separated "Goony Golf" from the driving range. The lagoon was actually a retention pond, and the pair
looked over the bridge's railing at the bubbles in the water and the submerged scuba diver with a sack of golf balls.

Sleigh bells jingled as Paul and Jethro opened the door to the driving range office. The man behind the counter scooped balls into wire
baskets and plopped them on the counter.

Paul pulled a hundred-dollar bill from his pocket.

"We don't take hundreds."

"I'm sorry," said Paul. "What if I let you keep the change?"

"Then we have a new policy." The man plucked the bill from Paul's hand, stuck it in his back pocket and pushed two baskets of balls across the counter. Paul and Jethro went to select clubs from a large oak barrel of bent irons and woods.

"We close in a half hour," said the man. "You can still play, but you'll be in the dark."

"Ah, such is the challenge of life itself," said Jethro.

"No problem," added Paul. "Anything you say."

"And replace your divots," said the man. "This ain't a sod farm."

Actually, it was a sod farm, at least on documents at the zoning office. The state was under drought restrictions, which meant only sod farms could water, and the driving range wanted to keep its sprinklers going.

"Right. Replace divots," said Paul. "Sure thing."

"I remember it well," said Jethro. "Grand traditions of Scotland, the noble but curious land of plaid . . ."

"And stop talking like that. Both of you. It's getting on my nerves."

"You got it," said Paul. "No problem-o."

The pair left the office and headed to the last tee, number twenty-two.

Jethro spilled his bucket on the ground and used the head of a four iron to rake a few red-banded balls over to his feet. "DiMaggio would have been a formidable golfer. You could see it in his dark Italian eyes, etched with the scars of life." Jethro swung hard and hit the ball with the toe of his club, slicing right, scampering through traffic on A1A and ricocheting off the manager's door at the Orbit Motel. An old Honduran opened the door, looked around, closed it.

Paul lined up his own shot. He looked out at the range signs, marking distance in fifty-yard increments. In between were small greens with flagsticks.

"What's the objective here?" asked Paul. "Hit it as far as you can or get it close to the flags?"

"Neither, my worthy companion. It is but to hit the range cart."

"The what?"

"You do not understand now, but you will in time."

Paul and Jethro swung through their ration of balls, which took off at random adventures in geometry. They were accompanied by a score of other golfers whose graceful swings resembled the chopping of fire-wood, and a spray of balls curved, sliced, bounced and whizzed across the range, some hooking high over the safety netting and into the retention pond, where a scuba diver trespassed with a mesh gunnysack full of balls in one hand and a twelve-gauge bang-stick for alligators in the other.

One of the golfers noticed something. Out near the left hundred-yard marker, a small tractor started moving across the range. The driver's seat was enclosed in a protective wire cage, the tractor pulling a wide scooping device that sucked up balls and squirted them into the collection bin.

The golfer on tee number three sounded the alarm.

"Range cart!"

The customers began hitting balls as fast as they could, a rapid series of twenty-one-gun salutes. Most were wildly off target, but through sheer volume the range cart began taking heavy fire. The driver was used to it by now, a community college student reading *Crime and Punishment* and drinking a Foster's as the fusillade of Titleists and Dunlops pinged off the vehicle. A lucky shot smashed one of the red plastic light covers. A small voice in the distance: "I got the taillight! I got the taillight!" A two-wood clanged off the outside of the cage protecting the driver, who was inside a depressing nineteenth-century Russian apartment. He turned the page. Balls flew by.

Paul topped another drive fifty yards. "How does anybody play this game?"

Jethro addressed his ball with a three wood. "Think of it as bull-fighting and you will see the truth in it." He knocked a TopFlite into the Checkers drive-through.

Bianca and Johnny held hands as they crossed the footbridge over the retention lagoon next to the driving range. She giggled and squeezed his arm. "I'm getting wet just thinking about it."

Johnny choked on some saliva and grabbed the railing for balance. "You all right?"

He nodded. They continued walking, coming to a fence and meeting a third party in the dark. Johnny paid the man in twenties. The couple began wiggling into position behind a control panel.

"Look! I can see people over there!" said Bianca. "Oh, my God!" She ripped off her bra and plunged her tongue down Johnny's throat. Her hands went for his zipper.

"Are you ready?" she whispered.

Was Johnny ready? He had the kind of erection SWAT teams could use to knock down doors on crack houses. He fumbled to operate the control panel like he'd been shown.

The man waved goodbye as Johnny and Bianca departed. "Have a safe trip."

Bianca gave Johnny a hickey as she slid off her panties. She looked over her shoulder at the little people in the distance and her stomach fluttered. She bit Johnny again. "You're going to remember this the rest of your life. . . ."

The couple had just gotten the rest of their clothes off when they heard a tiny voice in the distance.

"Range cart!"

Bam. Bam. Bam. Bam. Bam. Bam.

Bianca jumped off Johnny in alarm. "What the fuck was that?"

Bam. Bam. Bam. Bam. Bam. Bam.

A shower of dimpled balls pelted the range cart with the two naked people.

"They're trying to kill us!" yelled Bianca.

"No, they're not," said Johnny. "It'll just make it better. Come on, baby."

Bianca lost it, clawing at the inside of the protective cage like a drowning cat. "I have to get out of here!"

"Don't open that door!"

She opened it, took a Maxfli in the forehead and fell back unconscious in Johnny's lap.

Rush-hour traffic lurched along Route 836 through hardworking Hialeah, past the horse track and indus-
trial park. In the third warehouse off Exit 7, men in back braces pushed handcarts of brown boxes marked THE STINGRAY SHUFFLE through beams of exhaust-filtered sun, loading trucks and vans, which pulled out of the shipping bay toward the highway ramp.

In a windowless room next to the dispatcher's office, a young man scrolled down his computer screen. He stopped, hit *print* and waited for a sheet of paper to come off the inkjet.

The supervisor's office had windows, but they overlooked the load-ing dock and the men hoisting cases of bestsellers at one of the biggest book wholesalers in the Miami–Fort Lauderdale statistical hub. The young man stood in the doorway.

"What is it?" asked the boss, staring at his own computer screen, squeezing a stress ball advertising a new stress-free-diet book.

"I'm getting some strange sales figures on this one title."

"Down?"

"Way up."

The young man handed his printout to the supervisor, who grabbed his reading glasses.

"That *is* strange. You sure these are right?"

"Triple-checked."

"Must be an explanation. Maybe a publisher's promotion. Contest or something."

"Nope. Already called them."

"What about the author? Is he touring? Speak at a local college?"

"Hasn't been seen in years. Could be dead for all we know."

"Anything on *Oprah*?"

The young man shook his head.

"Maybe it's one of these local book clubs. Look—see how the sales are all just at this one bookstore in Miami Beach, The Palm Reader?" He took off his glasses and set the page down. "That has to be it. Must be someone's selection-of-the-month, and they're all buying at this store."

"Three months in a row? The numbers are bigger than any ten book groups could account for. Besides, The Palm Reader is a dump. No self-respecting club would set foot inside with all the classier places nearby."

The supervisor scratched his head. "Then there's simply a strong word-of-mouth pocket. The book's taking off on its own."

"Sir, *The Stingray Shuffle* has been out eleven years."

"This is a crazy business. I've seen stuff out twenty years with nothing to show, then someone makes a movie and *bang!*"

"There's no movie."

"The point I'm making is you can't account for consumer behavior. These things sprout at their own pace, the gestation of the pyramid progression, a classic equation of the hundredth monkey. Revenues are cruising horizontally along the X axis, then suddenly demand reaches critical mass and sales make the all-important vertical swing up the Y axis."

"Sir?"

"Yes?"

"What are you talking about?"

"Making some money," he said, picking up the phone. "Let's call the other bookstores, see if we can't help this thing along. And beat the other wholesalers while we're at it."

The supervisor got the entire staff in on the act, and they canvassed the bottom half of the state, pushing the title, then working their way north. The stores were receptive. They could always send the books back if they didn't sell. "Sure, we'll take a few cases." The title started moving in several markets. Not like at the first store, but respectably, and multiplied by hundreds of outlets, it began adding up to real numbers.

An overcast summer morning in New York. A Friday. Midtown Manhattan, the nerve ganglion of the global publishing industry, and by noon everyone was consumed with the same crisis: how to beat weekend traffic heading out of town to the Hamptons after lunch.

On West Fifty-third Street, at a sidewalk restaurant of obscure nationality and no prices, a man and a woman sat across from each other in identical business suits. A waiter in a red turban set a plate in front of each of them. They had ordered the same, pan-seared sponge on a bed of pollen.

"Pepper?" asked the waiter.

They nodded. The waiter twisted a metal tube over their plates.

"Sir," said the woman. "We have a sleeper on our hands. Just got the sales report yesterday. Red-hot—might even crack the *Times* bestseller list."

"Whose book? Allister? Byron? Sir Dennis?"

She shook her head. "Ralph."

"Ralph!"

The waiter held a pump bottle. "Moisture?"

They nodded.

"I didn't know Ralph was even still alive."

"We're trying to confirm that."

"When did we publish a new title?"

"We didn't. This is his last one."

The waiter put on safety goggles. "Blowtorch?"

They nodded.

"But his last book was ten years ago."

"Eleven."

The man shook his head. "This is a crazy business."

"No crazier than any other."

A troupe of midgets surrounded the table, Cossack dancing.

"I just can't get over it. I mean, Ralph! How did this start?"

"A sales fluke out of Miami Beach. A bookstore called The Palm Reader, then it snowballed."

"The Palm Reader?"

"One of those new crime and mystery specialty shops. A local wholesaler got wind of it and spread the word . . ."

The waiter clapped his hands twice, and the midgets dispersed. "Dessert?"

They nodded.

"Okay, throw some money at promotions," said the man, jabbing his sponge with a fork. "And find Ralph. We need to get him back on tour. Talk to his agent."

"He isn't represented anymore, not that we know of."

"Try the last one."

The dessert hovercraft arrived.

The day Paul and Jethro found the five million dollars
and took off across the state had started out pleasant enough. No
rain in the forecast, the mercury hovering under eighty at the Lakeland
airport, halfway between Tampa and Orlando. Two long lines of cars
sat stationary in the eastbound lanes of Interstate 4, hundreds of
traffic-jammed vehicles stretching endlessly over the gentle central
Florida hills, all the way to the horizon.

In the middle of the right lane was a blue '74 Malibu. Jethro was
driving, Paul in the passenger seat with an open briefcase in his lap,
counting wads.

"How much farther to the cruise ships?" asked Paul.

"Eighty miles," said Jethro. "How much money?"

"Three million. A lot left. Hope there's a ship leaving today."

"We can always put up in a motel. Nobody's going to find us that fast. It'll be weeks before they even realize anyone has found the money, and longer, if ever, before they connect it to us."

Five miles behind the Malibu, a pink Cadillac Eldorado was stuck in the same lane.

"What's the global-positioning tracker say?" asked Lenny.

Serge looked down at the beeping box on the seat beside him. "The briefcase is stuck in traffic, too. About five miles ahead."

The Cadillac held four people, two men in front, two women in back. Airbrushing down the side of the convertible: LENNY LIPPOWICZ— THE DON JOHNSON EXPERIENCE. One bumper sticker: REHAB IS FOR QUITTERS.

"What's the delay?" said Serge, grabbing the top of the windshield and standing up on the driver's seat to see as far as he could. He plopped back down and punched the steering wheel.

"Maybe a wreck?" said Lenny in the passenger seat, wearing a pastel T-shirt and white Versace jacket.

"Should have known better," said Serge. "Never take I-4 when you have to get anywhere."

A female voice from the backseat: "Can we have another joint?"

"No!" snapped Serge. "No more dope for you!"

Lenny passed a joint back.

Serge threw up his hands. "I just told them they couldn't have any more."

"Doper etiquette," said Lenny. "Mellow out."

"You know my personality type," said Serge. "I can't take boredom. And I especially can't take some kind of huge holdup where you don't know what's going on!"

One of the women offered the lit joint over Serge's shoulder. He pushed it away. "Just give me a ballpark of how long the wait is! I don't care if it's four hours—I need something I can mentally whittle on, compartmentalize, break down and digest. Or give the reason. Let me know what the hell's going on! This out-of-the-loop, can't-see-the-front-of-the-line shit is making me crazy!" He punched the steering wheel again.

"Look," said Lenny. "I think they're starting to move up there."

They both leaned forward and watched closely. They sat back again.

"Sorry. Just an illusion," said Lenny. "Heat waves from the road."

The backseat: "Ahem . . . can we have, like, another joint? It'll be the last one. Promise."

"See what you started?" said Serge. "They're hooked."

"How was I to know?"

Serge turned around and put his arm over the back of the driver's seat and stared at the women, City and Country, college-age babes from Alabama. "You say you never got high in your life until last week? Not a single time until Lenny turned you on back at Hammerhead Ranch?"

The women nodded, one hitting a roach clip, the other holding her smoke.

"At least try to be a little more discreet. We're in a convertible." Serge turned back around and hit the steering wheel again. "C'mon!"

"Must be a wreck," said Lenny.

"It would have to be a ruptured tanker of liquid phosgene to take this long. Otherwise, they'd already be sweeping up glass."

"What do you think?"

"It's I-4. Take your pick," said Serge. "I've seen sinkholes, armed assaults, forest fires that flushed wildlife into traffic. And then there was the cow."

"The cow?"

"There was this one cow. She liked to stand alone all day up to her tits in the middle of this little lake off the side of the road."

"That was a driving problem?"

"Everyone slowed down and watched. They thought she was in trouble. Hundreds called the highway patrol, wanting them to send a rescue helicopter with a canvas sling harness and a winch."

"Did they?"

"No. There was nothing wrong. But the calls kept pouring in and tied up all the emergency lines. So the highway department put up a sign, one of those big mobile things on wheels, a bunch of flashing orange light bulbs that spell out stuff like RIGHT LANE CLOSED AHEAD. Except this one said, THE COW IS OK. True story."

"What happened?"

"Made everything worse. *Everyone* slowing down to watch."

Lenny nodded, then pointed ahead at the stationary lines of cars. "Might as well turn the engine off and save gas."

"And put The Club on."

"I've been meaning to ask you," said Lenny. "How come you always put your Club on backward, with the lock facing the dash?"

"Fuckin' kids—they stick machine screws in the lock and yank the mechanism out with dent-pullers. But they don't have the necessary clearance if I reverse the bar. The things you have to do to survive in this state."

A BMW blew by in the breakdown lane and kept going, passing the entire line of cars and disappearing over a hill.

"That's the fourth guy who's done that since we've been here," said Lenny.

"It's just not right," said Serge.

"We could do that, too, but we don't," said Lenny.

"Because rules are important," said Serge. "Otherwise, everything starts breaking down."

The backseat: "Um, do you think we could have, you know, another . . ."

Lenny passed a doobie back.

"If we're going to be here much longer, I'll have to occupy my mind," said Serge. He turned off the Cadillac and walked to the rear of the car.

"What are you doing?" asked Lenny.

"Getting my toys." He opened the trunk, removed a gym bag and got back in the driver's seat. "I bought you a present." Serge pulled something out of the bag. He could have easily handed it across the seat to Lenny, but he threw it, the way guys have to.

Lenny dropped it on the floorboard.

"Nice catch."

Lenny picked up the red-and-white canister. "Cruex? What are you trying to tell me?"

"No, you dingleberry, unscrew the bottom."

Lenny struggled to figure out the can, twisting with everything he had. "You know what a dingleberry actually is?"

"I've heard the rumors," said Serge. He reached over. "Here, let me."

Serge grabbed the can and twisted off the bottom, revealing a secret compartment.

"Cool," said Lenny. "A stash safe."

"I bought it at Spy vs. Spy."

"What's that?"

"A new chain that sells a bunch of espionage and counterespionage stuff, but it's really a toy store for guys—useless gadgets men can't resist. Night-vision scopes, walkie-talkie pens, voice-activated bomb-disposal robot/beer caddy . . ."

Lenny stuffed a baggie of pot up the bottom of the can. "Why'd you have to pick Cruex?"

"Had a friend who went to college in Boston. His roommate was from Colombia, and during spring break, the roommate says, 'Hey, why don't you come visit back home with me?' My friend says sure. It's a legitimate visit—no drugs or anything—and he's coming back through Miami, and Customs goes ape. What's an Anglo kid doing on vacation in Bogotá? They rip his luggage apart, make him take a laxative and shit on a clear toilet in front of all these people . . ."

"They actually have clear toilets?"

"The government does. But they seem to be the only ones who want them. I think that speaks volumes. Anyway, get this—they grabbed my friend's can of shaving cream and sprayed some out and tested it."

"That's spooky," said Lenny.

"*Drugs* are spooky," said Serge. "But jail is spookier. That's why I got you that can. Use it and stay free, my friend. Shaving cream is one thing, but nobody wants to mess with a guy's Cruex. DEA, Customs— they don't get paid enough."

Serge removed another canister from his bag and began shaking it. A metal ball rattled inside.

"Spray paint?" asked Lenny.

"Spy spray paint." Serge got out of the car and walked back to the rear bumper. He bent down and sprayed the license plate.

"What are you doing?" asked Lenny.

"The paint's clear, reflective," said Serge, rattling the can again. "Standard technique for operatives attending state dinners in case any spies try to photograph license plates in the parking lot of the embassy while you're upstairs stealing files. The clear coating reflects any flash photography, and all the spy will see when he gets his pictures back from the drugstore will be a bright, all-white license plate, completely blank."

Lenny rubbed his chin. "Is this a problem you anticipate us having?"

Serge climbed back in the car and pointed up the road toward Orlando. "It also works on those new cameras the state installed to catch people running tollbooths. I'm tired of paying these motherfuckers every time I want to go see a shuttle launch."

Serge pulled something else from the gym bag. A few little poles covered with spikes.

"What are those?"

"Stop sticks," said Serge. "Police use them at roadblocks to puncture the tires of fleeing suspects."

"Why do *you* need them?"

"To throw out the window in case the police are chasing me," said Serge. "Two can play this game."

Serge casually tossed the sticks over Lenny's head, out the right side of the car, and began rooting around again in his bag. "Let's see—what else do I have in here? . . ."

Pow, pow, pow, pow.

A new set of Michelins blew out on a Corvette racing by in the breakdown lane, and it cascaded down the embankment.

". . . Here we are." Serge removed a heavy egg-shaped object wrapped in orange silk. "My ace in the hole." He carefully folded back the silk to reveal a scored olive-green metal hulk—an antique hand grenade.

"Is it live?"

Serge nodded.

"Also get that at Spy versus Spy?"

Serge shook his head. "eBay."

A chorus from the backseat: "We're hungry."

"Again?" said Serge.

"Why don't you drive to a restaurant or something?" asked Country.

"Good idea," said City. "Drive us to a restaurant."

Serge turned around and pointed at the empty boxes in their laps. "You just ate. You both got the jumbo taco salad."

They looked down at their shirts and hands covered with grease, shredded cheese and strands of lettuce. Country looked up. "We're still hungry."

"I'm feeling like barbecue," said City.

Serge gestured around them at the sea of parked cars boxing them in, then searched for any hint of understanding in their bloodshot eyes. "Fuck it! Never mind!" He turned back around and sat silent a minute. He smacked the inside of the door. "What can be taking so long?"

"It's funny how when you're high, time seems to slow down," City told Country.

"Absolutely," said Country. "It just creeps. Everything takes forever. The least little thing becomes an eternity . . . Tick, tock, tick, tock . . ."

Serge slowly turned his head toward the passenger seat and glared.

"Don't look at me," said Lenny. "It was *your* idea to bring them."

". . . *Tick, tock, tick, tock* . . ."

"I thought it would be fun," said Serge. "Get the women's perspective for a change instead of the same old barbarian stuff I'm used to. But it's gone horribly awry, and now I'm being held prisoner in a Cheech and Chong marathon."

"I'm soooo hungry," said City.

"Does this car have music?" asked Country. "Let's play some music."

"Yeah, crank up the tunes," said City.

Lenny reached for the radio.

"Only classic album rock," said Serge. "It's all I can handle right now."

The car began to throb with bass.

"What about contemporary urban?" asked Lenny.

Serge shook his head. "I respect the rapper, but I need to be in the proper mood to appreciate social and economic polemics about who can play a turntable better."

Lenny twisted the dial to another station. The Beatles came on, "All You Need Is Love."

Serge nodded his approval. He took a deep breath and closed his eyes, trying to relax with the soothing music.

"You know, they're absolutely right," said Country. "All you *do* need is love. It's the most profound thing I've ever heard in my life . . ."

"They get straight to the heart of the matter," said City. "You've got love, what else do you need? . . ."

"Think about it, one small word, just four little letters, yet they make all the difference . . ."

Serge turned around and faced them again.

"What?" said City.

A weather-beaten seventeen-foot flats skiff motored slowly through the first light of day in the upper Florida Keys. It was a falling tide, and orange and pink and green Styrofoam balls dotted the water. Flocks of spoonbills glided low over the shallows, timing the tide to the minute, heading for feeding grounds as they had for thousands of years. Tiny, low mangrove islands punctuated the horizon, which disappeared toward Cape Sable and the Everglades.

An old man stood in the back of the skiff, his hand on the outboard throttle, a "Sanibel Biological Supply" fishing cap on his head. Yellow rubber waders with suspenders. The man had risen at precisely four-thirty, as he did every morning, and stepped onto the porch of his stilt house, eye level with the coconuts in the trees, barely visible in the blackness. Unseen water lapped the rock revetment; palms rustled.

He grabbed the balcony railing and concentrated on being thankful. Then he went downstairs and turned on the Weather Channel. There was a rim of light on the horizon when he headed down the dock with a mug of Sanka and an insulated sack of tuna sandwiches. He mixed gasoline and oil in the two-stroke fifty-to-one ratio and jerked a bucket of frozen mullet from a dockside freezer. He pulled the cover off the outboard, wiping spots with a rag, spraying points with silicone, replacing the cover. The davits clicked as he cranked the skiff down into the water. Soon he was planing up across the bay, snaking between the islands, until he was in the thick of the floating Styrofoam. The man throttled down.

He idled the boat and reached for one of the balls with a long-handled gaff, grabbing it and pulling up the crab trap tied underneath with rope. He pushed the outboard throttle stick to the side, turning the propeller starboard and putting the skiff in a perpetual clockwise circle as he shook blue crabs out of the trap and into a seventy-gallon cooler. Then he reached in a gray bucket for a dead fish and rammed it into the empty trap's wire-mesh bait hole and threw it all back over the side, the Styrofoam ball bobbing in the wake a few times as the trap settled back to the bottom. The man motored up for the next float and repeated the process, again and again, float after float—the whole time drinking coffee, eating sandwiches, juggling gaff, bait, traps, throttle. Back-country ballet. But he only stopped at the green floats; the orange and pink belonged to the other guys, and you didn't mess with them unless you wanted to get shot. Back-country justice. The man tossed his last trap in the water and headed home. He knew he was getting close when he saw the toilet seats.

On the north side on Plantation Key, the approach from the bay was extra shallow and rocky, and a channel had been cut long ago. The pass was known as Toilet Seat Cut or Little Stinker. It was originally designated with regular nautical markers, but the locals had since hung toilet seats on all of them. They were painted in vibrant colors, with names and dates and little drawings of people and pets. The old man looked off to the side. Spoonbills chiseled at tide-exposed oysters; tarpon fins slit the surface. An ibis stood frozen in an inch of water among the mangrove roots, then snapped its neck forward, spearing a fish with its beak. A pink toilet seat went by.

The sun finally rose as the old man cranked the skiff back up the davits and flushed fresh water through the lower unit with rabbit ears. He hoisted the cooler of crabs into the back of a pickup and headed for market.

The man had come into a modest amount of money in the sixties and bought a house and several commercially zoned parcels in the Florida Keys. Now their worth was in ransom range. The rental checks from the gas stations and seashell shops were steady, and the man no longer had need for the crab money. That wasn't work; it was religion.

He loved the stilt house. Two stories, tin roof, screened-in wrap-around balcony. Inside, you couldn't see the walls for all the built-in bookshelves. You knew he was a book guy by the way the shelves were filled, not just packed rows of vertical spines, but more books crammed in on top. It might have been a space problem except the man only collected one other thing: beer signs. The shark Bud Lite sign, the palm tree Corona, the flamingo drinking Miller. At night, the neon came on, and so did the strands of white Christmas lights tracing the porch's eaves. People driving by on US 1 often mistook it for a tavern and pulled over. "Hello? Anyone here?"—climbing the stairs and knocking on the screen door—"Is the bar open?"

The old man would trudge across the porch and reach for the handle. "It is now."

That's how he started his third collection. He collected friends, many of whom he met when they were on vacation and initially thought his place was a pub. They returned year after year. He kept a refrigerator on the porch, stocked with beer. There was a basket of colored markers on top, and he told his visitors to "sign the guest book," and the refrigerator was now covered with names and hometowns from across the USA and parts of Europe.

He was a big hit with the neighbors, too, something of a local celebrity. But that had taken a little more time. The man may have been old, but he wasn't weak or withered. In fact, he was scary. A burly, tight fist of a man, he kept fit swimming in the bay and pulling crab traps. His face was hard and leathery, and the shaved skull made him look like Mr. Clean. The neighbors were afraid of him at first; they aggressively avoided his property and gave him wide berth in town. There was talk he used to be a professional wrestler or a Green Beret or a bagman for the mob. But then they saw all the people dropping in from the highway, laughing on the porch late into the starry night. The bravest neighbor tiptoed up to the porch during one of the happy hours and knocked timidly.

"Frank! Come on in!" said the old man. Expansive smile and expansive, muscular arm that went around the neighbor's shoulders and jerked him off the steps into the party.

"You know my name?"

"Sure, Frank. You're my neighbor. I was wondering when you were going to drop by. Beginning to think you were afraid of me or something. . . . Hey, everybody! This is Frank!"

"Hi, Frank!"

"Frank, you want a beer? There's the fridge. Help yourself. And write something if you want . . ."

Another knock at the door.

"Gotta get that. Make yourself at home . . ."

The old man became an institution. So did his parties, which sometimes lasted days, people sleeping or passing out all over the house, prompting the man to install a bunch of hammocks. Half the time strangers were cooking breakfast in his kitchen when he got back from crabbing.

"I grabbed some of your eggs. Hope you don't mind," said a young woman in a long University of Miami T-shirt and nothing else, stirring a frying pan. "Want some?"

"Sorry, can't stay. But have at it."

During his gatherings, the man was content to sit on a stool in the corner of the porch, smiling, not saying anything, letting others have the spotlight. It only grew the legend. When a shrimpy guy is humble and quiet, well, that's just pitiful, but when it's a genuine tough guy, people can't resist building the story. The neighbors took to him like a lovable circus bear. That he was. Except when someone was being bullied; then he became a grizzly.

The old man liked the Caribbean Club at Mile Marker 104, where signs still made a big deal about a snippet of *Key Largo* putatively being filmed there. The usual crowd had gathered around the man's stool one Friday night when they heard a woman's protests from the pool tables.

"Ow! You're hurting me!"

A tall young man in a workout jersey had her by the arm. "We're leaving."

"Let me go!"

Nobody intervened as he dragged her out the door.

"Excuse me," said the old man, setting down his draft and getting off his stool. "I'll just be a minute."

Sixty seconds later, the woman ran back into the bar, followed by the old man, who casually returned to his stool and picked up his beer. "Where were we? . . ." Then they heard the ambulance siren.

The rumors spread, and the man got credit for ten times what he ever did, once driving off an entire motorcycle gang armed only with a bullwhip.

After dropping his crabs at the market each morning, the man always drove up to Mile 82 and the Green Turtle Inn. He stuck quarters in the news boxes out front and carried the stack of papers inside.

"Hey, it's Ralph!" "Hi, Ralph!" "How the crab business treatin' ya, Ralph?"

It didn't seem the man's reputation could get any bigger until one of the breakfast regulars came across an old paperback at the Islamorada Library. "What's this?"

She thumbed down the row of books. There was another, and another, finally a whole bunch, all with Ralph's name on the cover.

The next morning at the restaurant, everyone had books, wanting autographs. "Ralph, why didn't you tell us you were a writer?"

"What's to tell? That was another lifetime ago."

They talked about him after he left. "Wow, a tough guy who's sensitive *and* writes books."

"Just like him not to mention it."

"That's so *cool!*"

Ralph Krunkleton had seen life the way other people only dream. He had an uncanny knack for being at the right place at the right moment, an almost perfect sense of literary timing. Almost. He always seemed to be one human skin removed from huge success. The problem: Ralph wrote mysteries, which got no respect.

In 1958, he was twenty-seven years old and fifty pounds lighter. Goatee and turtleneck. It was San Francisco, drinking coffee at the City Lights Bookstore and listening to bad poetry. The beatnik movement was exploding, and he knew them all. Ginsberg, Burroughs, Ferlinghetti. Ralph wrote his first novel, a quixotic tale of wanderlust on America's highways and living in The Now, a stream-of-conscious bohemian murder mystery called *B Is for Bongo*. Another book came out that same year, and Jack Kerouac's career took off.

Ralph was still in San Francisco nine years later when the Summer of Love broke out at the corner of Haight and Ashbury. He began taking notes at the Fillmore, where he hung out with Jefferson Airplane and giant pulsing amoebas. He wrote a zeitgeist tome about hippies traveling the country in a brightly painted school bus, dropping LSD and getting murdered one by one. It was called *Bad Trip*. Tom Wolfe's career took off.

New York two years later, Ralph was thrown in the back of a paddy wagon with Norman Mailer during an antiwar demonstration.

"I suppose you're going to write a murder mystery about *this!*" said Mailer.

"Maybe I will!" Ralph shot back.

The Naked and the Murdered was published the following year and faded quickly after a single printing. Mailer became an asshole.

Ralph was last represented by the renowned agent Tanner Lebos. Ralph met Tanner in 1969 at a Simon and Garfunkel concert in Central Park. Tanner was wearing a Simon T-shirt; Ralph a Garfunkel. It was meant to be. They started talking. Tanner was struggling to get his literary firm up and running. He took Ralph on, and they were together almost twenty years. By the mid-seventies, however, their careers were on clearly diverging trajectories.

Ralph began spending more and more time in Florida until he was there year-round. He split his days between his homes in the Keys and Sarasota, where he played liar's poker with John D. MacDonald, McKinley Kantor and the rest of the gang at Florida's version of the Algonquin Round Table.

"Stick to mysteries, kid," said MacDonald. "Trust me. You'll see."

In the late seventies, Tanner paid Ralph a visit. They did lunch poolside at the Polo Lounge in Palm Beach. Ralph came in a corduroy leisure suit; Tanner wore tangerine sunglasses and an ascot. The conversation didn't go well.

"One favor," said Tanner.

"What's that?"

"One book that's not a mystery. Just one."

"I don't feel it."

"You louse up more good books by throwing bodies around. Look at Fitzgerald—where would *The Great Gatsby* be if it was a mystery?"

"Technically, it *is* a mystery."

Tanner began to simmer. "Let's enjoy our food."

While Ralph stayed down in the bargain bins, Tanner went on to become one of the hottest literary agents in Manhattan, eventually branching into theatrical representation. As they say, he was going places. Ralph was not. It continued another ten years until the big split-up in 1987. There had been a loud argument in the parking lot of a Longboat Key seafood restaurant, complete with police cars and women screaming and Tanner and John MacDonald wrestling at the base of a grinning lobster in a chef's hat.

The phone was ringing in the stilt house when Ralph got back from morning coffee at the Green Turtle. He picked it up.

"Ralph, it's me, Tanner. New York."

Silence.

"Ralph? You there?"

"Tan?"

"Bet you didn't expect to hear from me."

"It's been a while. What? Ten years?"

"Eleven."

"Good to hear your voice."

"I love you, too. Listen, you're not going to believe this, but I just got a call from your publisher. Your book's taking off. They're going back to press."

"Which book?"

"*The Stingray Shuffle*. But the others are starting to catch the draft, too. It could be big."

"Is this a joke?"

"They want you back on tour."

"But that book's been out for years. You said yourself it was dead."

"It's a crazy business."

"I don't want to tour. I like it here."

"Don't be a shmuck. Why did you write in the first place? So people would read your books. Well, now they're reading them. And they want to talk to you. You owe it to your fans."

Ralph was a stand-up guy. When Tanner put it that way, he couldn't refuse.

"What are they talking about?"

"Twenty cities, plus a few book festivals, a little TV and a celebrity mystery train."

"Could you repeat that last part?"

"It's the new thing. Mysteries are big now—who would have thought? They have all these fancy dinners and cruises and train rides where people pay a fortune to act all this shit out. Don't worry about the details—you'll be getting faxes."

"I don't have a fax machine."

"Doesn't matter. I have one of the new faxless fax machines. And you'll need some clothes."

"When is this supposed to start?"

"They were planning next Thursday. But that was before *Publishers Weekly* hit the stands. Have you seen it?"

"I'm in the Keys."

"There's an article on you, page sixty-seven. They've made you out like some kind of tropical Salinger. Nobody can get in touch with you.

They can't find anyone who's seen you in years or even has a recent photo. There's talk you're keeping some dark secret, but they're not even sure you're still alive."

"That's crazy. I'm in town all the time. Have coffee at the same place every day. There are no secrets—"

"I've told the publisher I want to push back the tour a month so we can grow the ambient buzz about your bizarre need for privacy and seclusion, and when the public appetite is too much to stand, *then* we put you on the road."

"The publisher isn't going to go along with this foolishness."

"They already have a team working on your mystique. They want everyone wondering who or what it is you're hiding from."

"I'm not hiding from anything—"

"Start."

"What?"

"Don't leave the house, and don't answer the phone. Unless it's me."

"How will I know it's you."

"Caller ID."

"I don't have caller ID."

"Even better. Adds to the myth. The recluse completely out of touch, shunning the new technology. We'll build you up like those Japanese living in island caves who think the war's still on. Maybe you've even gone *insane* . . ."

"There's nothing wrong with me."

"Let me worry about that. You stick to the books. Later."

Ralph put down the phone. "Unbelievable."

It rang again.

"Hello?"

"I thought I told you not to answer the phone."

"I didn't know we had started yet."

"We have."

"Sorry."

"While I've got you on the line, I want you to grow a beard. And start getting drunk in public."

"I thought I wasn't supposed to go out . . ."

"You can for that. It's pretty important."

"Anything else?"

"Do you think you can get arrested? I mean, do you know any local cops, some minor thing where you can arrange beforehand to get out immediately on bail? Do you have any drug connections?"

"Tanner—"

"I'm just thinking out loud now. I'm excited. Are you excited? Because I'm excited. Later."

Click.

7

Bok Tower stands 205 feet upon the highest point in peninsular Florida. It is an unforgettable sight, a stone monument rising alone on a pristine ridge called Iron Mountain, near the center of the state.

"The Singing Tower," as it is known, features a fifty-seven-bell carillon, the centerpiece of the tranquil Bok Tower Gardens, a meditative retreat of unmatched serenity.

A car engine roared. People screamed. Tires squealed. A beat-up pink Cadillac convertible patched out of the parking lot. Serge and Lenny turned around in the front seat and looked back at the two young women called City and Country as they ran and yelled through a dust cloud, trying to catch the Cadillac as it pulled back on the highway and sped off.

"Hated to ditch them like that," said Lenny.

"They left us no choice," said Serge.

"Our sanity had to come first," said Lenny, pushing the gas all the way to the floor, watching the women grow smaller in the rearview mirror.

"They never stopped talking," said Serge. "I couldn't hear myself think."

"They were smoking up all my weed." Lenny held a can of Cruex to his eye to gauge the damage. "And they were starting to get fat."

"Of course they were getting fat—they never stopped eating. I thought I was watching some kind of unnerving nature special on the Discovery Channel, constrictor snakes dislocating their jaws to ingest small mammals headfirst."

"That's what the munchies do to you."

"I'm glad I was never part of the drug culture," said Serge, loading an automatic pistol in his lap.

"This isn't about the drug culture—it's about *women*," said Lenny. "Oh sure, it always starts with a lot of Technicolor orgasms, and the next thing you know you got matching dishes in your apartment . . ."

"If we let them stay, pretty soon they'd be telling us what to do . . ."

"Making us wipe our feet . . ."

"Getting mad at us all the time for things we do not understand . . ."

Serge and Lenny looked at each other and shook with the heebie-jeebies.

"Still, I'm disappointed we had to leave the tower so fast," said Serge. "I haven't been to Bok since I was a kid."

"You're really into this history stuff, aren't you?" asked Lenny, lighting a joint.

"Fuckin'-A. Built by Dutch immigrant Edward W. Bok, who dedicated it in 1929 to all Americans."

"Nice gesture," Lenny said through pursed lips.

"Guess what publication he was editor of."

Lenny shook his head.

"*Ladies' Home Journal.*"

"Get outta here."

"I shit you not. And guess who he had write for him?"

Lenny shook his head again.

"Rudyard Kipling and Teddy Roosevelt."

"Not too shabby," said Lenny. "But how do you find out all this stuff? How do you *remember* it?"

"I assign each fact a geometric shape and then string them together in a crystalline lattice in the image center of my brain."

Lenny exhaled a hit and nodded. "Works for me."

"You see the funky colors in the masonry?"

Lenny nodded, although he didn't know what masonry was.

"Pink and gray marble from Georgia and native coquina rock from St. Augustine," said Serge, shaking the geopositioning tracker.

"What's it say?" asked Lenny.

"The signal's fading in and out, but it's consistently pointing east, so the transmitter in the briefcase must still be working." He put the tracker down on the seat beside him. "I'm pretty hacked I didn't get to the gift shop. You know I'm always required to buy an enamel pin for my archives."

Lenny reached in his shirt pocket and pulled out a Bok Tower lapel pin. He turned it back and forth to glint in the sunlight before passing it across the front seat.

"You're humble and lovable," said Serge. He removed a small plastic box from the gym bag at his feet and tucked the Bok pin inside with dozens of other pins.

"What are those?" asked Lenny, glancing over.

"Recent acquisitions. Sea World, Silver Springs, plus lots of train stuff, like the Flagler Museum."

"Trains?"

"Yeah, I kind of got into them a little bit last year, because of the direct linkage to Florida's evolution."

"You? Getting into something a little bit?" said Lenny. "More like you completely obsessed, right?"

"I like to call it disciplined study habits."

"I don't buy it," said Lenny.

"Neither did the cops."

"You were arrested again?"

"It's so unfair," said Serge. "All these misunderstandings happening to the same person. What are the odds?"

"How did it happen?"

"Well, I'll tell you," said Serge, reaching in the glove compartment and taking out novelty glasses with 3-D spirals on the lenses and little pinholes in the middle.

Lenny looked over at him. "You going to do a flashback?"

Serge nodded. "I'm all about flashbacks."

He slid the glasses on his face and raised his chin in concentration. "I can see it like it was just yesterday—a warm summer morning, the overnight dew burning off fast, mixing with the smell of just-mowed grass. A dark blue Buick LeSabre drove slowly down Cocoanut Row on the island of Palm Beach . . ."

Inside the Buick, two retired women sipped coffee from travel mugs. The passenger read the *Palm Beach Post* to the driver: an update on the "Spiderman" burglary trial out of Miami, then the arrest of a man who was looking up women's dresses in Burdines with a video-camera concealed in the toe of his shoe.

"Must have been a small camera," said the driver.

"Technology," said the passenger, turning the page.

They took a left on Whitehall Way, toward a sprawling lawn and twin palms flanking a tall iron arch. The two museum volunteers parked and unlocked the gate, then the front door of a century-old mansion. They flipped on lights, adjusted the thermostat, opened the gift shop. One headed outside through the south door. There was an old banyan tree near the seawall, overlooking the Intracoastal Waterway and the mainland, where the servants lived in West Palm Beach. In the middle of the lawn was a brief stretch of railroad track that led nowhere. On the rails sat a forest green Pullman passenger car custom-built in 1886. There were historical plaques and gold letters down the side. *Florida East Coast.* And a number, 91. The woman climbed the steps at the end of the car and unlocked the door on the observation platform. She walked through the dining room, then down a narrow hallway past the copper-lined shower. She got to the sleeping compartment and froze in the doorway.

One of the pull-down sleeping berths was open, holding a pile of blankets covering a human-sized lump.

The woman took a meek step backward.

The lump moved.

The woman seized up. She wanted to run, but her legs wouldn't respond.

The lump moved some more, and a head of mussed hair popped out of the blankets.

"Are we there yet?"

The woman stood paralyzed.

"Are we there yet? Key West?"

The woman finally managed a light, trembling voice. "Key . . . West? . . ."

"Key West," repeated the man. "This is my big day. The biggest day of my life."

There was a pause. The woman's voice quivered again. "Uh . . . what day is that?"

"January twenty-second!"

The woman looked through the windows at the beautiful summer day outside. "January?"

"Of course," said the man, "1912."

No reply.

"If we're not there yet, I could use some more sleep."

"We're . . . uh, not there yet."

"Good," said the man, rolling over and covering his head with the blanket.

Two officers in a squad car were en route to a report of golf rage at a local country club when they received the intruder call from the Flagler Museum and made a squealing U-turn. The officers reached the museum's south lawn and found a garden hose stretching across the grass to the side of the train car. They drew service pistols and quietly climbed up the observation platform. As they filed down the car's tight hallway, they heard water running. Then singing. The first officer reached the door of the shower and peeked in. The curtain came up to the shoulders of the intruder. His eyes were closed as he rubbed shampoo into his scalp.

"Everybody's doooo-in' a brand new dance, now! . . ."

The officers looked at each other.

The intruder opened his eyes. "Oh, my VIP escorts. Be with you in a minute."

"Henry Morrison Flagler was born of humble roots in 1830 and, with John D. Rockefeller, founded the Standard Oil Company. By the time he retired at the relatively young age of fifty-three, profits and interest were building up in his bank accounts faster than any human could spend. Some say what Flagler did next was out of guilt from the brutal business practices and obscene profits of his oil company. Others say the man was like one of those ants that spend all day lifting ten times their own weight, and Henry had no choice but to build, build, build!—"

"Objection!" said the prosecutor, jumping to his feet in courtroom 3C, Palm Beach Judicial Circuit.

"What grounds?" asked the judge.

"Your Honor, this is a simple trespassing case. A bum sleeping in a train car at a museum. The court has already been overly generous letting this man represent himself, but now he's abusing the privilege and turning the proceedings into an utter travesty."

The judge turned to Serge at the defense table. "What do you have to say?"

"The historical underpinnings of this case go directly to my motivation. I must be given wide latitude to establish my state of mind in order to defend myself against these unfair but highly imaginative charges."

"Your Honor," interrupted the prosecutor. "It's clear the defendant needs psychiatric attention. He's already wasted enough of the people's time and resources."

The judge looked at the defendant. "Tell me, are you Henry Flagler?"

"Of course not," said the defendant. "That would be crazy."

"What's your name?"

"Serge. Serge Storms."

"I'm going to allow it," the judge told the prosecutor. "After hearing your legal arguments for the last few years, I find the change of pace rather refreshing."

The prosecutor sat down and fumed. The judge faced the defendant again and got comfortable in his big chair. "You may continue."

"Thank you, Your Honor. Now where was I? Oh, yeah. Henry looked south and saw Florida, an empty canvas. The Spanish, French and English had been at work on the place for three centuries with nothing to show. The massive St. Johns River, just below Jacksonville, was the natural barrier preventing serious progress. The first crucial thing Flagler did was bridge that gorge. It changed the whole ball game. He began laying train tracks like nobody's business and built a string of luxury hotels down the coast. Northerners came in droves. By 1904, Flagler's railroad ran all the way to Homestead, south of Miami, the very bottom of Florida. Most people would have stopped. But did Flagler?"

Serge turned toward the prosecutor's table. *"Did he?"*

The judge was grinning now. He looked at the prosecutor. "Well, did he?"

The prosecutor rolled his eyes. "I'm sure he didn't."

"That's right!" said Serge, slapping the defense table. "With the Spanish-American War just over, that freed up the sugar and pineapple crops in Cuba. Flagler could load it all on ships and sail to Key West. If only he had a train station there. But surely a railroad couldn't be built a hundred miles out to sea, facing the open ocean and hurricanes, right?" Serge slapped the table again. "Wrong! Flagler heard of a man named J. C. Meredith, who was doing new things with reinforced concrete down in Mexico, and brought him in on the project. Ten thousand workers came south. The cost blew the mind. This was something on the level of the pyramids, the Manhattan Project and the moon program. But no government was behind it—just one man. They said it couldn't be done. Flagler's Folly, they called it. And it looked like they were right." Serge began pacing and gesturing. "All types of setbacks and geological barriers—they had to invent new kinds of engineering on the spot. Flagler himself was falling apart, almost blind, a year to live, tops. Didn't look good. But on January twenty-second, 1912, *The Extension Special*, pulling Flagler's private train car, rolled into Key West as bands played and schoolchildren cheered and threw roses on the tracks."

Serge looked around the courtroom and dabbed his eyes with a handkerchief. "As he pulled into the station, Flagler said, 'I can hear the children, but I cannot see them.'" Serge sat down at the defense table, buried his face in his arms and began sobbing.

The judge cleared his throat. "What does the court psychiatrist have to say?"

"Your Honor, the defendant obviously needs treatment. He's on a variety of medications, and when he takes them, he's fine. But when he stops, he has episodes, like the other day at the museum."

"Is he dangerous?"

"Only to himself. There's nothing violent in his record . . ."

"Nothing *yet*," interrupted the prosecutor.

". . . Only a string of night burglaries," continued the psychiatrist. "Cypress Gardens, Trapper Nelson's Pioneer Home, the Marjorie Kinnan Rawlings Estate."

"What does he do? Take stuff?"

"He leaves stuff."

"Come again?"

"He leaves stuff."

"Like what?"

"Little historic artifacts and souvenirs he's collected over the years. He finds them at swap meets or on the Internet or even with a metal detector," said the psychiatrist. "He told me he wants to make sure they're preserved by the appropriate authorities."

Serge raised his head and nodded urgently in agreement.

Over the prosecution's vociferous objections, the judge suspended sentence and ordered the defendant to perform fifty hours of community service polishing the brass on Henry Flagler's private railroad car. Then he headed for his chambers, chuckling to himself, *"Wide latitude."*

8

he sun hung just below the Atlantic horizon on another clear Florida morning. Cigarette wrappers and cellophane bags blew across a grimy alley on the sour north end of Miami Beach. Another ocean gust, and a Burger King cup started rolling toward the gutter and was flattened by an all-weather tire. The tire belonged to a white Mercedes Z310 that drove down the alley and backed up to a service door behind a strip mall. Five men in tropical shirts got out and unloaded brown cartons from the trunk and carried them in the back door of The Palm Reader.

The owner checked his wristwatch. A minute till ten. He parted the strings of beads under the Employees Only sign and walked to the front of the store, flicking on fluorescent lights that revealed a skimpy, outdated selection of dusty books. He checked his watch again. Ten on the nose. A long line had already formed outside. The man flipped the CLOSED sign over, unlocked three large bolts and pushed the front door open.

Back in the storeroom, the staff was busy with box cutters, slicing open a dozen cases of paperbacks, 576 books in all, every one the same title.

The customers were not browsers. They went straight to the counter.

The owner stood behind the cash register and smiled. "Can I help you?"

"Uh, yes," said the first customer. He leaned forward and lowered his voice. "I'd like *The Stingray Shuffle*."

"I think we might have one left," said the owner, reaching under the counter and producing a paperback. "Yes, here it is. But it's a rare collector's item. First edition. A hundred dollars."

The customer handed over five twenties, took the book and left quickly.

The next customer stepped up.

"May I help you?"

The customer opened his wallet. *"The Stingray Shuffle,* please."

"We might have one left," said the owner, reaching down. "Yes, here it is . . ."

The line still had a dozen customers left when the owner felt under the counter and found an empty shelf. He yelled toward the bead curtain in the back of the store: "Need some more books up here!"

One of the workers burst through the beads and trotted up to the register with a fresh box. The others in the storeroom were hard at work with box cutters, slicing secret compartments into the middle of the paperbacks and inserting grams of cocaine.

A half hour later: "We need more books again!"

"We're almost out."

"So reorder," yelled the owner. "Call the distributor."

The phone rang in the back room. It never stopped ringing. Always the same question. "Yes, we have that title."

But this call was different.

The employee who answered it got a nervous look. He cupped his hand over the receiver. "Boss! Come quick!"

The owner stuck his head through the beads. "What is it?"

"Some nosy person asking a lot of questions about books. Really suspicious."

"Who is it?"

"Says he's a publisher."

"You idiot! Of course it's a publisher! This is a fucking bookstore. Just get rid of him."

"Right." The employee uncovered the receiver and had a short conversation, jotting something on a scrap of paper before hanging up.

"What did they say?"

"They wanted an author to do a book signing here."

The boss started laughing. "Here?" He broke up again. "That's a riot!"

The employee started laughing, too.

The laughing gradually tapered off, and the boss caught his breath. "How'd you get rid of him?"

"Said Tuesday would be fine."

"What! We can't have a book signing here!"

"You just told me to get rid of him. You didn't say no signing."

The boss pulled a gold bullet of coke from his shirt pocket, stuck it under his nose. "Who's this author, anyway?"

The employee checked his piece of paper. "Ralph Krunkleton."

The boss sniffled and bunched his eyebrows in concentration. "Ralph Krunkleton, Ralph Krunkleton. Where have I heard that name before? Hmmm . . ."

The others continued slicing books.

". . . Ralph Krunkleton, Ralph Krunkleton . . ." The boss looked down at the table full of paperbacks. "Oh, my God! Not Ralph Krunkleton!"

"Who's Ralph Krunkleton?"

"The guy who wrote this book!" The owner snorted up again, and the coke began marching him in a circle. "We don't need this kind of attention! We've worked hard to develop this book as our code title—one of the worst-selling novels in history, one that no law-abiding customer would ever, ever ask for. A signing is the last thing we need—it'll screw up the entire procedure. And there'll be press, TV . . ."

An employee slit into another paperback. "We'll need snack mix."

*A*t the end of the twentieth century, major drug cartels were displaying enormous ingenuity and limitless finances. Cocaine was found encased in concrete posts, dissolved in soda pop, injected in breast implants.

But nobody expected what was discovered one cool morning high up the mountains twenty-eight kilometers west of Cartagena. Police were tipped off by farmers in a remote village, who said three strangers had moved into an old warehouse, never came out and appeared to subsist entirely on takeout delivered from God knew where. They heard drilling sounds at night.

There was no sign of the three men when the *policia* swarmed the warehouse in a coordinated predawn raid and found precision tools, welding tanks and Russian engineering manuals. But nobody was looking at that stuff. They were staring up at The Tube—the arc-welded, double-hulled, twenty-foot-wide steel cylinder running the entire length of the building. It couldn't possibly be what they thought it was, not at this altitude.

Military experts soon confirmed their worst suspicions: a nearly complete military-class submarine that could dive to three hundred feet and carry ten tons of cocaine. The sub was to be built, then dismantled and trucked to the coast for reassembly. The estimated cost: twenty-five million U.S. dollars. The police had to shake their heads with grudging admiration. This was even more ambitious than the previous high-water mark in 1995, when the Cali Cartel attempted to purchase a used Soviet navy sub before the deal was uncovered and scuttled. But that was dismissed as a grandiose scheme doomed from the start. This, on the other hand, was frighteningly close to fruition. There was a wave of relief. Thank heaven they'd arrived when they did.

A police captain with as much imagination as the cartels deflated the mood. "How do we know there aren't other subs already in the water?"

A tall, rugged man in a white linen suit stood on a sandy beach near the southern end of the Windward Islands and looked out to sea with binoculars. It was a beautiful horseshoe harbor of clear blue water, the shore ringed with quaint pastel buildings. Behind the man, the island rose quickly through coconut palms and a rain forest to the volcanic peak of Mount St. Catherine, the highest point in Grenada.

The man kept his binoculars trained on the water and for some reason remembered reading that Grenada had 154 TV sets per thousand residents. He looked a little like Gene Hackman and wore an expression of grave concern. Nobody knew the man's name, but they all called him Mr. Grande, head of the infamous Mierda Cartel.

The cocaine business had always been a tricky proposition, and everyone knew the risks. The absurd amounts of money made it worthwhile. Except for the Mierda Cartel. It was the sixty-eighth-largest cartel in the world, which was last place, and it was broke. The other cartels fought extradition; the Mierda gang was hounded by bill collectors.

Everyone naturally assumed that all cartels were extremely rich and ruthless, and the residents of Grenada initially treated their hometown traffickers with the appropriate mixture of respect and fear. But a different picture soon emerged. The cartel was running up tabs all over town. Nobody wanted to say anything at first. They had heard the stories. But when the cartel couldn't pay for transmission work on a Mercedes, and the mechanic impounded the car—and was still alive a week later—everything changed. The merchants started getting nudgey, and the cartel began avoiding town.

It was eating at the Mierda organization. The newspaper stories touting the triumphs of the other cartels only rubbed it in. The cocaine business was an intensely competitive one, with a pecking order as rigid as the seating chart at the Oscars. Word of the submarine discovered in the Colombian highlands had reached Grenada, and it got under Mr. Grande's skin.

This called for a sit-down.

Mr. Grande drove his golf cart up the winding road to cartel headquarters, a top secret mountain hideaway concealed in the thickest part of the rain forest, near the top of Mount St. Catherine. He stopped at the mailbox and removed a stack of threatening collection notices. His men were already waiting in the study, submachine guns hanging from shoulder straps. They stood when Mr. Grande entered, and they sat when he sat. When they did, one of the submachine guns accidentally went off, a quick burst of bullets whistling across the room into the saltwater aquarium.

"Who did that?" demanded Mr. Grande, clownfish flopping on the floor.

They pointed at Paco.

"Give it!"

"But—"

"Now!"

Paco shuffled across the room, head down, and handed the weapon to Mr. Grande, who stuck it in the bottom drawer of his desk and closed it.

Mr. Grande then held up the newspaper with the submarine article. He slapped the page with the back of his hand. "This is what we should be doing!" He picked up the phone.

After a brief conversation, he hung up and turned to his men. "Our problems are solved."

Mr. Grande had phoned the cartel that lost the submarine. He knew the raid had put them behind schedule, and he made a persuasive argument to subcontract his own boys for rush delivery of a new thirty-million-dollar sub.

"Where are we going to get a sub?" asked Paco.

"*Estupido!*" yelled Mr. Grande.

The men crowded around as their boss rolled his office chair over to the computer and logged onto Yahoo! Five minutes later, he stood at the printer. Out came a crosshatch schematic blueprint of the submarine *H. L. Hunley*. What attracted Mr. Grande was the *Hunley*'s elegant simplicity.

"We can build one of these with our eyes closed," he said. "Then we'll have all the money we need . . . and some respect!"

The phone rang.

"What now?" said Mr. Grande.

It was the power company.

"Do you have any idea who you're talking to?" he screamed in the receiver. "I could have you killed just for saying that! One word from me and your whole family will be blown up! . . . Hello? Hello? . . ."

Mr. Grande put down the phone, and the lights went out.

A month later, the Mierda Cartel packed themselves into a convoy of pickup trucks and drove down from their mountain headquarters to the coastal capital of St. George's. The curious townspeople came out of the shops and restaurants as the cartel backed a trailer up to the water. The residents faintly recognized the object on the trailer but couldn't quite place it.

One of the cartel stood knee-deep in the surf and motioned to the driver, who watched in the side mirror as he backed up.

"Keep coming. Keep coming. Keep coming . . ." He held up a hand. "Stop!"

They untied the restraining straps, and a large, bulbous object slid gently into the water. Then they opened a hatch on top and the entire cartel got inside except Mr. Grande, who stood on the beach focusing binoculars.

The onlookers inched forward and formed a semicircle around their local kingpin. Mr. Grande didn't look at them, but he knew they were there, and he swelled with pride. Finally, respect.

The craft began its maiden voyage, moving under its own power at modest speed until it reached deeper water and submerged, just the periscope showing. The impressed crowd murmured.

Mr. Grande had become supremely confident the moment he saw the *H. L. Hunley* on the Internet. He immediately recognized the shape and knew exactly where he could lay his hands on something watertight to use for the pressure hull. He cajoled Grenada Power & Light to turn the electricity back on and talked a local merchant into extending credit one last time. "You won't be sorry."

The cartel took delivery of the "hull" the next afternoon and worked round the clock with drills, jigsaws and rivet guns, carefully following their computer diagrams. They attached hand cranks to underwater paddles with axles fitted through greased nylon gaskets in the hull, and they employed a similar shaft design for the rudder. They bought plastic fifty-gallon outboard gas containers for ballast tanks, which also acted as the keel. A shuttlecock valve let water into the tanks, and an air-mattress foot pump pushed it out. And finally, they installed a periscope, a hatch and a series of portholes in the hull, which was a fiberglass septic tank.

Mr. Grande's smile broadened as he watched through the binoculars. The crowd's approval grew louder until cheering broke out. The sub moved into deeper and deeper water, until the periscope finally disappeared. Bubbles. Then nothing.

They waited.

The reason for the *Hunley*'s simplicity: It was the first submarine ever used in combat. Built during the Civil War, it was launched off Charleston in 1864.

The Mierda Cartel couldn't read English, so they didn't know the vintage or history of the *Hunley*, but they had no problem with the diagrams. They followed them perfectly. Too perfectly, in fact, and, like its historic predecessor, the cartel's sub promptly sank on its maiden voyage with all hands.

Mr. Grande lowered his binoculars. "Damn."

The crowd was silent. The cartel owed all of them money, but they decided it was an awkward time to bring it up, and they parted and let Mr. Grande pass through unmolested.

A pink Cadillac sat quietly at the end of an empty parking lot, catching shade from some jasmine. Lenny sat alone in the car, head back over the headrest, exhaling smoke straight up, flicking the nub of a roach out on the pavement. He turned and squinted toward the long, bright-white building with the string of Mediterranean arches facing some train tracks. The building had twin cupolas in the middle, topped with Moorish domes, and between them, curved over the main arch: ORLANDO.

"Will you come on!" yelled Lenny.

Serge's shout came back faintly: "A couple more seconds!" Lenny watched him in the distance, standing in the middle of the train tracks, snapping photos of the back of a departing Amtrak heading south to Kissimmee. A handful of weary passengers had just gotten off and carried suitcases across the pavement toward the depot. Otherwise, the place was deserted, the Florida sun directly overhead without clouds.

No wind. Crickets, sandspurs. The stagnant heat seemed to have weight.

"Will you come on! I'm getting something on the tracker!"

Serge took a couple parting shots, then sprinted back to the car and vaulted into the passenger seat without opening the door.

"What the hell were you doing?" asked Lenny.

"I've decided to completely dedicate my life to the study of trains and things that look like trains."

Lenny started up the engine. "I knew I should never have asked you about trains. Now we'll never catch up with that briefcase."

"This was on the way to the briefcase—sort of. And besides, we've got them cornered with the five million."

"Really?" said Lenny. "I thought this was just fucking around. Not that I'm against that."

Serge pointed his arms in two different directions. "The logical escape routes are Daytona and Miami. But the tracker's pinging due east, which can only mean the port and the cruise ships out of the country. The next one leaves Friday."

"How do you know?"

"I have the schedule memorized," said Serge. "I go over my own escape routes all the time. To survive in this state, you have to think like the French Resistance."

Lenny took the entrance ramp for I-4, and Serge stood to snap a final elevated photo back toward the train station. He sat down and stowed the camera. "I can't believe nobody visits that depot anymore. They're all too busy heading for the Tower of Terror or the Aerosmith roller coaster. What's happening to us as a people? . . ."

"They have an Aerosmith roller coaster?"

". . . The depot's barely changed since it was built in 1926. This is where the town began, for heaven's sake. People should be flocking here whether they're taking a train or not. But now the only people who still come are forced to after making a horrible mess of their lives through a series of gross miscalculations until they can't scrape together airplane money."

"Now I can see how you got arrested that time in that old train car."

"You mean the first time."

"There were others?"

"I'm telling you, it's like life is out to get me," said Serge, reaching in the glove compartment for his novelty 3-D glasses.

"Flashback?" asked Lenny.

Serge nodded, slipping on the glasses. "Courtroom scene."

"You ever watch *The People's Court*?" asked Lenny.

"Shhh," said Serge. "The flashback is starting . . ."

One year earlier, courtroom 3C, Palm Beach County Judicial Circuit.

The judge levied a stiff fine and probation on a retired banker for killing a prize swan with a pitching wedge at a local golf course.

"Bailiff, call the next case."

"Number six-nine-seven-two-five, *People versus Serge A. Storms.*"

"Will the defendant please rise . . ." The judge stopped midsentence and took off his glasses. "Back already?"

"I can explain, Your Honor," said Serge. "This is all a tragic miscarriage. A mockery of justice. If what I did was wrong, I don't wanna be right! . . ."

"Your Honor," interrupted the prosecutor. "The defendant is charged with burglary, trespassing, disturbing the peace, resisting arrest and vandalism, to wit: applying paint to an object of historic national importance."

"What does that mean in English?" asked the judge. "Spray-painting graffiti? Throwing paint balloons?"

"Not exactly."

"Then what exactly?"

"Uh, um . . ."

"You're mumbling," said the judge.

"He was in a historic railroad car, restoring some detail work that was chipping."

The bailiff handed the judge an evidence bag marked "Exhibit A," an extra-fine camel's-hair brush with dried gold paint on the tip.

"There I was," said Serge, "minding my own business . . ."

"Your Honor," said the public defender. "This is really a mental-health case. The defendant needs professional care. He shouldn't be in criminal court at all."

"Why is he in *my* court?" asked the judge. "As I understand it, this all happened in Miami's jurisdiction, at the . . ." He paused and flipped through some papers. "The Gold Coast Railroad Museum."

"Your Honor, this violates the conditions of the probation that you placed upon him last week for breaking into the railroad car at the Flagler Museum, so it throws it back here," said the prosecutor. "Most disturbing is the resisting-arrest charge."

"What's that about?" asked the judge.

The prosecutor picked up a copy of the police report. "When officers arrived, the suspect was applying paint in the dining compartment of an antique passenger car. When said officers attempted to effect arrest, the suspect dove from the car and ran across the museum, where he proceeded to climb into a nearby locomotive engine, refused to come down, and began singing, and I quote: 'Riding that train. High on cocaine . . .'"

The judge ran his fingers through his hair and turned to the public defender. "Is your client on drugs?"

"That's just the problem, Your Honor. He refuses to *take* his drugs."

"That locomotive was number one fifty-three, Florida East Coast Railway," said Serge, "which pulled a rescue train out of the Keys during the Labor Day hurricane of 1935 . . ."

The judge held up a hand for Serge to stop and turned to the public defender. "So what's with all the trains, anyway?"

Serge kept talking in the background: ". . . and that railroad car I was painting was the famous Ferdinand Magellan, built in 1928 and later retrofitted with armor plating and bulletproof glass for none other than the president of the United States! . . ."

"Your Honor, Mr. Storms, like so many other unfortunate Americans, is battling severe mental illness. He's going through a phase right now."

"A phase?"

". . . You see," said Serge, "this was in the days before Air Force One, when the president had to travel by rail. The Magellan was first used by Franklin Roosevelt in 1942. And it was on the rear platform of this very car that, on November 3, 1948, a grinning Harry Truman held up the *Dewey Defeats Truman* newspaper in the now-famous photograph . . ."

"Your Honor, he gets on these compulsive tangents," said the public defender. "He has to find out every single thing there is to know about a subject, talk to as many experts as he can, see and touch everything . . ."

"I object!" said Serge, jumping to his feet. "He's making it sound weird."

"Weirdness isn't grounds for an objection," said the judge. "And that's your own attorney."

"Then I respectfully withdraw." Serge sat back down and turned to the public defender. "Proceed."

"Your Honor, why is this man even being allowed to speak?" complained the prosecutor. "He's not even representing himself anymore, and he's completely out of line. As a matter of fact, we're not following any of the procedures at all!"

"First thing—relax," said the judge. "This is a minor case. Second, this is *my* court, and third, I kinda like the guy. Is that okay with you?"

The prosecutor sat down and sulked. The judge turned back to the public defender. "Continue."

"He'll go days without sleep, covering incredible distances on foot, and he only stops when he passes out from sheer exhaustion."

"Interesting," said the judge. "And right now it's railroads?"

"Railroads."

Serge raised his hand.

"You're not in school," said the judge.

"May I?" asked Serge.

The judge leaned back in his chair and got comfortable again. "Go ahead."

The prosecutor snapped a pencil in two and threw the pieces on his table.

"You see, the railroads *made* Florida," said Serge. "They played a major role in most states, but not like here, where their influence was an iron fist, the train companies owning much of the land and businesses along their routes. I'm not saying it was wrong or right; I'm just saying it worked. Completely opened up the peninsula."

"What about air-conditioning?" asked the judge. "I understand that when Mr. Carrier went into mass production, it jump-started all kinds of development."

"Your Honor," interjected the public defender, "Mr. Storms had, uh, a number of arrests last year dealing with the air-conditioning and refrigeration industry. I don't think we want to go there."

"Understood," said the judge. "Continue, Mr. Storms."

"Thank you, and Your Honor's point is well taken. But that never would have been possible if it wasn't for the rail pioneers. It all started with Flagler . . ." Serge began pacing in front of the empty jury box. "Time? The Gilded Age! Place? Jacksonville! The rich valued their leisure, and the railroads went down to Florida just to get to the new luxury hotels, which were built just for the railroads. After traversing the St. Johns, Flagler erected the Ponce de Leon in St. Augustine, then the Alcazar, and remodeled the Cordova and Ormond, laying tracks all the way. The Royal Poinciana and the Breakers went up in Palm Beach, more tracks, still going south, right through the big freeze of 1895—*chug-a-chug, chug-a-chug . . .*"—Serge shuffled across the courtroom, arms going in circles like pistons moving the wheels of a steam engine—"*. . . chug-a-chug, chug-a-chug. Woo-woo!* The tracks reached the bottom of the state, and residents were so happy they wanted to name their town Flagler. But did Big Henry accept this honor? Hell, no! He said, 'Why don't we name this place after the Indian word they use for the river.' That little town? Miami! Fresh produce moved north, tourists south, the Florida East Coast Railway kept on going, right up to the beach, then into the sea. He had to be crazy to keep going—crazy like a fox! . . . *Chug-a-chug, chug-a-chug . . .* Another Henry, Henry S. Sanford, ran the South Florida Railroad down the middle of the state in the 1880s. And on the Gulf Coast, yet another Henry—where were they all coming from?—this one named Plant, built a third railroad and more hotels. His line made it down to Cedar Key, and the little fishing village exploded as it became the southernmost port at the end of the tracks. But then the tracks continued south, and Cedar Key was forgotten. The tracks stopped again at another tiny outpost. Its name? Tampa! . . . *Bang, bang, bang!* War breaks out in Cuba! Troop trains to Florida, Teddy Roosevelt, the Rough Riders, Hearst, José Martí. The war ends! We win! More trains, more tourists, more hotels! The Boca Grande Line, the Gasparilla Inn, hope and prosperity for all! . . . *Chug-a-chug, chug-a-chug* . . . Train fares drop, the bourgeois climb on board, everyone riding south on *The Havana Special, The Florida Special, The Orange Blossom Special.* Then, daring! Railroads unveil the deco streamliners! In 1939, *The Silver Meteor* debuted its New York–Miami night runs with a sleek Electro-Motive diesel. The Atlantic Coast Line countered with *The Champion* and Illinois Central rolled out *The City of Miami* . . ."

The judge looked over the top of his bifocals. "Don't you mean *The City of New Orleans,* like the song?"

"And a great song it is. But no, I mean *The City of Miami.* Few people realize there ever was such a train, but what a train! The trademark orange-and-green paint scheme, the coach cars with those wonderful names: Bougainvillea, Camellia, Japonica, Palm Garden, Hibiscus, Poinsettia and the Bamboo Grove tavern-observation car—very popular. . . . *Ridin' on The City of Miami . . . Don't you know me? I'm your native son . . .*"

"No singing in court, Mr. Storms."

"Sorry. Then came the twin enemies of the iron horse—airlines and interstate highways. The trains hung on gallantly until the 1960s, when all appeared lost. . . . But wait! A last-second reprieve! The government stepped in, and Amtrak was born in 1971. The old *Silver Meteor* came back into service, now joined by *The Silver Star, The Silver Palm* and *The Silver Stingray.* But then, the stake through the heart—apathy! Nobody gave a damn. The depots deteriorated, and Overseas Railroad spans were torn up and sold off. A few noble groups fought uphill. They restored Union Station in Tampa, and my heart just goes pitter-pat every time I see that cute little spruced-up depot in Lake Wales. Unfortunately, it's looking like too little, too late. Amtrak isn't making the grade, and there's been talk of pulling the plug in a couple years. Our kids will probably only see the pictures in the history books. Right now could be your last chance to head up to New York, hop a train in the snow and take the slow ride south to the Sunshine State, *the way you're supposed to . . .*"

A half hour later, everyone in the courtroom was silent, leaning forward on Serge's every word.

"... So in conclusion, Your Honor, and the good people of this courtroom, I may not have had a right to do what I did, but I had a duty. I did it for all of us, not just those alive here today, but for the memory of our ancestors and the future of our unborn descendants." Serge's lip began quivering and he sat down.

The judge took off his glasses again. "Mr. Storms, I'm going to give you yet another chance. Probation and community service. But I never want to see you in my courtroom again."

Courtroom 3C, Palm Beach County Judicial Circuit.

"Bailiff, call the next case."

"Number nine-three-five-one-two, *People versus Serge A. Storms.*"

Serge smiled and waved at the judge.

"You were just here yesterday!"

"There's a very simple explanation. Then we can all laugh about it and go home—"

The judge stopped Serge and turned to the prosecutor. "What's the charge?"

The prosecutor glanced at his docket. "There are any number of possibilities, but we've decided to file under disturbing the peace."

"What exactly did he do?" asked the judge.

"I think you need to see the video. Words cannot do justice."

A bailiff wheeled a twenty-seven-inch Magnavox and VCR to the front of the courtroom.

"This was shot at a local funeral. It was taken by one of the mourners, the deceased's only brother, who was later x-rayed for chest pains."

The bailiff inserted a tape and handed the remote to the prosecutor. The courtroom saw a tent in the middle of a sunny lawn full of tombstones. Folding chairs, people in black, a preacher.

The prosecutor hit *pause* and pointed to the right side of the screen. "This is where Mr. Storms enters the picture and takes a seat in the back row of chairs." He hit *play*; on the screen, a wiry man in swim trunks and tropical shirt joins the mourners.

"Hit *pause* again," said the judge. He folded his hands and looked toward the defense table. "I know I'm going to regret asking this, but did you even know these people, Mr. Storms?"

"Never met them in my life."

"What were you doing in the cemetery?"

"Taking rubbings of a historic headstone, a famous train engineer. Suddenly, a funeral breaks out."

"And you just walked over and helped yourself to a seat?"

"I like people."

The judge nodded at the prosecutor, who restarted the tape. "Okay, now here's the point when Mr. Storms approaches the podium and tells the preacher he'd like to say a few words."

"Hit *pause* again," said the judge, turning. "You never even met these people before! What on earth could you have to say at a time like this?"

"Anything," said Serge. "The preacher was bombing. You should have seen the long faces, people crying . . ."

"It was a funeral!"

"That's the whole problem," said Serge. "Everyone takes that view. I don't buy it."

The prosecutor started the tape again. "Mr. Storms opens with a few jokes, talks about the deceased in generic terms, praises the Greatest Generation, blah, blah, blah, a few more jokes . . ."

The judge pointed at the TV. "It doesn't look like the audience is too distressed. A few are even beginning to smile. What he did may have been highly inappropriate, but I don't see any criminal disturbance of the peace here. . . . See? He's even starting to get some laughs."

"Hold on. The good part's coming up," said the prosecutor. "Mr. Storms wraps up his little talk and steps away from the podium. That's the urn that he's picking up now, and he starts walking away. The audience is confused. They begin to realize they better do something. They go after him. Mr. Storms begins running. The funeral party starts running—that's all the bouncing and jiggling you're seeing from the camera now. This is the ditch at the edge of the cemetery. Mr. Storms takes the lid off the urn. An uncle grabs him by the arm, and now the full-scale free-for-all gets under way. That's some off-camera screaming you're hearing, and this is where the ninety-year-old mother accidentally gets punched in the eye by the uncle, and Mr. Storms breaks free and runs to the edge of the ditch and yells—we've had an audio technician verify this—'It's for your own good. You need closure.' And, as you can see . . . he dumps the ashes in an open sewer."

"How was I supposed to know it was a sewer? I thought it was a little river," said Serge. "It was supposed to be very symbolic. Obviously it didn't work out that way, but at least I tried. These are the kind of people who cling. It's not healthy."

The judge's face was in his hands.

He finally looked up. "Mr. Storms, this doesn't give me any pleasure, but you leave me no choice but to commit you to the state hospital at Chattahoochee for a period of observation not less than three months."

They dragged Serge from the courtroom, kicking and yelling.

The judge banged his gavel. "You're out of order, Mr. Storms!"

"I'm out of order? You're out of order! And he's out of order! They're out of order! This trial's out of order! The whole courtroom's out of order! . . ."

The bailiffs pulled Serge into the hall, and the double doors swung closed.

In the fall of 1960, five very special little girls entered the fourth grade in five different schools across Florida.

A nine-year-old girl in Fort Lauderdale named Samantha told her father she wanted a baseball glove.

"You mean a softball glove."

"What's that?"

He was a kind father, and the next day he brought home a nice pink Spalding softball glove and a ball the size of a grapefruit.

"It's pink," said Samantha. She knew baseball gloves weren't pink.

"I know," said her father, smiling fondly. "Isn't it pretty?"

Samantha could see her dad's happiness, and she didn't make a fuss about the color and hugged him.

"Thanks, Daddy."

She stuck her little hand inside.

"I can't move the fingers."

"That's because you have to break it in first."

"How do you do that?"

"You oil it up good and put a softball in the palm and wrap twine around it and set it aside overnight. Then you have to play lots and lots of catch so the leather takes on the shape of your own hand, and pretty soon it fits like a glove."

"But I don't want to wait that long. I want to play right now."

Her father laughed. "Life's not like that."

After dinner they oiled and wrapped the glove, and when her father came home from work the next evening, Samantha and her glove were waiting on the front porch to play catch.

"Okay, let me set my things down first."

That was the beginning of a lot of catch. Samantha got pretty good. Soon she could even move the fingers. One afternoon, she ran outside with her glove and down the street to the park, where the boys wouldn't let a girl play ball, pink glove or not. They were practicing for the big Little League tryouts that weekend. They all wanted to be on the Yankees.

When Samantha's father came home that night, she told him she wanted to try out for Little League.

Her father laughed and crouched down and rubbed her yellow hair. "Honey, girls don't play Little League."

"But I want to."

"Life's not like that."

That Saturday, her parents thought Samantha was down at the playground, but she had taken her bike and ridden to the Little League park, where she lined up with the boys waiting to take the field and catch grounders, pink ribbon in her hair and pink glove on her hand. The boys weren't happy.

"Get out of here! You're a girl!"

"Yeah, get out of here!"

Samantha dug in and snarled.

"What are you waiting for?"

"Yeah, *girl*. You don't even know how to play baseball."

"That's not even a baseball glove!"

"Is so!" said Samantha.

"Is not!"

The coaches on the infield heard a commotion by the dugout. "Is that a girl?"

They came over. The boys were playing keep-away with the pink glove.

"Gimme my glove!" Samantha ran back and forth.

"Missy," said one of the coaches, "where are your parents?"

"At home. . . . *I said, gimme my glove!*"

"What's your name? . . ."

"Samantha." Running back and forth after the glove. Why wouldn't the grown-ups help her?

"Samantha what?"

"Samantha Bridges. . . . *Give it!*"

The coaches didn't help retrieve her glove because the boys were within rights, provoked as they were by Samantha's presence, which threatened to cheapen their whole ritual.

Samantha finally caught up with her glove. The coach's son had it and they were tugging. The boy shoved her to the ground.

"All right, that's quite enough, Missy," said the coach. "You've caused your share of trouble today."

No she hadn't. She got up from the dirt and punched the boy in the nose, drawing tears.

The public shame of his son crying at the hands of a girl was too much, and before the coach knew it, he had grabbed Samantha by the arm and slapped her face hard enough to make any of the boys cry.

Samantha didn't.

She kicked him in the shin.

"Ow! Shit!"

Samantha struggled for the coach to let go of her arm, and the other men had to help restrain the thrashing child. Everything else stopped. A crowd gathered. They looked up her parents' phone number, and her father arrived in minutes.

"What are you doing to my daughter?" her dad yelled, jumping out of his car.

"She disrupted the whole tryout!"

"She's just a little girl!" he said, walking quickly toward the group. "Let go of her right now!"

"Only if she promises not to kick me again."

The father turned his angry glare toward Samantha. "Did you kick him?"

"After he slapped me."

"You slapped her?" asked her father.

"She hit my boy. She was out of control—"

The tooth-loosening right cross sent the coach to the ground. Her father took Samantha by the hand, and they walked away.

The police showed up in Samantha's driveway after they got home, and there was a big stink. But the cops talked everyone out of pressing charges and suggested Samantha stay away from the ballfield.

Dinner was pork chops and mashed potatoes and beets. Samantha asked for the beets in a separate bowl because the beet juice ran into the potatoes and made them pink.

"I just don't understand these people," Samantha's father told her mother across the table. "What's the big deal?"

"You know what you always say? Life's not—"

"I know, but this is so petty. Why can't they just let girls play? It's stupid."

Samantha wasn't saying a word and wasn't eating, just following the conversation back and forth with her eyes.

"You know what I should do? I should file a lawsuit!"

"Oh honey, please don't," said her mother, reaching across and putting a hand on her father's arm. "Isn't it bad enough that everyone already calls her Sam?"

There was a successful court challenge, and girls were allowed to play Little League. But the challenge didn't come from Samantha's father and not for another ten years, until Samantha was in college.

Samantha had a growth spurt when she was thirteen, and she would always be among the tallest in her class, either sex. By high school she found an outlet in girls' basketball. She became what's known as an "enforcer," delivering retribution for rough play against her smaller teammates, fouling out of every game.

"You elbowed me on purpose! That's not fair!"

"Life's not like that."

In Daytona Beach, another nine-year-old girl, this one named Teresa, sat in her classroom drawing airplanes. It was the first day of the new school year.

"And what do you want to be when you grow up?"

"Fireman." "Football player." "Nurse." "Mommy."

"Teresa, what do you want to be?"

Teresa looked up from her planes. "A pilot."

"You mean a stewardess."

"I don't want to be no stewardess."

"I don't want to be *a* stewardess," said the teacher.

"Me neither," said Teresa.

"No, I mean you used a double negative."

"I'll be a stewardess," said a boy named Billy, whom the teachers were already concerned about.

"Boys can't be stewardesses, and girls can't be pilots."

"*I'm* going to be one," said Teresa, coloring in the airplane and nodding with conviction.

"But you can't, dear."

It came out of the blue. Teresa threw all her crayons on the floor and ripped up her picture and knocked over her desk. The teacher tried to calm her, but Teresa spit at her. She was still stomping and crying when they led her to the principal's office.

Compared with Teresa, Samantha was living a fairy tale. Teresa's mother and stepfather were called in for a conference, and they decided to put her in a special school. Nobody could understand it. Teresa had been such a marvelous child the previous school year, before the incest had started that summer.

"Do you have any idea what might be causing this?"

"Not a clue," said her stepdad.

They tested for dyslexia, tried some autism drugs, sent her to camp, where a counselor fondled her. Funny, but she was only getting worse.

Teresa began smoking when she was twelve and drinking at thirteen. Her stepfather was out of the picture now, and her mother blamed Teresa for the breakup. He left them with a pile of bills and without warning. Teresa's mom took up a minimum-wage job and sudden fits of hysterical crying. Teresa became fat.

She stayed away from the house as much as possible, becoming what you'd call a loner, hanging out next to the airport and watching the planes land, cutting herself with razor blades.

Nobody saw the warning signs because her grades had rocketed to straight A's. Everything had to be exactly right, and once it was, it wasn't good enough for Teresa, who worked some more.

Teresa didn't become promiscuous, but she wasn't frugal either. She was more or less desensitized, losing her virginity at fifteen to a boy who was also a virgin, behind a movie house, in a defining moment that was memorable for its clumsiness.

"Is this it?" Teresa asked herself, although the boy seemed to be having an out-of-body experience: "I can't feel my legs!"

"Do you want to stop?"

"No!"

Meanwhile, an undersized child named Paige was growing up in Okeechobee, near the lake. She didn't speak much.

Paige kept bringing home stray and injured animals.

Her mother had died from postdelivery infections that would mean a seven-figure malpractice verdict today. Her father was killed by a drunk driver when she was two. She lived with her grandparents. They were nice, but man, were they old. They took lots of naps and didn't have any idea what Paige was talking about half the time. But Paige rarely spoke as it was, and nobody seemed bothered by the arrangement.

Her grandparents were understanding enough with the little birds and frogs, which she kept in boxes on the porch, but a dog or cat was out of the question, because they had heard something on *Paul Harvey* about germs. Paige loved her grandparents, who weren't permissive as much as just plain tired. By the time she was nine, they were going to bed before she was, and Paige stayed up late watching *Laugh-In* and Carson.

Children are natural explorers, and they're influenced by the media material they discover around the house. Paige grew up in a museum. What were these records? Guy Lombardo and Mario Lanza? There was also about nine hundred pounds of old *Reader's Digests* and a few stacks of *Life* that her grandparents wouldn't throw out. They never threw anything out. It had something to do with the Depression.

They left Paige to the orphaned and wounded animals in her room, which was crowded with fish tanks and terrariums and plastic turtle ponds and hamster wheels and a maze of interconnecting gerbil tubes that ran all over the place like berserk plumbing.

When Paige was fifteen, her grandparents died within a month of each other, and Paige was passed around the family, attending four different high schools in four years, and she started talking even less. There are many roles in a high school: star quarterback, prom queen, class clown, brain, stoner. Paige was an extra.

Maria's parents would have loved Paige.

Maria learned to talk early, and she never stopped.

"What's this?" "What's that?" "Why is that?" "Can I have one of those? What is it?" "You know what I think? . . ."

It accounted for her parents' permanent expression of having teeth cleaned.

Maria demonstrated at age four her talent for mismatching clothes. "Can I dress myself?" "I want to dress myself." "I'm going to dress myself now." She ran into her bedroom and came out in a raincoat and bikini bottom. "I'm ready to go to school now."

Maria had lots and lots of accidents, big scary-looking tumbles, skinned knees, twisted ankles—her parents awakened every other night by a loud thump, Maria falling out of bed in her sleep again, then yelling down the hall, "I'm okay!"

They thought she might need glasses, but the tests came back twenty-twenty. The spills seemed to bother Maria less than her parents, who would jump out of their chairs on the porch and grab their hearts before Maria dusted herself off and guaranteed nothing was broken. It finally dawned on them that Maria never cried, no matter what, going over the handlebars of her bike, popping right up, "I'm okay!" Jumping back on the bike and taking off again into the side of a parked van. "I'm okay again!"

Maria seemed to have a high threshold for pain, and she could definitely take a punch, which were administered by boys everywhere. *Ooomph*, the wind leaving her. "I'm okay!"

Maria's true passion lay in the arts. Maria was a frustrated painter, a frustrated musician and a hopeless romantic. She tried oils, pencils, watercolors, all to no avail. That hemisphere just wasn't firing. Same problem with music, made that much more glaring by her fondness for the tuba. She was an open book, all things to all people, wanting to be liked and trying to become whatever you wanted, except quiet. She dated a lot, but was saving herself for marriage. Trying to at least. But boys will be boys, and there were lots of struggles in backseats of cars outside dances and burger joints, a car door finally popping open and the other students seeing Maria tumble out of the car with a broken bra strap. "I'm okay!"

You couldn't help but like her. And hate her. She was the kind of gentle person who made you feel horribly guilty every time you lost patience with her. She made the other members of the pep club suicidal. Then there was the cheerleading squad, where her natural zest won her the top position on the human pyramid—each game the parents pointing in alarm, "Jesus, did you see the fall that girl just took?"

"I sure hope she's okay."

"She said she was."

Rebecca had talent coming out her ears. Her first teachers couldn't believe it. They quickly took her off finger paints and gave her oils and acrylics. Everything was a photograph. Same with music. She skipped reading sheets and mastered the scales by ear—piano, flute, guitar.

Rebecca was one of the most well adjusted children you'd ever meet, which meant she was weird. Her parents were semiprofessional folk musicians, playing in bars and coffeehouses in the Tampa Bay area, taking Rebecca along since she was five.

The nightclub experience made her a bit precocious, and life in the sandbox was never quite as exciting after that. She spoke a different language from the other children, refusing to play dodge ball because it was "too much like Vietnam." But she was able to duck the menu of neuroses that afflicted her peers, mainly because her parents were so well adjusted and weird, too.

Her friends' bedrooms were covered with the usual teeny-bopper pinups, but they didn't recognize any of the posters on Rebecca's walls: Dylan, the Mamas and the Papas, Donovan, Joan Baez. "Who are all those old people?"

It was a stress-free life, and Rebecca was content to just lie in a field and watch the clouds. That was Rebecca all over, ephemeral and surreal, like some kind of unicorn. Not quite of this world, catch it while you can because it won't be here for long, and it definitely can't be possessed.

"Daddy, how come poor people are poor?"

"I don't know, dear."

"But that's not fair."

"Life's not fair."

"It should be."

"I know, dear."

Her parents were remarkably youthful and good-looking, and you could tell that she was going to be beautiful, too. Rebecca was one of the few individuals who actually deserved to be pretty, because it wasn't going to make her full of shit. She took after her parents that way.

People generally hated the whole family.

A *de Havilland twin-engine turboprop* banked at four thousand feet over the turquoise water of Florida Bay and lined up its approach. Samantha Bridges pressed her face to the window and looked down at the A1A traffic, moving only slightly slower than the plane.

Samantha felt a Bogart sensation of intrigue as her plane landed on the single, short runway with faded markings, bleached and hot, carved into the salt flats and coconut palms. The terminal was smaller than some houses in her neighborhood and needed paint.

Key West International Airport. *International*—they used to fly to Havana once upon a time. Propeller plane was the only way in now; local ordinance prevented jet noise from disturbing residents and wildlife.

Stairs flopped down from the side of the plane, and Samantha appeared in the hatch. Two women waited on the edge of the runway outside the Conch Flyer Lounge, grinning, hoisting fruity drinks in toast. Sam almost didn't recognize Teresa in the lavender dress. She was thin. And blond. Maria looked great, too, despite the fashion error of matching vertical stripes with gila monsters.

A pair of Beechcraft B100s landed in quick succession, Paige and Rebecca, and suddenly they were all there, piling in an airport shuttle van.

It started two months earlier, a chance occurrence. Samantha Bridges was now an assistant state attorney in Miami, and her youngest daughter had just left for Florida State. She turned the extra bedroom into a home office with a new computer and AOL account.

Sam began fooling around with search engines one Sunday evening. Midnight came and went. She still couldn't believe her screen. She had plugged in the names as a lark, and it had become a chain reaction of long-distance phone calls. Then they all hung up and hopped back on their computers, five women typing nonstop in the new Books, Booze and Broads chat room. Layoffs, surgeries, relocations to Boston and Belgium, a total of four new marriages that had gone south. Then, full circle, all back in Florida and single again. With one big difference. Empty nests.

"Let's revive the book club."

"Have a reunion."

"What do you want to read?"

"Where?"

"What?"

"The reunion."

"Slow down!"

"Let's pick a book and visit where it's set."

"Or pick a place and find a book that's set there."

"I like the first idea better."

"They're the same."

"No they're not."

"Whatever."

First stop: Key West, Cayo Hueso, The Rock, Island of Bones. Rebecca had recommended the book, passed along by her parents. It was about a bunch of Jimmy Buffett fans on a pilgrimage to the Keys, and they spend the whole trip wasted on frozen drinks until they're mysteriously murdered one by one. *Parrot Droppings,* by Ralph Krunkleton. The women liked it so much they had torn through four other Krunkletons before boarding their planes.

The courtesy van pulled up in front of the Heron House on Simonton Street. The women wheeled luggage through the orchid garden and past the mosaic of a big wading bird tiled into the bottom of the swimming pool. They entered their suite through the sundeck, and there was no doubt where they were. Watercolors everywhere. Paintings of tropical plants, bedspreads with tropical fish. Rattan, marble, French doors, stained transoms. They crossed "the fulcrum"—that long-anticipated turning point when you're traveling to a party town and finally get in your room and drop the suitcases, and it all lifts off your shoulders with a sudden buoyancy. This called for a meeting of the book club. They headed out the door to find one of the taverns in their Krunkleton paperbacks.

The five started north on Duval Street, past the Lost Weekend Liquor Store, into the drinking district. Freaks on the street, squares in the bars. Bars with plastic bulls crashing through walls, parrots and flamingos on the counters, sailfish over the taps, pinball machines in back and pitchmen out front barking about double-jointed strippers upstairs. People who should never limbo doing so, reggae bands joined onstage by bald drunks from Cincinnati, derelicts riding bicycles with iguanas in the baskets and big snakes around their necks, drunk couples necking, transvestites on stilts, dogs wearing sunglasses, college students falling off mopeds and vomiting all over their SEE THE KEYS ON YOUR HANDS AND KNEES T-shirts.

The women came to the end of Duval and headed up a twisting garden path behind the Pier House, through schefflera and hibiscus, onto a boardwalk next to a lagoon where hotel guests were throwing Chicklets to a school of feeding tarpon, then winding back to the patio until they finally stood near a hall tucked under the hotel by the supply rooms and the mops.

"This can't be it," said Teresa.

Sam pulled a paperback from her purse and opened to a bookmarked passage. "That must be the door." She grabbed the handle.

A row of faces along the bar squinted at the silhouettes of five women backlit by bright sunlight. The BBB stood still in the doorway a few seconds—that awkward, territorial moment when newcomers first set foot in a regulars' bar. They started moving again toward a table in a corner of the tiny room, hanging purses over the backs of chairs.

"So this is the Chart Room," said Maria, shifting in her seat, straightening panties. She looked around for a waitress.

"I think this is the kind of place where you have to go to the bar," said Sam, getting up.

Teresa turned her paperback over, scanning blurbs on the back— "*. . . Stunning . . .*" "*. . . Dazzling . . .*" "*. . . Important . . .*"—the kind of terse praise surgically lifted from the bodies of damning reviews. Sam returned with a pitcher of Michelob. They poured, clinked glasses and checked out the interior, mostly bare, except for a pair of nautical charts and a black-and-white photo of an early Key West street scene. But there was all kinds of stuff on the wall behind the bar, overlapping Polaroids of bent patrons making faces and hugging, business cards, newspaper clippings, scribbled-on dollar bills and a handmade sign: TIP BIG.

Maria reached out and touched the plain cinder-block wall. "So this is where Buffett got his start?"

"Right here in this corner," said Paige, referring to her own paper-back. "Arrived with Jerry Jeff Walker. Played six-string for tips while writing his early songs."

"Wow," said Rebecca, and they all gazed at the ground under their feet with a sense of reverence usually reserved for mangers.

Teresa stood up. "I'll get the next pitcher."

And so it went. Another pitcher. Then another. Then liquor.

"How'd we get so drunk?"

"It's a fuckin' mystery," said Rebecca, slamming a shot glass down on the table.

"Sam, how come you aren't drinking as much as we are?" asked Teresa.

"Lost its luster. Half the men I prosecute are wife-beating alco-holics."

"Prosecute? I thought you were a public defender."

"Was. But I kind of got tired interviewing clients in jail who asked me if I liked to take it in the ass."

"I can see how that would get tedious," said Rebecca. Then she asked if any of the others owned an SUV. They said they didn't and asked why. Rebecca wanted to know if anyone else had a problem with men who liked to pull up at stoplights next to female drivers in taller vehicles so the women have a clear view of them beating off.

"How often does this happen?" asked Maria.

"More like how often *doesn't* it happen." She turned to Paige. "So what kind of work do you usually get as a vet?"

"Patch up cats shot with BB guns and dogs set on fire and pelicans who've been thrown fish filled with needles and M-80s."

"Who would do such things?" said Teresa.

"Obviously the work of women," said Sam.

"I wouldn't necessarily go easy on our own kind," said Maria.

"You're right," said Sam. She raised her glass for a toast. "Fuck Dr. Laura."

"Hear! Hear!"

The alcohol got the best of Maria. "Do you remember . . ." she said, then stumbled into forbidden territory.

The other four glowered at her. "We never talk about that!" snapped Teresa. The others nodded.

"Excuse the hell out of me."

They all sighed and sagged.

"Nothing exciting ever happens to us," said Rebecca.

Teresa suddenly straightened up and got out her organizer. "We should make a list."

"Of what?"

"Things to do as a group to break out of our ruts. Adventures, risks." Teresa clicked her pen open. "Okay. New bylaw. Everything that goes on the list we all have to do together. No exceptions."

"Sounds like disaster," said Sam.

"The psychology of group behavior. It'll embolden us to do things we'd never attempt as individuals."

"That's how we got suffragettes," said Rebecca.

"And lynchings," said Sam.

"I don't think I want to lynch anyone," said Maria.

"What about your ex-husbands?"

"New bylaw," said Teresa. "Those in favor?"

"Aye." "Aye." "Aye." "Aye." "Nay."

"What sort of things do we put on the list?" asked Paige.

"Stuff like sky-diving," said Maria.

Teresa sat poised with pen. "Item number one. Anybody?"

"Sky-diving," said Rebecca.

"*Sky-diving,*" Teresa repeated as she wrote. "Number two?"

"Okay, I've changed my mind. Let's lynch my husbands."

"I'm being serious."

"So am I."

"Who's got ideas, besides Maria, who needs to get in the proper spirit?"

"Get a tattoo."

"Use a powerful man before he uses you."

"Watch the New Year's ball drop in Times Square."

"Skinny-dip."

"Shoplift."

"That's going too far," said Sam.

"We'll give the stolen item right back," said Teresa. "It's the principle of the thing."

"I know," said Rebecca. "Let's get arrested at a protest."

"What kind of protest?"

"Rocks and bricks and Molotov cocktails."

"No, I mean what cause?"

"World peace."

"Anything else?"

"Let's meet Ralph Krunkleton."

"That's a great idea," said Teresa. "We've read what? Five of his books now?"

Rebecca nodded hard. "He's our newest favorite author, now. New."

"You might want to slow down on those shots."

"Why for?"

Sam grabbed the purse off the back of her chair. "I'm going to the rest room."

"It's outside around the corner," said Paige.

Sam walked down the corridor under the lobby, mumbling to herself; they were her friends and all, but their judgment was stinking up the joint. Sam found the door to the men's room, stopped and looked around for the women's. They were usually in pairs; she was hoping this wasn't one of those places with some artsy unsymmetrical layout. She kept walking. Where was it?

A man came around the corner. She could ask him. As he walked closer, Sam got a better look. Trim, muscular, flowing black hair, tight tennis shirt, solid chin. *Rrrrrrrow!* This could be two birds with the same stone. She'd ask where the women's room was, and it would also be a perfectly innocent icebreaker.

The man smiled as he got closer, great teeth.

"Excuse me," said Sam. "Can you tell me where—"

The man took off running.

"My purse!" Sam broke into a sprint.

People lounging by the pool sat up and turned as the pair raced by the tiki bar, the man glancing over his shoulder, darting down the garden path, crashing through palm branches. He came out in the alley for the service vehicles, climbed up on a Dumpster and jumped over a fence. He ran another few yards, slowed up and turned around to see Sam jump down from the fence. He cursed and took off again. They were soon running along the wharf, past oyster bars and sailboats and antique shops. Sam was twenty yards back, not gaining but not falling off the pace either. They came around a street corner, running up a sidewalk by a multilevel parking deck with fresh graffiti: *They paved over paradise and put up a parking lot.* The man looked back again. Sam was still there. What was her problem? He ran through the streets of Old Town. Historic wooden cottages, gingerbread trim. He stopped and panted in front of a picket fence with pineapple-shaped holes. He looked back. Finally lost her. No, wait, there she was, coming around the place with the Bahamian shutters. He took a deep breath and charged south on Elizabeth Street, coming to an iron fence too tall to scale. He ran along it until he found an open gate. Ten seconds later, Sam dashed in the gate. They zigzagged through the cemetery, Sam catching glimpses of him between palm trees, above-ground crypts, whitewashed mausoleums and royal poincianas. The man stumbled, chest heaving. Sam cruised at the comfortable aerobic pace of daily after-work runs. The man finally put out his arms as he crashed into a crypt with a cement cherub on top. He turned and braced his back against it and flicked a stiletto knife open. Sam broke stride and stopped a few feet away. The man waved the knife weakly in the air, his back slowly sliding down the side of the crypt until he was in the sitting position, gasping for breath, the knife resting in a hand on the ground that he no longer had the strength to raise.

Sam stepped forward and picked up her purse without interference. She turned and started walking away, the sound of desperate breathing behind her, then a single, barely audible word.

"Cunt."

Oops.

Sam stopped and stood a few moments with her back to him. The man was beginning to catch his breath and pushed himself to his feet. He picked up the knife. "Yeah, you heard me."

Sam spun around. She took a half-hop step at the start of her run, like a gymnast beginning a floor exercise, and galloped toward him with measured strides. She hit the brakes three feet away, where she correctly anticipated the knife swing. It lacked energy, and the blade floated by without menace. Before the man could begin the backslash, Sam planted her left foot and cocked her right leg to her flank, the way they taught her at the police academy when they let the prosecutors work out. The man only saw a blur as the side kick punched his lower ribs. Something snapped inside. He flew back against the crypt and went down to stay this time. The show was over, but Sam took the keychain tear gas out of her purse anyway. She heard gagging and high-pitched screaming as she soaked him down good, for instructional purposes.

When Sam got back to the hotel room, the others were mixing something in the blender, all wearing T-shirts from Captain Tony's. Paige's face had been painted by a street artist.

"Where the hell'd you go?" asked Maria.

"We thought you were taking a big dump or something," said Rebecca. "But we couldn't find you in the rest room."

"I went for a walk."

Teresa threw some more ice in the blender. "You missed all the fun."

The pink Cadillac raced east out of Orlando on the Bee Line Highway.

Unfortunately it was in the westbound lanes.

Serge and Lenny screamed their lungs out as honking, swerving dump trucks and tractor-trailers passed by on both sides. All four of their hands tightly gripped the steering wheel, Serge pulling one way, Lenny the other.

Serge: "Ahhhhhhhhhhhhhhh!"

Lenny: "Ahhhhhhhhhhhhhhh!"

The stretch of highway was currently undergoing roadwork, and cement retaining walls on both sides of the highway prevented the Cadillac from escaping down the grassy shoulders. Pickup trucks and Harleys split and passed around them.

"Ahhhhhhhhhhhhhh!"

The Cadillac began weaving back and forth across all three lanes of highway, dodging head-on collisions. A minivan came straight at them; the Caddy veered left. Then a PT Cruiser; they swung right.

The construction zone ended and Serge pulled hard on the steering wheel, taking the Eldorado down into the median strip, bounding back up the far side and into the correct lanes. He gave the wheel back to Lenny, who put on his right blinker, slowed and pulled over in the breakdown lane. He and Serge stared at each other, both sheet-white, feeling their hearts pound through their chests like the coyote after the roadrunner almost runs him off a cliff.

"What happened?" said Lenny, taking shallow breaths.

"How much of it do you remember?"

Lenny shook his head.

"You don't remember anything?"

He shook his head again.

"It all happened pretty fast . . ."

Ten minutes earlier.

Lenny stubbed out a joint in the Cadillac's ashtray. "Are we there yet . . . *hic* . . . ?"

"A half hour to the Atlantic Ocean, then we swoop down on the money," said Serge, holding the global tracker in both hands like he was flying a model airplane. "We have a solid transponder lock now, which means we should be able to pinpoint the briefcase's signal within a half meter. We're 'go' all the way!"

"What do you plan to do with the money? . . . *hic* . . . Crap. These hiccups won't go away . . . *hic* . . . Maybe if I smoke another joint and calm down . . . *hic* . . ." Lenny stuck a twistie in his mouth and fired up.

"You know, I actually thought of taking up drugs once," said Serge.

"I thought you were against getting high . . . *hic* . . ."

"I wouldn't do it to get high," said Serge. "I just like the sneaking-around part. You have to gain the confidence of your connection, set up the meeting, make the buy, hide your shit, make preparations whom you're going to do it with, where, how, all without detection. Sort of like being a secret agent."

Lenny beamed proudly. "You mean like me? . . . *hic* . . ."

"Afraid not, Condor. It's just a matter of time before you gift-wrap yourself for the police. You're the guy who gets caught after triggering a twenty-car pileup on the freeway by simultaneously trying to shotgun a beer and fire up a six-foot Cambodian bamboo peace pipe."

Serge opened a book.

"What are you reading? . . . *hic* . . ."

Serge showed him the cover of the book. *Hypnosis Made Easy*. "I got the idea from reading *The Stingray Shuffle*."

"The what?"

"This novel by my favorite author. I first picked it up because it had a lot of stuff about Florida. And trains. Lots of trains. But it also had a bunch of hypnosis stuff, so I decided to research further."

"What kind of a name is *Stingray Shuffle*, anyway?"

"You've never done the stingray shuffle?" asked Serge.

Lenny shook his head.

"When it's stingray season in Florida during the summer, stingrays lie on the bottom of the water near the shore, under a thin blanket of sand, and you can't see them. The stingrays would much rather flee than fight, but if you walk normally in the water and step on one, you pretty much pin it to the bottom and leave it no choice but to hit you in the leg with its poisonous tail barb."

"That'll wreck a buzz."

"So instead of walking normally when you're in shallow water, you shuffle your feet along. That way, if you accidentally come across a ray, you just bump it on the edge, and it spooks and swims away. It's also a perfect metaphor for the on-your-toes, aware-of-your-surroundings, ready-to-jump-any-second dance you have to do every day in Florida to stay alive and ahead of the dangerous *humans*."

Serge opened his hypnosis book again. Lenny leaned across the front seat and looked over his shoulder, trying to read along.

"Why are you reading about hypnosis?"

"Because I'm into it now. I've decided to completely dedicate my life to the study of hypnosis."

"I thought you'd dedicated your life to trains."

"Trains and hypnosis."

"That's an odd combination."

"I've learned not to question my muse . . ." Serge pointed forward at the road. "Will you please?"

"What's the book about? . . . *hic* . . ."

"I told you. Hypnosis."

". . . *Hic* . . . I know that from the cover."

"That's what it's about. I can't change it."

"I mean, what specifically about it? . . . *hic* . . ."

"Well, there's a story here about a hypnotist in Europe who killed a woman onstage in 1894 by commanding her soul to leave her body. She had a heart attack."

"Oh . . . *hic* . . . right!"

"I wasn't there, but that's what it says. . . . Lenny, you can't read over my shoulder and drive at the same time. Pick one."

Lenny reluctantly returned to his side of the car and the approved ten-o'clock, two-o'clock steering-wheel grip.

"Okay, Mr. Skeptic," said Serge. "Want to get rid of those hiccups?"

Lenny nodded. *"Hic."*

Serge turned sideways in his seat and spoke in a monotone. "Concentrate on my voice."

"What are you going to do? . . . *hic* . . ."

"Make your hiccups leave your body."

"Not with my soul! . . . *hic* . . ."

"Good point. I'll try to make sure I get the pronouns right in the incantation."

"Don't you need to swing a pocket watch . . . *hic* . . . or have me look at a pinwheel or something?"

"That's bullshit. Besides, you're challenged enough with just the road."

"Hurry up," said Lenny. "I hate hiccups . . . *hic* . . ."

"Focus on my voice. Relax. Take deeper and slower breaths. Hiccups cannot survive at low rates of respiration. . . ."

". . . *Hic* . . . I still have the hiccups."

"Shhhh! Don't listen to the hiccups. . . . Only my voice. . . . You will continue to relax, the interval between hiccups growing longer each time. . . . Each hiccup is one less until they're gone for good. . . . Okay, I'm not talking to Lenny anymore. Hiccups, do you hear me? I'm talking to you now. I command you—in the name of Christ, leave Lenny's body!"

Serge heard a rattling sound. He turned forward and saw they were off course, running over the raised reflectors as they crossed the inside breakdown lane, then down into the narrow median. Serge looked over at the driver's seat and saw Lenny's head slumped to his chest. He reached over and grabbed the wheel, but it was too late. They had already entered the construction zone, and the temporary cement retaining walls funneled them into oncoming traffic.

"Lenny! Wake up!"

"Huh? What? What is it? . . . Ahhhhhhhhhhhhhhh!"

"So that's what happened," said Lenny. "I hate it when I wake up driving."

"How are your hiccups?"

Lenny thought a second. "They're gone."

"What do you think about hypnosis now?"

"Gimme a break," said Lenny. "That didn't do it."

"What do you mean? It did it and then some. You were fuckin' *out.*"

"That was the weed," said Lenny. "It was already making me feel like nappy time."

"Atheist."

Lenny lit another joint, started up the car and pulled back on the road. Serge put down the hypnosis book and picked up the morning paper as they passed a thousand-acre brush fire.

"Anything good?" asked Lenny.

"Second-grader brings gun to school. Jesus, what ever happened to just sticking out your tongue?"

"I still do it."

"Here's an item on a drunk bridge tender who sent a car airborne," said Serge, oblivious to the wall of flame down the side of the highway. "And someone stole the Picasso cat again from the Hemingway House. A funeral home is being sued for putting voodoo dolls in a chest cavity. Eleven more Floridians die from smoke inhalation trying to stay warm by barbecuing indoors. Man convicted of killing his dog because it was homosexual. . . ."

"How did he know?"

"It says the Yorkshire made advances on another terrier named Bandit. That's when the owner decided to put a stop to the godlessness."

"What is it about this state?" asked Lenny. "All my friends up north keep asking me: Does the freak show ever take a break down there?"

"I have no idea what you're talking about." Serge looked back down at his newspaper.

Up ahead, Lenny saw a small stampede of flaming rabbits running from the brush fire and into the road, where they were snatched up by turkey buzzards circling overhead, whose claws were singed by the burning fur, and the rabbits began dropping by the dozen on passing vehicles, one splattering on the Cadillac's windshield and bouncing over Lenny's head.

Serge looked up from his newspaper at the sound of the thud. "What the hell was that?"

Lenny's jaw fell open, the joint sticking to the spit on his lower lip.

Serge pointed at the bloody stain on the windshield. "What kind of bug did you hit?"

"It was a bunny."

"How'd you hit a bunny with your windshield?"

Lenny pointed up at the sky.

Serge shook his head. "You're higher than a motherfucker." He went back to his newspaper.

Lenny took the joint out of his mouth, looked at it a second, then threw it out of the car.

"Serge."

"What?"

"Do you think I'm dysfunctional?"

"No, Lenny. You know those nagging sensations you're always having? Total alienation, utter lack of self-worth, chronic-masturbation guilt and perpetual dread of impending death?"

"Yeah?"

"That's all normal. Feel better now?"

"I'm not sure."

"Your problem is you lack focus. The key to life is hobbies, otherwise you're asking for trouble. You know what they always say—if Hitler only had a train set . . ."

"Who says that?"

"Nobody ever says that. I have no idea where I get some of these thoughts, and you know what? I don't care! Because I'm alive and the sun is shining!" Serge reached in his back pocket and pulled out a folded-up piece of paper.

"What's that?"

"It's my Life List."

"What's a Life List?"

"The list of things you want to accomplish before you die. The idea is to keep you planning for the future or else you end up seventy years old on your porch with a rusting chain-link fence around a front yard full of barking Dobermans and a dismantled Skylark, and you never know why."

"Where'd you come up with this list idea?"

"First heard about it from Lou Holtz. 'Become coach of Notre Dame' was on his list, and you know what?"

"He became coach of Notre Dame?"

Serge nodded. "I said to myself, 'I gotta get me one of them lists.'"

"So what's on yours?" asked Lenny.

"Item number one: space flight."

"You're too old to join NASA."

"That's why I'll have to deal with the Russians. After the Soviet collapse, everything's for sale over there."

"What else?" asked Lenny.

Serge held up his piece of paper: "Swim the Florida Straits, communicate with the monkeys on Key Lois, steal the DeLong Ruby, break a bull at the Okeechobee Rodeo, get into a Disney ride in less than an hour, locate the Fountain of Youth, win the Daytona 500, bring the panthers back to healthy numbers, travel in time . . ."

"But time travel's impossible."

"I know," said Serge. "I wanted to keep the list realistic, so that's why I only want to travel one week. And that way, if something goes wrong with the time ship and I can't get back, I'm not stuck in some strange future land where the government makes everyone wear tunics and report unwelcome behavior."

"I hate that," said Lenny.

"Tell me about it."

Serge stuck the list back in his pocket and got out the global tracker.

"How's the signal?" asked Lenny.

"Real strong. Solid all the way." Serge pointed at a traffic sign. "Take the causeway. It's our best bet."

They crossed US 1 and the Indian River, then went down the bridge onto Merritt Island.

"Are those real alligators in that canal?" asked Lenny.

"That's what those are."

The pair began seeing the tips of shiny metal tubes over the trees.

"Look," said Lenny. "Kennedy Space Center."

"And there's the new shuttle mock-up they put on display at the visitor center." Serge grabbed his camera from under the seat and snapped half a roll of film as they went by. He faced forward again. "Oh my God!"

"What is it?"

"The signal!" said Serge, holding up the tracker. "It changed direction. It's pointing back at the visitor center. Turn around!"

Lenny swung across a break in the median and headed back. The Cadillac turned in the entrance of the space complex and parked next to a row of idling Gray Line buses. Serge jumped out and tucked a pistol in his waistband. He reached back in the car and grabbed the global tracker off the passenger seat. The signal pointed toward the admission gate.

"This is it! Payday!"

They took off running.

nother month, another book club meeting. Miami
Beach this time. Books, Booze and Broads cruised down A1A in a
rented Grand Marquis.

"We're finally going to meet Ralph Krunkleton," said Maria.

"Not at this rate," said Sam, checking her wristwatch. "Just look at
this traffic jam."

"We've still got plenty of time," said Teresa.

"How much farther?"

"Twenty miles."

Twenty miles ahead, a strip mall:

"Get a move on!" the owner shouted in the back room of The Palm
Reader. He leaned over and did a line. "We have to close up and clear
out before that stupid author shows up for his stupid signing!"

The buzzer at the rear service door rang. The boss jumped. "What
was that?"

"The door."

He opened it a crack. Four people stood behind hand trucks stacked with brown cartons. In the background, a white commercial van from a book distributor in Hialeah.

"Hi, I'm your wholesaler," said a smiling woman holding a dachshund.

No response. The door stayed open only a slit.

"Is everything all right?" she asked, trying to see inside.

"Fine. Go away."

"But we brought some more books."

"We didn't order any."

"I know," said the woman, smiling again. "We got so much more press than we expected that I was afraid you'd run out. I took it upon myself to bring extras. You've been such good customers . . ."

A pause.

"Go away."

"If you don't need them, then we do. We'd like to get them signed for our other stores. This is our hottest title."

One of the tropical shirts tapped the boss from behind. He jumped again. "What?"

"Someone's out front asking for you."

"Get rid of them."

"I think it's the author."

"Shit!"

"What should I tell him?"

"Tell him we're out of books."

"You're out of books?" said the woman at the back door. "Then I'm glad we came."

The employee tapped the boss again. "I don't think I can get rid of them."

"Why not?"

"There are others."

Blinding lights came on in the front of the store, the strings of beads breaking them into hundreds of bright shafts that showered the back room. The boss shielded his eyes. "What the fuck is that?"

"TV cameras. I was trying to tell you. . . ."

"Who called the TV station?"

"I did," said the woman. She had pushed the back door open and was directing hand-truck traffic. "Just set those cases over there."

The tropical shirts scrambled to hide cocaine. A man stuck a microphone through the beads. "Sir, can I get a quick interview?"

"No! Go away!"

More TV people arrived, then writers from the *Herald*, the *Sun-Sentinel* and the *Post*.

The boss burst through the beads. "Everybody out!"

A long line of regular patrons waited at the cash register, and they weren't leaving until they got what they came for. Neither were the reporters. A TV camera panned down the customers, who for some reason were all covering their faces. The camera swung to a newswoman: *"As you can see, the rising popularity of Ralph Krunkleton seems to cross all economic, ethnic and social lines . . ."*

"Turn that camera off!"

The boss grabbed the newswoman's arm, but she jerked free and stomped on his instep with a high heel.

"Ouch!"

"You, sir, what does Ralph Krunkleton say to you?" The woman held her microphone toward a businessman, who froze in the lights, then broke from the line and sprinted out of the store.

"Obviously camera shy. . . . What about you, sir?"

"Uh, good plot?" said a schoolteacher, grinning nervously.

"Good plot. That seems to be everyone's verdict tonight at The Palm Reader, where author Ralph Krunkleton will be signing copies of his latest bestseller in just a few moments. Back to you, Jerry . . ."

The camera lights died, and the newswoman spun on the store's owner. "Don't you ever fuck with me while I'm on the air!" She jammed her microphone in his stomach, knocking the wind out of him, and walked away.

The owner doubled over. "Can this get any worse?"

"Hi, I'm Ralph Krunkleton." A big man in a fishing cap extended a hand.

"The signing's off. We don't have any more books."

"What are those?" asked Ralph, pointing at three tall stacks of his books behind the counter, selling quickly at a hundred dollars each.

"Those are special. They're on reserve. People have already bought them."

Ralph took out a pen and stepped toward the piles. "I'd be happy to sign—"

"No!" The owner grabbed him by the arm. He stopped and lowered his voice. "I mean, no, that won't be necessary."

A college student had just purchased a book. Ralph reached for it. "How about you, son? Would you like an autograph?"

"Touch it and I'll kill you!" The student jerked the book away and left the store.

The owner turned and gasped. "What the hell do you think you're doing?"

People were unfolding Samsonite chairs. "Setting up for the reading," said the woman with the wiener dog.

"No!" shouted the owner, grabbing a chair out of someone's hand. "No reading! Go away!"

A TV cameraman looked through his viewfinder, talking to his news director. "There's something strange about these people. I can't quite put my finger on it. . . ."

"I know what you mean," said the director. "I've never seen an author appearance where nobody gets an autograph or stays for the reading. Smells fishy, like this is some kind of front. . . ."

The owner overheard them and began clapping his hands sharply. "Okay, we're about to start the reading. Everybody take a seat."

A debutante paid for a book and started for the door. The owner blocked her path.

"Where do you think you're going?"

"My boyfriend's."

"You're staying for the reading."

"I've been waiting all day to get off."

The owner lifted the edge of his tropical shirt to reveal a pistol tucked in his Dockers. "Have a seat."

The owner kept lifting his shirt at departing customers, and the chairs began filling with fidgeting, sniffling people.

Unsuspecting readers who had seen the TV spot started arriving, a few at first, then dozens. The parking lot overflowed. Police officers came into the store.

"Are you the owner?"

He fell into a chair and grabbed his heart.

"We'll take care of traffic. The chamber of commerce already called and is paying for the overtime, so there's no charge. Just wanted you to know." They went back out into the street, waving lighted orange batons.

The legitimate customers began mixing with coke fiends in the book line. The books kept selling, although the cost dropped sharply to the regular cover price when the new customers expressed outrage and the cashier panicked. Everyone was happy again, especially the dopers, who discovered the price of cocaine in Miami Beach had just fallen to $6.99 a gram.

The normal people took their new books and joined the others in the audience until it was standing room only.

"I guess we were wrong," the TV director told his cameraman. "They're staying for the reading. Some of them still seem a little weird, but on average it's about what you'd see in any mall around here."

The owner slid up to the cashier and whispered out of the side of his mouth, "How are you keeping the books with the cocaine separated from the others?"

"How am I doing what?"

Ralph stepped to the front of the chairs. "Good evening and thanks for coming. I'd like to start by reading one of my favorite passages—"

"What the heck's this?" interrupted a woman in back, holding up a little white baggie.

"There's one in my book, too," said a man on the other side of the room.

"Me, too!"

"It looks like cocaine."

"What's going on here?"

The owner stood on a chair in the corner, holding a match up to an emergency sprinkler head.

"Come on! Come onnnnnnnnn!"

Teresa leaned over the steering wheel of the rented Grand Marquis. "I think I can see the bookstore on the next block. I told you we'd make it."

"Why are all those police jumping out of those vans?"

*C*ollins Avenue.

The BBB lounged behind dark sunglasses and recovered with morning coffee on the front patio of the Hotel Nash.

Sam stared into her decaf.

"Sam, were you listening?" asked Rebecca.

"What?"

"I was saying you missed all the fun."

"Where'd you run off to?"

"After missing the book signing, I decided to head back to the room and call it a night."

"It was because you didn't want to skinny-dip with us in that hotel pool, wasn't it?"

"I can't put anything over on you."

"We only did it for ten seconds," said Maria.

"Just long enough to check it off the list," said Rebecca.

"We were careful," said Teresa. "Slipped our clothes off, held them in our hands, slipped 'em back on again. No big deal."

"It was the alcohol," said Sam.

"Of course it was the alcohol," said Teresa. "That's the whole *point* of alcohol."

Sam pointed at their rented Grand Marquis, parked at the corner. "What's wrong with our car?"

"What do you mean?"

"The back end's riding low. And dripping."

Maria stood up and smiled. "I was going to surprise you. Come on."

They walked over to the car and Maria popped the trunk. A mountain of ice cubes covered dozens of beer cans and mini wine bottles.

"I discovered something new about rental cars," Maria said proudly. "The trunk is a self-draining cooler."

They went back to their spot on the patio and looked up as the shadow of an inbound 747 crossed Collins Avenue and their table. Men sat at other tables, behind Porsche sunglasses, leering at the book club. The café society was in full swing, everyone aloof, clandestinely checking each other out, posing, trying to get laid by acting like people who got laid way too much. The bouillabaisse of sexual tension caused those least likely to have sex to play their stereos at top volume, and the street was quite noisy. But the designers at Mercedes-Benz had anticipated this, and the interior of a white Z310 was virtually soundproof as it rolled north up the avenue, the air conditioner set at a nippy sixty-six. A red light stopped it outside the Nash. Five dark-haired men in tropical shirts filled the Benz, two in front, three in back, eating ice-cream cones, nodding heads slowly to easy-listening hits. Its trunk was also dripping, holding five soggy cartons of paperbacks.

"Boss, what are we going to do about all those books?"

"Shut up!" said the driver. "I don't want to hear about books right now."

The light turned green; the driver prepared to go. Before he could, a horn blared and a purple Jeep Wrangler whipped around the Mercedes and passed in the oncoming lanes. The Benz's driver hit the brakes. He felt something cold and stared down at the ice-cream cone squashed on the front of his tropical shirt.

The Jeep accelerated toward the intersection at Hispañola, but it got boxed in behind a slow-moving Oldsmobile. The light ahead turned yellow, plenty of time to make it, but the Olds slowed to a crawl and stopped.

"Motherfucker!" screamed the Jeep's driver, punching the roll bar. He and his three passengers were muscle-bound from constant weight lifting and creamy protein shakes, and they experienced considerable difficulty turning their torsos to exit the Jeep. They walked toward the Olds, arms swinging well out from their bodies because trapezius muscles were in the way. All four were in their early twenties, wearing baseball caps and T-shirts from a "world-famous" little-known sports bar.

They reached the front door of the Oldsmobile and began kicking it, causing the tiny old man behind the wheel to turn up his hearing aid and look around. He got the Beltone adjusted in time to hear, "Come out of there, you fuck!" The Oldsmobile's door was jerked open and the old man dragged into the street. They threw him to the pavement and began stomping him in the stomach. People froze in horror. An elderly woman dropped groceries on the sidewalk and screamed.

"Where'd you learn to fucking drive!" Kick.

Tires screeched. The Jeep guys looked up. Four doors opened on a Mercedes; ice-cream cones flew out. Easy-listening music piped into the street.

"*. . . On the day that you were born, the angels got together . . .*"

The Jeep's driver stopped kicking and began laughing. He turned to his pals. "Look at the funny guys with ice cream on their shirts!"

The Mercedes's driver walked up to the Jeep and saw a baseball bat sticking out of the back. He grabbed it.

The young driver loved his Jeep, with the Fold-and-Tumble rear seat and legendary off-road prowess. His smile dropped. He pointed at the vehicle, then at the man with the baseball bat. "Don't even *think* of messing with it!"

He didn't. He walked past the Jeep and swung with a sharp uppercut, catching the driver under the chin. Teeth scattered across the intersection like a broken pearl necklace on a wooden dance floor.

The other punks fled, but the slowest was caught from behind and swarmed. The tropical shirts knocked him to the ground and formed a tight circle for synchronized groin-kicking.

Mr. Grande sat alone in the mountain hideaway of the Mierda Cartel, tapping his fingers on a wicker desk, gazing out the window at fruit trees. A cockatoo strutted across the porch. It was quiet except for the ceiling fans and a gibbering monkey somewhere in the hills that Mr. Grande had come to believe was personally mocking him.

The phone rang. It was the cartel in Colombia, and they wanted to know where their submarine was.

"There's been a setback," said Mr. Grande.

"Setback? It sank with your whole fucking cartel! You're an embarrassment to the industry!"

"I just need a little more time."

"You've got a week. Then you know what happens." Click.

It had been a rough year for the Mierda Cartel. It hadn't started out that way. They had been riding high with five million in the black, all laundered through a Tampa insurance company called Buccaneer Life & Casualty. To make the insurance company appear legit, they employed legit, unsuspecting adjusters, who accidentally paid out all of the cartel's money in a fraudulent disability claim.

Mr. Grande had dispatched every cartel member to Florida to get the money back, but they were all dead now, the money last seen in a briefcase in Key West. Mr. Grande had replaced the deceased cartel members by recruiting a handful of trusted smugglers, and he had intended to send them back to Florida for the money, but they were now all at the bottom of St. George's Bay in a modified septic tank. Turnover was getting to be a problem for Mr. Grande, who could no longer get anyone to underwrite group health except Buccaneer Life & Casualty in Tampa.

Complicating matters was the language barrier. The Mierda organization was the only cartel that wasn't Latin. It was Russian. Following the collapse of the Soviet Union, mobsters from Moscow and Leningrad flooded south Florida and the Caribbean, which was a good thing. It infused the region with fresh blood and new ideas. Plus, everything of value in the former republic was being dismantled with cutting torches, crated up and shipped to the West for quick sale. You could buy absolutely anything—suspension bridges, nuclear triggers. The Russians quickly became valued partners. But, as they say, ten percent of all college students graduate in the bottom tenth of their class, and the same held true for the new wave of criminals. Mr. Grande had to take what he could get.

The timing of that last phone call from Colombia was not good. What the hell did they expect him to do, *buy* a sub?

Wait, that's it! Soviet subs were all over the place. The Cali gang had tried to buy one a couple years ago, but they had gone about it all wrong. Mr. Grande was Russian. He knew all the right people, where every pitfall lay. He wouldn't make the same mistakes. What was a sub going for these days, anyway? Mr. Grande checked the Blue Book. *Ski lift, styptic pencils, subatomic centrifuge* . . . Here it is: *Submarine, like new, never fired, five million dollars, firm. Call Yuri, afternoons.* Hmm, thought Mr. Grande, that's the same amount of money we lost in Florida. That sure would come in handy now.

Mr. Grande flipped open his address book, then picked up the phone.

The old man who had been driving the Oldsmobile regained consciousness in the middle of Collins Avenue. He moaned and grabbed his stomach and fought his way to his feet. The tropical shirts saw him staggering, and they steadied him by the arms and walked him over to the punk from the Jeep.

"Go ahead," said the tallest.

The old man began kicking. "You ungrateful little prick! I fought in the Big One for you! . . ."

A phone rang.

The Mercedes's driver pulled a cell from his pants. He cupped a hand over it and turned to his colleagues. "I have to take this." He stepped onto the sidewalk and covered his other ear to block out the screaming.

"Mr. Grande, an honor, sir. . . . I'm sorry, but you'll have to speak up. Miami Beach is pretty noisy this time of day. . . . I see. . . . I see. . . . No, that won't be a problem. . . . Thank you for the opportunity, Mr. Grande. You won't regret this. . . ."

The driver closed his cell phone and turned back to the street. "We have to go."

Police sirens grew louder as they piled back in the Mercedes and sped away.

The old man was still kicking when the cops arrived. The first officer realized what was happening and jumped out of the squad car. "No! Stop!" he yelled, running toward the old man and pulling his nightstick. "Here—use a baton."

16

An astronaut in a pressure suit heard his own ampli-
fied, labored breathing as he slowly navigated his moon buggy
over the treacherous terrain.

The buggy rolled past a man in a tropical shirt, banging the side of
his handheld global tracker.

"What's it say?" asked Lenny.

"The vector's gone haywire," said Serge. "Must be jammed by all the
space transmissions here."

"In a tourist attraction?"

"No, but the attraction is in the middle of a working launch complex, and next to a pair of classified Air Force installations."

"What'll we do?"

"We simply have to start canvassing," said Serge. "There's the gift
shop."

"You just want souvenirs."

They pushed open the glass doors. No briefcase in immediate sight. Serge walked rapidly down the aisles, spinning display racks of pins, magnets and key chains. He picked up a stack of official launch photos and discarded them one by one: "Already got it, got it, got it, got it, got it . . ." He scanned the rows of personalized NASA coffee mugs, *Adam* to *Zelda*. "They never have *Serge*."

"I think that last joint is wearing off," said Lenny.

"Hang on. I just found something I don't have." He grabbed it off the wall, paid at the cash register and went into the rest room. He came out ten minutes later wearing a royal blue astronaut jumpsuit. "How do I look?"

"Babe magnet."

"It's not about sex. It's about the human spirit," said Serge, tucking his folded Life List in a zippered utility pocket on his shoulder.

"I thought it was about sex," said Lenny.

They left the gift gantry and began combing the exhibits. It was a thorough, time-consuming search, from the IMAX theater to the walk-through space shuttle. The crowd was heavy, getting autographs from authentic NASA astronauts who were assigned public relations duty on a rotating basis. One of the astronauts zipped by on a replica moon buggy. A family from Minnesota flagged him down for photos. Other families stopped Serge in his royal blue jumpsuit, asking him to pose with their kids.

"Come on!" yelled Lenny.

"Hold up," said Serge. "I cannot deny the children."

They worked their way through the Gallery of Manned Spaceflight, taking a break to peer down into a dimly lit bulletproof display case.

"That moon rock looks awfully familiar," said Serge.

"I need a joint," said Lenny. "I'll crouch down behind the lunar module."

"I'll stand guard," said Serge.

Paul and Jethro stopped in front of the Astronaut Memorial with their Cocoa Beach travel guide and silver briefcase.

"I can't take the stress anymore," said Paul, gazing up at the polished granite monument. "We've got a whole twenty-four hours before our ship leaves."

"Character is grace under pressure," said Jethro. "Consider the early astronauts. Those were the days of giants, when destiny did not choose men, but men chose destiny."

Paul and Jethro heard shouting in the distance. They turned and saw a security guard chasing two men—one in a royal blue jumpsuit—away from the Gallery of Manned Spaceflight. But the guard was in mall-cop weight range, and he quickly became winded and broke off pursuit.

Serge peeked out from behind a ticket booth. "I think we lost him."

"I'm fairly sure I have the munchies now."

Serge began gently rubbing all the official space patches on his shoulders and chest.

"Must have snack," said Lenny, feeling his tongue with his fingers. "And beverage."

Serge unzipped and rezipped the dozen utility pockets on his thighs, knees and forearms.

Lenny grabbed his throat. "Parched! . . . *Can't . . . breathe!* . . ."

"Don't embarrass me." Serge zipped a pocket.

"Life . . . functions . . . terminating . . ."

"Okay, let's get a bite."

"Cool."

They entered the Launch Pad Café. Lenny got a chili-cheese dog. Serge sat across from him in his jumpsuit, eyes closed, sucking on a foil pouch of astronaut ice cream.

"Serge . . ." said Lenny.

"Shhhh! Don't talk. I'm having a *moment.*" Serge stuck the metallic pouch back in his mouth and squeezed it dry. He opened his eyes. "Okay, what is it?"

"Isn't this the best chili-cheese dog you've ever seen in your life?"

"I've never felt comfortable about any cheese that comes out of a condiment pump."

"I need another joint."

"You're too high as it is."

"That's what I mean," said Lenny. "I need to smoke myself down."

"It's all in your head," said Serge, unzipping a pocket and pulling out his Life List. "You have to learn how to master your quirks."

Lenny chewed and pointed with his chili dog. "You left off with time travel."

"Let's see, what's next? Ride Shamu, tend the Jupiter Lighthouse, dive the Atocha, perform my one-man salute to Claude Pepper at the Kravis Center, become a surf bum in Jensen, join the harvesting of the oysters at Apalachicola, take a billfish on flyrod, double-eagle at PGA National, ride with the Blue Angels from Pensacola, deliver peace and justice to my Cuban exile community . . ."

"I didn't know you were Cuban."

"Lenny, my name's Serge."

"So you're part of the Miami Mafia?"

"No, Tampa Cuban, different gang, much earlier. We're the group that came up by way of Key West when they opened the cigar factories in the 1880s. My great-great-grandfather was the noble Juan Garcia. Used to be a reader in Ybor City."

"Reader?"

"They sat in tall chairs and read stuff, newspapers, magazines, so the workers wouldn't get bored rolling stogies. Then he started reading D. H. Lawrence, *Lady Chatterley's Lover*. Production increased, but the owner didn't like the idea. Then he bounced around a bit and ended up working the bolita games by the time of the big trouble."

"What's bolita?"

"The old Latin street lottery. Illegal but winked at. They put a bunch of numbered ivory balls in a sack and Juan would reach in and pick one. No way to cheat, right? Wrong. The crime bosses would tell Juan which number they wanted, and he'd freeze that ball in an ice-box. At drawing time, he'd just feel around in the bag for the cold ball."

"You said there was trouble?"

"One Friday he thought they said thirty when they actually said *thirteen*. Froze the wrong ball. It got ugly. They had stacked their bets, and a fortune was lost. They decided to ice him."

"They shot him?"

"No, they stuck him in an icehouse. One thing about Cubans—we love our irony."

"Froze to death," said Lenny, nodding. "I hear it's like going to sleep."

"What about you?" asked Serge. "Any interesting background?"

"Not really," said Lenny. "Born in Pahokee. Family never kept up with their roots, so I didn't hear much. Did a little bit here and there. Worked in an airline parts depot in Opa-Locka because I got to fly around the country for free. I'm a Jets fan but the games aren't broadcast here, so I'd fly up to La Guardia or Newark every Sunday to watch them in the airport lounge and fly right back after the game. Then one Wednesday I'm at the airport here. I'm driving the parts van on the edge of the runway and I hear yelling. 'Stop him! Stop him!' I see some guy in a silk shirt and gold chains running from a Cessna being chased by a Jack Webb type. So I blocked him off with my van at the corner of a building. The guy reaches in his pants. I think he's going to blow me away, but he pulls out a kilo bag and throws it at my window and it explodes in this white cloud and I can't see anything. The federal agent tackles the guy from behind and his face comes through the cloud and smashes up against my window, a big blood streak where his nose hit the glass and dragged down. The agent cuffs him and starts yelling his head off, punching the guy in the liver: *'Don't . . . you . . . ever . . . make . . . me . . . run! . . . '* They haul the guy off and he's shouting that he'll come back and get me, and the other employees said I should leave town, so I head to Broward and get a job cleaning the inside of cop cars because of all the drugs you find where handcuffed suspects stuff them in the backseat crack. I moved again when my dad died and the will gave me a little condo they used to rent out in Kendall. I was up visiting some friends in Georgia one weekend, and I'm coming home at sunset on a Sunday and the other side of I-95 is jammed with cars heading north, barely moving. But there's absolutely nobody on my side of the highway. I mean *nobody*. I must have driven a hundred miles without seeing another car. And the people crawling along in the northbound lanes are pointing at me. I'm thinking, That's odd. Is there something going on I don't know about? But I dismiss it and keep going. I get to my neighborhood and it's ghost town. Even the twenty-four-hour convenience stores are closed, plywood on the windows. Now I'm thinking, Okay, something's definitely up. I turn on the TV, and they're talking about this Hurricane Andrew. I try to find some sports or cartoons, but every channel is the hurricane. So I figure screw it—I'll go work on my car. Which is real drudgery unless you're high, so I'm out there at midnight laying on the ground, blowing a fat one and draining my oil pan, and the wind starts to pick up and I begin getting this sideways rain under the car, really hard, stinging like hundreds of little pins. But I'm thinking it's just really good dope. A fence picket tears loose and hits the car, then something else breaks the passenger window. I finally put two and two together—can this Hurricane Andrew be what all the hoopla's about? I make a mental note to start reading the papers. I head to the house, but there's no power and my sliding glass doors have buckled, but luckily I've got two twelve-packs in the fridge. So I sit down and start drinking. But after a while it's not fun anymore. With the sliding doors down, there's way too much wind in the room, and everything's flying around and hitting me. I start to take a real beating. My beer can collection, CDs, Playboy videos. I'm getting my butt kicked by my own shit. I don't need it. I say, Fuck this, and I go out in the stairwell. It is one of those sturdy concrete jobs with a padlocked storage area underneath for bicycles and lawn mowers. I crawl in there with the rest of my beer and a radio and a candle. I'm not sure exactly when I passed out, but the next morning the only thing left standing was that stairwell. The insurance company paid for everything, and I spent the money on a six-month kick-ass cocaine party. I've never had so many friends. Then I was living in my car for a while. I got like a million parking tickets, and I was towed once while passed out in the backseat. They must not have noticed me. I woke up, climbed over into the front and drove out of the towing yard when they opened the gate for one of the trucks. Did you know you can get all your parking tickets canceled just by mailing in your death certificate? Doesn't matter how many you have—they erase every one. But after I died three times, they got really upset. So I had to leave town again. . . ."

Serge was staring with his mouth open.

"Serge?"

"What?"

"Why are we here?"

"That's an awfully big question, Lenny. I guess if you believe in God, it's a little easier. If not, you might have to go with the unified field theory."

"No, I mean, why are we here right now? Why did we come to this place? I forget."

"We came here to . . ." Serge stopped. "Why *did* we come here?"

Serge and Lenny looked at each other, then at the ground, then back at each other, scratching their heads, looking off in the distance, across the concourse, where two men walked toward the exit with a silver briefcase.

Serge and Lenny looked at each other: *"The briefcase!"*

They jumped up and took off after the men, rounding the corner of the building and sprinting through the Rocket Garden, giant silver and white tubes towering skyward all around.

"That's an Atlas. Had a sixty percent fail ratio before John Glenn climbed in. This is the suborbital Redstone that took up Shepard and Grissom . . ."—Serge breathing hard, not breaking stride—". . . and the big one is the incredible Gemini Titan, an ICBM converted for human flight. Pulled some serious Gs off the pad . . ."

They made it to the car and patched out. Serge grabbed the tracking device. "It's working again! Must be because we've left the complex!"

Serge was driving now, pushing the Cadillac across the causeway, accelerating as they rounded A1A by Port Canaveral. "Take the wheel."

"Man, I'm way too fucked up to drive, especially from the passenger side."

But Serge had already let go and was pointing the tracking device out the side of the car. Lenny began steering with his left hand.

The tracking signal grew stronger. Serge aimed it at each passing building. ". . . There's the Durango steak house, formerly the Mousetrap. Legendary astronaut hangout. If those walls could talk. . . . And there's the Econo Lodge, which used to be the Cape Colony Inn owned by the Mercury Seven. There's still a little commemorative sign out back by the oriental restaurant. . . ."

"Who's your favorite astronaut?" asked Lenny.

"I'd have to give the edge to Frank Borman or John Young. What about you?"

"Major Healy."

"Ah yes, the master thespian from *I Dream of Jeannie,* a very strange TV show," said Serge. "The one that always made me wonder was *The Flying Nun*. Think about it. There was actually a prime-time show on a major network about a nun whose hat made her fly."

"They did a lot of drugs back then," said Lenny.

"That might explain the Sid and Marty Croft stuff, but this idea was brain-dead on arrival. I would have loved to have sat in on that pathetic pitch meeting. I mean, what the fuck were they *rejecting*? The wacky yet sexually frustrating escapades of the disembodied-head-in-a-jar sharing an apartment with three voluptuous flight attendants?"

"I'd watch that show," said Lenny.

"I'm in the wrong business."

They passed the Orbit Motel. The tracking signal went nuts. Serge stomped the brake pedal with both feet, leaving a big cloud of dust and burned rubber as the convertible screeched to a halt in the middle of the road.

A Mazda honked and swerved around the Cadillac. "Asshole!" The driver gave them the finger but quickly retracted it when he saw Serge slamming an ammunition clip into the butt of a .45.

"Let's hit it," said Serge. They turned around and headed back toward the Orbit Motel.

17

There was trouble brewing elsewhere in the United States. Which could mean only one thing. It would eventually come to Florida.

This time, Nevada. The caked desert changed colors five times after sunset, from burnt orange all the way to an eerie purple. A horned lizard lay belly up on a rock and blinked.

A towering sign with a thousand colored bulbs came on, a man in a cowboy hat holding up a big gold nugget. Some of the bulbs flashed on and off, making the cowboy wave at cars.

The Gold Rush Hotel stood outside Reno. Way outside. Just desert and cactus and cattle skulls. It was out on the highway toward California, designed to catch the people coming in, who couldn't wait to get to Reno, and those leaving, who hadn't learned. There were slot machines at the reception desk, a slot machine in each booth of the restaurant, and long lines of clanging machines against the walls in the Sapphire Room.

The Sapphire Room held forty dark nightclub tables, each with its own tiny cocktail lamp. Two keyboards sat onstage, facing each other.

Rock groups are notoriously lax about protecting names and trademarks, which often revert to record companies. By the time the reunion tours roll around, all bets are off. If you're lucky, you might see a band missing only the lead singer. If not, you get half of Chicago. If you're really unlucky, you've paid to get in the Sapphire Room.

An emcee walked onstage with a microphone. Behind him, two men in tuxedos sat down at the opposing keyboards.

"May I have your attention? It is with great pleasure that I introduce Dave and Jeff on the Dueling Wurlitzers. . . ." The pair began playing a rousing number. "Ladies and gentlemen, the Sapphire Room is proud to present Bad Company!"

Jeff leaned to his microphone. ". . . *I feel like makin'—what do I feel like makin'? Can anybody out there help me?—that's right! love! . . . I feel like makin' love, oh yeah! . . .*"

Three tables got up and left.

Bad Company finished their concert, roadies packed up the Wurlitzers, others began setting up for the next act. They unfurled a silk banner. "The Great Mez-mo, amazing feats in mesmerization." A sinister eyeball gave off lightning bolts.

Preston Bradshaw Lancaster took the stage in a blue velvet tuxedo and powder-blue shirt with ruffles. Soon, four volunteers sat in a row of chairs across the stage, a family, their heads slumped to their chests. Disneyland T-shirts.

The forty nightclub tables now held exactly three people; one was passed out. Welcome to show business.

Preston snapped his fingers, and the family of four awoke and looked around disoriented.

"Have a nice nap?"

They nodded.

Preston walked around behind the chairs and put his hands on the father's shoulders.

"I sure am getting hungry," said Mez-mo. "I could really go for some *noodles.*"

"Quack, quack, quack," said the dad. Two people in the audience cracked up. Dad looked confused.

"Yes, sir," said Mez-mo. "I think I could eat a whole plate of *noodles!*"

"Quack, quack, quack."

"Thanks, Dad." Mez-mo took a couple steps and put his hands on the mother's shoulders. "Mom—the Great Mez-mo would like you to go to the blackboard and write the numbers one to ten."

She walked across the stage and began writing with chalk. "*1, 2, 3, I like to swim out to troop ships . . .*" Two people laughed again; Mom looked around.

"Thank you, Mom," said Mez-mo. "You can take your seat. . . . Oh, by the way, would you happen to have a spare *paperclip?*"

She looked down. "Dammit!"

Mez-mo handed her some paper towels, and Mom began wiping invisible dog poop off her shoes.

"Sonny," said Mez-mo, putting his hands on the shoulders of a nine-year-old butterball. "What's your name?"

The boy thought he was saying Benny, but instead he answered, "Agent X-18, the Dreaded Mongoose."

"And Mr. Mongoose, do you know who your assigned targets are today?"

The boy nodded, and Mez-mo handed him a starter's pistol.

"Mr. Mongoose, did you know I just bought a new *telephone?*"

Benny got up from his chair and began firing blanks at his parents. "Die, you bastards!"

"Hey," the father yelled at Mez-mo. "That's not funny!"

"Not as funny as, say, *noodles?*"

"Quack, quack, quack . . ."

"That leaves just you, little lady." Mez-mo put his hands on the teenager's shoulders. "What's your name?"

"Jessica."

"Jessica, did you ever learn to play the *harmonica?*"

Her eyes got big, and she put a hand over her mouth. "Oh, my God! It's Brad Pitt!"

The Great Mez-mo walked to the front of the stage and raised his hands for the room to hold down its non-applause.

Behind Mez-mo, the parents were growing angry over the shooting incident. "What gives you the right! This is the most outrageous . . . !"

"You've been a great audience!" said Mez-mo. "And now I have to order some *noodles* on the *telephone* and clean my *harmonica* with a *paperclip.*"

Benny opened fire again on his parents, who quacked and wiped crap off their shoes. Jessica jumped up and down next to Mez-mo, begging for his autograph.

". . . Thank you and good night!"

Mez-mo ran down the stairs on the right side of the stage, slapping hands tag-team-style with the next performer coming up the steps, Andy Francesco, the Pickpocket Comedian.

Preston headed down the hall to the Flash in the Pan Restaurant.

"There he is! The Great Mez-mo!" someone yelled from the corner booth. "Oooo, oooo! Don't look in his eyes! He has supernatural powers! . . ."

Preston turned toward the voice. It was Spider, the one-armed juggler. Preston hated Spider. He hated them all—all the other performers. Look at them, sitting there so smug in that booth. Wearing the same fancy blue velvet tuxedos, the snap-on bow ties hanging from their collars, elbows over the backs of the seats. Preston still couldn't believe he had been reduced to associating with these losers. After all, he had a Ph.D. in hypnosis.

The corner booth was their turf. Big and curved, shiny red vinyl, it was where all the performers waited while the other acts were onstage, comparing notes, trying out new material, drinking coffee, smoking, maybe ordering a steak when it started getting light out.

"Scoot over," said Preston.

The guys slid around to make room, Spider; Bruno Litsky, America's Favorite Jay Leno Impersonator; the Saul Horowitz Tribute to Vaudeville; Frankie Chan and His Incredible Hand Shadow Revue; Xolack the Mentalist; and Bad Company.

"How'd it go tonight?" asked Saul.

"Like fuckin' death out there," said Preston. "I need a smoke."

Bad Company handed him a cigarette. Xolack gave him a light. The waitress refilled coffee. "Can I get some eggs?" asked Preston. "Not too runny."

"Maybe if you worked on your script," said Spider. "The way you weave the hypnotic trigger words into the conversation—seems a little forced."

"The script's fine," said Preston. "The script's perfect."

"It's a perpetual non sequitur," said Spider. "You're talking about wanting a bowl of noodles, then you have to borrow a paperclip and answer the phone. If I'm in the audience, I have to ask myself, where the hell is all this going?"

"There's nothing wrong with my script!" said Preston.

"It doesn't make any fuckin' sense!"

"Oh, pardon me, Mr. Entertainment, Mr. 'I can juggle with one hand. Everybody, look at me!'"

"I'll kick your ass with this one hand!" said Spider. "Let's go!"

Spider jumped out of the booth and stood next to Preston. "I know what you're thinking. 'He's just got one arm—I can take him!'" Spider began bouncing on the balls of his feet, throwing quick left jabs in the air. "You want a piece of me? I'll fuck you up!"

"Sit down, Spider," said Preston. "I respect you as a performer and a man."

"All right, then." Spider tugged his left lapel defiantly and sat back down.

"I think he's right about the script," said Frankie. "What you need is a good story line."

"No!" said Preston. "No story! It's just a goddamn hypnosis show!"

Frankie turned to his left. "What do you think, Xolack?"

Xolack shrugged and went back to bending spoons with his hands against the edge of the table.

Sparse applause filtered down the hall. Spider nodded at Bruno. "You're up."

Bruno Litsky, America's Favorite Jay Leno Impersonator, stood and straightened his suit. "How do I look?"

"Not remotely like Jay Leno. Break a leg."

Andy Francesco, the Pickpocket Comedian, came back to the table. "How was it out there?"

"Fuckin' oil painting. Give me a cigarette."

Frankie passed him a Winston. They heard a punch line down the hall: "*. . . sounds more like a night out with Bill Clinton and Charlie Sheen!*"

The waitress arrived with Preston's eggs and another pot of coffee.

"Did anyone read where Steppenwolf's coming to town?" asked Frankie. "Man, I love Steppenwolf."

"So what? It's not really Steppenwolf," said Spider.

"What do you mean?"

"Ask Bad Company over there."

"What are you getting at?" Jeff said defensively.

"Nothing that everybody here doesn't know already." Spider lit a cigarette and threw the Zippo on the table.

Preston stabbed his egg yolks with a corner of toast. He picked up his fork, stopped and looked at it, then checked the rest of the utensils around the table. "They're all bent . . . Fuckin' Xolack!"

"Are you vaguely implying we're not Bad Company?" asked Jeff.

"No, I'm saying it directly," said Spider. "Watch my lips. You're not fucking Bad Company."

"We played session on one of the albums," said David.

"In the *studio*."

"That counts."

"Sure it does. In your little make-believe rock 'n' roll castle."

"You son of a bitch!" David jumped up to slug Spider, but the other half of Bad Company grabbed him. "Are you nuts? You can't hit a guy with one arm!"

"Is that so?" said Spider. He sprang out of his seat and began bouncing around next to the table again. "Let's go! You and me—right now!"

"Knock it off!" yelled Preston.

"Make him take it back," said Jeff.

"No, *he* has to take it back," said Spider, still bounding in the aisle.

"Everyone's going to apologize," said Preston. "Then we sit down and act like fuckin' grown-ups. . . . You first, Spider."

"All right," Spider said reluctantly. "I'm sorry I even brought it up. If it's that important to you, you're really Bad Company."

"Damn straight we're Bad Company!" said Jeff, nodding and leaning back in his tuxedo.

"Your turn," Preston told Jeff.

"Sorry," said Jeff. "I'm sure you have a helluva left hook . . ."

"That's better," said Spider, sitting back down.

". . . But your right's a little weak."

"That's it!" Spider dove across the table at Bad Company, knocking over ice-water glasses and ketchup bottles before the others pulled him back down.

"Look at this mess," said Frankie. "Waitress!"

"My wallet! My wallet's gone!" Preston patted his jacket and pants pockets, then stopped and stared across the table. "Give it!"

The Pickpocket Comedian grinned and handed Preston his wallet.

Preston snatched it out of Andy's hand and stuffed it inside his jacket. "Very fucking funny!"

"*The Little Mermaid*," said Frankie.

"What?"

"That's got a good story. You could use new hypnotic code words like *enchanted* and *sea horse* . . ."

Preston lost his appetite. He threw a bent fork down in his plate and pushed it away.

"Frankie, try to stay up with the class," said Spider. "That was six fuckin' subjects ago."

"I didn't know it was closed."

"Just work with us, okay?" said Spider.

"Will you guys shut the fuck up! You've already ruined my break-fast!" yelled Preston. "I can't believe I've been reduced to associating with you people. I have a Ph.D., for Chrissakes!"

"What are you saying? Because I have only one arm, I'm stupid, too?"

"I'm just saying it's the same shit every night. Frankie starts up with *The Little Mermaid*, and you and Bad Company knock over all the drinks, and thanks to Xolack and his spellbinding silverware tricks, I can't take a bite of eggs without almost putting my fuckin' eye out!"

Bruno Litsky came back to the table.

"How was it?"

"Like a goddamn wake," said Bruno. "Cigarette me."

"Frankie, you're up."

Frankie went down the hall and climbed onstage for his hand-shadow rendition of *The Little Mermaid.*

A gaggle of young girls entered the restaurant.

"Hey, Preston," said Andy. "Isn't that girl on the end the one you had onstage tonight?"

Preston turned around. "So it is."

He cupped his hands around his mouth and yelled across the diner: *"Harmonica."*

The girls turned around. One of them began shrieking. She ran over to the corner booth and begged Preston for his autograph again.

Preston stood up and put his arm around Jessica's shoulder. "I think that can be arranged. Let's go back to my suite."

He winked at the other guys as he led her away from the table, toward the men's room.

Bruno shook his head.

"What's the matter with you?" asked Spider.

"There's a line you don't cross," said Bruno, pointing at Preston and the teenager. "That's just not right."

"It's not right because you're not getting it," said Spider.

"Speak for yourself," said Bruno.

"What is that supposed to mean?"

"What does what mean?"

"Oh, I know what you're thinking. 'He's only got one arm—I'll bet he doesn't get any.'"

Preston held the men's room door for Jessica. Nobody inside except one guy playing a slot machine over a urinal.

"Wow!" she said. "I've never been in a presidential suite before. This must cost a fortune!"

Preston pushed open a stall. "Let me show you the bedroom. . . ."

Preston Bradshaw Lancaster had gotten nine women pregnant. That was by his own count. Who knew the true total? That

Preston—such a life-giver. Maybe that was why he was against abortion.

The first pregnancy—and again, this is all inexact science—came during his junior year in college. Preston was working on his undergrad in abnormal psych when he became fascinated by the subject of hypnosis. He soon learned the technique itself really wasn't that difficult; the trick was finding the right personality type, someone in the twenty percent that researchers had identified as highly susceptible to mesmerization.

He walked around the lobby of his dorm approaching women, swinging a pocket watch. "You are getting sleepy."

"What the hell are you doing?"

"This is for a class project."

"Get away from me, you pig! I'm studying!"

Preston went to the next woman.

"Get lost!"

To his benefit, Preston couldn't take a hint. He figured it was all in the numbers. He waited until a party, when everyone had been drinking. The first woman laughed but let him try anyway. She went under quickly. Preston led her to his room. He swung the pocket watch again. "You want to have sex with me."

Even under hypnosis, the woman laughed.

It happened three more times at the party, three different laughing women. Preston had hit a wall, the so-called Svengali effect. He couldn't get them to do something under hypnosis that was against their nature in real life, and having sex with someone like Preston was against the universal nature of women everywhere.

Preston thought about it and read his textbooks. Something in the espionage chapter caught his eye, the way the CIA and KGB liked to turn the tables during hypnotic interrogations, making the subject believe they're from the other side in order to uncover double agents. Preston decided to tinker with the scenario.

The next party. A woman was in his room. A watch swung. "I'm Richard Gere."

Bingo.

Preston couldn't believe the amount, quality and unusualness of the sex he started getting.

Two months later, back in his room. "I am Robert Redford—"

A knock at the door.

"Go away."

More knocks.

"I said, go away! I'm doing homework!"

"It's me, Becky. I have to talk to you. It's an emergency."

"Damn it!"

Preston opened the door a crack.

"I'm pregnant."

"You can't be."

"I am."

"It wasn't me."

"Yes, it was."

"Your word against mine. Who knows how much you sleep around?"

"I was a virgin."

"Trying to trap me in marriage? I know what I'm worth! Don't think I can't see through this."

"I don't want to get married. I need an abortion. I don't have any money."

"Oh, so this is about money! You have sex and now you want me to pay. There's a name for women like you."

"I need two hundred dollars."

"Go to hell!"

He slammed the door.

Becky began calling, and knocking again.

"Stay away from me!"

She didn't. Preston got nervous. Two hundred might just be the start. And what if she had the kid? There could be child support, no end in sight, and all because she was fucking around.

Preston went to his parents, who called their minister. They met in the family's living room.

"Son," said the reverend. "You have to tell her you'll marry her."

"But I don't want to marry her."

"Don't worry, son," said the preacher. "You're not marrying anyone. This is just to prevent her from having an abortion."

"Preston," said his father. "The minister and I have already discussed this. There's no point in letting some bimbo ruin your life."

"You have a bright future," said the preacher. "We're not going to let this woman destroy it. We just need you to make her believe you'll really marry her."

"Say whatever you have to," said the father.

"Just string her along until the third trimester, when it'll be illegal," said the minister.

"Isn't that lying?"

"You'll be doing God's work."

"Preston, obviously you're not completely blameless, but we know how it is," said his father. "You're a devout young man. You go to church. You're just the type they're looking to lead astray."

"She had sex before marriage, so she's a harlot," said the minister.

"But I had sex before marriage, too."

"Because she used her harlot ways. You were obviously seduced."

"Well, there was a little of that."

"Of course there was. Now go and do the right thing."

Preston was convincing. She had gotten him into this, and now it was up to him to prevent a double tragedy. Preston saw it as a test of character, kind of a proud moment. His parents even helped; they had both of them over for Sunday dinners and talked about the future.

Becky bought the act, even started looking at wedding and nursery stuff. A few months later, she went up to Preston's dorm room with exciting news. She had the sonograms—it was a girl!

The door to the room was open. She approached slowly. "Preston?" She looked inside.

Empty. Stripped to the walls.

Becky drove to his parents' house and rang the doorbell. His mother opened the front door, but the screen door on the outside stayed latched.

"Yes?"

"Where's Preston? His dorm room is empty."

"Who are you?"

"What?"

"We don't know anyone named Preston."

". . . I don't understand . . . what—?"

"Never come back here, tramp!"

The door slammed.

They had shipped Preston across the country to finish up at another college in Nevada. That was years and years ago. Where was his daughter today? Preston had never really given it any thought. He went on to postgraduate work in the East, then teaching, building an impressive résumé of being fired from some of the most prestigious institutions in the country. He could pull the hypnosis-for-sex stunt as a student, but it was receiving less than enthusiastic applause now that he was on faculty. Women from other parts of the country began showing up on campus looking for him, pushing strollers. In three short years, he was drummed completely out of the teaching field.

His life fell apart in short order, and he ended up living in a Reno flophouse working nights and weekends as a dishwasher. He called his parents for money.

"Didn't you hear?" said his mother. "We gave it all to the church. And we sold the house, too. We're going to become missionaries. Isn't that great news?"

A week later, Preston saw his first stage hypnotist. He was taking a break from scrubbing tureens, standing in the swinging kitchen doors, watching this incredible guy onstage. Some poor salesman from Omaha was making out with an inflatable woman.

Preston returned from the men's room at the Flash in the Pan, tucking in his shirt. An ecstatic teenager emerged behind him and ran to her friends.

"Scoot over," said Preston.

Xolack the Mentalist was onstage bending spoons.

"How do you do that, anyway?" asked Andy.

"Do what?" asked Preston.

"Get all these women to fuck you. I thought you couldn't get people to do things under hypnosis they wouldn't do in real life."

The audience down the hall grew angry. *"Hey! He's using his hands! He's not even trying to hide it!"*

"You mean the Svengali effect?"

"I don't know what it's called. I just watch a lot of TV."

"The popular notion you can't get someone to do something against their nature is a myth. If you rearrange the context, you can get anyone to do anything."

"Bullshit," said Spider.

"True story," said Preston. "The CIA was messing around with hypnosis about the same time they were losing people out high-rise windows on LSD. They were able to get one of the office secretaries to pick up an unloaded gun, point it at another secretary and pull the trigger."

"How do you know they didn't hate each other?" asked Andy. "Secretaries can be vicious."

Preston shook his head. "It's all documented in government files released under the Freedom of Information Act. These guys were reckless cowboys. They had no idea what they were fooling around with. They should have left this stuff to the universities, where we handled it cautiously and professionally."

"By screwing your students?" asked Bruno.

Preston ignored him. "Did you know you can place a cold needle in the palm of someone's hand and tell them it's red-hot, and it will leave a burn mark?"

"You've done that?" asked Saul.

"Hundreds of times."

"People actually leave your stage with burns?"

Preston nodded proudly.

"You guys are a bunch of rubes," said Spider. "I don't believe any of this hypnosis garbage!"

Preston whispered: *"Parsley."*

Spider's eyelids snapped a couple times like he had just awoken from a long nap. He looked around the table. "What's going on? Why are all of you staring at me like that?"

The others tried to keep straight faces, but when Andy cracked up, they all fell apart.

"Is somebody going to tell me what's going on?" Spider demanded.

Andy wiped tears of laughter. "Sorry, we're really laughing *with* you. Preston hypnotized you to think you were a one-armed juggler . . ."

"With a complex," added Saul.

"That's ridiculous!" said Spider. He held out both his arms, like evidence.

They laughed even harder. "You should have seen yourself," said Jeff. "Trying to pick fights with everyone, holding one arm behind your back."

"You're making this up! All of you! I've never been hypnotized in my life!"

That just made them laugh more.

"Who ever heard of a one-armed juggler? Fuck all of you!"

Spider stood up and marched away from the booth. Preston yelled *parsley,* and Spider tucked his right arm behind his back and stormed out of the restaurant.

18

It was a dark and starry night down the long, straight road through the mangroves, miles from anything. A white Mercedes sat at the dead end.

Five men in tropical shirts got out of the Benz and went to the trunk. Ivan, Igor, Pavel, Nikita and Leonid, all former KGB now gone free-lance, working for themselves in the land of opportunity, most recently running The Palm Reader bookstore in Miami Beach before landing a contract with Mr. Grande. South Florida was a natural fit for them. Lots of ex-spooks around, CIA, MI6, Mossad, and nobody held grudges. Couldn't afford to. With constantly shifting political terrain, they depended on each other to network for gigs. Still, there was a loose hierarchy. The Russians were considered among the best. Most of them.

These five began their intelligence careers in different branches of the service, but soon distinguished themselves. Pavel accidentally sat on a plunger, blowing up an elite demolition team. Nikita was the helicopter pilot who misjudged crosswinds during a labor riot and sent a commando unit rappelling down the chimney of a Ukrainian steel foundry. Assigned to protect an emissary to Kazakhstan, Leonid offered him an after-dinner mint—no, wait! That's my suicide pill! Igor was driving a specially equipped limo in the big May Day parade, past the VIP bleachers on the Kremlin Wall, trying to get something on the radio when he inadvertently flipped up the machine guns and took out the back two rows of a marching band. Their leader was Ivan, who had done something either less stupid or grossly more stupid than the rest. He slept with the wife of someone in the Politburo.

Only one thing to do with people of such intelligence: put them on the torture squad.

Ivan's boys were well suited to their work, able to blithely perform tasks that made even the most veteran agents queasy. After all, someone had to work with the electric prods and pliers and train the sexual attack dogs. But there were the good times, too. They had been together a decade now, and when they started reminiscing—oh, the memories. Like how about the time Nikita drank too much vodka and passed out and got raped by one of the German shepherds? Whew! They laughed until they cried about that one!

Tonight would be another for the scrapbook. The Mercedes had made good time across the state and now sat at the end of Cockroach Bay Road on the southeast shore of Tampa Bay. The nearest house was four miles; the only reason the road went this far was to reach one of the most remote boat ramps in the state. There were no streetlights and rarely any traffic this far back except the occasional pickup with blood-spattered upholstery engulfed in flames. You stayed far away from here at night unless you were getting rid of human evidence, which faced accelerated swamp decomposition and what detectives liked to call "animal interference."

On this particular evening, all was quiet except croaking frogs and the weeping coming from the trunk of the Mercedes. Ivan unlocked it.

"But I'm only an insurance adjuster! Please let me go!"

They carried him to the shore, which had that low-tide smell. They drove long stakes into the muck and began tying the man down.

"Please don't kill me!"

"You work for Buccaneer Life and Casualty?"

The man nodded.

"Tell us what we want to know."

"But I don't know anything! I don't know what you're talking about!"

Nikita walked over to Ivan, standing by the Mercedes. Ivan lit a cigar. "Has he said where the five million dollars is yet?"

"No, but I think he's about to crack."

"What method are you using?"

"Crabs."

Ivan winced. "Terrible way to go."

"The worst," said Nikita. "Let's go watch."

They strolled back over to the insurance man.

"Tell us what we want to know!" snapped Nikita.

The man couldn't stop crying.

"All right then!" said Nikita. "We'll just leave you to the *crabs*!"

The man whimpered a couple more times, then stopped and looked side to side at the little mangrove crabs dancing around the shore, darting in and out of their sand holes as each wave from the bay advanced and retreated on the rising tide. The insurance man looked up at Nikita. "That's it?"

"Don't even try asking for mercy!"

"Okay," said the man.

"Why isn't he scared?" Ivan asked Nikita.

"He's so scared he's in shock!"

Ivan bent over and picked up one of the little crabs, which repeatedly pinched his thumb and forefinger.

"Watch out!" said Nikita. "Built to scale, those claws have the crushing power of a great white shark!"

The crab continued pinching Ivan. "I barely feel anything."

"Maybe it sliced clean through your nerve endings."

"It's not doing anything."

"That's because it's just one," said Nikita. "They're like piranhas. It's all in the numbers. Imagine hundreds of those crabs!"

Ivan stared at his hand. "It's just leaving little red marks."

"But imagine hundreds of little red marks!"

Ivan smacked Nikita in the back of the head. "You idiot! They're the wrong kind of crabs!" Ivan pointed at the insurance man. "And he knows it. He lives around here."

"What now?"

"Break into the insurance office," said Ivan, handing Nikita his car keys. "Get the Mercedes."

"Right." Nikita jumped behind the wheel as the others waited on the side of the mangroves.

They noticed the Mercedes's engine was racing, but it wasn't going anywhere.

"Does he have it in neutral?"

"I don't think so."

The Mercedes was backed too close to the boat ramp, and the rear tires were spinning on algae.

"Nikita! Give it more gas!"

Nikita gave it more gas.

"I think he's starting to go backward."

The others watched curiously as the sedan slowly slid down the boat ramp and into the water. It was three-quarters under when the panic hit—Nikita struggling in the dark bay with his safety harness and the shorted-out child-safety locks. Then a gun started firing out the roof, letting the air pocket escape, and down she went.

"Well," said Ivan. "That was certainly different." He turned to the adjuster. "You know the way back to town?"

He nodded.

"Untie him."

"*I promise I* won't tell anyone," said the adjuster, tied up again, this time to an office chair in the headquarters of Buccaneer Life & Casualty in downtown Tampa.

The Russians didn't answer. They dumped out desk drawers, pulled paintings off walls, smashed vases and cut the stuffing out of couches and chairs.

"What are you looking for? Maybe I can help."

No answer. They ripped acoustical tiles from the dropped ceiling and pulled up carpet. They checked the toilet tanks, unscrewed wall sockets. They gouged the drywall with a fire ax. They used an acetylene torch to cut into the plumbing and electrical conduits.

"No use," said Igor, wiping insulation dust off his shoulders. "It's not here."

"What's not here?" asked the adjuster.

"The file on the five million you paid out in September."

"In the filing cabinet."

Ivan looked sternly at the others. "You didn't check the filing cabinet?"

They removed their hard hats and shrugged.

Ivan walked over to the cabinet and retrieved the thick file. It had everything—names, dates, addresses, bank accounts. Then it ended abruptly.

Ivan walked back to the adjuster. "It's not complete. Just stops cold. There's no current address for the guy."

"I know. He fled. He was last seen at a local bank. Witnesses told police he made a withdrawal and stuffed the money in a silver briefcase."

Ivan cursed under his breath and turned to the others. "I thought you interrogated him!"

"We did."

Ivan looked at the adjuster again. "Where is he now?"

"Six feet under. They never found the briefcase."

"When did this happen?"

"Couple months ago."

"Where?"

"In a motel room in Cocoa Beach."

"You wouldn't happen to know which motel, would you?"

"The Orbit. Room two fourteen."

"And you just happen to know all this because . . . ?"

"It was in the papers."

Ivan dropped his head in exasperation and closed his eyes. He slowly looked up again. "Why didn't you tell us this down at the boat ramp? You could have died!"

"Your guys never asked," said the adjuster. "They just kept saying, 'Tell us what you know!' What the hell does *that* mean?"

Ivan looked at the others. "Do we have to go over this every time?"

"I think it's a trick," said Igor, putting his goggles back on and firing up the acetylene torch again. "Pull down his pants. I'll find out what he *really* knows."

"Igor! Turn that thing off before you hurt yourself!"

Leonid stepped forward holding the live electrical conduit. "I think Igor's right. It sounds like a trap. Let me attach these wires to his nuts, just to be safe."

"Bend him over," said Pavel, squeezing the trigger on the concussion drill.

"I can't believe you guys!" said Ivan. "You're the most perverted bastards I've ever met! Leonid, what's with always wanting to put wires on a guy's nuts?"

Leonid grinned and blushed. "I've never seen it done before."

"Can I use the torch if I'm extra careful?" asked Igor.

"No! No! No!" yelled Ivan, pounding his fist on the file cabinet. "We kill him normal! Nothing fancy! Nothing sick! He keeps his pants up! That how all the trouble started *last time*."

The men sagged with disappointment.

"Igor. Shoot him," said Ivan.

"All right," Igor said reluctantly. He turned the valve on his acetylene torch. Only he turned it the wrong way and a flame shot out and caught some drapes on fire.

"Sorry."

They stood and watched the curtains burn.

"Is somebody going to put that shit out, or do I have to do everything?" said Ivan.

Igor grabbed the fire hose off the wall and hit the drapes with a stream of water. He also hit Leonid, holding the five-thousand-volt electrical conduit, who departed the planet in a bright flash and a shower of sparks.

19

"We're in Cocoa Beach," Ivan said in his cell phone. "We're at the motel right now, Mr. Grande." He slid bills through a slot in thick Plexiglas.

"Yes. . . . Yes, sir. . . . As smooth as can be expected, except we lost two men. . . . No, it couldn't be helped. . . ."

Jethro and Paul locked up their motel room and headed out with their silver briefcase. They walked past the office window of the Orbit Motel.

"I don't think I can make it," said Paul. "I'm gonna crack up for sure."

"Relaxation," Jethro said as they reached the edge of A1A. "That's what golf is all about."

The traffic let up and the pair started across the street for the driving range.

Ivan held the cell phone with one hand and stuck a paper cup under the water cooler with the other. ". . . Yes, sir. . . . Yes, sir, Mr. Grande. . . ."

Pavel tugged on Ivan's sleeve and pointed out the window.

". . . Yes, sir. . . . Hold on a second, sir. . . ."

Ivan covered the phone. "Not now!" He nodded with importance at the phone in his hand. "I'm talking to *You Know Who!*"

He uncovered the phone. "No, sir. . . . There's no problem. . . ."

Pavel kept looking out the window and kept tugging. Ivan swatted him away.

Serge and Lenny locked up their motel room. They ran past the office window.

Pavel tugged harder. Ivan covered the phone again. "What is it?"

Pavel pointed again. Jethro and Paul were halfway across the highway with the briefcase, followed by two other guys they didn't recognize.

"That's them!" yelled Ivan, dropping the phone.

Three Russians ran out of the motel office.

"We're home free," Jethro said as they reached the other side of A1A and the miniature golf complex. "Nothing can go wrong now."

Paul heard footsteps. He looked back and saw Serge and Lenny.

"Run!"

They sprinted for the Japanese footbridge over the lagoon by the driving range.

Serge stopped and grabbed Lenny by the arm. He pointed at hole number five, the pink elephant on the surfboard. "Split up! You go that way! We'll ambush on the other side!"

"Right!" Lenny ran for the elephant, and Serge took a hard left at the T Rex.

Jethro and Paul looked back as they reached the bridge. The two guys were gone, but now there were three others, way back, their colorful shirts visible through the trees. Jethro and Paul started up the bridge. Serge had made a complete circle and was closing fast on the far end of the span for the ambush, but Lenny was tired from all his pot smoking and had to sit for a moment on a plastic turtle.

Jethro and Paul hit the crest of the bridge. Jethro was still looking back, but Paul faced forward again.

"Aaauuuhhhhh!"

Serge was charging full speed. Paul panicked. He threw the briefcase as hard as he could up in the air. They all stopped and watched it sail end over end, tumbling weightless at the top of the arc, reflecting in the sunlight, then falling again, over the bridge's railing and splashing next to the scuba diver collecting golf balls.

There was some yelling from behind a cluster of palm trees. Russian accents. "I think I saw them go over there!"

Everyone started running again. Paul and Jethro continued down the far side of the bridge, away from the tropical shirts. Serge kept charging in the opposite direction, up the bridge, letting them pass, concentrating on the briefcase. He never slowed as he reached the top of the bridge, swan-diving over the railing into the murky lagoon.

The scuba diver had mistaken the briefcase's splash for a feeding alligator diving into the pond, and he surfaced and jerked his head around, standing at the ready with his bang stick. Just then, another big splash, some guy diving into the water next to him.

"What the hell?"

It had been a long footrace, and the Russians were spread out along the path according to endurance. Pavel was the fastest, the only one who had made it around the last bunch of palms at the base of the bridge in time to see Serge dive over the railing.

The scuba diver stared dumbfounded at the rippling water where Serge had gone in. Serge stayed submerged for the longest time, and the diver started thinking he might have drowned. Just then, Serge broke the surface of the water with an irrepressible smile, holding the briefcase over his head like the Stanley Cup. "I got it! I finally got it!"

From the top of his vision, Serge saw the fastest Russian dive off the bridge. "Uh-oh."

Boom.

The Russian belly-flopped on the end of the upright bang stick, and a shower of red hamburger rained on Serge and the scuba diver.

From down the path: "They went that way!"

Serge grabbed the scuba diver by the arm and pulled him under the Japanese footbridge. He put a finger over his lips for the diver to be quiet as feet clomped across the wooden boards above. The footsteps faded. Serge looked up at the slits of sunlight coming through the bridge. "I think the coast is clear."

He looked back down, but the scuba diver was already scrambling up the far bank of the lagoon.

Fog rolled in from the ocean. A deep steam horn sounded from across the dark, night water. A cruise ship headed for the Bahamas.

Paul was not on it. He was strapped to a lawn chair at the deserted end of the Port Canaveral jetty.

"Where's the briefcase?" said Ivan.

"I told you, I threw it in the lagoon!"

Ivan backhanded him across the face. "We already checked. I'll ask you again. Where's the briefcase?"

"That's where I threw it!" said Paul. "Someone must have grabbed it!"

Slap.

"All we found was Pavel floating facedown, his lunch in the trees. Where's the briefcase?"

"I don't know!"

Slap.

A new Mercedes drove up, with dealer stickers still in the windows, headlights slicing through the fog, shining in Paul's eyes. Igor got out and unlocked the trunk. He took the blindfold off Lenny and dragged him to the front of the car.

"Where'd you find him?" asked Ivan.

"Hiding in the windmill."

"Any sign of the fat one with the beard?"

Igor shook his head. He tied Lenny to a second lawn chair next to Paul.

"Where's the briefcase?"

"I never saw the briefcase," said Lenny. "Can I go?"

"Sure thing," said Ivan. "And would you like some cab money?"

Lenny smiled. "Yeah."

Slap.

"We can do this all night," said Ivan. "I don't have to be anywhere."

"I do," said Lenny.

Slap.

"Let me pull his pants down!" said Igor, holding up a cage of scorpions.

Ivan smacked the cage out of Igor's hand. "What is wrong with you? I mean it! You're not normal!"

Igor pointed at the ground. "They're getting away! Give me a piece of paper or something to scoop them up."

Slap. "Forget about the scorpions!"

Igor rubbed his sore cheek. A foghorn blared. "Is that a cruise ship?"

"Probably," said Ivan. "They go out of here all the time."

"Ever been on one?"

"What?"

"Ever taken a cruise?"

"A couple times."

"I heard you can eat all you want all the time, that they keep refilling the buffet twenty-four hours."

Ivan stared at him.

"Do they really do that? If they do, that's a pretty good deal."

Ivan put a hand to his own temple and closed his eyes. "Don't talk anymore. I have a headache. Just turn the car around and we'll stick them in the trunk and handle this later at the motel."

"You got it." Igor hopped back in the Mercedes and started the car.

Ivan cupped his hands around his mouth and yelled over the engine: "Remember, you have trouble with English . . . R is for—"

Igor ran over Paul.

". . . reverse."

Igor put the car in reverse and backed over Paul. He got out and walked around the front of the car. "Is he okay?"

"Absolutely. Ready to dance all night."

"But he looks dead."

Slap.

"He *is* dead! You ran over him! Twice!"

Igor picked up a crumpled lawn chair and tried to unbend it, then turned quickly. "What was that?"

"What was what?"

"That noise. I heard something."

"We're outside in a park. There's a million squirrels and birds."

Igor stepped forward and peered into a palmetto thicket. "I could have sworn I heard someone."

Two Russians still alive. Ivan and Igor. They drove back to the motel in silence.

"What do you want to eat?" asked Ivan.

"I don't know. Something different." Igor turned on the radio.

"It's after midnight. We only have so many options."

Igor thumbed through his CD wallet. "But we always go to the same place."

"It's a good place."

Mosquitoes buzzed around fluorescent lights. Outdoor speakers played faint Muzak. A deep, rhythmic pounding came up the street, quiet at first, but getting louder. A white Mercedes Z310 came around the bend on A1A. The tinted windows were down, Igor's head bobbing.

". . . *Everybody Wang Chung tonight* . . ."

Lenny tried to adjust his eyes in the jet-black trunk. He screamed and he banged. The car came to a stop and Lenny listened carefully. The engine turned off. Lenny started screaming and banging again.

The trunk lid suddenly opened, bright light. Lenny shielded his eyes.

"Seven-Eleven," said Igor. "What do you want?"

Lenny crunched his eyebrows in thought. "Jumbo dog . . . no, chicken salad. And a cookie. But if they don't have chicken, don't get the tuna—"

The trunk lid closed.

Ivan and Igor hit the chips rack, then the beer case. Hiding Paul's body in the underbrush hadn't been easy, and they still had quite a bit of blood on their shirts, but no more so than the other customers.

"Coors good?" asked Ivan.

"It's all right."

"You want me to get it or what?"

Igor scanned the rest of the display. "Have you had the new Killians with the pressurized ball in the can for real draft taste?"

"Come on! We're fogging up the door!"

Coors it was. They moved on to the deli. Ivan grabbed the first sub he saw. Igor picked up three in succession, put each back. He waved at the cashier. "Are these salads fresh?"

"Made this morning."

"What time?"

Ivan grabbed a salad and jabbed it in Igor's stomach. "Take it and let's go!"

They dumped their purchase on the counter. The cashier began ringing.

"The slot for the little bags of croutons was empty," said Igor. "I don't think I should be charged full price for the salad."

"I have to charge what the label says."

"But I didn't get my croutons."

"We're out."

"I know."

"All I can do is void it."

Ivan smacked the back of Igor's head again. "Pay the man and get in the car!"

Further into the night. A1A became deserted, the last decent people straggling home. Traffic lights cycled through their colors with no cars. Next shift. A hooker rode to work on a bike with a banana seat. A police cruiser slowly rolled by, shining a search beam down each alley. A pack of wild dogs came out from behind a muffler shop, fighting over a large piece of unidentified meat, scattering when headlights hit them and a Mercedes turned into the parking lot of the Orbit Motel.

Ivan and Igor carried plastic convenience store bags to their room. The dogs took off down the street after a banana bike.

"I don't know why you're in such a grouchy mood," said Igor.

Ivan stopped walking. "Did your mother, like, fall down several flights of stairs when she was pregnant?"

"No."

"Get kicked by a horse?"

"No."

"Handle a lot of plutonium?"

"No. Why do you ask?"

Ivan resumed walking to the room. He unlocked the door, and they dumped their stuff on the dresser.

"Go get him out of the trunk," said Ivan. "You think you can handle that?"

Five minutes later, Ivan stood in his socks in front of the TV, looking for something with the remote and shaking a bag of sunflower seeds into his mouth. Then he remembered Igor was taking a long time.

Ivan opened the door and stuck his head out. "Igor? . . . Igor? . . ."

Igor hadn't blinked for five minutes. His hands were bound, mouth taped.

Serge snipped away with heavy-gauge metal shears.

"It's important to have the right tool for the job." Snip, snip. "They're Sears, you know. Lifetime guarantee." Snip, snip. "Aren't you just fascinated by the place we're at?"

Igor didn't blink.

"Me, too," said Serge. "Cape Canaveral, from the Spanish for 'cape of canes' because of all the reeds the sailors saw. Say the name today, and people think modern, futuristic, space travel. Yet it also has one of the oldest histories of any place in the country." Snip, snip.

Serge stepped back to inspect his work, then nodded to himself and began snipping again. "The cape jutted out so much, it became Florida's most prominent navigational feature for early explorers. That's why there are so many shipwrecks around here. Hence, the Treasure Coast."

Serge switched to bolt cutters. Snap, snap.

"The area was mapped as early as 1502. The Spanish tried to establish their first settlement here, but the Indians were too savage, so they moved a bit farther north to a little place called St. Augustine. Isn't that a fun fact? Did you know they had to bulldoze historic Indian grounds when they were building some of the launch pads? Talk about your symbolism overload."

Igor finally figured out Serge's plan and started screaming under the mouth tape.

"You're right," said Serge. "It *was* a tragedy. All kinds of archaeological opportunities lost."

Serge snipped a few last times and stood up straight. "There!"

He reached down next to Igor's leg and turned a key. A quiet electric motor came to life. "You realize you kidnapped my best friend. I saw you with that cage of scorpions. You weren't exactly planning a Hallmark moment."

Serge produced a pistol with a silencer, took aim, and shot out four floodlights in the distance. He picked up a concrete block and placed it in front of Igor's feet, on a pedal. The electric motor grew louder, and Igor slowly pulled away from Serge.

"Don't forget to write."

Ten p.m. A homicide detective and the county medical examiner stood on a Japanese footbridge, interviewing witnesses. EMTs were down on the bank of the retention pond, zipping up Pavel's body in a black plastic bag.

The detective took notes on a spiral pad. "And you say you were scuba diving in the pond for golf balls." The detective looked up. "Is that actually a job?"

The diver nodded.

"And the deceased just came out of nowhere and jumped on the end of your bang stick?"

The diver nodded again.

"Hey!" the complex's owner yelled over to the detective. "Can I open the driving range now? I'm losing a lot of money!"

The detective said it was okay.

"Go ahead!" yelled the owner. Twenty golfers began swinging.

They loaded Pavel's body into the back of the coroner's van.

"Range cart!"

The golfers dumped out the rest of their buckets and began swinging as fast as they could, dozens of balls clanging off the side of the cart. But other shots, which appeared to have found their mark, didn't make much noise at all. With the floodlights shot out, the golfers couldn't see that the driver's protective metal cage had been cut away.

The police and medical examiner had to drop Pavel's body off at the morgue and head right back to the driving range.

The detective wasn't happy when he met the owner in front of the windmill. He pointed at the range. "They're still hitting golf balls!"

"I have to make a buck."

"This is a crime scene!"

"They're not aiming at the cart anymore."

"Tell them to stop!"

The owner stuck two fingers in his mouth and whistled toward the driving tees. "Hey! The police say you have to stop!" Most of them did, although some tried getting in a few last balls.

"Stop hitting!" yelled the detective. "What are you, children?"

The detective and coroner walked out to the two-hundred-yard marker and peeked in the range cart at Igor. The detective cringed. The coroner threw up.

The detective offered him a handkerchief and tapped the corner of his own mouth. "You got vomit."

The coroner dabbed it.

"Other side."

The EMTs carefully extracted Igor from the range cart.

The detective stared off in thought and shook his head. "What the hell kind of Goony Golf are they running here?"

A golf ball whizzed by.

Ivan sat in his motel bathroom with a cell phone.

"Calm down, Mr. Grande. . . . Please calm down. . . . Nobody feels worse about this than I do. . . . No, someone else has the briefcase now. . . . We're still trying to find that out. . . . Look, I know this is a bad time to bring this up, but I need some more men. . . . I ran out. . . .

What do you mean, what happened to the ones I had? They're all dead. . . . Stop shouting. . . . Please stop shouting. . . . I'd like to point out that they died trying to recover your five million dollars. . . . Yes, that's right, the five million I still don't have. . . . If you can just send some more guys, I think we can wrap this up pretty quickly. . . . Okay, I'll meet them at the airport. . . ."

The next morning Ivan headed west on the Beeline Expressway, listening to books on tape. He took the exit for Orlando International and parked in short-term, then got on a moving sidewalk for the new airside. He found a seat and folded his hands in his lap.

A wide-body pulled up to the terminal. Ivan stood and walked over to the gate. Passengers poured off the plane. Couples embraced, children cried, others ran for the smoking area. Ivan got on tiptoe in the middle of the human stream, craning his neck for a better view, holding a white sign in front of him with both hands: MIERDA CARTEL.

Four men in tropical shirts walked up and introduced themselves. Dmitri, Alexi, Vladimir and Chuck.

"We're on a tight schedule," said Ivan. "We have to head to an address right now. Then drinks on me."

Jethro was back in his room at the Orbit Motel, sitting on the foot of the bed. He had decided to end it like a man. There was no other choice. The money was gone and so was his little buddy. He had already read the grisly details in the paper. Jethro blamed himself. He drank straight from a bottle of George Dickel and muttered as he loaded the shotgun he had purchased at Space Shuttle Pawn for twenty-five dollars.

"If only I had not run like a coward, possibly I could have prevailed in the struggle and offered protection and comfort. Instead, I abandoned my faithful traveling companion. Men do not do such things. Not even dogs do such things. . . ." He took another swig. "I am not even a dog. Where was my grace under pressure? There is no honor in this anymore. Just the burning sting of truth like a morning urination in Madrid. *Galanos!*"

He braced the butt of the shotgun on the floor and placed the other end in his mouth. He kicked off his right sandal and stuck his big toe in the trigger guard.

He pressed down with his toe.

Nothing.

He pressed again. Still nothing. The damn thing wouldn't budge. He took the barrel out of his mouth and looked down. The safety was still on. He reached for it but the gun was too long, and he couldn't get to it with his toe still in the trigger. He tried to pull the toe out, but it had swollen and was stuck.

Jethro sulked on the end of the bed, hanging his head pitifully, his big toe turning purple. He grabbed the bottle of Dickel again. "Exquisite," he sighed. "Even in suicide I have become a buffoon."

The motel room door crashed open. Five tropical shirts stood in the doorway.

"Where's our briefcase!"

Jethro screamed. He jumped up and ran for the bathroom.

"Get him!" yelled Ivan.

It was difficult for Jethro to run, dragging the shotgun. The sixteen-gauge swung out and hit the bottom of the dresser, knocking off the safety.

Jethro took another step for the bathroom.

Bang.

Another step.

Bang.

Jethro hobbled as fast as he could, the shotgun firing with each step, spraying a tight pattern of lead pellets at everything within six inches of the floor.

The homicide detective was conducting follow-up interviews at the driving range. His beeper went off.

The detective parked behind the Orbit Motel and trotted quickly toward an upstairs room but slowed when he noticed five sets of bloody footprints coming down the steps.

A paramedic was inside, trying to get Jethro's toe out of the shotgun with Vaseline.

"Ah, yes, you drive the ambulance," said Jethro. "Like the courageous young men of the Parisian countryside during the Great War . . ."

"Jethro, straighten your leg out some more," said the paramedic. "I can't get leverage."

"Did you check to see if it was still loaded?" asked the detective.

"Of course."

Bang.

"Jethro? . . . Jethro? . . ."

The detective pulled out his notebook. "This is going in your file."

*S*pider came back to the Sapphire Room after storming out that night. He always came back.

Preston promised not to do the one-armed gag anymore. He always lied.

The Sapphire Room was the Devil's Island of lounge acts. The gang wanted out. They all had the same agent, and they complained every chance. On a Saturday night in September, they got the phone call. Their agent had come through with an ambitious schedule of engagements cutting clear across the country from the desert southwest to the northeast industrial corridor. The itinerary came over the fax at the Gold Dust Motel.

"These places look worse than the Sapphire Room!" said Spider. They called their agent.

He advised patience. This was résumé-building time. They needed to get some polish from the road, put together recommendations and audition tapes. And if all went well . . . the agent told them what he had in mind next.

"Shit," said Preston. "What are we waiting for?"

They hit the highway in Spider's brown DeVille with bad suspension, pulling a U-Haul, dragging the trailer chain and making sparks. It was tight quarters. Spider, Andy, Saul, Preston, Frankie and Bad Company, shoulder to shoulder in blue tuxedos. They were surprised to discover they actually liked the road. It got in their blood: the gas stations and the greasy spoons and the greasier motels with The Paper Strip of Total Confidence across the toilet seat. They worked the circuit of small hotel bars in second-shelf cities bypassed by the big acts. No interstate travel. Just two lanes across America. The big, open sky and rolling plateaus and tumbleweeds across Arizona and New Mexico, putting in a lot of car time. Preston kept them going with hypnosis stories.

"There was this guy in Switzerland back in the eighteen hundreds who used to hypnotize his wife into becoming completely rigid. And he would set up two chairs and lay her on her back, head on one chair, feet on the other, nothing underneath . . ."

"I've seen that one," said Andy.

"It gets better," said Preston. "This guy put concrete blocks on her stomach and invited people from the audience to smash them with sledgehammers."

"I know what's coming," said Spider. "She came out of the trance at the crucial moment?"

"Worse," said Preston. "One of the volunteers from the audience— he misses the block completely. Kills her."

"That's fucked up," said Spider, lighting a cigarette.

"Still a fun story," said Preston.

More miles. Texaco road maps, flat tires, bad coffee, farts. But things were looking up, moods improving. They were seeing their country. And they were getting better. Acts began to sharpen during the night-in-night-out lounge march east, Tempe, Tucson, Tombstone. "Any cliff dwellers in the audience tonight? I got a joke for you . . ."

Albuquerque, Carlsbad, Roswell, Lubbock, Abilene, the landscape slowly transforming, cattle ranches and oil derricks replacing the mesas and buttes and UFO people. San Antonio, Austin, Corpus Christi, the Alamo Room, the Lone Star Supper Club, the downtown Galveston Skate-O-Rama, which they would be discussing with their agent.

"Here's a good one," said Preston. "This is what got me interested in hypnosis in the first place, and it's definitely true, completely documented. All the scholars know the details. In the late 1800s, another hypnotist in Europe had regularly been hypnotizing an assistant for stage demonstrations. He usually instructed her mind to leave her body and enter another hypnotized subject, in order to cure ailments. Then she'd leave that person's body and take the ailment with her."

"Did it work?"

"The medical part is hocus-pocus, but the power of suggestion is very real. One night, the guy got sloppy or something and instead of telling her mind to leave her body, he told her *soul* to leave."

"What happened?"

"Heart attack. Died."

"No!"

"Yes."

"Bullshit!"

"We only find it amazing because we're cynical Americans. We've never really accepted hypnosis over here," said Preston. "The French know all about this."

"The French?"

"If it can be used for sex, the French are all over it. A hundred years ago, stage hypnotists were screwing everything that moved in Paris. It got out of control. Everybody knew what was going on. The subject dominated French publishing. De Maupassant wrote about it. So did Alexandre Dumas, author of *The Three Musketeers.* Then, in 1894, the same year that assistant got killed onstage, George du Maurier kicked the door wide open with his international best-selling novel *Trilby,* featuring the cowardly-cruel villain Svengali, who exploits his subjects."

"A hypnotist who exploits his subject?" said Spider. "What a shock."

Onward, turning north, heavier coats, autumn leaves changing. Knoxville, Lexington, Akron, Wilkes-Barre, Schenectady. The regional accents and politics morphing, but not the clubs, which even had the same names, repeating over and over in a neon Möbius strip: the Flamingo, the Satin Club, the Stardust Room, the Horseshoe Lounge, Fast Eddie's, the Sands, the Surf, the Algiers, the Copa, the Aladdin, the Riviera, the Flamingo . . . These were the good times, barnstorming Vegas Nation, laughter again filling their lives, even if it was at someone's expense from another hypnosis prank. None of them would admit it, but they genuinely began enjoying hanging out together, encouraging each other, going to movies at old Main Street theaters. They went to see *Saving Private Ryan* in Bridgeport and Preston said *asparagus,* and Frankie Chan went up to the screen and made shadow puppets during the beach landing, and they all got chased down the street.

With such a heavy schedule, it was bound to happen. Casualties. In Poughkeepsie, they lost Saul Horowitz and his vaudeville tribute to varicose veins, replacing him with Dee Dee Lowenstein "as Carmen Miranda." Then, in the Tango Room in Scranton, Bad Company was served a footlocker of lawsuits for trademark infringement.

But they were professionals now, no looking back, pressing forward, toward the final prize. The odometer turned over. Spider dialed their agent in New York. "When do we get the replacement musical act for Bad Company? . . . But they were our anchor on the marquee. . . . You said to be patient last time. . . ."

The DeVille pulled into their Thursday-night engagement.

Dee Dee Lowenstein finished her Carmen Miranda set. She returned to the corner booth in the restaurant and set her fruit hat on the table.

Spider lit her cigarette. "How'd it go?"

She exhaled. "Fuckin' morgue."

Frankie reached for her hat. "Can I have a banana?"

"No, you can't have a banana! What are you, fuckin' simple?"

"But you got a whole bunch."

She pointed at his hand. "Move it or lose it!"

A stranger approached the table wearing a tuxedo and carrying a small musical case. He took a piece of paper from his pocket and read something.

"Can we help you?" asked Andy.

"I'm supposed to meet some people. I'm not sure I have the right place." He reread the piece of paper.

Andy reached. "Let me see that."

Spider finished his juggling set and came back to the table.

"How'd it go?"

"Fuckin' granite. Gimme a cigarette."

Andy handed the paper back to the new guy. "Yep, you're in the right place. What's your name?"

"Bob. Bob Kowolski."

Andy motioned back and forth. "Bob—the gang. . . . The gang—Bob."

"What's your act, Bob?"

Bob told them.

Frankie lit a cigarette. "Better than nothing."

The emcee came up to the table and jerked a thumb over his shoulder. "What's going on here? We got an empty stage."

Spider pointed at the new guy. "Looks like you're up, Bob. Cherry-poppin' time. Break a leg."

Bob hurried off with his musical case.

Spider chain-lit a Viceroy. "I didn't think it was possible, but Bob may just make us long for the days of Bad Company."

Bob climbed onstage and pulled a stool up to the microphone.

The emcee motioned for a soft spotlight. "Ladies and gentlemen, Caesars Palace of Hoboken is proud to present Steppenwolf!"

Bob leaned to the microphone. *"Get your motor runnin'! . . ."* He began playing the pan flute.

A cell phone rang in the corner booth. Spider answered. He mostly listened. He hung up.

"Who was it?" asked Preston.

"Our agent."

"Jesus, Spider, you're white as a sheet!"

"That was the call we've been waiting for our entire lives."

"What call?"

"We've made it. No more playing dumps like this. We're going right to the very top."

"You don't mean . . ."

"That's exactly what I mean."

21

They're in a pink Cadillac, for Chrissake!" Ivan yelled into his cell phone. "How hard can it be to find? . . . Shut up! That was rhetorical! . . . Look, here's what you're going to do. Tell all your hookers and pimps on US 1 to keep their eyes open for a pink Eldorado. They're out there twenty-four hours anyway. If the Caddy ends up anywhere on US 1 from West Palm to Miami, at least a dozen of your people will see it. . . . What do you mean, how do I know they'll end up on US 1? They're scumbags!"

A metal clanging sound.

Eyelids fluttered in morning sunlight.

Clang, clang.

Lenny sat up in the rigid motel bed and looked around.

Serge was at the sink, shaving, singing Estefan, "*. . . I live for lov-in' you. Ooooooo, la, la, la—la, la, la, la . . .*"

Lenny rubbed his eyes and went over to the window. He pulled back a burlap curtain. Cars raced by on US 1, past a big sign out front, SAHARA MOTEL. Someone had thrown a brick through the camel. He looked across the bent fence at the source of the clanging, the body shop next door.

"Where are we?"

"Riviera Beach," said Serge. "My hometown."

Clang, clang.

"This motel is on the skid," said Lenny.

"I know. Isn't it great?" Serge pointed at a wall. "And they still have the original cheesy beach painting from the sixties." Serge grabbed one side of the frame and began pulling.

"You're stealing the painting?"

"Yes, this is *The Thomas Crown Affair,*" said Serge. "Why do they have to bolt these things to the wall?"

Lenny came over and tugged from the other side, and the painting came down along with two drywall anchors and a tiny cloud of plaster dust. Serge reached in his shaving kit and pulled out a travel squeeze bottle and began squirting red liquid on the bedsheets.

"What's that?" asked Lenny.

"Chicken blood." Serge squirted the pillowcases and splattered the wall.

"It looks like someone got hacked up in here."

"Exactly," said Serge. "Takes their mind off the missing painting. Works every time." He stuck the bottle back in his shaving kit. "C'mon, we have to check out."

"I think I need a shower," said Lenny. "I can smell myself."

"No time," said Serge. "We have to get to the hideout."

"The what?"

"The hideout. We need to lay low until the heat is off."

"Why?"

"Because we're on US 1 and this is a very distinctive car. The network of hookers and other human cockroaches has no doubt already been alerted to be on the lookout."

"So that's why you covered it with that thing."

Serge tucked the painting under an arm and picked up the silver briefcase. "Let's rock."

They went around behind the motel. Lenny pulled the beige tarp off the Cadillac, and they got in.

Serge made a quick left onto North Thirty-seventh Street and pulled up to the curb in front of a small clapboard house, number 28.

"Is this the hideout?"

"I wish!" said Serge, snapping pictures without getting out of the car. He lowered the camera to change the f-stop. "No, this is Burt Reynolds's childhood home. His dad was police chief here, and the family used to have a restaurant on Blue Heron Boulevard by the old drawbridge."

Lenny fired up the morning fat one. "Why are you so into Burt, anyway?"

"Because we're homeboys. I grew up on Thirty-fifth Street, two blocks over."

"Far out."

"Think of it," said Serge. "Just two streets. Do you have any idea what that means?"

Lenny shook his head.

Serge held his thumb and index finger an inch apart. "It means I was *this close* to being in *Boogie Nights*."

A hooker approached the car. "Hey, sugar."

Serge pointed at the house. "What time's the next tour?"

"The what?"

He snapped a couple more quick pictures and looked around the yard, then back at the hooker. "Where's the historic marker? They've put one up, haven't they? Don't tell me someone stole it! . . . Yeah, that has to be it. There's no way they'd let Burt's place go unmarked . . ." He raised the camera again. Click, click.

"Wait," said the hooker, slowly backing away from the convertible. "This is the pink Cadillac. This is the car!" She quickly pulled a cell phone from her leopard purse.

"We've been made!" said Serge, starting up the car. "To the hideout!"

22

Well after midnight on the island of Palm Beach. The streets were empty; the people with five-hundred-dollar sweaters tied around their necks had all gone home. Waiters mopped and turned chairs upside down on the tables at Ta-boo, a popular piano bar on Worth Avenue.

It had been quiet outside, but now the windows shook, and the help looked up to see a purple Jeep Wrangler fly by with a pulsating stereo producing the kind of sound used by surgical instruments to pulverize gallstones. The Jeep continued west, past the showroom windows, Cartier, Tiffany, Gucci, Saks, ten-thousand-dollar purses, framed autographs of Sigmund Freud and Woodrow Wilson, handcrafted figurines depicting the Boer War. Past Via De Mario, Via Roma, Via Parigi, Renato's and the Everglades Club. Across Hibiscus Avenue, weaving erratically over the yellow center line. But the car was local, and the attention of the police was directed elsewhere, outward, defending the social perimeter from the unwashed mainland people.

The Jeep rounded the corner at South Lake and turned up a winding slab driveway to a private waterfront residence inspired by the Acropolis. The Jeep's doors opened; two men in loafers got out. Cameron and Brandon, home for semester break from the Ivy League. They had started vacation as a group of four frat brothers, but the other two had been beaten to pâté in a Miami Beach traffic misunderstanding and were respectively undergoing orthodontic surgery and groin reconstruction.

"Don't forget the beer."

"Whoops."

They were fairly good-sized boys, 215 pounds each at the start of the year, now 240 with the anabolics—stars of the sculling team and Greek intramural touch football. Everything was going their way. They had just made it home without a DUI, and that called for a celebration. Time to get out the speedboat.

According to the manufacturer's literature, the thirty-three-foot Donzi Daytona can reach speeds of a hundred miles an hour, but it was only going sixty when it ran over the pelicans in the darkness under the Royal Palm Bridge and spread a wide wake across the Intracoastal Waterway.

"Do you think we're going too fast?" Brandon yelled over the wind and spray.

"What?" yelled Cameron. "Go faster?"

He pushed the throttle forward and headed for the next bridge, Flagler Memorial. The draw spans were up and a yacht was coming the other way.

"There's a bunch of cars stopped up there," said Brandon. "Can you do a rooster tail?"

"In my sleep," said Cameron. He slowed and hit a switch, raising the pitch of the propellers, and a small geyser of water shot a couple feet into the air behind the boat.

"This is going to be so great!"

They didn't go under the draw spans, instead picking a solid span three to the left. When they came out the other side, Cameron slammed the throttle all the way forward, and a giant rooster tail shot thirty feet in the air, up onto the bridge. Ninety gallons of salt water flooded the interior of a convertible BMW, killing the electronics and the engine.

Cameron and Brandon looked back and saw the Beemer's headlights flicker and go out. They were still giggling as they idled the yellow-and-white boat up to the seawall just past the bridge. That was the thing about Palm Beach—all the best off-limits places were wired tighter than Fort Knox. You couldn't get near them from the street. A different story from the water.

The brothers only banged the prow of their father's boat into the seawall four times as they moored and climbed over the wall into the backyard.

"You remember the beer?"

"Yep. You remember the spray paint?"

Brandon rattled the can in his right hand.

Cameron pointed. "There it is!"

"This is going to be so excellent!"

It was a huge yard, and their target of opportunity stood alone in the middle. They stumbled across the grass and giggled some more and began spray-painting something ungrammatical about a rival fraternity sucking donkey dicks.

They finished and stood there looking at the dripping paint. They felt empty. That's it? This is as fun as it gets? They stood there some more, in case it would change, drinking and smoking, but no luck. Cameron got an idea. What if they broke something? That usually felt good.

They climbed some stairs and smashed a pane in the back door. They found their way around inside from the moonlight coming through the windows. Brandon put a cigarette out on a century-old sofa. "What's a train car doing out here anyway?"

"Do I look like a fucking conductor? Here—help me break this."

Legs snapped crisply off the antique divan.

"Let's go get the baseball bats," said Cameron.

"Good idea."

They ran back to the boat. The brothers always took baseball bats with them in case they came across someone in traffic who needed a licking, but they also brought gloves and balls, on the advice of their attorney father, to disprove premeditation.

They found some more Budweiser and decided it would be a good idea to bring that, too. Soon they had returned with the bats and beer, ready for a successful future.

"Hold it," Cameron said in the middle of the train car. He stopped and peed on something.

"That was great! Watch this!" Brandon dropped his trousers.

"You're going to pinch a loaf?"

Brandon nodded.

"Radical!"

Brandon finished his business and pulled up his pants.

Cameron raised the baseball bat and smashed the arm off an Elizabethan chair.

"Let me see that." Brandon shattered the cherry top of a library cabinet, gold-edged books spilling. The end of the bat got stuck in the hole through the busted-up wood. He braced his left arm against the cabinet to free the bat. "Hold it a second. There's something shiny in here."

He swept the rest of the books off the shelves, and Cameron helped him pull the shelving out. In back was a silver briefcase. They opened it up.

"Holy God!"

They picked up the briefcase and headed out of the train car.

Brandon spun around. "What was that?"

"What was what?"

"I heard something."

"You're imagining things."

"Up there."

They were in the sleeping compartment. The top bunk was down, holding a big pile of blankets.

"I saw it move!"

"I did, too!"

The blankets shifted some more and a sleepy head finally poked out and looked around.

"Dig it!" said Cameron. "Some old bum is sleeping in here!"

"I hate bums!"

"Get a job, bum!"

Movement in a second bunk. Another head poked out. Then a whisper: "Serge, someone's in the hideout."

"Look! There's two of 'em!" said Brandon.

"You know," said Cameron, picking up his baseball bat and slapping it in an open palm, "they're trespassing."

"That's right," nodded Brandon, slapping his own bat in his hand.

"We're going to teach you bums a lesson!"

Serge raised his hand. "Pardon me, but I think you're making a mistake—"

"Shut up, bum! If you don't have any respect for yourself, why should we?"

"Yeah! You make us want to puke with your laziness, your begging on street corners . . ."

"Your rude, unambitious, filthy lifestyle and your disgusting habits . . ."

"Time out," said Serge, sitting up and making a T with his hands. He pointed out in the hall. "Which one of you brought the dog in here?"

"What dog? There is no dog," said Brandon.

"But there's a big pile of shit on the floor," said Serge.

"Oh, that's Brandon's," said Cameron.

"Will you shut up, bum?" yelled Brandon. "You interrupted me! Now I can't even remember what I was saying!"

"You were talking about my disgusting habits," said Serge.

"Right!" said Brandon. "You sicken us! We don't want your kind near our island!"

"We're going to make sure you two think twice before you ever break in here again!"

The pair advanced and raised their bats.

"Don't even think of asking for mercy, bum!"

They stopped. Brandon tapped Cameron. "Is that a gun in his hand?"

Serge had their undivided attention. Brandon's and Cameron's eyes were open as far as they would go, their mouths taped. They were tied to straight-back chairs, wondering what all the pails were for—dozens of open buckets around their feet, filled with some kind of granular material.

Serge sat on the other side of the room, legs crossed, reading a copy of *Historic Railroader Monthly*. He was a lot more clean-shaven and fit—and armed—than they had expected a bum to be.

Serge looked up. "I hope you've learned your lesson."

They nodded quickly and hard.

"And that lesson," said Serge, "is that you never really know whom you're fucking with, so best not to do it at all."

More nodding in agreement.

Serge patted the briefcase on the floor next to his chair. "And thanks for returning this. The little sucker almost got away from me again."

He got up and walked over to one of the brick walls, gently touching the surface. "This is a pretty historic place itself. We're out by the switching yards near the old West Palm depot. The mainland—I'm the local now. This used to be a major warehouse until they boarded it up twenty-five years ago. This room here was a giant humidor used to store cases of cigars that were boxcarred over from the factories in Tampa." Serge ran his fingers along the doorframe. "It's held up pretty well. The seals are in good shape. Except we're not going to keep anything humid. We're going to do the opposite."

He picked up one of the granule-filled pails so they could read the side: "DampRid."

"This stuff is incredible," said Serge. "Sucks all the damn moisture out of the air. I mean *all*. If you reside in Florida, you can't live without it. Until I found this stuff, my shower curtains were mildewed, the cabinets full of mold, all my album covers warped. But no more!"

An empty five-gallon bucket sat near the door. Serge picked up one of the smaller pails of granules and tipped it slowly so the water that had collected in the bottom trickled into the larger bucket. He repeated the process until he had drained all the pails. Then he grunted as he hoisted the big bucket.

"That sure is heavy," said Serge. "I'll be right back."

He dumped the bucket outside the room, then crossed the warehouse and opened a jimmied door to the street. Lenny was under a broken awning, toking a roach down to his fingertips.

"Hi, Serge."

"How's lookout duty?"

"No problem except I'm almost out of dope, so I'm trying to conserve."

"That's being responsible." He went back inside.

Serge repeated the pail-emptying exercise a dozen more times over the next twenty-four hours. He also drank two entire eighteen-packs of Perrier. Cameron and Brandon stared in terror as Serge knocked back another bottle and thumbed through his magazine. He set the empty green container on the floor. "You're looking at me like, 'Is he crazy or something, drinking so much water?' No way—you have to make sure you take a lot of fluids in here or you'll dehydrate, and you don't want to die like that. It has a way of creeping up on you. Did you know that toward the end, you cry tears of blood? . . . Hey look! Here's our train car!"—pointing at a photo in his magazine. "The one we were in last night. It's called the Rambler. Bet you're glad you got a chance to see it, huh?"

Serge got up and paced like a cheetah. "Actually, we're lucky to have that car at all. In 1935, the Florida East Coast Railway sold it off to the Georgia Northern Railroad, along with a bunch of other stuff. Henry would have turned in his grave. They used the Rambler a few years and sold it again, and it eventually disappeared. When people finally realized its historic value, it was nowhere to be found."

Serge stopped walking and fanned himself with the magazine.

"Damn, it's hot in here!" Then he smiled. "But it's a dry heat."

By the fourth day, there wasn't any more movement from the two young men. They were technically still alive, able to hear and understand, but that was about it. Serge had moved them up to the top of the warehouse, out on the flat pebble roof, where they now lay naked on top of two ultrareflective silver survival blankets. Serge walked to the edge of the roof and looked down; Lenny was still on lookout, helping a bag lady cross the street. Serge went back to his captives.

"You didn't actually think I was going to let you die of dehydration, did you?" said Serge, wearing mirror sunglasses and a Miami Dolphins umbrella-hat. "I'm not that kind of guy."

He sat back down in his lawn chair and tried to find something good on his beach radio. "WPOM ruled when I was in puberty here, Alice Cooper, 'School's Out for Summer' and everything, right up until someone got the bright idea to make it all-news. . . . WPOM, get it? *West Palm?* Damn, that's clever!"

Serge had a little cooler and a canvas beach bag beside his chair. He reached in the bag and pulled out a bottle of Hawaiian Tropic, squirting it on his arms and rubbing. "The key isn't just the sun-protection factor, but also how well it blocks UV. The opposite would be, say, coconut cooking oil, which would accelerate the sun's effects. . . ."

The two men listened intently, their nostrils filling with the aroma of coconuts coming off their chests.

"You know, I never finished telling you about the Rambler. Sorry for leaving you in suspense. When we last left our tale, it had vanished from the face of the earth. Then, in 1959, they tracked it down miles from the rails, out on a Virginia farm where it was up on blocks, beaten all to hell, being used ironically enough as a tenant farmer's house. Must have been a tear-jerking sight, like when those kids found E.T. near death by that creek. Years later, they located the original wheel trucks in Tennessee—talk about your detective work!—and with a lot of time and TLC, they restored it to original condition. So I'm sure you can understand my emotional reaction to all the vandalism, banging my head like that on the side of the car when I saw the graffiti. You wouldn't have any idea who would do such an inconsiderate thing? It would have to be someone with a really low IQ, judging by the syntax and the reference to *Equus asinus* genitalia. . . ."

Serge glanced at his wristwatch. "Whoa! I almost forgot. Time to add more salt. . . ."

He picked up an extra-large blue Morton's canister, walked over to the men and began sprinkling.

"You know what they say: 'When it rains, it pours.'"

The medical examiner stepped out of the autopsy room and removed his surgical mask.

The homicide investigator got up from a chair in the hall and walked over. "What the hell happened to those two poor kids? The bodies must not have weighed an ounce over eighty pounds."

"Seventy," said the examiner.

"I had six cops lose their lunches back there when we found 'em," said the detective. "What kind of a monster . . . ?"

The examiner pulled off his latex gloves. "I wouldn't have believed it if I hadn't seen it with my own eyes. I always knew it was theoretically possible, but I've never actually heard of it being done to humans."

"Are you gonna tell me or what?"

"Someone literally turned them into jerky."

23

A white Mercedes ℨ310 cruised down US 1. Ivan was driving, pulling sandwiches from a fast-food sack in his lap. "Who had the cheddar melt?"

"Here," said Alexi.

Vladimir leaned forward from the backseat and tapped Ivan on the shoulder. "Did you know there's a disproportionate incidence of auto-erotic strangulation among hockey players?"

"What?"

Vladimir sat back in his seat. "If you pass out, there's still a chance you can come back to life, right?"

Ivan glanced at Vladimir in the rearview, then back at the road. "Who the fuck did they send me this time?"

A hand with a sandwich came up from the backseat, next to Ivan's head. "I asked for no pickles."

Ivan slapped it away. "Just keep your eyes peeled for a pink Cadillac. A pimp saw them pulling out of the old train depot."

Serge was driving south on US 1 again. Actually Lenny was driving; Serge was just sitting in the driver's seat.

"My arm's getting tired," said Lenny, steering from the passenger side.

"Just a few more pictures," said Serge. "I can't believe how much has changed. The Dairy Belle's still here, but not much else." Click, click.

Lenny tried lighting a joint with his free hand but couldn't get it going. The car began swerving.

Serge lowered his camera and looked over. "What the hell do you think you're doing?"

"What?" said Lenny, taking the joint out of his mouth.

"You're driving, for Chrissake!"

They ran a yellow light, followed by a white Mercedes.

"Where are they going?" asked Dmitri.

"That's what we're trying to find out," said Ivan.

"They keep changing lanes for no reason."

"Classic evasion tactic," said Ivan.

"Woah!" said Lenny. "I almost hit that bus. I think I'm too high to drive."

Dmitri snapped pictures of the Cadillac with a spy camera. "Did you see how he angled around that bus?"

Ivan nodded. "Must have been trained by Israelis."

Lenny reached under the seat and yanked a Bud off a plastic ring. "I need a beer to level out."

"That's where Indian River Citrus used to be," said Serge. Click, click, click.

"Those two poor bastards back at the depot," said Lenny, shaking his head. "On one hand, I feel sorry for them. On the other, we almost lost the briefcase. Did you really have to kill them like that?"

"They handled the briefcase."

"But only for a second."

"I told you it was cursed."

Lenny took a swig of beer, wiped his mouth with the back of his arm and looked up at the sky. "What a great place to live!" The car swerved.

Click, click, click. "That's where the Publix used to be, and that's where they tore down the bazaar tower, and they closed Spanish Courts over there and . . . oh my God! . . ."

"What is it?"

Serge focused the camera. Click, click. "They bulldozed the porn theater!"

"You're nostalgic about a porno joint?"

"No, but it used to be the regular Main Street theater back in the sixties when I was going to parochial school. That's where the nuns took us to see *The Sound of Music* when it first came out."

"You were taught by nuns?" said Lenny.

Serge nodded. "That's how I became an altar boy."

"Wait a minute. Hold the fuckin' phone. *You* were an *altar boy*?"

"Good one, too. Right up until I was defrocked." Click, click, click. "There was absolutely no reason for them to expel me from the program like that."

"This is explaining a whole lot," said Lenny. "Now it's all starting to make sense."

"It was Easter Mass, and we were wearing all those heavy vestments, the cassock and surplice. There were extra stage lights, and the place was packed—really hot. I had never fainted before, so I didn't know what it felt like. I'm kneeling on the side of the altar ready to ring the bells and everything starts getting dim, and I'm wobbling around on my knees like a duckpin. Then it goes completely black. I'm right on the verge of fainting but for some reason I didn't. The conditions were just perfect so I remained on that cusp, semiconscious and upright, but lights out. I'm just a kid—what do I know? I think some kind of miracle is going on. I feel around the ground and push myself to my feet and face the congregation. They say the priest was in the middle of the consecration when I raised my arms in the air and yelled, *'I'm blind! God has made me blind!'* Then I fainted in the Easter lilies."

The Cadillac sailed through the intersection at Okeechobee Boulevard, then Southern, Lake Worth, Lantana, Hypoluxo, down into Boynton Beach, Delray Beach, Deerfield Beach.

"Lenny, you're from this area. Know any good safe houses?"

"Yeah, why?"

"Because I'd like to get this car off the road. It's probably not a hot idea to keep driving it."

"Didn't you say the people were looking for us on US 1?" asked Lenny.

Serge nodded.

"Then why don't we just switch to a different road?"

"Because I love US 1, and besides, most of the people on lookout are really, really, really fucked up. They can probably correctly make out the color pink, but after that it gets dicey. We drive by them, and maybe they see a Cadillac, maybe they see a giant laughing vulva with whitewall tires."

Lenny unwrapped a Twinkie. "I don't see what's so great about this road."

"It's tradition. This is the same road that Magluta took when he was on the run."

"Who?"

"Magluta, as in the Falcon and Magluta. Augusto 'Willie' Falcon and Salvador 'Sal' Magluta, local boys made good. Went to Miami High and struck it rich in the coke biz, something like five hundred million dollars, took up speedboat racing before the feds closed in. Magluta jumped bail, and they finally found him right here along this stretch of road, driving a Lincoln Continental, wearing a wig and carrying twenty grand in cash and a fake passport. US 1 has all kinds of character like that." Click, click, click, Serge snapping photos of condemned motels and discarded malt liquor bottles in piles the size of ancient shell mounds. "I'll take this any day over the suburbs and your Bed Bath and Beyond."

"What a horror show," said Lenny.

"Out here on US 1, life is close to the skin. Anything can happen at any time." Serge knelt backward in the driver's seat and took pictures out the rear of the car. Click, click. "This is where the armored car thieves shot it out with the FBI, and the raccoon jumped off that garbage truck and crashed through the windshield of those tourists, and they found the tractor-trailer full of pirated stone crab claws, and the box of Tide detergent fell out the back of a van and split open and three hundred thousand dollars blew all over the place except the local residents told police it was only like eleven dollars." Click, click. Serge lowered the camera. "Is that Mercedes following us?"

"Don't fuck with me, man. I'm so high, *everything's* following us."

24

"**S**hit. That Mercedes is still behind us," said Serge. "This car's getting too hot. Is that safe house you know any good?"

"One of the best," said Lenny. "Not only that, but a quick phone and they'll come pick us up, extract us from just about anything."

"Can they be counted on?"

"Stone-solid. Used 'em dozens of times."

"I'm impressed. Very good, Lenny. . . . Dump truck."

"What?" Lenny looked up. "Woahhh!" He cut the wheel, narrowly missing the truck making a slow left turn, forcing Lenny to make his own hard left across several lanes of braking, blaring cars.

The traffic light turned red; a white Mercedes eased up and stopped at the intersection as the Cadillac disappeared around the corner.

• • •

Lenny stepped up to the concession stand. He turned to Serge. "Espresso?"

"Better not."

"It's good."

"Okay."

"Two espressos, please."

"You say the safe house is nearby?"

"Real close, but they're still not answering the phone."

"Try again."

Lenny dialed and listened. "I think I'm getting through."

"Ask them to send the extraction team."

Lenny nodded. He said a few words in the phone and closed it.

"Well?" asked Serge.

"They're on their way."

"That should give us time for a race. I love the races here!"

Serge and Lenny walked down a ramp and through the glassed-in lobby, lines of people at teller windows, the floor covered with torn paper stubs. A big funky sign on the wall, POMPANO BEACH HARNESS RACING.

"Let's go out to the grandstand. We absolutely must go to the grandstand," said Serge. "I love the people, the culture, the smell of the food, the insane betting strategy conversations. We have to go to the grandstand! It's the only way!"

"What about the briefcase?" asked Lenny, glancing at Serge's hand. "We don't want to attract any trouble."

"Don't worry," said Serge. "Not only will there not be trouble, but a parimutuel park is the one place where they *want* you to arrive with a briefcase full of money."

Lenny looked around at the numerous other people scattered across the lobby with silver Halliburton briefcases—standard for carrying cash around Florida—each being graciously waited on by track staff.

"Good evening," said a uniformed man, smiling at the briefcase, then at Serge and Lenny as he opened the door for them.

Serge smiled back. "We absolutely, positively must go to the grandstand."

"I understand," said the man.

A fresh night breeze caught them as they headed across the patio.

"Forget the grandstand," said Serge. "I just remembered I hate the fucking grandstand. We're going all the way down to the railing, where you can see the little pieces of dirt flying off the hooves. We need to be as close to the horses as possible, breathing the same air."

A dozen hard-core Type AAA personalities had already assembled along the railing when Serge and Lenny took their spot at the end. The starting gate filled up with horses pulling jockeys in small harness carriages.

"I want to place a bet," said Lenny, opening his racing program. "Number eight sounds good."

"What's the name?" said Serge. "It's all in the name."

"Entry Withdrawn."

"Sounds like a winner to me."

Serge chugged his espresso. "Uh-oh, pole time. You'll have to wait for the next race to bet."

A bell rang, the gates flew open. *"They're off!"*

Identical descriptions of an unusual pink Cadillac began to crop up in crime scene reports from Tampa to Cape Canaveral to Palm Beach. The all-points bulletin went out with a warning in tall letters: "Call for backup."

A patrol officer was making routine afternoon rounds in a quadrant west of 95, south of Atlantic Boulevard. He swung through a parking lot on standard auto-burglary sweep. Something caught his eye in the third row. He called for backup.

Police were everywhere. Seven cruisers clustered around the pink car in Section D, Row 3, of the Pompano Beach harness track. Evidence handlers with gloves went through the convertible; other officers questioned the valets.

"Look, Ivan! There's the Cadillac!" said Alexi.

"The place is crawling with cops!" said Dmitri.

"So it is," said Ivan. He eased the Mercedes slowly past the end of Row 3, then turned in the VIP parking lot. Five men with bandaged feet got out.

The horses went into the first turn.

Serge was strangely quiet. Lenny noticed the empty, crumpled paper espresso cup clutched in his fist. "Are you okay?"

Serge shook himself vigorously like a dog coming in from the rain.

"What's the matter?" asked Lenny.

"Can't you smell it?"

"Smell what?"

"The air. It's crackling with the electricity of memories." Serge's arms went up to the sky, his fingers wiggling like he was feeling two big tits. "It's overwhelming. I'm not sure I can stand it."

"You all right?"

"I feel like this every once in a while when I get hit with a memory bolt."

"Memory bolt?"

"My folks used to come here in 1964. Each time I blink, for a microsecond I see the way it looked back then on the inside of my eyelids . . ."

Lenny nodded. "I've gotten acid like that."

The horses went into the second turn.

"What triggers it?" asked Lenny.

"Espresso and déjà vu. Like a light afternoon rain at the beach, or the sound of lawn mowers on a hot Saturday morning in July, or just before sunset when I'm on the turnpike and I go through those fucking great tollbooths made of coral, or I'm driving back from Miami International on the Dolphin Expressway, and I pass the Orange Bowl and accelerate for that magical skyline, no longer in control, suddenly finding myself in this crazy interchange, then I'm flying south, faster and faster, up on the raised highway, looking out across the sea of coconut palms and orange roof tiles and crime lights, and I'm pulled down a ramp into the city, vibrant murals on the sides of ethnic corner groceries, billboards in Spanish, kids rolling tires up the sidewalk with sticks, radios playing, flowers blooming—and it's too much beauty, both my eyes feeling like they're having simultaneous orgasms, an aching inside because I want to consume it all at once, like Van Gogh in Kurosawa's *Dreams,* and I race over the Rickenbacker, through the sea grapes out to Cape Florida, jumping from the car, running along the seawall and screaming out to sea: 'Touch one splinter of Stiltsville and I'll rip your carpetbagging nuts off!' and then I'm usually asked to leave."

The crowd roared as the horses came out of turn number three. A knot of five husky men hobbled through the harness track lobby.

"Keep your eye out for a silver briefcase," said Ivan.

"There's one!" said Dmitri.

"There's another one over there!" said Alexi.

"And there's another one!"

"Of course," said Ivan. "We're at a parimutuel facility. These guys are good."

"Ivan! Down by the track!"

The horses rounded the fourth turn, into the homestretch.

Lenny had a two-handed grip on the back of Serge's belt as he hung over the railing near the finish line. "C'mon, Entry Withdrawn!"

Five men with bandaged feet came out a door on the left side of the building and began moving toward the track. On the right side, up by the grandstands, police officers questioned members of the track's staff, who pointed at the finish line.

"Whew! What a race!" Serge jumped down from the railing. He saw something out the corner of his eye. "When's the extraction team due?"

Lenny checked his wristwatch. "Just a few more minutes."

"Start walking for the exit, real casual."

I van pointed across the spectator deck at the Pompano Beach harness track. "They're heading back to the main building."

"They're not the only ones," said Dmitri, looking over at the cops closing in on Serge and Lenny.

"We have to head them off," said Ivan. "Walk quickly but don't run. We still have the advantage. None of them has seen us."

Serge and Lenny began moving faster as they approached the glass exit doors.

"Walk quickly but don't run," said Serge. "They don't know we've seen them."

Lenny checked his watch again. "The extraction team hasn't had enough time. We're not going to make it."

Serge glanced furtively over his left shoulder. The cops had picked up the pace, too, walking as fast as possible, still trying to look nonchalant, approaching that critical moment when everyone chucks the charade and starts running and pulling guns.

From Serge's right side, five men with bandaged feet hobbled as fast as they could.

"Now!" yelled Ivan. They broke into a hobbling sprint.

"Now!" yelled Serge. The pair made a run for it.

"Now!" yelled the police sergeant. The cops pulled guns and charged.

Serge and Lenny burst through the exit doors and ran out to the empty curb. "They're not here yet!" yelled Lenny. Suddenly a black, windowless van skidded up in a fire zone. The sliding side door flew open; Serge and Lenny dove in. The van took off.

Five Russians ran out on the sidewalk, looking around, soon joined by panting police officers.

Ivan scanned the parking lot. No people, no movement . . . wait, over there. A black van slowly pulled out of the parking lot and disappeared around a corner toward the interstate.

"To the Mercedes!"

Lenny climbed forward into the van's passenger seat. The driver was a large older woman with a poufy gray hairdo and a goiter. Lenny leaned over and kissed her on the cheek.

"Thanks for picking us up, Mom."

"You know I'm always happy to give you a ride home."

"Mom?" said Serge. A Chihuahua bounced up from somewhere and landed standing in Serge's lap, facing him. Serge jerked his head back. "What the—?"

The dog barked.

"That means Pepe likes you," said Lenny.

"Who's your friend?" asked the driver.

"That's Serge," said Lenny. "He's . . . my new employer."

Serge and the dog were having a staring contest.

"That's nice." The driver looked up in the rearview at Serge. "Thanks for giving Lenny a job. He's a good boy. So what do you do? Work at the harness track?"

Lenny spoke preemptively. "No, we were just out for some fun today."

The van accelerated down the middle lane of I-95.

"Lenny, you haven't called for weeks, you haven't shown up," said his mom. "You know how worried I get."

"Any mail?" asked Lenny.

"A little. I put it in your room."

Serge looked up from the dog. "You live with your mother? You never mentioned anything."

"I'll explain later."

"What's to explain?" said Serge. "Either you live with your mom or you don't."

"Lenny, you're not ashamed of me, are you?" asked the driver.

Lenny turned around. "Yeah, Serge, I, uh . . . I live with my mom. But only until I get a little older, you know, until I'm ready."

"You're forty-two," said Serge.

Mom looked in the rearview again. "So what is it you do, Serge?"

"I run my own new-economy entrepreneurship. Involves a lot of driving."

"Like traveling salesmen?" said Mom. She put on a blinker for an exit ramp. "Lenny, that explains why you were gone so long. You should have told me."

Lenny leaned over and kissed her cheek again. "I wanted it to be a surprise."

"I'm so proud of you."

The van pulled up the driveway of a single-story concrete ranch house next to the interstate ramp. White, baby-blue trim. The lawn was overgrown, a big teardrop oil stain in the driveway. Three people and a dog headed up the walkway. Lenny's mom unlocked the front door and they went inside. Serge looked around the living room filled with religious paintings, crucifixes, ceramic Madonnas, votive candles and a Ouija board.

"Serge, don't waste your money on a hotel tonight," said Mom. "You can stay in Lenny's room."

"Why, thank you, Mrs. Lippowicz," said Serge. "Let's see your room, Lenny."

"Well, it's not really my *room* room. I just use it for storage. I rarely stay here."

"What are you talking about?" said his mother. "You stay here all the time."

They headed down the hall. Serge stopped in the doorway. "Bunk beds?"

"Mind if I have the top?"

Serge set his briefcase on the dresser and walked over to the closet. "Let's get started."

"Get started what?"

"Checking out your stuff."

"I still have most of it."

Serge opened the closet door. "Wow, you're not kidding."

He started taking down boxes. Lenny lit a joint and went over to the window and exhaled outside, where a Mercedes had been parked a half block up the street for the last ten minutes.

Vladimir leaned over the backseat and pointed at the van in the driveway. "What are we waiting for?"

"I told you," said Ivan. "We have to be patient. We can't just rush in there like we usually do."

"Why not? It's just some old woman's house."

"That's what a safe house is supposed to look like," said Ivan. "The doors are probably steel-lined and booby-trapped. All kinds of sophisticated surveillance electronics."

"I wonder what's going on in there?" asked Vladimir.

"Probably some big strategy meeting," said Ivan.

"My turn," said Lenny, sitting cross-legged on the floor and drawing a card. "'Remove wrenched ankle.'"

Bzzzzz.

"I'm tired of playing Operation," said Serge.

"How about Hot Wheels?"

Lenny got out a shoebox of little cars and began laying tracks. Serge got out the Legos.

"What are you doing?" asked Lenny.

"Making the Brick Wall of Death," said Serge. "Where's your lighter fluid?"

"I don't have any lighter fluid."

"How can we play Hot Wheels without lighter fluid?"

Lenny's mom sat in the living room reading the *Enquirer*. Lenny kept walking by at intervals.

Lenny held up a roll of aluminum foil. "Mom, can we use this?"

She looked up and nodded. Lenny headed back to the bedroom.

A minute later, Lenny held up a large cardboard box. "Can we use this?"

She nodded.

A minute later Lenny sprinted by in the background, then ran back to the bedroom with a fire extinguisher. Lenny's mom put down her paper and went into the kitchen. She slipped on Jeff Gordon pot holders and opened the oven door. She set a ceramic serving dish on the table.

"Dinner's ready!"

No answer.

She headed down the hall. "I said, dinner's ready!"

Still no reply.

She stepped into the bedroom doorway. Nobody in the room. Just a big cardboard box in the middle of the floor. The box was covered with aluminum foil.

"I said, *dinner's ready!*"

A voice from the box: "Mom! Shhhhh! We have to maintain radio blackout!"

"You can play later," said Mrs. Lippowicz. "Food's getting cold."

The foil-lined top of the cardboard Gemini capsule flipped open, and Serge and Lenny stood up. They followed Mrs. Lippowicz into the kitchen.

"It's hot, so don't touch the dish." She stuck two big serving spoons in the casserole.

Serge got up and held her chair.

"Why, thank you, Serge."

Lenny began chowing. Serge tucked a napkin into his collar and cleared his throat. Lenny looked up. "Prayer," Serge whispered.

"Sorry." Lenny put down his fork, folded his hands and bowed his head.

"May I, Mrs. Lippowicz?" asked Serge.

"Of course. Thank you, Serge." She turned to Lenny. "Your friend has such nice manners."

Serge bowed his own head and closed his eyes. "God, please protect us from your followers. Amen."

They began serving.

"Good prayer," said Lenny.

Serge piled his plate. "It's from a bumper sticker." He took a bite. "This is delicious, Mrs. Lippowicz. You're an incredible cook."

"Thank you. It's tuna noodle casserole with browned Tater Tots on top."

"The Tater Tots make it," said Serge.

Mrs. Lippowicz passed Lenny the salt and pepper. "Why can't you be more like your nice friend Serge?"

Midnight, Lenny's bedroom.

Serge's eyes opened in the bottom bunk. Something had awoken him. He looked around, then noticed the bed was vibrating. His eyebrows furrowed in puzzlement. The vibrations increased.

Serge looked up at the bunk above him. The shaking got worse. "What on earth—?"

He tried to sit up, but the bed pitched and knocked him back down.

"Lenny, what the hell are you doing up there?"

No answer. The bed started rocking violently, the bottoms of its four wooden legs rattling and tapping on the floor. Serge grabbed the sides of his mattress and hung on as the bunk began to slowly slide and rotate across the terrazzo bedroom floor like a puck on an air hockey table.

"Lenny! Take it easy! It's not going anywhere!"

Serge stuck his head out the side of the bed and looked up. The bed bucked again and tumbled him onto the ground.

The rocking stopped.

"Lenny? You okay?"

"I'm pretty thirsty now."

"No kidding. You were going at it like Chuck Yeager trying to pull an X-15 out of a terminal spin."

Lenny swung his legs over the side of the bunk and jumped down. "I'm completely awake now." He went over and opened a dresser drawer and took out a baggie. "And I'm out of weed. We have to go get some."

"I'm not going to a drug hole, especially not at this hour."

"How about a restaurant or a lounge? I'm pretty good at connecting on the fly."

"My choice?"

"Sure."

"Then I have a historic place in mind."

Lenny checked the Magilla Gorilla clock on his dresser. Almost one. "Is this place still open?"

"Not even hopping yet."

Two dark figures came out of the ranch house and walked down the driveway toward the van.

Ivan reached over to the Mercedes's driver seat and shook Vladimir's shoulder. "Wake up!"

"Wha—what is it?"

"They're on the move!"

The Benz fell in line six cars back as the van merged southbound on I-95. They passed the executive airport, then Oakland Park and Sunrise Boulevard, the van accelerating the whole time, changing lanes.

"Keep up with them!" yelled Ivan.

"I'm trying!" said Vladimir.

The van cut left across three columns of traffic and squeezed between a Dodge pickup and the median retaining wall.

"Lenny, we're not in a lane anymore," said Serge. "You can't drive with your head below the dash."

"Just a sec. My beer rolled under the seat."

Ivan pointed. "They're getting away!"

"Hold on," said Vladimir. He floored it and passed a BP tanker on the right shoulder. The van suddenly accelerated again. It seemed to fake right, then shot to the left and into a tight space that briefly opened between a Lexus and a Probe GT. Then another jump left, swerving a couple times within the lane, braking fast and sliding right again, almost going up on two wheels.

"You're losing them!" said Ivan.

"They're just too good."

The van fishtailed as it came out of a banking maneuver. A fierce spray of suds shot around the inside of the vehicle, covering the windshield.

"Lenny, I told you not to open the can. It was bulging."

"I didn't think it had been shaken up that much." Shooting streams of beer hit both of them in the face.

"Get it out of here!"

Lenny cut off a honking Bronco and rolled down the window.

"They're going for the exit," said Vladimir. "Stay close."

"They just threw something out the window. . . . It just exploded . . ." Vladimir swerved around it.

"Foaming diversionary device," said Ivan, nodding with respect. "Israelis."

The Mercedes swung back in time to take the same exit and made a skidding left turn through the yellow light at the bottom of the ramp. They stayed with the van when it turned on Federal Highway and again when it grabbed the St. Brooks Memorial Causeway. Then, suddenly, nothing.

"Where'd they go?" asked Vladimir.

"Shit," said Ivan. "He's probably heading for a meet in one of the beach motels. That's standard."

Vladimir raced up the bridge over the Stranahan River, then slowed as they coasted down the far side, everyone looking around. Rippled reflections of white condo lights in the Intracoastal Waterway. Red and green running lights from sailboats.

They came off the bridge. Vladimir pointed. "There it is! There it is!"

They pulled up the hotel driveway, got out and headed across the valet parking lot. Ivan walked up to the van and looked through the windshield at the valet ticket hanging from the rearview. "It's for one of the restaurants, not the hotel, so that narrows it. Igor, Dmitri—you wait here with the van, in case they come back. The rest of you, follow me!"

The inside of the elevator was brass. Ivan and the others couldn't place the Muzak as they rode up to the top of the hotel. The doors opened into the big revolving rooftop bar with a raised, obstructing bandstand in the middle. Ivan directed them to split into two groups and go in opposite directions to sweep the place. They met back up on the far side, empty-handed.

"This is the only restaurant left open. They must have stopped in a rest room or something," said Ivan, taking a chair at one of the few empty cocktail tables. "We'll wait." He turned and looked out the window, down at his men waiting by the black van.

Serge and Lenny watched the numbers climb inside their elevator car.

"I thought it was going to be a new place," said Lenny. "We come here all the time."

"How can you get too much of Pier 66?" said Serge. "If it was good enough for Travis McGee."

"I can't believe they detained us in the security office like that just because you were taking all those pictures."

"History-haters."

The elevator doors opened as a cell phone rang at the Russians' table. Ivan answered it. Serge and Lenny headed around the opposite side of the bar.

"Yes, we received the flowers, Mr. Grande. . . . That was a very thoughtful gesture. . . . No, still no sign of the money, but I've got this feeling. . . ."

Serge and Lenny grabbed two chairs. Serge laid the briefcase on top of the cocktail table. "Now watch carefully. This was the infamous Sea of Hands Play."

Serge used a finger to draw a diagram in the dust on the side of the metal case.

"The date: December twenty-first, 1974. But it seems like just yesterday. The stage is set. The Dolphins are leading twenty-six to twenty-one with thirty-five seconds left. Looks like they're on their way to a third straight Super Bowl title. But they were about to get bitten by the Snake."

"The Snake?"

"Kenny 'the Snake' Stabler, quarterback of the Oakland Raiders, a diabolical little shit from Mobile, Alabama." Serge drew some more on the briefcase. "The clock is ticking. The Dolphins secondary is all over the mighty Fred Biletnikoff. Stabler has no place to throw. The Miami linesmen are closing. The heat is too much! . . ." Serge's finger zigzagged in the dust. "The Snake lunges forward into the pocket and rolls left. But the legendary Dolphin defensive end Vern Den Herder stays with him, gaining fast from behind! Vern dives and tackles Stabler around the knees, and the Snake goes down! Dolphins win!"

"Wow," said Lenny.

"But wait! What's this?" said Serge, making an arc with his pinky. "As Stabler is halfway to the ground, he throws the ball toward the end zone. It could never even politely be called a pass. It was a desperation release, like someone flinging a bag of dope out a car window."

"What happened?"

Serge drew three X's and one O. "A trio of Dolphins surround the lone Raider receiver. Eight hands reach for the ball, the now famous *Sea of Hands*. But the two that come down with the pigskin belong to Oakland's Clarence Davis . . ." Serge furiously erased everything on the briefcase fast with both hands. ". . . Touchdown! Oakland wins! The Dolphin Empire crumbles!"

He pounded the briefcase with his fists—"Why! Why! Why!"—then his forehead.

"Why! Why! . . ."

"So you were kinda into that game?" asked Lenny.

"Stabler might as well have stabbed me through the heart with one of the yardage poles! . . . Lenny? . . . Lenny, are you listening?"

"Why's that guy at the bar looking at me?"

"Probably because you're looking at him."

"He looks familiar. Doesn't he look familiar to you?"

"No."

"Of course! I know who it is! That's the drummer for ———."

Serge studied the man some more. "You know, you might be right."

Lenny waved for their waitress. "Who's that guy at the bar?"

"The drummer for ———."

"I knew it! I'm getting an autograph." Lenny grabbed a napkin and went to the bar. "Aren't you the drummer for ———?"

The man killed a whiskey on the rocks and smiled. "Yes, I am."

"Can I get your autograph?"

"Sure thing." He took the napkin from Lenny and wrote his name.

"Thank you." Lenny stuck the napkin in his pocket. "Mind if I sit here?"

"Go ahead."

"Man, I can't believe I'm meeting you! I loved you guys! Whatever happened to the band?"

"We're still together."

"Maybe it's because you don't have any new albums."

"We've released one every year."

"I don't really go in record stores a lot. You guys should start touring again."

"We tour all the time."

". . . Gee, sorry. . . . Well, anyway, I love you guys!"

"Thank you."

"Can I buy you a drink?"

"Sure."

Lenny waved over at Serge. "Buy this guy a drink. And can I get one, too?"

Serge got out his wallet.

Three drinks later, they were all back at Serge's table.

"Serge, do you know who this guy is?"

"You told me."

"I did? Well, let's buy him a drink! . . . I'll take one, too."

Two more. Lenny turned to the drummer. He put his thumb and index finger together and put them to his lips and sucked. Then he raised his eyebrows in a question.

The drummer nodded.

"You get high?"

"Yeah, you?"

"Yeah, wanna get high?"

"Yeah, let's go."

"Okay, let's go."

They got up from the table and headed for the men's room.

"Uh-oh," said Serge. "Here we go."

Lenny checked the stalls. No one there. He met the drummer back at the sink and rubbed his palms together in anticipation.

"Okay, break it out," said the drummer.

"What do you mean?"

"Break out your shit."

"I don't have any shit. I thought you had it."

"You said, 'You wanna get high?'"

"So?"

"So that's the guy that's supposed to have the shit."

"No, no, no," said Lenny. "You said, 'Let's go.' That's the guy with the shit."

"Usually, but you said the other thing first, and that's the thing that counts, first."

"I've been doing this for a while, thank you."

"So you don't have any shit?"

"No!"

They sighed and left the men's room.

"How'd it go?" Serge asked as they sat back down.

"Miscommunication. . . . Wait! I almost forgot! I have some emergency money in my sock. Let's buy some dope!"

"Great!" The drummer got his own money out. "How much you got?"

Lenny pulled crumpled bills from his sock and piled them on top of the briefcase. "Looks like forty-three dollars. How much you got?"

"Sixty," said the drummer. "That ought to cover us. A quarter's still a hundred, right?"

"Last time I checked."

"You're not a cop, are you?"

"You kidding?"

"I'm a target, you know. They're always looking for high-profile busts to get on the news."

"Tell me about it."

"So you're not a cop?"

"Not remotely."

"Okay, we'll meet right here in, say, an hour?"

"Here in an hour?"

"Yep. You sure you're not a cop?"

"Yep, you sure you're the drummer for ——?"

"Yep."

"Then it's all set."

"Let's do it!"

"We're on!"

They sat there staring at each other.

"Well?" said the drummer.

"Well what?"

"Why are you just sitting there?"

"I thought you were going."

"I thought you—"

"Shit."

"But you were the one who said, 'Let's buy some—' "

"Stop," said Lenny, shaking his head. "This is getting way, way too complicated. Let's back up and start over."

"Okay."

They each grabbed handfuls of money off the briefcase and stuck it back in their pockets.

"How much you got?"

"Forty-three dollars. How much you got? . . ."

Serge smacked himself in the forehead. He slid the briefcase off the table and set it down on the floor between his leg and the wall. Except he unwittingly set the briefcase on the ledge of the wall. The bar was revolving. The ledge was not. The briefcase began rotating away.

"I know this pot dealer with a scar . . ." said Lenny.

"I know him, too!" said the drummer.

The briefcase kept moving, rotating past the legs of unsuspecting customers. Table after table, typical south Florida hotel bar culture, three airline pilots from Ithaca, pharmaceutical salesmen hooked on their own samples, a Dutch tour group, headhunters, plastic surgeons, food photographers, four motivational speakers in town for a seminar on how to make one hundred thousand dollars a year repairing cracks in windshields with a simple tube of adhesive. The briefcase kept going, past the legs of two men sipping goblets of vodka and grapefruit juice.

"You've gone into another printing!" Tanner Lebos told Ralph Krunkleton. "Have you seen the new cover?"

Tanner passed the glossy prototype across the table to Ralph, who noticed some additional words across the top: *New York Times Bestseller!*

"It made the bestseller list?" asked Ralph.

"Haven't you heard?"

"I didn't see anything in the papers."

"That's because they only print the top ten or fifteen titles."

"What number am I?"

"One hundred ninety-four."

"That's on the list?"

"The list is actually thousands long. Theoretically, *every* book is on the list, but for the sake of integrity, we cut it off at five hundred. . . ."

"We have honor."

"You know, I just reread the book," said Tanner. "I'd forgotten a lot of it. It's even better than I remembered."

"Thanks."

"Like that character the urinal guy. How'd you think that up? What an imagination!"

"Imagination nothing. I *did* that. I was on a roadtrip in college. This was before credit cards. I ran out of money and couldn't get back. . . ."

The briefcase kept going, more legs. Conventioning oncologists, conventioning lapidaries, conventioning Mary Kay sales leaders with pink cars in the garage. Another quarter of the way around the bar, under another table, a heated discussion, Russian accents.

"Dammit!" said Ivan. "We were this close to that money! *This close!* . . ."

Still rotating, more legs. Diamond dealers on sabbatical, gigolos on the make, Panamanian strongmen, Brazilian bombshells, American tragedies. The briefcase went past the legs of five women with five glasses of Sex on the Beach.

"I can't believe you haven't finished *The Stingray Shuffle,*" said Rebecca.

"I've been busy," said Sam.

"You won't believe what happens to the five million dollars."

"Don't give it away!"

Teresa stood and took a snapshot out the window. "So this is Travis McGee's old stomping ground." Another snapshot. "Let's read a Travis book next."

"Let's not and say we did," said Sam.

"What are you talking about?" said Maria. "They're great!"

"The women are always objects," said Sam. "In fact, the more I read, I'm not even sure I *like* Travis."

That rocked the whole table.

"What?" said Maria. "You mean, you wouldn't have slept with Travis?"

"Are you kidding?"

"I would have," said Paige.

"I'd have slept with Meyer," said Rebecca.

"Ewwwwww!" said the other four.

The briefcase kept going, more legs, litterbugs, bookworms, social butterflies, midlife counselors, postmodern sculptors, premature ejaculators.

Serge looked up. "Oh no."

Two large-chested men in black suits, black shirts and pointy shoes. They walked quickly toward Serge's table, coats over their arms concealing something.

Serge's eyes locked on the men. His right hand slowly reached for the pistol in his waistband, his left felt blindly under the table and grabbed the handle of the briefcase as it came rotating by. "I knew this would happen," he whispered to himself. "I knew they were bound to send someone sooner or later."

The men were twenty feet away, then ten. Serge cocked the pistol under the table. The men turned and climbed onto the musicians' bandstand. They pulled a flute and a mandolin from under their coats and began playing Kenny G.

Serge fell back in his chair with a breath of relief. He set the brief-case back down, not on the ledge this time.

". . . We meet back here in an hour, okay?" asked Lenny.

"How will I know who you are?" asked the drummer.

"I'll be wearing this shirt."

Serge smacked his forehead again.

"What's the matter with your friend?" asked the drummer.

"I need some air," said Serge. He picked up the briefcase and headed around the curved side of the bar and pressed the elevator button. He overheard conversation fragments behind him. ". . . *Nyet!*" "*Vladimir!*"

Hmmm, Serge thought, Russian mob. . . .

He walked back to his table and handed Lenny the briefcase. "I need you to hide in one of the stalls with this and wait for me."

"*I don't believe* it," said Ivan.

"What is it?" asked Dmitri.

"I think it's him. Dummy up!"

Serge approached the table. "Hi guys. You the Russian mob?"

The Russians reached under the table for ankle holsters. Ivan discreetly waved them off. He turned to Serge. "No, we're with Amway."

"Right," said Serge, winking. He pointed. "What happened to your feet?"

"Amway accident."

"Mind if I join you?" Serge pulled up a chair before they could object. "I have a proposition for Amway."

A half hour later, everyone was laughing, shaking hands and slapping backs. Serge stood. "Then it's all set?"

"All set."

"Sunday at midnight," said Serge. "You remember the place?"

"We remember."

26

Serge sat with Lenny at the bar in the B&H Deli near
Cape Canaveral. Lenny dialed a number on his cell phone. No
answer. He hung up and dialed again. It began ringing again. He turned
to Serge.

"I still don't understand why we had to pay for a taxi from Pier 66
when we had the van."

"I told you already. Because they were going to ambush us in the
parking lot. That's standard. Didn't you see the two guys waiting for us?"

"But I thought you made a deal with them."

"I did. We're still on."

"I don't understand."

"You'd never make it in the business world."

Lenny hung up and dialed his cell phone again. He put the phone
to his ear.

"Will you stop that?" said Serge. "You've been doing it all night. It's getting on my nerves."

"I have to reach the drummer for ——. He's supposed to get me some weed."

"I hate to tell you this, but it's not going to happen."

"But he's got my forty-three dollars."

"Write it off as the stupidity tax."

"No way," said Lenny. "The drummer for —— would never rip me off."

"Lenny, he's not trying to screw you by not coming through. It's because he's hapless, just like you."

"He's not coming back?"

Serge put his arm around Lenny's shoulder. "It's a cruel world."

"I don't believe you." Lenny hit a series of numbers again on his cell phone. No answer.

Serge swung around to face the barstool on his other side and began hitting on an off-duty stripper. . . . Well, not really hitting on.

"Did you know that after every successful liftoff, the launch team eats the exact same thing—biscuits and beans?"

"Don't talk to me," said the dancer, lighting a Camel.

"It's tradition!" said Serge. "You look like a bright girl. Ever think of going out for the space program?"

"You're drunk."

"Drunk with enthusiasm for life!" said Serge, hoisting a briefcase onto the bar.

Lenny punched numbers on his phone. "Why doesn't he answer?" He dialed again. "Hold on! Someone's picking up!"

A woman's sleepy voice answered. "Mmmm, uh, hullo . . . ?"

"May I speak to the drummer for ——?"

Serge and the stripper heard the yelling from Lenny's phone. "What are you, a fucking comedian? . . . (Click.)"

Lenny closed the phone with a stunned look. "The drummer for —— gave me the wrong number."

"Lenny, this is how bad you've gotten. Almost everyone else goes out partying and they wake up the next morning and look in their wallet and say: 'Where the hell did all my money go?' But you're such a mess you invert the paradigm. People get wrecked and run into you and the next morning they go, 'Where'd all this money come from?' Do you understand what I'm getting at here?"

Lenny nodded.

"Good."

"So how do I get my forty-three dollars back?"

Serge turned to the stripper and slapped the top of his briefcase. "Guess what's in here."

"I don't give a shit."

"Five million dollars! You know what I'm going to use the money for? Want me to tell you?"

"No." She blew out a big stream of smoke.

"It's been my lifelong dream. I'm going into space!"

"Goodie for you."

"Haven't you read the Dennis Tito articles? Everything's for sale now in the former republic. Tanks, bombs, Fabergé eggs. I met some mobsters in Lauderdale. Turns out they also do some work for the Russian space agency. The deal's all set up. We make the swap at the rendezvous tonight. I give them the money and they give me my space suit, to show good faith. Then I fly out to the Baikonur Kosmodrome, go through six months of intense training, blast off on a Soyuz, and next thing you know I'm in the International Space Station helping mice copulate in zero gravity."

She stubbed out her cigarette. "Buy me a drink."

"Don't have any money."

"Thought you said you had five million."

"They might count it."

"Your whole story's horseshit," she said. "I've fucked people in the space program, and they won't even give me a damn launch viewing pass. There's no chance you could bribe your way onto the Space Station."

"Not through NASA, but it's a totally different culture over in Russia," said Serge. "They're Communists, which means it's all about money."

Serge stood with Lenny in the dark at the rendezvous point, checking his illuminated wristwatch: 12:01 A.M. "Where can they be?"

"How can I get my forty-three dollars back?"

"Sometimes you just have to let go."

A slight breeze came off the ocean. A twig snapped.

"Ivan?" Serge whispered. "Is that you?"

Out of the distant shadows came a silhouette, then a second, a third, a fourth, and finally five dark forms stood abreast thirty yards away.

"You got the money?"

"Right here," said Serge, tapping the briefcase.

"Put it on the ground."

"Where's my space suit?"

"It's in the car."

"Forget it," said Serge. "First I get my space suit, with my name over the pocket. Spelled right. That was the arrangement."

"You really *are* crazy."

"No space suit, no deal."

The five pulled automatic weapons. "The deal's changed," said Ivan. "Put the money on the ground and step away."

Serge pointed at them. "Hey! You're not really with the Russian space program!"

Bullets began flying.

"I'm hit!" Lenny yelled, going down and gripping his leg. Serge grabbed him by the armpits and pulled him to cover. Bullets pinged off the missile they were slouched behind in the Rocket Garden at Kennedy Space Center.

"Stop it! Stop shooting!" yelled Serge. He ran out from behind the rocket and threw himself across the front of the Titan, spreading his arms wide, a human shield. "I'm begging you! This is our history!"

Ivan grinned. He turned and fired at a Juno II.

"No!" screamed Serge.

Then an Atlas-Agena got it right between the tail fins.

"Please!" yelled Serge. "Anything!"

Ivan walked over to the next rocket and pressed the muzzle of his gun against the first stage.

"Hand over the briefcase or the Mercury-Redstone gets it!"

Serge felt down in the zippered leg compartment of his royal blue jumpsuit. He wrapped his fingers around the antique grenade, his ace in the hole. He looked up at the rockets. They were bound to take shrapnel. Too risky. He removed his hand from the pocket.

"Okay! Okay!" said Serge. "Just don't shoot!"

He took the briefcase by the handle and twirled himself in a circle three times like a discus thrower and let the briefcase sail. The moonlight caught the metal finish as it tumbled through the air. It landed a few feet in front of the Russians. Vladimir ran up, flipped the latches and raised the lid. He looked over his shoulder at Ivan. "It's all here."

"Good," said Ivan, looking up at Serge and breaking into a smile. "Now you die!"

The foot pursuit was slower than a three-legged race, Serge helping Lenny limp along, the Russians hobbling after them on bandaged feet. Serge and Lenny took off across the visitor concourse. The Russians fanned out to form a net and flush them into the courtyard. They encircled the pavilion and cased the IMAX theaters, Gift Gantry and Nebula Café. But they were no match for Serge, who knew the grounds of the space center like a womb. Soon it was quiet again; the Russians stood bunched together on the lawn, in front of a giant viewing window at the welcome center, scratching their heads with their guns.

There was a tremendous crash. A shower of broken glass sprayed the Russians, who ducked and shielded their faces as a moon buggy flew through the shattered window, sailed over their heads, and began bounding away. The Russians started shooting, but the vehicle had already made it to the edge of the Merritt Island Wildlife Sanctuary and disappeared into the swamp grass. The Russians ran for their Mercedes.

The moon buggy may have been a tourist attraction replica, but it was fully functional, with the same big moon tires and moon suspension—about the only vehicle around that could handle the spongy bog terrain of the sanctuary. The Mercedes's back wheels spun into the muck before it had gone twenty feet.

Two EMTs loaded an empty stretcher and closed the back doors of an ambulance parked in front of an emergency room in Titusville.

A moon buggy pulled up.

"Can you give Major Nelson here a hand?" said Serge, getting Lenny out of the rover. "He usually sees Dr. Bellows."

The EMTs helped Lenny through the automatic glass doors. One of them came back out as Serge started up the moon buggy. "Hey! Wait a minute!"

"Big problem at the Cape," said Serge, waving and pulling away. "They need me."

The Moon Hut restaurant, "Where the Moon People Dine," is a Cape Canaveral institution.

Built in the Sputnik era, the small-town diner sits near the ocean at the bend in A1A where the road swings west from Cocoa Beach toward the Kennedy Space Center. It opens before dawn every morning, when NASA workers and civilian contractors jam the place. The neon sign out front depicts a thatched hut sitting on the Sea of Tranquillity. The diner has two themes. Space flight and country arts and crafts. The traditional American menu has an unexplained number of Greek dishes. Everyone eats at the Moon Hut. Astronauts, politicians, movie stars.

A waitress led five big men and a briefcase over to a table.

Ivan took a seat next to a blastoff photo. Dmitri sat down under a spinning loom.

"Be right back with your water." The waitress left.

Ivan peeked over the top of a laminated menu, then ducked back down. "That's Annette Bening."

"Where?" asked Dmitri, turning around.

Ivan smacked him with his menu. "Don't look!"

"Why not?"

"Everyone looks!"

"What's she doing here?"

"Getting coffee to go."

"If that's Annette, where's Warren?"

"Must be in the car with the kids. They've settled down, you know."

The five men were peeking over the tops of their menus when the waitress returned.

"Is it too early for the flaming Greek cheese?" asked Ivan.

She shook her head no.

"Flaming Greek cheese. Five," said Ivan. "And five coffees."

She collected the menus.

"Excuse me," Ivan whispered. "Is that Annette Bening?" He tilted his head slyly toward the register.

"I don't know," said the waitress. She turned to the front counter. "Hey, Annette!"

The woman at the register looked around.

"That's her," said the waitress.

Coffee arrived, then cheese. A phone rang. Ivan flipped it open.

"Good morning, Mr. Grande. . . . Yes, I have good news. . . . That's right, we've got the *you-know-what*. . . . We're at the Moon Hut. . . . No, the *Moon Hut*. . . . No, you get breakfast here. . . . Because it's America. . . . Excuse me a minute, they're setting the cheese on fire. . . . No, I haven't been drinking. . . ."

The waitress came to refill coffee. Ivan put a hand over his cup.

". . . No, that won't be a problem, Mr. Grande. . . . A submarine? . . . Yes, I've seen them. . . . No problem, ask for Yuri. I'm writing the name down now. . . . That's in New York, right? . . . I understand completely. . . . We won't let you down. . . ."

Ivan closed his phone and stood up. "Waitress? We'll need this to go."

In the very back of the Moon Hut, in the history room, a waitress prepared to refill a glass of ice water. "That won't be necessary," said Serge, standing up and taking out his wallet.

It may have been December 30, but nobody told Palm Beach.

The mercury hit eighty by noon. The BBB was using a Krunkleton paperback again as a bar-hopping guide. They nursed ten-dollar drinks in the back of the Breakers.

Paige stared down at an angelfish swimming under her napkin. An orange-and-purple damsel swam the other way through coral. "I've heard of bars that had aquariums, but I've never been in one where the bar actually *is* an aquarium."

"The Kennedys used to jog over there," said Teresa, looking out the huge windows behind the bar as sea foam rolled in from the Atlantic.

"What a beautiful day," said Maria.

"Just one more day left until the new year," said Rebecca, raising her drink. "Here's to a new year with old friends."

Glasses clinked.

"What are your resolutions?" asked Maria.

"You know what? I've had it with resolutions!" said Rebecca. "No more resolutions!"

"That sounds like a resolution."

"I have an idea," said Teresa. "Let's make antiresolutions."

"I want to eat something fat at midnight," said Paige.

"C'mon, let's think big," said Teresa.

"Let's do something crazy," said Rebecca.

"Yeah," said Maria. "Really irresponsible."

Teresa stood and grabbed her purse. "Come on."

"Where?" said Maria.

"I don't know yet."

They headed back through the hotel lobby, stopped by the front desk and began going through the rack of tourist brochures. Teresa picked up and put down pamphlets. "Dreher Park Zoo, nope; Norton Gallery, nope; Clematis Concert Series, nope; Polo Club, definitely nope . . ."

"Wait a minute," said Maria, slowly opening a brochure with a silver Amtrak train on the cover. "Look at this."

"What is it?"

"A mystery train. New York to Miami. Departs New Year's Day."

"What's a mystery train?"

"You know, they act out whodunits, passengers participate."

"Oh my God!" said Maria, folding over the pamphlet and holding it out to the others. "Look at the book they're going to perform."

"The Stingray Shuffle!" said Teresa. "That's too much of a coincidence."

"We're meant to get on that train," said Rebecca. "We'll kick ourselves if we don't go."

"It's only two days away," said Sam. "We don't have tickets, we don't have plans . . ."

"Exactly," said Teresa. "It's so impulsive. We'll get one-way plane tickets, see the ball drop in Times Square like we always wanted, then take the train back the next day."

"Hold everything," said Maria, pointing out something else in the brochure. "Look at this list of celebrities onboard."

"No way!" said Rebecca.

"That seals it," said Teresa. "Now we *really* have to go."

Teresa fished in her purse for the valet ticket. "So we're finally going to catch up with him."

"*I still can't* believe we're actually on this plane," said Maria.

"Look at that sunset," said Rebecca.

They all leaned and stared out the left windows as the sun left a scarlet stripe across the bed of clouds. They could see another jet, miles away and tiny, moving across the horizon in the same direction.

Seat 24B in that other plane was ticketed to passenger Serge A. Storms, who leaned across the businessman traveler in the window seat next to him to take twenty pictures of the setting sun. Click, click, click . . .

The sun finally disappeared and Serge sat back in his seat. "Thanks for letting me do that. I think I got some great shots. It's important to record every sunset I can."

The businessman looked at Serge a second, then went back to his book.

"Yes, sir! Flying to the Big Apple! Goin' to Gotham! Matriculatin' to Manhattan! New York, New York, the city so nice they named it twice . . ."

The man took a deep breath and put his book down.

"I love flying but I hate airlines!" Serge told the man. "Who can keep all the fares and discounts straight? Frequent flyer miles, three hundred and nine dollars if you order fourteen days in advance, two fifty-nine if you stay over a Saturday, one nineteen provided you don't get off the plane . . ."

The man looked at Serge another moment, then picked up his book again.

"Oh, trying to read, eh? Don't let me distract you." Serge faced forward for thirty seconds. "So what are you reading?"

The man turned the book over and showed Serge the cover.

"Ralph Krunkleton?" said Serge. "I *love* Ralph Krunkleton. Read all his stuff back in school. Personally, I think that's his best book, balances surrealism with traditional murder mystery machinations. But don't worry, I won't give away the ending."

The man smiled politely and went back to reading. Serge stared forward another thirty seconds. Then he leaned over and whispered the ending.

The man dropped the book in his lap in exasperation.

"What?" said Serge. "I just did you a favor. That's the big mistake people make reading Krunkleton. They get all caught up in the suspense plot. Now you can concentrate on the prose, lyrical language selection and social nuances. And don't forget the five million dollars that's floating around. You'll never guess who gets it. . . . Oh, I just told you. Sorry."

The man put the book away.

"Good idea," said Serge. "They're preparing the serving cart. You wouldn't want to spill anything." Serge lowered his tray and folded his hands on it and smiled. Then he started tapping his fingers. He stuck his head out in the aisle. "What's taking them so long?"

He reached up to the overhead console and twisted a nozzle. A blast of cold air began blowing the man's hair around. He turned slowly toward Serge.

"Whoops, wrong one." Serge twisted the nozzle shut and twisted another, then closed his eyes and stuck his face up in the chilly stream. The man picked up an airline magazine.

Serge opened his eyes and turned off the vent. He pressed other buttons. Lights flashed on and off the magazine the man was trying to read.

"Need a reading light?" asked Serge. "Don't want to ruin your eyes." Lights continued flashing on and off.

"Here comes the cart! I love the cart!" said Serge. "All the choices— so hard to decide. There's the spicy Bloody Mary mix and orange juice and soda. They only pour half the can in those little cups, but you can ask them to leave the whole can. That's what I do."

Serge leaned into the aisle and looked forward toward Row 11. The sleeve of a tropical shirt and the bandaged foot were still there. He leaned back.

The attendant came to their row, and the businessman handed her eight dollars. "Scotch. Double."

"Coke," said Serge. "Please leave the can. And can I have one of those huge, huge bags of peanuts—I haven't eaten in days! Ha, ha, ha, ha . . ."

He turned to the man. "Oh, a drinker, eh? It's weird how times changed about that. One day you're Mr. Sophistication, and the next you're a social leper with a stigmatizing disease. . . ."

The man chugged his scotch and set the glass on his tray next to two empty airline miniatures.

"You might want to go easy on that stuff," said Serge. "I don't mean to preach, but there are all kinds of new federal aviation rules about in-flight behavior. You don't want to annoy other passengers."

Serge stood and got a box down from the overhead compartment. He sat and placed it in his lap. "Want to see my trains?"

Serge opened the box of model railroad equipment. "See? That green-and-orange engine there is *The City of Miami*. I painted it myself. Here, hold this. . . ." Serge rummaged through the box, cabooses, tracks, water towers. ". . . There she is! This baby is precisely to scale. It's Flagler's personal car, the Rambler. Built her from scratch. Hold this. . . ." More rummaging. "And this is the observation car from *The Silver Stingray*. That's one of the great trains that take the snow-birds to Florida. Hold this. . . ." He picked up a passenger car, looked in the windows, put it back down. "You should have seen them at the X-ray machine when this baby went through. About ten people crowded around the screen. They took the box off to a special area and had a dog sniff it." Serge grinned impishly. "It was partly my doing. I arranged some of the metal tracks and trains in the shape of a machine gun, just to keep them on their toes. I have to make sure I'm safe when I fly. . . . Darn it, did I remember to pack my diesel? . . ." More rummaging.

The man spoke for the first time. "You know, the rest rooms on these things have all kinds of levers and buttons and secret compartments."

Serge stared at him a moment, then quickly grabbed all the trains from the man's arms, repacked the box and returned it to the overhead. He got up and trotted toward the back of the plane.

Twenty minutes later, a stewardess had Serge by the arm and escorted him back to his seat over his protests. "I told you, I wasn't trying to disable the smoke detector. I was *exploring*. . . ."

Serge reluctantly sat down. He thought a second. He reached under his seat for his camera.

The businessman was typing on his laptop. He could feel Serge's eyes drilling into the side of his head.

"Listen . . ." said Serge.

The man sighed and closed his laptop.

"I'd like to take some more pictures again when we land. Will that be okay? If it isn't, I'll understand. Life is so fleeting I want to capture every moment. I'll just set the motor drive on automatic and let 'er rip."

The Boeing 737 banked over Long Island for its approach. The landing gear went down. Serge leaned across the man again and pressed his lens to the pressure window. Click, click, click. "I'm getting goose bumps." Click, click, click. "This is just like that U2 song. . . . You like U2? . . . Of course! Everybody does! . . . *It was a cold and wet December day when we touched the ground at JFK . . .*" Click, click, click.

The Boeing taxied up to the terminal. Serge unlatched the overhead bin. "I only take carry-ons. Checking your luggage is playing with fire. . . ." He turned, but the businessman was already halfway up the aisle.

"Hey!" Serge yelled. "We forgot to exchange phone numbers. . . ."

*N*ew *York City. Manhattan.* East Side.
Eugene Tibbs was blue. That was his job.

He had always been blue.

He was blue back in his days on the Mississippi Delta, in those cotton fields, and he was blue in Memphis, on Union Avenue, recording for Sam Phillips at Sun Studio. He was blue after selling his soul to the devil late one night at the crossroads. And he was blue because he didn't sell his soul for talent and fame but for a sandwich. That's what cheap liquor will do to you. That's what the blues does to you.

Tibbs sat in the last car of the 4-5-6 subway line as it clattered and sparked under Grand Central Station. Well after midnight, Eugene was alone in the car, reading a paperback by Ralph Krunkleton. He looked out the scratched window at a group of laughing people in the seedy yellow light on the Fifty-first Street platform. They couldn't fool him. They were blue, too. He could tell. He knew the blues.

Tibbs had just returned from Florida. More like fled. He had been let go from a steady run at Skipper's Smokehouse, the legendary blues joint on Tampa's north side. His last night there had started blue enough, but there was trouble waiting down the tracks for Tibbs. He sat in a chair onstage, wearing a neat black tuxedo and cradling his faithful hollow-body Epiphone guitar, Gertrude. That's when trouble walked in the door.

Eugene performed as Blind Jelly Doughnut, and his sunglasses were so dark he could safely watch a solar eclipse. They made him bump into things, and people thought he really was blind and his music, therefore, the bluest of all. If you were blind and not blue, something was wrong.

But even with the sunglasses, Tibbs recognized the man who came in the club that night. He'd recognize him anywhere, and it might as well have been the devil himself, wanting to talk about that sandwich. Damn the blues.

The man came right down to the stage and took a seat at a cocktail table in the front row. He set his glass of ice water down and pulled out a notepad. It was that damn Atkins fellow from Alabama, the blues historian who'd been stalking him for an interview. The man just wouldn't take no.

It unsettled Tibbs seeing him sitting there, quietly confident, watching, waiting for a slip—the man could ruin everything. It became a war of nerves. Eugene broke out in a sweat. After the third song, he began to cough. The man in the front row stood and silently offered Tibbs his glass of water.

"Thank you," said Eugene, taking the glass.

The man jumped back and pointed. "He can see! He can see! I knew it!"

The audience was horrified, houselights came on, a scuffle broke out. Eugene barely escaped, running three blocks and ducking into an adult theater. He peeked out the window at the mob running past the theater with torches and clubs. Don't mess with the blues.

Tibbs caught the first flight back to New York. He took a bus to the Port Authority Terminal, then tried to use the subway, but he didn't have the right change. When you're blue, you never have the right change. That's the way it works. Rock and roll gets the limos. The blues makes you walk. It was another dozen blocks across the Village back to his loft apartment in SoHo, next to the nineteenth-century carriage house on Crosby Street where Billie Holiday used to live.

At times like these, Eugene liked to read himself to sleep with his favorite author. He picked up a paperback, the one with the stingray on the cover. It was his favorite author because his books were always in the bargain bin. Eugene opened the book to a folded-over page and lay down on the cold mattress in his skivvies. But tonight, the book did not make him sleepy. It spoke to him. He got out of bed, dressed, put on his boots. He stuck the book in his back pocket, scratched around a dresser drawer for correct change and headed back to the subway.

That's where he was now, in the last car of the 4-5-6, standing up, approaching the Eighty-sixth Street station. It was almost five a.m. when he reached Park Avenue. The Upper East Side was still and dark except for puffs of steam from the grates that drifted slowly across the empty street. There wasn't much time left before the garbage trucks would come. Eugene began grabbing Glad bags of trash off the stoops of million-dollar apartments, taking as much as he could carry and running two blocks to Central Park and into the woods. He began sorting through the trash, the lion's share worthless to him. But shortly after sunrise, he had what he'd come for: six empty bottles of the most expensive cologne from Saks and Bloomingdale's. He jammed them into his jacket and headed for a drugstore on Seventy-ninth.

Soon he was climbing out of the subway on Bleecker Street with four bags from Rite Aid. Back in his apartment, he spread the contents on the floor. Economy sacks of green mints, red-and-white hard-candy mints, peppermint patties, Tic Tacs, mouthwash, a big pouch of disposable Bic razors, shaving cream, combs, Aqua Velva, toenail clippers, files, No Doz, Sominex, a two-liter bottle of generic cologne and a large pickle jar of discontinued condoms.

He poured the generic cologne in the designer bottles from Park Avenue, then packed everything into an old briefcase he'd pulled down from his closet. He got out his paperback again, to make sure he'd done everything just the way the character in the book had. Then he lay back in his bed and waited.

Limos arrived at the curb outside the Hotel Carlyle on East Seventy-seventh.

Eugene Tibbs approached on foot from the south. He was wearing the tuxedo from his blue days and carrying his briefcase. He made one last stop at a print shop.

"Yes, I'd like your Fifteen-Minute Instant Business Card Special."

"What do you want them to say?"

He pulled the paperback from his pocket, opened it to a dog-eared page and pointed at something he'd underlined. "This right here."

"You got it."

"And can I have my change in ones?"

Fifteen minutes later, he left the print shop and walked the last few blocks to the Carlyle. A long line spilled out of the café. Inside was a hospitality industry ant farm: service people moving in all directions, maître d', greeters, coat checkers, table captains, waiters, water pourers. Tonight there was also an armed guard because Woody Allen was playing the clarinet. Eugene still couldn't believe anyone would pay the sixty-dollar cover charge. He decided he'd never understand white people.

Eugene walked past the coat line.

"Excuse me," said the guard. "Where are you going?"

Eugene produced a business card from his jacket. The guard studied it and handed it back. "Go ahead."

Eugene stuck the card back in his jacket and wound his way through the hotel to the men's room. He set the briefcase on the counter next to the sink and opened it. He removed the contents, setting out mints and aftershave and cologne in precise arrangement. Then, the final touch: the tip basket with a few ones from Eugene's own wallet.

Three hours later, Eugene counted up his tips. The paperback had been right—there must be five hundred dollars here. Eugene heard the rest-room door opening, and he stashed the money in his pocket.

A small, redheaded man with a clarinet case walked into the men's room. He finished his business; Eugene handed him a paper towel.

"Do you need anything, sir?"

The man looked around to see if anyone else was there, then pointed.

"Mint?"

The man shook his head.

"Condom?"

He nodded.

Eugene opened the jar. "How many?"

"Five . . . no, six."

The man stuffed the foil pouches in his instrument case, threw a twenty in the tip basket and left quickly.

That was just the beginning. Eugene Tibbs pulled down five grand in the next month, making two- and three-night stands at the Four Seasons, the Waldorf, Tavern on the Green, constantly rotating to avoid suspicion. There were enough four-star restaurants and hotels in Manhattan that he could change locations every night and not run out for the rest of his life. As long as Eugene didn't deviate from the plan in his paperback, everything went smoothly. Oh, sure, there was the occasional skepticism, but the book had anticipated that. Eugene compiled a list of restaurant owners' names from the department of health, and he called ahead each night to ask the name of that evening's maître d'.

"Nobody told me about this!" said the maître d' at Sardi's, studying Eugene's business card.

Eugene didn't say anything, just stood there holding his briefcase like he was bored, staring at caricatures of Liza and Anthony Quinn.

"And I've never heard of your company either." The maître d' read the card again: *Big Apple Urinal Guys—restaurants, hotels, weddings, bar mitzvahs. Bonded, references.*

The maître d' turned the card over. He saw two names in pencil: his own and that of the restaurant's owner.

"Where'd you get these names?"

"My boss. Those are the people I'm supposed to ask for if there's any trouble."

The maître d' began to perspire. He stuck a finger in his collar to loosen it. He picked up the phone under the brass lamp on the reservation podium and dialed the number on the card. He got Eugene's answering machine. ". . . Big Apple Urinal Guys, we're not in . . ."

The maître d' hung up. His Adam's apple stuck out.

Eugene remembered what the book had said. There's a point in conflict resolution when the next person who talks loses. You're ready to play with the big boys when you can recognize that moment.

The maître d' coughed. "I, wait, uh . . ."

"I won't need an escort," said Eugene, moving past the man for the men's room.

The money rolled in. The Essex House, Trattoria, the Brasserie. Eugene experimented by wearing his dark sunglasses and offering paper towels in the wrong direction, but the increase in sympathy tips was offset by people who waved a hand in front of Eugene's face and then took money *out* of the basket.

He couldn't complain. The hours and money were great—it was working out just like it did for the character in his paperback. Eugene was making a fortune as the Wildcat Urinal Guy.

It being New York, however, the scheme did have limits. One night in a regional French bistro on Amsterdam Avenue, Eugene learned the hard way that the mob had a hand in the urinal guy rackets on the West Side, and he was toilet-dunked by two guys in sharkskin suits. He got home and found his loft apartment had been tossed.

So he stuck to midtown and the East Side. He began taking other precautions he'd learned about in his paperback. When he left his apartment each day, he lightly sprinkled talcum powder on the doorknob and some more in front of the threshold, only enough to notice if you looked. He went out on the fire escape and taped a human hair across the base of the window.

A week went by without incident. He was working Rockefeller Center that Friday when he was approached by a capo in La Cosa Nostra. They made him an offer he couldn't refuse. Eugene was a pro by now, and the mob had taken notice. They'd also become increasingly unsatisfied with their own soldiers assigned to urinal duty—guys whose heart wasn't in it, slouching against the sink in Naugahyde jackets, smoking, listening to Knicks games on transistor radios.

"Excuse me, could I have a mint?"

"You want a mint? Sure, I'll give you a mint. I'll shove it up your fuckin' ass, you fuckin' douche bag!"

For some reason, the mob wasn't seeing a lot in tips. Not the kind of money Eugene was making. They proposed a split. Eugene would be allowed to expand into their territory. He'd return a piece of his action from Hell's Kitchen, and they'd give him a taste of Little Italy and protection from the crazy Jamaican gang that was already running a wicked urinal guy operation in Jersey and Queens.

Business boomed. Le Cirque, the Ritz-Carlton, the River Café. In the middle of an eight-hundred-dollar night in the Russian Tea Room, he pulled the paperback out of his pocket again and smiled at the cover. Eugene decided that if he ever got the chance, he'd make sure he thanked Ralph Krunkleton in person.

December thirtieth in New York is no time for shorts and tropical shirts. The Russians stood rubbing their arms in the cab line outside JFK.

"Screw this," said Ivan. "I know a trick."

They went back inside and followed the arrows to curbside check-in. They waited until a taxi dropped off a fare, then sprinted outside.

"Manhattan!" yelled Ivan.

"It's against the rules. I'm supposed to go back to the pickup zone and wait at the end of the line . . ." The driver stopped and looked around quickly. "Get in!"

They pulled away from the airport. Ivan looked out the window and saw a giant metal sphere flickering through the trees, the old '39 World's Fair globe in Flushing Meadows. He sat back in his seat and noticed a thin ribbon of incense smoke by the dashboard, but it was no match for the foul human smell. Strange, mystical music came from the radio. The driver had oily hair and a scraggly beard.

Ivan leaned to the partition. "Are you an immigrant?"

"No. College student."

The driver made an unexpected turn, and Ivan was pitched against the door. A recorded message came on in the backseat. "This is Paul O'Neill of the New York Yankees asking you to hit a home run for safety. Please buckle up."

They entered the Midtown Tunnel under the East River and came out in Manhattan. Then the fun. Thrills, spills, the driver bench-testing axle strength, better than any amusement ride back in Orlando. They headed north, their taxi joining a sea of yellow cabs weaving up the Avenue of the Americas. The Russians saw there were lanes painted in the road, but that was clearly part of an ancient custom from some long-forgotten people.

The taxi screeched to the curb, tossing the Russians into the partition. "There she is," said the driver. "The famous Warwick. The Beatles used to stay there. And Cary Grant lived in one of the rooms for twelve years . . ."

The Russians dashed into the building and stomped their feet for circulation as they waited at the registration desk. They took hot showers and had the bell captain send up a clothier. They checked the time. Four hours until the meeting Mr. Grande had set up with Yuri.

"I'm hungry," said Vladimir.

"Me, too," said Dmitri. "But I'm tired of all this American food."

Five smartly dressed men in new fur coats walked down West Fifty-seventh. The one carrying the silver briefcase gestured, and the rest followed him into a restaurant under a red sidewalk canopy. The Russian Tea Room.

"Get a load of this place," said Alexi, slowly turning around. Bright red carpet and red leather banquettes, gold firebirds on the walls, gold on the ceiling, and gold samovars on the counters, for tea. The Moscow skyline carved in ice.

"Incredible," said Vladimir, studying a scale model of the Kremlin.

Ivan watched a sturgeon swimming in a fifteen-foot revolving aquarium shaped like a bear. "Everyone back home should get a chance to see America. We certainly don't have anything like this where we come from."

They waited in the lounge for their table. The bartender came over. "What's your pleasure?"

"What should we get?" Dmitri asked the others.

"When in Rome . . ." said Ivan.

"Manhattans?" said Dmitri.

"Try the Russian Quaalude," said a stockbroker three stools down.

"Never heard of it," said Ivan. "What's in it?"

"Not sure," said the broker, turning to the bartender. "Hey Bob, what's in a Russian Quaalude?"

"One second," said the bartender, walking to a wall phone by the stemware.

Alexi got nervous and stood up. "Who's he calling?"

"Relax," said Ivan. "This is America. He's on the bartender hotline."

The man hung up and returned. "Frangelica, Baileys, vodka, layered in that order."

"Five," said Ivan.

The bartender grabbed a bottle of vodka by the neck. "I was a technical adviser for the movie *Cocktail*." He swung the bottle up quickly like he was going to twirl it in the air but didn't release, for liability reasons. "The trick to twirling bottles is to pick ones with only a little liquor left. The cast tried to twirl full bottles. Liquor flew everywhere. Had to edit it out."

Dmitri whispered to Ivan: "You meet everybody in New York."

Their table was ready when they finished the drinks. They all got the hot borscht and Stroganoff, except Dmitri.

"How's the chicken Kiev?" he asked the waiter. "I hate it when it's tough."

The waiter said it wasn't.

Sevruga caviar and gazirovannaya vodka arrived, then the main course. The men ate with gusto as they admired winter paintings above their booth by Surikov and Kustodiev. Dmitri poked his chicken with a gold fork. "It's tough. I knew it."

In the back of the restaurant, a visitor from Florida sat alone, sipping tea, reading a paperback.

The check arrived. Ivan patted his full stomach. "We better get going for the meeting. Who has to take a leak?"

They went downstairs to the men's room. After finishing business, Ivan set the briefcase on the floor and turned on the ornate gold faucets. The others lined up at adjacent sinks and turned more gold faucets.

Eugene Tibbs handed out paper towels.

Ivan lifted the lid off a jar. "Mint?"

"Take as many as you want."

The Russians each took one of the round, hard, red-and-white mints. They liked those.

Ivan threw a five in the tip basket and picked up his briefcase.

The Russians started across midtown on foot, the temperature dropping fast. They picked up the pace, passing twenty consecutive windows with pictures of restaurant owners and Giuliani. Icy gusts blew down the Seventh Avenue canyon. More windows, more pictures. Pauly Shore, Ron Howard, Julie Newman, Goldie Hawn, Kim Basinger, Mike Tyson, Damon Wayans.

Ivan pointed across the street at a blue-and-yellow sign, LATE SHOW WITH DAVID LETTERMAN. "We're getting close."

They went around the south side of the Ed Sullivan Theater, over to Fiftieth Street and down the stairs into the subway.

"Where is it?" asked Alexi.

"Not sure," said Ivan, reading his own scribbling on a Moon Hut matchbook.

"You said we were supposed to meet Yuri and make the submarine deal at a clandestine KGB document drop station."

"That's right. It's disguised as a little subway bakery—bagels and stuff for morning commuters."

Dmitri looked across the subway platform. Nobody else except a man in a trench coat playing the tenor sax in a rueful way that made people want to forgive Third World debt. A deep rumbling noise grew out of the darkness at the end of the platform, then a bright light. A late train on the 1-2-3-9 roared out of a tunnel and stopped. The doors opened. Nobody got on or off. The doors closed. The train left.

Vladimir studied a map on the wall. "I think that was the red line."

A gravelly voice: "Are you looking for Siberia?"

The Russians turned around. A homeless face poked out of the shadows from a dark corner of the platform.

"What'd you say, old man?"

"You looking for Siberia? That Commie place?"

The Russians glanced at each other. The document drop station was a tightly guarded Soviet secret. Just great. Even the bums knew about it. And he was calling it Siberia, adding insult.

"I'll tell you for a dollar," said the bum.

Ivan handed him a folded George Washington.

"Go over this platform and around to the other train. Don't worry if you think you've gone too far—just keep going. It's way down in the bowels of this thing. You'll find it, just keep going down. . . ."

They started walking away. Ivan stopped and turned and called back to the old man. "How do you know about this place? It's supposed to be a secret."

"It *is* a secret," said the bum. "But the in-crowd knows about it. They're always coming by to check it out, usually on the weekend if there's nothing else to do."

"It's become idle amusement?"

"Pretty much," said the bum.

"Wonderful," said Igor.

The Russians went farther down into the subway. And down. And down.

"Where the hell is it?" asked Vladimir.

"He told us to just keep going," said Ivan, trotting down another flight of stairs. "If we . . . hold it, what's that?"

They saw a dark glass door and approached slowly. The door had a little sign. In small, plain black letters: SIBERIA. Ivan thought he heard something. "Is that music?"

Next to the door were several large windows, also dark, wallpapered from the inside with newspaper clippings. The Russians began reading the articles, all about the discovery of a Soviet document drop station. Their hearts sank. Ivan continued reading: in the mid-nineties, someone had leased the shop for a pub, and they started knocking out interior walls for more space. That's when they found all the KGB documents and Russian passports and rubles inside the studwork. The clippings said the station was traced to a Soviet agent known as Yuri, who had fled long before the FBI swarmed the place. Other articles chronicled the new, literally underground, coolest bar of the moment that had since sprouted at the location. One story explained that the city's Metropolitan Transportation Authority doesn't allow bars in the subway, but this specific location fell in a jurisdictional crack because of complex subterranean rights with foreign corporations in the area of Rockefeller Center.

"There goes the rendezvous," said Ivan. He took several deep breaths of subway exhaust. "What the hell—let's get something to drink." He opened the door.

Inside was a dive's dive, like if the producers of *Animal House* rejected a set for being too slovenly. Nobody picked up the empties, which collected on tables with cigarette butts and got knocked over and rolled under broken chairs and sofas. There were two undependable jukeboxes, a novelty photo machine, and cases of Amstel and Red Stripe stacked high against walls with profane graffiti. Behind the bar, a row of Russian military hats hung from the shelf that held the liquor bottles, over a picture of Hillary and the owner.

The bartender yelled over the Clash on one of the jukes: "What can I get you guys?"

The Russians began draining longnecks.

"*. . . The shareef don't like it . . .*"

Ivan heard a familiar voice. He turned around. In the darkness, at one of the tables, a squat old man made a sales pitch to a pair of Juilliard students. He held up a painted wooden figure, twisted it apart at the middle, and took out a smaller figure. Then he twisted that one apart and took out an even smaller one, and so on until he had six figurines of descending size lined up across the table. The man gestured proudly.

"Twenty dollars is a lot of money," said one of the students. "I don't know."

"What's not to know?" said the man. "These are genuine Romanov nesting dolls. Almost a century old, worth a fortune. This is the bargain of a lifetime!"

"Then why do you have them? How can you sell them so cheap?"

"I told you, after the breakup, the whole country's for sale. You name it, I can get it. Rocket launchers, cadaver parts, tsarist dinnerware . . ."

"No, thanks," said the students, getting up and leaving.

"Wait! Let me show you how they reassemble. . . ." The man desperately pieced the dolls back together. "That's the genius of these things. That's the whole beauty . . ." His voice trailed off. ". . . shit."

". . . *Rock the casbah!* . . ."

Ivan walked up from behind. "I hear you're the sorry bastard I'm supposed to see about a submarine."

Yuri turned around and his eyes lit up. "Comrade!" They gave each other big, slapping bear hugs.

Ivan gestured around the room. "Love what you've done with the place."

"It's a crazy story," said Yuri. "After the big Soviet collapse, there was no money. The KGB got behind on the rent, evicted. They wouldn't even bring me home—just cut me loose over here."

"They laid you off?"

"Can you believe it? And after all the microfilm I smuggled in my ass for those guys. I said I'd appeal. They just told me to take a powder—a cyanide powder, and they laughed. Personally, I don't think that was very professional."

"But what are you still doing here?" asked Ivan. He pointed back at the articles in the window. "They said you had fled. Nobody knew where you went."

"Yeah, I heard that, too. Isn't that weird? I've never left. Even when the FBI was here. I kept tapping them on the shoulders and asking if there was anything they wanted to know, but they just told me to stay out of the way and went back to tearing out the walls with demolition saws. I even tried to get asylum. Back when the Cold War was hot, you got asylum, you were set. Nice house, credit cards. Today, if you used to be KGB, you can't get arrested. The CIA won't return my calls. The people who own this place keep me around like a novelty, all my drinks are free. I can't complain. Speaking of which: Bartender! Stoli!"

The bartender placed six shots on the table, the surface of the clear liquor vibrating as another subway train thundered by on the other side of the wall.

"So this place went from being a document drop to a bar?"

"Not directly. After the Kremlin lapsed on payments, it first became a hip-hop kung fu video store. They had these stereo speakers pointed out the door at top volume twenty-four hours, and passing commuters heard all this crazy urban martial-arts screaming: 'Eeeeeee-yahhhhh, motherfucker!' Jesus, was I glad to see that go. I couldn't hear myself think in here. I was trying to get résumés out at the time. The Canadians were hiring in the Tribeca office."

"The Canadians spy on the United States?"

"Not really, but they like to keep a few nominal cells active for national pride. They have this big inferiority thing, or so I've heard. They gave me an interview, and I told them I knew how to kill with a single sheet of typing paper, but they said they weren't interested unless I could hit Céline Dion, and then they laughed. Again, not funny."

Ivan nodded with empathy. "I hate to mix business, but there's this matter about a sub."

"We're all set for delivery," said Yuri. "It's a Perestroika Class attack submersible, one of the small ones but still nuclear, with beverage holders, so you're getting your money's worth. We sail in February from the North Sea, at four knots through the NATO array of hydrophones. But I wouldn't lose sleep. Even if we get caught, it's no biggie. Nobody cares anymore—all the rules are new. We've still got hydrogen bombs, but who knew the Internet would be the thing? Suddenly, rock *doesn't* crush scissors. 'Hey, we can blow you up!' 'So what? Your bandwidth stinks.' We're like organ-grinders to these people."

The bar's owner walked up to the table. "Hey, Yuri! I see you brought some of your Russian friends. I sure hope you're not doing any *spying*! Ha, ha, ha, ha . . ." The owner walked away, still laughing.

"See?" said Yuri.

"What I wouldn't give for a poisoned umbrella," said Dmitri.

Ivan lifted the briefcase and set it on the table.

Yuri smiled. He cracked his knuckles and licked his lips, then turned the briefcase around to face him. "This is what I've been waiting for." He flipped the latches and dramatically opened it with the lid facing the others.

Ivan was still smiling, but Yuri's expression changed. He looked up. "What is this, some kind of sick joke?"

"What do you mean?" said Ivan. "It's all there. Five million dollars!"

"Very funny." Yuri spun the briefcase around.

"What the hell's all this crap?" said Ivan. "Cologne, mints, condoms . . ."

The bar shook again as the subway rumbled by. It was late, only two people in the train: Eugene Tibbs in the first car, heading home with his silver briefcase, and in the last car, a tourist from Florida named Serge.

A sheet-covered body lay on the sidewalk outside a pizza parlor.

"Roll film!"

The location crew from *Law & Order* panned over the body and up to the actors talking on the curb.

Cars began honking and swerving as five Russians ran through the middle of traffic on Broadway, sprinting up the sidewalk past Jerry Orbach, hopping over the body and disappearing around the corner.

"Cut! Cut!" yelled the director.

The Russians crossed the street again, running up Fifty-seventh and back into the Russian Tea Room. They dashed down the stairs and burst into the men's room. Empty.

They ran back up the stairs toward the dining room.

The maître d' blocked their path. "Do you have a reservation?"

The maître d's head bounced on the steps as he was dragged back down the stairs by the legs. They pulled him into the men's room and slapped him around.

"Who's the urinal guy?"

"I don't know what you're talking about."

Punch.

"Who's the urinal guy!"

"I don't know!"

They upended him and shook him by the ankles. Pocket change and silverware clanged on the tiles. A business card fluttered to the floor. Ivan picked it up.

"Big Apple Urinal Guys," said Ivan. "Who's that?"

The maître d' shrugged upside down.

"There's no address. Only a phone number."

"You can use the reverse directory," said the maître d'.

"How do you do that?"

"Just call the phone company."

The N-R line squealed into the subway station below Houston Street. Eugene Tibbs stood up and grabbed a handrail. Tibbs's shift back in the Russian Tea Room had started like all the others, but the ending was a bit different. Tibbs had finished counting his tips and went to pack up his supplies for the night. He grabbed his briefcase from under the sink and opened it.

His blues were cured.

Tibbs slammed the lid shut and hurried out of the Tea Room. He'd been a paranoid mess ever since. He knew someone would come after the money, and they wouldn't ask politely. Even if he gave it back, he was still dead. Only one option: leave the city as fast as possible and retire in millionaire's style. He couldn't stop shaking and looking over his shoulder. Why couldn't he be cool like Ralph Krunkleton? What would the *real* urinal guy do in a jam like this?

The train doors opened, and Eugene stepped out of the car onto the Houston Street platform. He was quiet and alone. Then movement. Eugene's head snapped to the left. Way, way down at the opposite end of the platform, someone stepped out of the last car.

Tibbs stared at the man, standing there casually, reading a newspaper like he had nothing to do. The man looked up from the paper at Tibbs and looked back down quickly.

Uh-oh. Don't panic. Where did you see this once? Adrenaline spun the memory Rolodex in Eugene's head. Yes, I remember now. *The French Connection.* Tibbs took a single step backward, through the still-open door of the subway car.

At the other end of the platform, Serge looked up from his paper as Tibbs disappeared back into the train. So that's it, thought Serge. He wants to play *French Connection.* Well, two can tango! He took a step backward into his own car.

Tibbs stuck his head out of the train. The platform was empty again. Perspiration increased. He took a step out of the car and stared down the platform.

Serge's head popped out of the last car. He saw Tibbs. He stepped back on the platform. Tibbs jumped back into the first car. Serge jumped back into the last car. Tibbs jumped out again. Serge jumped out. On, off, on, off.

The subway system put an end to the game. The train's doors closed, and it pulled away into the tunnel.

Just Tibbs and Serge alone on the platform. They locked eyes. Eugene blinked. He took off running for the stairs up to Houston Street. Serge sprinted after him.

Eugene tripped and went sprawling on the steps. Mints, Bic razors, business cards everywhere. He turned around. Serge was gaining. He got up and started running again, coming out of the subway and reaching the street. Car noises, food smells. He evaluated each direction, then took off west.

Serge ran up the steps, grabbing a business card and reading it on the run.

They galloped all over lower Manhattan, through the Village and SoHo. Serge was faster, but Eugene knew the turf, running through restaurant kitchens and up service lifts. He crossed Bleecker Street and turned south, but Serge was still there, a block back.

· · ·

A yellow taxi-van drove five women up Hudson Street, a recorded message playing in back: "This is Mary Wilson of the Supremes asking you to *Stop! In the name of safety!* Please buckle up."

"Pull over," said Teresa. She checked the address against her paperback. "This is the place."

The BBB got out in front of the White Horse Tavern.

Rebecca pointed at the sidewalk. "Dylan Thomas bought it right there. The permanent hangover."

They stared at the pavement.

"Should we be feeling good about this?" asked Sam.

A tanker truck was parked at the corner, next to a crane dangling an array of metal wands over a vintage Checker cab.

"Look," said Teresa. "They're shooting a movie."

A technician turned on the rain machine, and the wands began to drizzle on the taxi.

"Roll film!"

Two people got out of the cab and kissed passionately.

Five Russians sprinted up the sidewalk. They ran through the rain, vaulted the hood of the cab and knocked over the embracing couple.

"Cut! Cut!"

The book club took a step back off the sidewalk as the Russians stampeded past them and disappeared into the darkness.

"Now we're seeing the real New York," Maria said cheerfully.

The Russians finally arrived at the address they had gotten from the reverse directory, using the urinal guy's business card. They stared up at the grimy brick building, and it reminded them of the factories back in Leningrad. But they had heard Americans liked to spend a lot of money to live in depressing places. They walked quietly up the stairs and came to a landing with two doors.

"Which one?" asked Alexi.

"Take your pick," said Ivan. "If it's wrong, we'll just try the other."

Alexi stuck a lock pick in the handle. The door opened easily, as if by itself.

"Don't be shy," said a smiling woman with a glass of Chardonnay, holding the inside doorknob. The loft was cavernous, full of people in tank tops and black turtlenecks, nibbling fondue and sushi. Three spotlights lit up a large, blank canvas propped in the middle of the room. The stereo was extra loud, playing a synthesized mélange of electronic buzzes, beeps, chirps and sirens, the newest Nihilistic German discotheque music designed to make people think, "Gee, it's got a great beat to dance to, but what would be the fucking point?"

The Russians mingled. More wine, more raw fish, more knocks at the door. The Eurotrash arrived. Someone rang a tiny brass bell; the crowd quieted and gathered around the canvas. The Russians strained for a better view from the back. A naked man came out of the bathroom spooled in Saran Wrap. He walked to the middle of the loft, produced his penis from the layers of plastic and whizzed on the canvas.

The crowd applauded to show they were hip, but not too much, to show they were hip.

Alexi turned to Ivan. "I think we have the wrong apartment."

Eugene Tibbs stood panting at the corner of Broadway and Houston, looking back up the street. Finally lost him. He returned to his apartment, sluggishly climbing the stairs. Nihilistic music thumped from the apartment next door. Eugene stuck his key in the knob.

Inside the apartment, the Russians heard Tibbs's key. "Someone's coming!" They packed themselves in a closet. Lots of jostling, "Shhhh!" "No, you 'Shhhh!'" They got settled in and peeked out through the slats in the accordion door.

Tibbs was ready to turn the doorknob when he noticed something. The talcum powder on his knob was smudged. He looked at the landing and saw footprints in the fine layer of white powder. Eugene tiptoed back toward the steps. He stopped when he heard someone at the base of the stairs. He slipped over to the landing's window and climbed out onto the fire escape.

"What's taking him so long?" asked Alexi. They slowly opened the closet door and ventured out. The place was a shambles. Drywall kicked in, wiring torn out, down feathers everywhere from slit pillows, jars of stuff dumped on the kitchen floor.

"Do we have to make such a mess every time we look for something?" said Ivan.

Alexi held a flowerpot in each hand and smashed them together. "We're looking for something?"

Serge made it to the top of the stairs. "Two doors, hmmm. Eenie, meenie, miney moe." He stuck a bobby pin in the lock.

"Someone's coming!" The Russians piled back in the closet.

Serge opened the door. "Anybody home?" He turned on the lights and looked around at all the dumped-out drawers and broken stuff. "I could never live like this."

He walked around the room, pawing through clothes, checking behind paintings.

"What's he doing?" asked Vladimir.

"Shhhh!" said Ivan, peeking out the slats, strips of light across his face.

Serge was checking under sofa cushions when he heard the doorknob. "Uh-oh. Someone's coming." He jumped into a second closet on the opposite side of the room and peeked through the slats.

The knob turned and the door creaked open. In walked five huge men in tuxedos with waist-length dreadlocks—the crazy Jamaican gang from Queens in a turf war over the urinal guy rackets. They had gone to the mattresses with the Sicilians over control of the West Side, and guess who got caught in the middle?

"Hey *mon*—anybody home?" The Jamaicans walked through the loft with TEC-9 machine guns at their sides.

Ivan peeked through the slats and whispered out the side of his mouth: "Silencers."

The Russians screwed suppressors on their pistols.

The last Jamaican stopped and stood still. The others turned around. He held a finger to his lips, then pointed at the closet. They raised machine guns.

"Hey *mon*! Looks like nobody's home." The Jamaicans clicked their safeties off. "We'll just have to come back another time."

The front door of the loft crashed open, and in rushed a crew from the Balboa crime family assigned to protect Tibbs. They opened fire on the Jamaicans. The Jamaicans shot back. The Russians let 'er rip through the closet door at the Jamaicans and the Italians, who both fired back at the closet in a confusing burst of triangulated fire. Music pounded through the walls.

The Jamaicans ripped off long, puttering bursts of small-caliber fire, the Russians blazed with nine-millimeter rounds, the Balboa crew rat-a-tat-tatted with fifty-caliber tommy guns. Serge sat down in the bottom of his closet and pulled a coat over his head.

Two of the Rastafarians were hit immediately, and they went down spinning, their machine guns still firing, strafing the walls, the lighting fixtures and the Russians' closet. Three of the Russians were hit, then two of the Balboas, then another Jamaican, lead flying everywhere. A burst of bullets cut through the kitchen, a line of bottles on the counter blowing up in succession: ketchup, olives, A.1., jerk sauce. The windows blew out; a sink faucet got hit and geysered. The closet door splintered above Serge. He covered his ears and gently rocked back and forth, singing to himself: "*. . . I woke up in a SoHo doorway, a policeman knew my name . . .*"

The shooting finally stopped. The room was still except for thumping German music. Nothing but a thick cloud of smoke, the smell of cordite, a spraying faucet and a swinging lamp that finally snapped and crashed. Almost everyone dead or dying. Ivan was left with just a flesh wound in the thigh, under a pile of dead Russians in the closet. He pushed them off, one by one, like sandbags, and finally pulled himself free. He fell through the closet door into the room.

There was a moan from the middle of the loft. One of the Jamaicans was coming around, pushing the fallen lamp off his head. Ivan limped toward him. The Jamaican saw the Russian coming and tried to get up, but couldn't. He dragged himself across the floor, begging. Ivan kicked him in the stomach, then the head. He picked up the Jamaican and slammed him into the door that connected the apartment with the adjacent artists' loft. The door gave way.

The Jamaican came crashing into the unit next door, distracting the crowd from a man in a pope costume defecating on the Sinead O'Connor CD box set.

Ivan entered the room next, kicking the Jamaican across the floor. He snatched a steaming fondue pot off the table.

"Pull your pants down! Now!"

The crowd applauded.

31

Eugene Tibbs knew he was past the fail-safe, his life forever changed. He couldn't return to his apartment. He had to get out of town right now, no looking back.

But which way? La Guardia, JFK, Newark, Grand Central Station? Every pore in his skin wide open. A clock ticked in his head.

Penn Station was the closest. Eugene made his way into Chelsea and north on Seventh Avenue, people pushing racks of clothes across the street. Eugene spun around. What was that? Everywhere he looked, he saw enemies. Is there something odd about that guy feeding the pigeons? That woman eating a sandwich in the park? The man pushing a shopping cart with a ten-foot ball of aluminum foil? His legs felt like lead; he forced them to carry him to Thirty-fourth Street.

Tibbs entered the train station and began browsing brochures. Where to go? It had to be far, far away. California? Arizona? Oregon?

He found an attractive pamphlet with palm trees and went to the Amtrak window.

Serge was on stakeout across the street from Tibbs's crib.

He kicked himself for losing Eugene's trail. This was his only chance. All he could do was hope that Tibbs came back, but he knew his chances were slim. He sat on a bench reading an article in the *Post* about Mariah Carey's secret source of inner strength. Serge turned the page and looked up at the SoHo loft. He still couldn't believe the police hadn't arrived yet. He had expected the place to be crawling, TV trucks, gawkers, the unit sealed off. All that gunfire—hadn't anyone called the cops? Actually, they had, but it was to report loud German party music that had drowned out the shooting.

The cops weren't anywhere to be seen, but Serge soon realized he had other company. Watching the apartment from the corner across the intersection were Ivan and a Jamaican, nursing hangovers. The pair were the newest toasts of the avant-garde art community, and the revelry had lasted till dawn. They even scored. Now they were paying for it, huddled in the cold over Starbucks.

The Jamaican's name was Zigzag, and he and Ivan had just gone into business together. With everyone else dead, there was no point continuing to fight. The deal was sealed when Ivan got the dawn phone call: The Colombians had just assassinated Mr. Grande by placing a bomb in his riding mower.

Serge had never been good at waiting. He was pacing manically now, and Ivan and Zigzag picked him up on their radar. Serge finally came to the end of his rope. He ran across the street, cars honking. He marched right up the stairs, kicked in the door and started going through Eugene's stuff as if the room wasn't full of bodies.

Ivan and Zigzag looked at each other.

"Come on!" said Serge. "There's got to be a clue where he's going! An address book with relatives! Anything! . . ."

The phone rang. Serge stared as the answering machine clicked on. *"You've reached Big Apple Urinal Guys . . ."*

Beeeeep.

"This is Amtrak calling to confirm your reservation on The Silver Stingray, *departing for Miami tomorrow at noon . . ."*

Serge casually walked back down the stairs, feigning an expression of futility. He sauntered around the corner until he was out of sight, then took off sprinting.

Ivan and Zigzag looked at each other again and shrugged.

Serge loping across the garment district. Thirty-seventh Street, Thirty-sixth, Thirty-fifth, flying through racks of clothes being wheeled across the street, people yelling and shaking fists. He ran past a pretzel wagon stand, which exploded, throwing a Bruce Willis stunt double through the air and into a parked car.

Serge stopped and helped him up. "Are you okay?"

"Cut! Cut!"

Serge took off again, charging down the steps at Penn Station and running to the Amtrak window.

"Miami, please."

Serge carefully tucked the ticket in his wallet and went over to the main concourse to check out the giant schedule board with the latest arrival and departure info.

"What do you want to do tonight?" asked Maria.

"It's Monday," said Rebecca. "Woody's playing clarinet at the Carlyle."

"That's a great idea!" said Teresa.

"I'm not sure I *want* to see Woody Allen," said Sam.

"Why not?"

"Because of what he did to Mia."

"We don't know Mia," said Rebecca. "What's she ever done for us?"

"He slept with her daughter, for heaven's sake!"

"It's not a sex show," said Teresa. "He's just going to play the clarinet."

"Mia went with the Beatles to see that Maharishi guy," said Rebecca. "And she married Sinatra and played the on-screen mother of Satan."

"So?" said Sam.

"The whole thing was shaky."

"There it is," said Maria. "There's the schedule board."

The BBB walked across the Penn Station concourse and stopped in front of the big board.

"That's our train, *The Silver Stingray*," said Teresa. "Leaves in twenty hours. Let's find the departure platform so we're not late when it's time to go."

"What about Woody Allen?" asked Rebecca. "Are we going or not?"

"Excuse me," said a man's voice. "Did I hear you say you're going to see Woody Allen?"

A limo pulled to the curb on the seven thousand block of Park Avenue.

The Café Carlyle doorman had a smile and white gloves. "Good evening, ladies." The women checked their coats and the maître d' led them to a table under muted frescoes. He bowed and left.

"Look how intimate the seating is," said Rebecca, gesturing at an empty chair beside a piano just feet away. "He's going to be sitting right there!"

Sam leaned and whispered to Teresa: "I can't believe we let him come along."

"Shhh! He'll hear you." They looked over and smiled at Serge, who was setting up a miniature digital recorder under a napkin to bootleg Woody.

A round of drinks arrived. Then a few more.

"Let's check out guys," said Rebecca. "Oooo, I like that one over there."

"Which one? The overaged hippie?"

"No, the business type in the turtleneck. I'd sleep with him."

"You would?"

"Sure, if I knew I wouldn't catch anything and wouldn't get pregnant again, and knew that he would still respect me and call, but not call too much and get cloying and possessive. And if he doesn't have a wife, and doesn't lie to me if he does, because I wouldn't want to wreck another woman's home, and . . ."

"In other words, in some fantasy astral plane in a parallel universe," said Teresa.

"Right," said Rebecca.

"Okay, Rebecca's an easy lay. Who else?"

"I'd do that guy over there," said Maria.

"The cheap Tom Selleck?"

"That's the one."

"Same terms as Rebecca?"

"Except that he also can't smell bad after an hour or two. Or bob his head in the car to some song that he tells me perfectly captures the kind of person he is. Either of those two things, and it's no Big O for Maria."

"Are you talking about Charlie?"

"How'd you know?"

"I warned you not to go out with him, but did you listen?"

"*Yuk* is not a warning."

"I'm starting to not want to date anyone who's eligible," said Paige.

"I know what you mean," said Maria. "It's like availability automatically disqualifies them. If they're single and never been married, they're either playboys or have some kind of psychological defect that prevents them from forming healthy relationships, like a private sexual ceremony you only find out about when you're innocently going through his dresser and find the baby pacifiers and vibrating butt plugs and he accuses you of spying . . ."

"Charlie again?"

"Did I use any names?"

"And if they've been married and gotten divorced, what did they do to deserve it?" said Paige. "You don't want to hire someone who's just been fired . . ."

"And if she was the bad unit in the marriage, then his judgment is suspect . . ."

"The only decent ones are married, and if they fool around, what does that say? . . ."

"That means the only guys worth considering are widowers . . ."

"And you can't go out with *them* because it's way too depressing. Every few minutes some little thing reminds them of their dead wives, like a certain brand of perfume or a car horn, and they either stare off for an hour or cry real loud in a crowded restaurant."

Sighs.

"So," Sam said to Serge with overt contempt. "What's with the tape recorder?"

"Preserving the show for future historians."

The chemicals were undergoing a tidal shift in Serge's head. He was now a man of mystery, currently involved in some kind of high-stakes smuggling game with the Russians. And these women . . . well, a good female agent will use any weapon at her disposal; Serge was determined not to let any of them lure him into the classic espionage "honey trap."

Sam snickered. "You're a historian?"

A historian was as good a cover as any. Serge nodded.

A tipsy Rebecca leaned toward Serge, brushing her shoulder against his. "Wow, a historian. I'll bet that takes years of study and hard work." Rebecca looked around at the others, and she could see it in their eyes: *Slut!*

This Rebecca could be the Mata Hari, thought Serge. But then, so could any of them. Watch your step.

A small redheaded man took the stage. Serge pressed a button on his recorder.

The Dixieland jazz began whimsically and slow but built with reckless precision. At one point, Serge had an uncontrollable urge to ask if he could sit in on trombone. Why not? It was a chance of a lifetime. But that would risk his cover because he didn't know how to play the trombone, and national security had to come first.

Rebecca leaned cozily into Serge again. "Can you believe what this is costing?"

"Believe it," said Serge. "You got your sixty-dollar entertainment charge, eighteen dollars for the appetizer if you want to cheap out, drinks, cab fare, coat check, tips. It never ends! Russell Baker was right. In New York, you hemorrhage money!"

The women smiled and tapped along with the music. With the exception of Sam, they were all starting to fall for Serge, so dashing and charming and funny—no clue he was crazier than a whirligig beetle—sitting there bouncing jauntily and playing the "air clarinet."

An hour later, the room erupted in applause as Mr. Allen packed up his instrument and left the stage. White noise of conversation filled the room. Serge asked where the women were from, and they told him.

"Really? I'm from Florida, too!" he said. "What about family?"

"Most of our kids also go to school there," said Teresa, "but a couple are out of state."

"You have kids?" said Serge. "Pictures!"

Teresa opened her wallet and handed it to Serge. "He's a fine one! . . . Okay, the rest of you!"

The others dug out wallets except Sam, who finally got moving after an elbow from Maria. Serge carefully lined the photos up on the table like a collection. "That sure is a blue-ribbon crop. You must be mighty proud parents! What do your husbands do?"

"We don't have any."

"Not anymore."

"Irresistible women like yourselves?" said Serge. "Available?"

"Please!" Sam said under her breath.

"So you're all single moms?" asked Serge.

They nodded.

"What the heck is this, a club or something?"

They nodded again.

"Well, you got all my respect. Single moms are my heroes. No tougher or more important job in America today, that's a fact! I was raised by a single mom. I didn't really think about it much at the time, but looking back—what she must have gone through! You may not know it to look at me today, but I was quite a handful."

Sam muttered again.

"Did you say something?" asked Serge.

She smiled. "Nope."

"Anyway, hats off to you. The country can't do enough—Congress should come up with a medal! . . ."

His stock with the gals was going through the roof. ". . . If it was up to me, you'd get hazardous-duty pay, yes sir! . . ."

Rebecca looked at the others. "He has to come with us!"

"Yes, you have to!"

"We've got a limo."

"How can a man say no to such lovely ladies . . ."

"I don't think that's such a good idea," said Sam. "No offense, but we don't know anything about him."

"She's right," said Serge. "I'm a complete stranger you've just met in New York. God only knows what I'm capable of."

"Who are you kidding?" said Rebecca. "You look so normal."

"It's the normal-looking ones you have to worry about," said Serge. "You're not going to end up in a sex dungeon because you went off with a *wacky*-looking guy."

Rebecca laughed and put a hand on Serge's shoulder. "You're so funny!"

32

A *small newsstand stood on* the corner of Madison and Fifty-fifth. No business. A thin Guatemalan shivered inside the booth and rubbed his hands together in their mittens. A small battery-powered TV sat atop a stack of unsold tabloids. John Walsh walked angrily toward the camera. *"Tonight on* America's Most Wanted, *we're on the lookout for a merciless serial killer who has been terrorizing south Florida and leaving a trail of bodies from Tampa to the Keys . . ."*

The clerk turned up the volume on his little black-and-white set as a stretch limo rolled by on Madison Avenue. Sam sat in the backseat, turning up the volume on the little color TV flush-mounted in the wet bar.

". . . We're going to get a rare glimpse inside the twisted mind of a psychopath with some astonishing footage that will be shown for the first time anywhere right here on America's Most Wanted! *. . ."*

Sam listlessly resumed watching TV with her chin in her hands. Her friends were acting like such fools. Look at them, standing up through the moon roof, whooping, hollering and dancing with that Serge guy, their hair blowing in the cool night wind below the skyscrapers.

"Hey, Sam," Paige shouted down through the opening in the roof. "Why don't you join us?"

"I'll take a rain check."

"*. . . In the next few moments, you will hear the actual voice and see real footage of the suspect from a chilling videotape seized by police in Miami. Pregnant women and those with heart trouble are asked to leave the room . . .*"

"Come on, Sam!" "Yeah, come on, Sam!" "Don't be a party pooper, Sam!"

"Oh, all right!"

Sam stood up and stuck her head through the moon roof as the image on the TV set switched to a thin, fortyish man sitting on a stool in front of a sky-blue portrait-studio backdrop. There was a banner over his head: SOUTH BEACH DATING SOLUTIONS.

An off-camera voice: "Ready anytime you are."

The man cleared his throat. "Hi. My name is Serge. Serge . . . uh . . . Yamamoto. And I'm looking for that special gal out there who enjoys quiet evenings, walks on the beach, fine wine, good conversation, fact-finding missions and exhaustive library research. . . . You must be fun-loving, have a sense of humor, an open mind, incredible stamina and experience at rapidly loading cameras and firearms under hectic conditions. . . . Smokers okay, no hard drugs. . . .

"I'm thirty-five, keep myself in reasonable shape. A spiritual army of one. No hangups that I'm comfortable talking about. Hobbies: genealogy, first editions, conch-blowing, my prize poinsettias, celestial navigation for the car, warning the populace about the impending social collapse. Scotch: Dewar's.

"Turn-ons: women who use big words, women who wear glasses, women who work in libraries and state forests, women who perform in theme park marine mammal shows, bedroom role-playing involving the first territorial congress.

"Turn-offs: women who react to big words like somebody cut the cheese, women who change the color of their hair, women who change the size of their breasts, women who want to change *you,* women who know the names of MTV personalities, women who go to bars in groups complaining about men while hoping to be approached by them.

"Turn-ons: growth-management plans, no-wake zones, the annual return of the white pelican, the tangy scent of the orange blossom, Spanish doubloons, Saltillo tiles, Marjory Stoneman Douglas.

"Turn-offs: the unexamined life, deep-well injection, people who call radio shows and say 'Mega dittos,' politicians who pretend to like NASCAR for votes, stupid Floridian jokes, stupid Floridians . . ."

Off-camera voice: "Okay, that's enough."

"I'm not finished."

"That was great. You'll do fine."

"But I have more to say. I have to present the whole picture."

"Please get up. We have to start filming the next guy."

"No!"

Two men appeared from behind the camera and approached. "Okay, buddy, on your feet."

Serge pulled a pistol from his waist and coldcocked one over the head, dropping him to the ground in front of the stool. He pointed the pistol at the other one, who raised his hands.

"Get back there and keep filming until I say to stop."

"You got it."

Serge tucked the gun away and sat back down, an unconscious man at his feet. ". . . So if you're searching for that special someone, if you're tired of the bar scene, generously misleading personal ads and blind dates that turn into restraining orders, look no further. . . ."

The limo beat a red light at Thirty-eighth Street, a tight cluster of people sprouting through the moon roof. "And there's the Chrysler Building," said Serge. "The spire contains the penthouse where Walter Chrysler once lived, lucky bastard, except he's dead. . . ."

Maria chugged a plastic glass of champagne and swayed. "Isn't he the best tour guide ever?"

Teresa blew a paper noisemaker, which unrolled and hit Sam in the side of the head.

After a quick series of stops on Serge's A-Tour of New York, the limo pulled up outside the GE Building. Serge jumped from the backseat. "To the Rainbow Room!"

They took the elevator to the exclusive bar on the sixty-fifth floor, facing the Empire State Building. "I saw them film Conan in this building. O'Brien, not the barbarian. And once I sat next to Katie Couric at the table right there. Scorcese opened his 1977 opus *New York, New York* in this room with Tommy Dorsey on the bandstand. . . . Let's go!" Serge heading for the elevators.

"We just got here," said Teresa.

"We just ordered," said Maria, holding up a full beer.

But Serge was off to the races. The women chugged a few sips and ran after him.

". . . And this is Sparks Steak House. Paul Castellano got whacked right there. . . . Back to the limo!"

They stopped at the corner of Broadway and Fifty-fourth; Serge ran down some stairs to a basement.

"And this is Flute, used to be a speakeasy. The acerbic writer Dorothy Parker came here all the time. Now that was a broad! Used to answer her phone: 'What fresh hell is this?'"

"I was just about to say that," said Sam. Teresa elbowed her.

"Back to the limo!"

"Slow down!" yelled Teresa. "Do you always move this fast?"

"No. When I'm alone, I move faster," said Serge. "Like when I came to see Conan last year. I arrived four hours early and still almost missed it. As usual, I built in a vast cushion of time because I always have a lot of anxiety that I'll be late. I didn't plan on the museums."

"The museums?"

"East side of Central Park, Museum Mile. You got the Met, the Frick Collection, National Academy of Design, the Museum of the City of New York, the Whitney, Cooper-Hewitt. I knew they were nearby. I just thought I had the willpower."

"But you just couldn't resist?" said Sam.

Serge nodded. "Which still wouldn't have been a time problem until I remembered the Museum of Natural History was on the other side of Central Park. That's where they have the Star of India, the world's largest sapphire, stolen in 1964 by flamboyant Miami Beach playboy Jack Murphy, portrayed by Robert Conrad in the delightfully campy *Murph the Surf.* After the arrests and a lot of negotiation, an anonymous phone tip led detectives to an outdoor bus locker in Miami, where the sapphire was recovered and later put back on display. The caper is so carved into my brain that I couldn't pass up an opportunity to see the gem in person. I made good time crossing Central Park to the museum, but then more trouble. To get to the gem room, you have to go through the Hall of Biodiversity. I really got hung up in there. Thousands of species on display, bacteria to great blue whales, phylums and families, marsupials, nocturnals, a rainbow of butterflies, blind fish from cold depths with no light, eels with scraggly teeth, bugs the size of your head, birds that can't fly, squirrels that can, some shit with webbed toes and all these eyes, something else with dangling prongs sticking out its forehead. Then the other rooms, ancient civilizations, Neanderthals, dinosaurs, geological forces, continental plates, the stars and the cosmos, and finally, the Big Bang Room. My time-management was shot; started looking bad for Conan. Then, complete panic. My consciousness was expanding, id shrinking, the exhibits making me feel utterly insignificant, that life was a mere flashbulb going off, and I had a sensation of falling, trouble breathing, and I realized what it was. All this knowledge and awareness—I was getting closer to God. Which can be stressful. Takes a lot of intellectual curiosity and courage, and also you'll get a bunch of heat from religious types because it involves evolution and science, which actually only points all the more to the existence of a deity, unfortunately not the kind you can use to boss others around. . . ."

"So did you see it?"

"See what?"

"The sapphire."

"Oh, the sapphire! Yes, I saw it. It was an unbelievable experience, the way the light breaks into six points across the oblate, azure surface. I got goose bumps. I was shaking so much I could barely hold the glass cutter steady."

"A glass cutter," said Rebecca, laughing. "What a riot!"

"Yeah, it was pretty funny. The guards had never heard that alarm before, and they didn't know what to do. Two ran head-on into each other. I was laughing so hard I couldn't finish getting through the glass. It's a lot thicker than you'd expect."

Maria tapped her watch. "Eleven o'clock."

"Right," said Serge. "We better get moving."

The chauffeur parked as close as he could to the blocked-off streets, and they all began walking west on Forty-sixth, working their way through the packed crowd to Times Square. They reached the corner of Seventh Avenue and looked up. In one direction, a twenty-foot cup of steaming ramen noodles. In the other, the lighted New Year's Eve ball.

"I'm hungry," said Maria.

"Me, too," said Rebecca. They went in a Sbarro's for pizza by the slice.

Except Sam. She withdrew. She stood outside the restaurant watching a sidewalk portrait artist with no customers working on a charcoal of Tina Turner.

Serge left the restaurant and stepped up beside her. She knew he would.

"You don't like me, do you?" he said.

Sam turned and looked him strong in the eyes. "I want you to leave my friends alone. I want you to start walking right now and keep going."

"What?"

"I know what you are. You've got a record somewhere, and if you stay I'll find it and turn you in. So get going!"

"That settles it," said Serge. "I'm in love with you."

"What?"

"I know what you are, too," said Serge. "Intelligence and confidence are always sexy in a woman."

Sam grabbed the back of his head and kissed him hard, then stepped back. "I have no idea why I just did that."

The other women came out of the restaurant with slices of pepperoni on paper plates, cheese stringing to their mouths.

"Where'd those two go?" asked Paige.

"Maybe we should go look for them," said Rebecca.

Teresa shook her head. "We'll lose our spot. We don't want to miss the ball drop."

Dick Clark was on TV, counting down.

Men's and women's clothes trailed across the carpet of the posh, dark room.

Serge was staying on the fifty-first floor of the Millennium Hotel. He was in bed, on top of Sam. Sam usually preferred the top, but Serge had flipped her with an illegal wrestling move. He reached beside the bed and yanked a cord, opening the curtains on the floor-to-ceiling windows. The night air was white with light, thousands of tiny people jamming Times Square far below.

Sam was a loud one.

"Oh yes! Oh no! Oh yes! Oh no! . . ."

"I like you, too," said Serge.

Sam reached up and grabbed him by the hair on the back of his head. "Oh my God! What are you thinking about? Tell me now!"

"The blooming of the tulips on Park Avenue, those little lamps in the New York Public Library, the lighting of the tree at Rockefeller Center, the playful audacity of the Guggenheim, the Babe, the Mic, Earl 'the Pearl,' Yoko, Prometheus . . ."

"Faster! Faster!"

Serge talked faster: ". . . The new Times Square, the Stork Club, the old Times Square, the Sunday *Times*, Black Tuesday, Blue Man Group, the '21' Club, the '69 Mets, *Breakfast at Tiffany's*, corned beef on rye, *My Dinner with André*, Restaurant Row, *King Kong*, Queen Latifah, Jack Lemmon, the Statue of Liberty, Son of Sam, the Sharks and the Jets, the Flatiron, 'Ford to City,' *Do the Right Thing*, 'Don't block the box' . . ."

"Oh my God! . . ."

"Here it comes," Dick Clark said on TV.

The ball began dropping outside, just over Serge's bouncing derrière, the mob down on the street counting down. *". . . Ten, nine, eight . . ."* Teresa leaned over to Paige as they watched the ball from the street. "Those two sure are going to be disappointed they missed this."

"*. . . Three, two, one . . . !*"

"I'm there!" screamed Sam, back arched and quivering.

Serge raised up and exploded: *"I did it my way!"*

"Happy New Year!" said Dick Clark.

33

The first day of the new year in Manhattan. Everyone hungover.

New York slowed to a crawl. The steam trays of oriental food in the corner convenience stores went untouched. Nothing selling except aspirin and stomach remedies. Others swore by ginseng. They sat on benches, trying to conserve movement, walking only when they had to, shuffling slowly through Times Square with the street sweepers.

Serge and Sam stepped over two people on the sidewalk in front of McHale's Café and continued up Forty-sixth to the Edison Hotel. They walked into the 1930s lobby, deco murals wrapping around the tops of the walls, Rockettes, *Twentieth Century Limited,* Bronx Bombers, Cotton Club.

"They said they'd meet us in the restaurant after they checked out of their rooms," said Sam. "Café Edison."

"I know the place well," said Serge. "Affectionately nicknamed the

Polish Tearoom, a simple yet culturally rich coffee shop for Broadway people in the know. Neil Simon's setting a play . . . Hey, there they are."

Four women waved from a table up front. Serge and Sam walked over. A waiter arrived with pancakes and eggs.

"Where did you two disappear to last night?" Teresa asked with a grin. They were all grinning.

"Knock it off," said Sam.

"We were beginning to worry you might not make it back in time for the train."

"Never a problem," said Serge. "I was keeping track of time."

"I thought you didn't want him along," said Paige.

"Yeah," added Rebecca. "We really don't know anything about him."

"Don't think I won't hit you," said Sam.

They poured syrup and sipped tomato juice.

"I'm impressed," said Serge. "You picked The Table."

"What table?" asked Teresa.

Serge looked around the group. "You don't know?"

They shook their heads.

"This is the table where Al Pacino shot those two guys in *The Godfather*. Remember when they taped the gun behind the toilet tank?"

"No way!" said Maria.

"Way!" said Serge. "Ask anyone." He waved at the waiter. "Didn't Pacino shoot those guys right here?" The waiter nodded.

The next thing the women knew, Serge was clutching an imaginary bullet wound in his neck with one hand, grabbing the tablecloth with the other, falling to the floor with all the dishes.

They were quiet for a time as they stood on the curb with their luggage, waiting for cabs.

"I've never been kicked out of a place before," said Teresa. "Taxi!"

Half the group got in the first one that stopped and headed for Penn Station. Serge flagged down a second and the rest got in. "Follow that cab! I've always wanted to say that."

The two taxis quickly covered the dozen blocks to Thirty-fourth.

"Here we are!" said Serge, helping the women out. The book club rolled luggage inside the building.

"You should have seen the original station, the historic one—they tore it down in 1963," said Serge, hand over his heart. "But there's a little silver lining. It produced a preservationist outcry. It's been said that Penn Station had to die so that Grand Central could live."

Their luggage wheels squeaked on the concourse. Serge rolled an overnight case and carried a box in his other arm.

"What have you got there?" asked Maria.

"This?" said Serge. "My trains."

"Your what?"

Serge stopped and opened the box.

"See? There's the engine, *The City of Miami*. They didn't actually have a model one, so I had to buy a Union Pacific and repaint it by hand. Took hours. And this is the Rambler. I'm really proud of that one. Built it from scratch, balsa wood and dowels and Dremel tools. Got the plans from historic collections in the Palm Beach Library. As long as you know the gauge conversion, which happens to be three-point-five millimeters to the foot, the rest is easy. These silver babies are the train we're walking toward. And you've got a hopper over here, a tanker, an old caboose, and a logging car that really tips sideways to dump its load. See the plastic logs?"

"When did you first get interested in trains?" asked Rebecca.

"Watching *Captain Kangaroo*. My favorite part of the show was a commercial. They had a train set on the soundstage, and the steam engine would come puffing out of a mountain, past Mr. Moose and Green Jeans and Bunny Rabbit, and stop and pour out a load of Rice Krispies from one of the cars."

"Those models are all quite nice," said Teresa. "But why bring them? Isn't actually riding on a real train enough?"

"No."

They resumed rolling luggage.

"They're going to build a new one," said Serge.

"New what?" asked Teresa.

"Penn Station. It's supposed to be an unbelievable piece of modern architecture—I've seen the models, and I can hardly wait! I saw the president's speech on C-SPAN during the dedication and took notes and committed it to memory: 'Whether you are a wealthy industrialist or just a person with a few dollars to your name, you can feel ennobled, as people did, in the old glass-and-steel cathedral that was Penn Station. People without tickets could come in the afternoon just to dream about what it would be like to get on the train.'"

The women noticed Serge wasn't walking with them anymore and looked back. Serge held up a hand as he composed himself. "I'll be okay."

Public announcements echoed through the station. Waves of people poured in from subway connectors. Overcoats and newspapers. Serge and the women continued until they got to the big train board and looked up. The letters and numbers clattered as they flipped over, updating arrivals. Three down from the top: "Miami . . . *Silver Stingray* . . . On Time . . . Track 12W."

"This way," said Serge. They took the escalator down to the departure platform. Ahead was a gleaming metal rocket, the pride of the Amtrak Corporation. They rolled luggage past the diesel and several silver cars until they came to the steps of their sleeper. The women climbed aboard; Serge stood in the doorway passing up luggage.

The BBB found their sleeping compartments, and Serge found his. He cranked down the upper bunk, cranked it up, flipped the sink open from the wall, flipped it back up, then down again just to be sure, flushed the toilet, hit the button for porter assistance, changed channels on the flat-screen TV, angled the vents up and down, left and right, adjusted the thermostat, cycled the reading and wall lights, turned on the radio, climbed into the overhead luggage compartment, let himself down, and finally clipped all his spy travel bags to the various handrails with spring-action mountain-climber D rings.

The porter showed up in the doorway. He had never seen a fully activated sleeping cabin before, TV and radio, lights, air, sink, toilet, Serge giving the upper bunk another quick up-and-down on the pulleys.

"Is everything okay?"

"Fine," said Serge. "Just a shakedown cruise."

"You hit the porter button?"

"It was a test. I'm happy to report your response time is excellent." Serge tucked a five in the porter's shirt pocket, then began unloading his box of trains on the floor. "That will be all."

When the porter was out of sight, Serge reached in his overnight bag and removed an egglike metal object wrapped in orange silk. "My ace in the hole." He stuffed the grenade in another cool storage nook.

More people headed for Track 12W. Tanner Lebos smiled and spread his arms wide when he spotted his old friend coming down the escalators.

"If it isn't that good-for-nothing Ralph Krunkleton!"

"Tan!" yelled Ralph. "There you are!"

They met in the middle of the platform and hugged and headed for *The Silver Stingray.*

"How you been?" asked Tanner.

"Never better."

"How'd the book signing go in Miami?"

"Raided by police."

"That's just Florida," said Tanner. "Some people exchanged fire at a Tom Clancy deal last month."

Out on Thirty-fourth, more cabs arrived. A woman in a floral dress got out, followed by a bunch of guys in blue velvet tuxedos. They stopped and looked up at the train station in befuddlement. The Pickpocket Comedian scratched his head. "But I thought you said we were going to play—"

"I know what I said!" snapped Spider. "There's been a big fuck-up, and I'm going to get to the bottom of it! C'mon!"

The BBB finished squirreling away possessions in their sleepers and headed out. They moved single file up the narrow aisle, hitting the automatic button that opened the door at the front of the car, passing through the connecting chamber, hitting another button, into the dining car. They grabbed a table and called the waiter. "What do you drink on a train?" asked Teresa.

"I don't know," said Sam. "A blue caboose?"

"What's that?"

"Whiskey and Irish Cream and something else, I think."

"Amaretto," said the waiter.

"Five blue cabooses," said Teresa.

"Don't look now," Rebecca whispered, "but I think that's Ralph Krunkleton."

"That's him, all right," said Maria.

"Doesn't look like the book photo," said Teresa.

"That was eleven years ago."

"He's shorter than I thought."

"I'm going to get his autograph," said Maria.

"It's too soon," said Sam. "Let him settle in. Don't embarrass us."

Ralph was joking around with his agent when a bunch of people climbed aboard. Tanner made the introductions. "Ralph, this is Preston Lancaster, also known as the Great Mez-mo, and Andy Francesco—you might have seen his stuff on *Showtime*—and Xorack the Mentalist . . ."

"Xolack."

"Sorry, *Xolack* the Mentalist, I can never keep that straight, and Spider—he juggles, quite good, too—and Dee Dee Lowenstein as Carmen Miranda." Tanner pointed at Bob Kowolski. "Of course you know Steppenwolf."

Ralph shook hands and smiled, wondering what he had gotten himself into. Tanner had told him he'd branched into live entertainment, but it didn't quite prepare him.

A new person with stringy long brown hair walked up. Tanner put his arm around the man's shoulders. "I have a surprise for you. Meet the newest member of your troupe, the drummer for ——."

Spider pointed at Steppenwolf. "We already got a musical act."

"I've decided to have them perform together as a super group."

Tanner turned to Ralph. "You're gonna get a chuckle out of this." He began pulling books from an overnight bag. "I found these when I went digging for bio material. They're your old novels. The jacket photos are a scream! Here's *B Is for Bongo*. Note the goatee and the fashionable suicidal look. And here's *Bad Trip*. What's with the flowers on that shirt? You look like you played tambourine in Herman's Hermits. . . . And here's *Murder at the Watergate*. Ralph, is that genuine polyester?"

The laughter finally subsided, and Spider stepped forward. "Mr. Lebos, I don't mean to sound ungrateful, but in your phone call, I thought you said we were going to play Carnegie . . ."

"Almost right," said Tanner. "The Carnegie *car*." He pointed up at a fancy brass sign on the bulkhead.

Preston turned to Spider. "That's even better! Who wants to play Carnegie when you can play the Carnegie *car*?"

"Shut up!"

"There's no slowing this career juggernaut now . . ."

"I said, shut up!"

". . . Next stop, the Hollywood Bowl . . . *public bus!*"

Spider grabbed Preston's collar, and there was a quick, wordless struggle in the aisle. A sleeve ripped.

"Break it up!" said Tanner. "We've got rehearsing to do."

Bruno Litsky cleared his throat. "Uh, Mr. Lebos. I'm still not clear on precisely what it is we're supposed to be doing."

"I'm not an actor," said Andy.

"I'm not even sure what a mystery train is," said Dee Dee.

"What's my motivation?" asked Frankie.

"All of you—relax or you'll give yourselves heart attacks," said Tanner. "Look at me. Who takes care of you? Huh?"

They stared at the floor and spoke in unison: "You do, Mr. Lebos."

"That's right!" said Tanner, holding up his briefcase. "Got your scripts right here. And the props."

"Scripts?"

"Props?"

Tanner nodded. "Fake guns, rubber knives, play money, stuff like that. Didn't you read Ralph's last book? I had some copy editors convert it to a script. You're going to perform it on the way to Florida, interact with the passengers. Do you have any idea how much money these people are paying for this? It's an incredible opportunity. If everything works out, we might even be talking cruise ships."

Preston nudged Spider. "The *Carnegie* ship."

"I'm warning you!"

Out on the loading platform, a train conductor in black slacks headed for Track 12W. He stopped at the front of *The Silver Stingray*, pulled a hundred-year-old gold Elgin pocket watch from his pants and flipped it open. He snapped it closed and returned it to his pants, then fit a conductor's hat on his head. "Allllllll aboard!"

Serge stepped up next to him. He wore his own souvenir conductor's hat and opened his own gold pocket watch. "Alllllll aboard! . . . *The Silver Stingray,* serving Dade City, Winter Haven, Delray Beach and *Coooo-ka-munnnnnga!*"

The conductor grabbed a handrail and climbed up. "I hate these fucking mystery trains."

In a rest room on the northwest side of Penn Station, Eugene Tibbs sat on a toilet in a locked stall with his knees and a silver briefcase tucked to his chest, the same position he'd been in for the last twenty-four hours. When the public address system announced final boarding for Miami, Eugene stretched out his legs. He slowly opened the stall door, looked both ways, then ran out of the rest room and across the station. He raced down the escalator and didn't stop until he had bounded up the steps of the train just as it started to move.

"Here come our drinks," said Teresa. The waiter placed five blue shots on the table.

"Cheers!"

The waiter held his empty tray to his stomach and Eugene Tibbs held the briefcase to his as they turned sideways and passed in the aisle. Eugene sat down at the last table in the car, his back to the wall.

Ivan and Zigzag were on day two of their stakeout at the SoHo loft. They were still on the same bench across the street, eating dollar hot dogs from a corner vendor, a pile of trash next to them, soda and coffee cups, bagel chip bags, lollipop wrappers. Growing impatience.

"We have to make a move," said Ivan. "It's now or never."

"You got mustard," said Zigzag.

Ivan touched the corner of his mouth with a paper napkin.

"Other side."

They headed across the street and up the stairs to the loft. Ivan picked the lock. They had begun sifting through the wreckage when Ivan saw the red light blinking on the answering machine. He pressed *play.*

The pair sprinted north on Eighth Avenue, pushing tailors to the ground, running through racks of clothes, Ivan yanking a mink stole off his face and throwing it over his shoulder, crossing Thirty-third Street, knocking over an elegant blonde in a strapless evening gown walking a tiger on a diamond-studded leash next to the luxurious new Mercury Sable with dual-stage air bags.

"Cut! Cut!"

They reached Thirty-fourth, down the stairs into the train station, looking around frantically, tracks to the left, tracks to the right . . .

"There he is!" yelled Ivan, pointing at Eugene Tibbs sprinting from the rest room to the escalators on the far side of the concourse.

Zigzag and Ivan bolted across the station. The train was already moving pretty good as they vaulted down the escalator, crashing into people, scattering luggage. Ten miles an hour, twelve, fifteen, the diesel engines roaring to life. They finally caught up with the last car, running alongside it as hard as they could, yelling and slapping the corrugated metal side, twenty miles an hour, still accelerating, gradually pulling away from the two men, who broke off pursuit and bent over and grabbed their knees, out of breath. When they looked up again, *The Silver Stingray* was a hundred yards down the snow-covered tracks, pulling away from New York's Pennsylvania Station for Florida, Serge waving from the back window.

Serge had his new digital camera ready, aimed out the window of the dining car, as the Philadelphia skyline came into view. Click, click, click. Running through to the lounge car in case it had a better vantage, taking pictures out windows along the way. Click, click, click . . .

That's when he saw it. He couldn't believe his luck. It was just sitting there in the aisle. A silver briefcase. It was next to a table full of people. Serge stayed cool, pocketing his camera. He scrunched down as he walked and dipped his left shoulder so his hand was at the same level as the briefcase handle. He snagged it without breaking stride and kept going, keeping the briefcase an inch off the floor as he moved away. When he was out of view, Serge brought the case to his hip and walked swiftly back to his sleeping compartment. He closed the door fast behind him, twisting the lock and pulling down the shades. He set the briefcase on the floor and tried the latches. He expected them to be locked, but they just flipped open. Serge broke into a broad smile. "We meet again!"

He raised the lid. His face changed.

"What the hell?"

He began removing plastic guns, plastic handcuffs, rubber knives, rubber candlestick holders, fake passports, packets of play money. He got to the bottom of the briefcase and removed a stack of stapled Xeroxes. He read the cover and riffled the pages.

"Scripts?"

Another skyline in the distance. *The Silver Stingray* pulled out of the Wilmington station, back into the snow. A bunch of guys in blue tuxes and Dee Dee Lowenstein stood in the aisle of the last sleeping compartment.

"We better find Tanner," said Spider. "We're supposed to go on in a few minutes and we still don't have our scripts."

They noticed for the first time that a large group of people had gathered behind them, suspiciously quiet. The performers looked at them. The people stared back and smiled. Some had notebooks and pencils out. One wore a T-shirt: "Mystery lovers do it by the book."

"This is creepy," said Preston. "Let's get out of here."

They went up to the next sleeping compartment and looked back. The doors opened and the group came in, slightly larger now. The performers headed for the next sleeper car. The group followed, picking up new members along the way. The performers walked faster; the crowd stayed with them. Preston hit a button and the automatic doors opened to the next car.

They were practically running when they reached the dining car. They turned around. The door in the back of the compartment opened, and in they came.

"Who the hell *are* they?" said Spider.

"What do they want from us?" said Andy.

Another voice: "There you are!"

They turned. It was their agent, Tanner Lebos, sitting at one of the tables with Ralph Krunkleton.

"Get over here!" Tanner bellowed, making an exaggerated waving gesture.

They approached the table. The crowd followed.

"I got your scripts right here . . ." Tanner's hand felt around next to the table but only found air. "Hold a sec."

Tanner stuck his head under the table, then came back up. "The scripts! They're gone!"

"Maybe you left them back in the sleeping car?" said Ralph.

"No, I'm sure," said Tanner. "I always know where that thing is—it's my favorite briefcase." Then Tanner started talking to himself, reenacting recent events. "Okay, I sat down, turned and put the briefcase right there, opened the newspaper . . ."

"There's got to be a simple explanation," said Ralph.

"No chance," said Tanner. "Something bizarre has happened. This is a real puzzle."

"Kind of like a mystery?" said Krunkleton.

Tanner glared. "Not now, Ralph." He went back to re-creating his morning. "Then I reached for the salt . . ."

An Amtrak porter walked through the sleeping compartment, knocking on doors. "Tickets. Check your tickets . . ."

He knocked on the number seven berth. "Tickets . . ."

"It's unlocked."

The porter opened the door and saw Serge sitting on the top bunk, legs dangling over the side, a conductor's hat on his head and an electric control box in his hands. On the floor, a miniature train chugged around a small oval of track.

"I need to check your ticket."

Serge pointed at the train. "It's coming around."

The porter bent over and plucked the ticket sticking out of the logging car as it went past his feet. He looked it over—"Thank you"—and stuck the ticket back in the logging car on its next pass. "Having a nice trip?"

Serge nodded without looking up from his controls. "Me ride big choo-choo."

"That's nice," said the porter, closing Serge's door. ". . . *Holy Jesus!*"

Back in the dining car, tables began filling up. Waiters set ice-water glasses on the linen and flipped open order pads. "Poached salmon or prime rib?"

"What are we going to do without scripts?" asked Frankie. "Look—they're already arriving."

"I got it," said Tanner. "You all have regular acts, right?"

They nodded.

"Do 'em," he said. "That'll hold us till tomorrow. We'll find the scripts and write it all in as back story."

Plates of fish and beef arrived. People buttered rolls. Preston and the others claimed the big rounded booth at the front of the car. When most of the people were finished eating, Tanner stood and tapped a glass of water with a spoon.

"May I have your attention. I want to thank you all for coming to this special production of *The Stingray Shuffle* . . ." Tanner paused until the clapping tapered off. "Since most of you have read the book, there really wouldn't be a whole lot of suspense. So we've played around with the story a little. The killer might not be who you think. And you'll definitely never guess who ends up with the five million dollars! With us tonight to bring the story to life are some of the finest entertainers in the business. Starting from my left, direct from Reno, Nevada, Frankie Chan and His Amazing Shadow Puppet Revue . . ."

The women at table number five ordered another round of blue cabooses.

"I'm having so much fun," said Maria. "This was a great idea."

"Where's Serge?" asked Rebecca.

"He'll show up sooner or later," said Teresa. "If I know him, there's no way he'll miss this."

". . . And finally," Tanner announced, "the reason all of us are here. The author of classics we've come to know and love—let's give a big hand for the one and only Ralph Krunkleton! . . . Ralph, stand up!"

Ralph stood self-consciously and waved to the applause. Baltimore went by the windows.

A half hour later, Frankie Chan was wrapping up his big finale, the St. Valentine's Day Massacre in hand shadows. The ovation was deafening. Frankie went back to the booth and bummed a cigarette.

"You hear that applause?" he said. "We should have been doing this from the start!"

"Who's up?"

"Dee Dee," said Spider.

Dee Dee Lowenstein took the stage and launched an uncanny rendition of "South American Way."

Serge walked up the center aisle of the dining car in a burgundy smoking jacket. "It's murder, I tell you! This man has been poisoned! Nobody leave the room!"

Dee Dee stopped singing and someone turned off her boom box. The audience began taking notes. Some filmed with camcorders. Serge pulled the script from his back pocket. "Wait a minute. There's no Carmen Miranda in this scene." He went back to the sleeping car.

Someone turned the music back on, and Dee Dee brought the house down with a medley from Carmen's Hollywood years.

The applause was off the meter. Dee Dee headed back to the rounded booth. The Washington Monument went by. "What a great room!"

"Preston, you're up."

The Great Mez-mo took the stage. "I need some volunteers."

Nobody responded. "You gals," said Preston, pointing at table number five. "Come on up here."

The women declined, but the audience was behind Preston: "Get up there!"

A few minutes later, Paige was scraping invisible poop off her shoe, Teresa said she swam out to naval carrier escorts, Sam quacked, and Rebecca begged Preston for his autograph.

Preston walked up to Maria.

"Are you a lesbian?"

"No," Maria said, trancelike.

He handed her a blow-up doll. "Then pretend this is one of the Baldwins."

The crowd roared.

Three hours later, Books, Booze and Broads were still in the dining car. They barely held a quorum.

"Where did the time go?" said Paige.

"Better yet, where did Rebecca and Sam go?" said Maria.

"I can guess where Sam is," said Teresa. "But Rebecca must have had some kind of luck we don't know about."

The Great Mez-mo closed the door behind him in his sleeping compartment. Rebecca looked around in wonderment. "I can't believe I'm actually in Brad Pitt's room!"

The next compartment: *"Oh yes! Oh no! Oh yes!"* Sam grabbed Serge by the back of the head. *"Oh God! Oh God! Tell me what you're thinking about! . . ."*

"The Great Train Robbery, The California Zephyr, The Wabash Cannonball, the Rock Island Line, Casey Jones, *Murder on the Orient Express,* the Atchison, Topeka and the Santa Fe, *Soul Train . . ."*

Ivan and Zigzag listened to Jimmy Cliff on the stereo of an orange '72 Dodge Charger. Zigzag rocked slowly with the rhythm, but Ivan wasn't convinced.

"What's so great about this music? It just makes me antsy."

"You need to learn how to relax, *mon.*"

It was after midnight. Ivan changed lanes, passing some farm equipment infarcting the southbound side of Interstate 95. They drove under a big green sign. Richmond, ¼ mile. Ivan took the exit ramp; Zigzag unfolded a map and navigated through the city to the train station. They skidded up to the curb and ran through slush to the Amtrak window.

"Two tickets to Miami, *The Silver Stingray.*"

"It's sold out," said the clerk.

"What about cancellations?" asked Ivan. "Standby?"

"Doesn't matter," said the ticket man, pointing down the tracks. "It just left."

"Why didn't you tell us in the first place?"

The pair dashed out of the depot and jumped back in the Charger. Zigzag pulled the map from under his seat and flicked a lighter to see. "What now?" asked Ivan.

"We might be able to get on in Fayetteville, or maybe Charleston."

"You heard the man. It's sold out."

"That's never stopped me and Louise here," said Zigzag, producing a shiny .380 automatic from the glove compartment.

"We can't just go in there blazing! We don't know where he is on the train. If we cause any commotion at all, he might jump off and we'll never see the money."

"You got a better idea, *mon*?"

"Well, if we try to get on at a depot, we risk problems from the Amtrak people, and they're the last ones you want to mess with. Plus, the train will be stopped, so it's easier for him to hop off. Which means we'll have to get on the train between cities, while it's moving. It's the only way we can . . ." Ivan stopped and stared at Zigzag, who was lighting a joint the size of a bowling pin.

"What the hell do you think you're doing?"

"Hopping on board the ganja train."

"Look at the size of that fucking thing!" Ivan glanced around in traffic to see if there were any cops. "Are you nuts?"

Zigzag exhaled, a small cloud enveloping their heads. "You're the one who wants to jump on a moving train."

"It's possible."

"It's suicide."

"I'm not talking about shooting ourselves out of a cannon at the thing. There are ways to trim risk. I just haven't figured out the right method yet."

Zigzag grinned. "I have an idea, *mon*."

The sleeping berths were wide enough for sex, if you had the right motivation. But there wasn't remotely room for a couple to sleep together.

Serge was in the top bunk, Sam on the bottom. She had fallen off fast after the lovemaking, but Serge was still wide open. He was way too wound up from being on a train. Plus, Sam snored like a lumberjack.

A little after two in the morning. Serge lay on his back, head propped with two pillows, looking sideways out the window as *The Silver Stingray* rolled through the backside of Virginia, rhythmic clacking, a faint train whistle ten cars up, then the crossing guard, the red-and-white bar across the road, caution lights flashing above a metal sign with buckshot dents, two pickups waiting on the other side of the gate. America was on the move, and it was moving away from the train tracks. Serge saw what was left behind, the late-night scenes repeating, Virginia becoming North and South Carolina. Raleigh, Southern Pines, Hamlet, Camden. Crime light, barbed wire, warehouses and liquor stores, alleys, a flashlight in the face of someone pulled over by police, then another tiny train depot from the 1940s hanging on for life, bleary travelers under the cantilevers. Serge hit radio buttons until he found jazz. Perfect. Watching America go by. Homeless people rubbing hands over oil-drum flames to the melancholy of Thelonious. He got out his new digital camera and rested it on his stomach, switching on the tiny monitor, replaying scenes from the last twenty-four hours. The gray Philly switching yards, the Maryland slums, the upscale parks in D.C., the Marine Corps hangar with the president's helicopter, the blur of a freight train passing the other way, a citadel, a rocky trout stream, a riverboat, a carnival, a fire station, a little girl with pigtails skipping rope in front of a church, a restored Victorian home in an anonymous town with train tracks running down the center of Main Street, and everywhere, smiling Americans waving back at the train like a Ford truck ad. Serge finally came to the last picture in the camera's memory and stopped: An old guy with a long white beard standing next to the tracks in the middle of nowhere, operating a big Hasselblad camera on a tripod, taking a picture back at Serge, his own future.

A loud scream startled Serge, and he bonked his head on the ceiling. It was Sam. "You bastard!"

Serge hung his head over the side of the bunk. "What'd I do?"

"You bastard!" she yelled again, talking in her sleep. There were more words, but he could only make out a few of them, and most of those were *bastard*. Then something about final exams.

"What year is it?" asked Serge.

"1973."

She twisted violently, a few more *bastards,* then: *"It's our secret, girls."*

"What's your secret?" asked Serge.

The sunrise sparkled through the trees as *The Silver Stingray* rolled into the quiet South Carolina morning. There was still a cover of snow, but now patches of ground poked through.

A bunch of tuxedos sat around the booth in the front of the dining car.

"Tanner find the scripts yet?" asked Andy.

Spider shook his head.

Dee Dee came back from the rest room.

"Hey! Who ate one of my bananas?"

An empty peel sat in front of Preston.

Dee Dee snatched her hat off the table. "If I ever catch you doing that again, I'll fuckin' kill you!"

Passengers at nearby tables perked up. They put down their forks and began writing in notebooks.

The BBB walked forward through the sleeping compartment.

"Is it me, or does this train seem to be going faster?" asked Teresa.

"Feels the same," said Maria. "The important question is why Rebecca won't tell us where she disappeared to last night. And why she's grinning so much."

"I just had a dream, that's all."

"What kind of dream?"

"A Brad Pitt dream. We'll leave it at that."

The BBB left the sleeper and entered the dining car. The people having breakfast turned around and applauded.

"You were great last night," said a woman in a sun hat.

"They didn't tell us more cast members would be hidden among the passengers," said her husband. "What a performance!"

"What are you talking about?" said Teresa.

"I got it all on video if you want to see."

"We do," said Sam.

They crowded around. The man adjusted the tiny crystal screen on his camcorder and played back Preston's hypnosis show. Sam quacking, Paige scraping her shoe and so on. The BBB began to boil as they watched. But it was nothing compared to Maria's reaction when she saw herself with the blow-up doll.

"I'll kill the son of a bitch! Who's got a gun?"

Passengers took more notes.

Suddenly, yelling and a struggle at the front of the car.

Dee Dee had demanded an apology about eating from her hat, and Preston had told her to go fuck herself with one of her precious bananas. Andy and Spider had to separate them. Passengers scribbled furiously.

"Preston, enough's enough!" said Frankie. "Sometimes it's just not funny anymore. Like back in Bridgeport when that mob chased us out of *Private Ryan*. I was ready to strangle you with my bare hands."

More writing in notebooks.

The book club marched angrily up the aisle, ready to read Preston the riot act. A woman in a red dress pushed by them and stormed to the front of the car.

"Preston?"

He turned around. "Yes?"

"You don't remember me, do you?" said the woman.

Preston squinted at her face. "Should I?"

"Albuquerque."

"Let's see . . . Albuquerque, Albuquerque . . . oh, *Albuquerque!* I remember now. Wait, don't help me . . ."—snapping his fingers—". . . Helen, Helga, Heloise . . ."

"Betty."

"I was just about to say Betty."

"I finally tracked you down, you worm! How dare you take advantage of me like that!"

"Take advantage of you how?"

"Hypnotizing me to think you were Brad Pitt so I'd have sex with you!"

"*Moi?*"

"You!" said the woman, pulling a gun from her purse and pointing it at Preston.

Some passengers ran out of space and had to break out new notebooks.

"Hold on a second! I can explain! I, I was trying to help you . . ."

"Help me! How was that helping me?"

"You obviously have a problem with men . . ."

Mistake.

Just before she pulled the trigger, Spider grabbed her arm, and the bullet flew out an open window. Andy and Frankie helped wrestle the woman to the ground, kicking and screaming.

Preston looked around with a fake grin. "Those blanks sure sound real!"

They got the gun away and hog-tied the woman with Andy's belt and waited to hand her over to authorities at the next stop.

The BBB looked at each other.

"Did she say 'Brad Pitt'?" asked Rebecca.

"Yes, she did," said Sam.

"Something's not kosher in Denmark," said Teresa.

"You used me!" the woman screamed from the floor. "You made it so every time I heard the word *harmonica,* I'd think you were Brad Pitt."

Rebecca began jumping up and down. "Look, it's Brad Pitt!"

"The trigger word is probably a toggle," Sam told Teresa. She grabbed the shrieking Rebecca by the arm. "*Harmonica!*"

Rebecca stopped jumping up and down. "Why are you holding my arm, Sam?"

"I think we need to have a talk."

The women stood in the aisle explaining things to Rebecca. Rebecca's head shook side to side. The other women nodded. Rebecca shook her head harder. The others nodded sadly.

Rebecca broke from the group and ran to the front of the car. "Wait!" yelled Teresa.

Too late. "Did you have sex with me last night while I was under hypnosis? I'll kill you if you did!"

"*Moi?*"

One passenger leaned to another. "That Preston's finished."

The second passenger nodded, still writing. "Too many enemies, plenty of motive. Now it's just a matter of creating the opportunity for murder."

The train slowed at the next depot. Only a few little patches of snow left. The Savannah police boarded and carried off the woman in the red dress, still kicking and screaming. "I'll kill you, you bastard! I'll cut your fucking dick off if it's the last thing I do!"

A passenger turned to a fresh page in her notebook. "This is the best mystery train I've ever been on."

36

The dining car began filling up again shortly after noon.

Waiters circulated, dropping off drinks, opening order pads. "Chef's salad or Caesar?"

It was a sunny day on the train; warm light poured into the dining car through the glass skydome.

Serge was sitting with the book club. "Chef's salad," he told the waiter. "Extra dressing on the side. Double-chop the lettuce. That is all." He still hadn't seen any sign of Eugene Tibbs. Surely he hadn't missed the train.

Paige pointed out the window. "Palm trees!"

They crossed the Florida state line as Tanner Lebos stood and clinked a glass of water with a spoon again, signaling the official start of the author's luncheon.

"Thank you once again and welcome." He shook his head and chuckled for effect. "This already has been quite an action-packed trip to say the least. And we have one person to thank for that! The author who thought all this up, Ralph Krunkleton!"

The audience began applauding. Ralph didn't know what the hell Tanner was talking about. He had no idea what was happening—this was the craziest damn train he'd ever been on.

Passengers began standing up, five, ten, twenty, until it was a solid standing ovation.

"Speech!" someone yelled.

"Don't worry," said Tanner. "The problem will be shutting him up."

Everyone laughed.

Ralph stepped into the aisle, and the crowd quieted.

"First, I'd like to thank the best agent money can buy."

More laughter. Tanner pointed at Ralph and smiled: Ya got me!

"Seriously. What a weird business. What a weird *life*. I still haven't figured it out. I'm getting to associate with a better class of people by writing about a worse class of people."

More laughs.

"But I'm glad to see the mystery genre finally getting its due. For the longest time, people automatically thought there was no meaning. That's simply not true. In my case, I'm on an internal journey, the crime plot just a pretext for me to explore the spiritual side of existence. Like when I used the urinal guy as a metaphor for Christ . . ."

The audience looked puzzled.

". . . pure humility, serving others," said Ralph. "And the tribulations of the people developing the first orange harvester are straight from the Twenty-third Psalm. I also borrowed some Eastern elements of cleansing and rebirth for the reunion of that women's book club after all those lost years . . ."

The audience exchanged glances. Were they reading the same books? Tanner saw what was happening; he gave Ralph a slashing gesture across his throat with an index finger.

Ralph saw him and nodded.

". . . Uh, and then I killed a whole bunch of people."

"Hooray!" the audience yelled.

Tanner stood up and slapped his hands together. "What do you say we sign some books?"

The passengers quickly formed a line in the aisle.

Ralph's little speech had been especially comforting to Serge. So he'd been right all along about the religious imagery in the book—it wasn't just more hallucinations. "After you," he told the BBB, who got up from the table and joined the autograph line. Then Serge stood and bumped into someone who didn't recognize him.

"Excuse me," said Eugene Tibbs.

The line began working its way down. The BBB finally made it to the front, and they heaped on the praise. "Your books have changed our lives," said Teresa.

Ralph blushed. "Maybe that's exaggerating a little."

"No, it isn't," said Maria. "What a path of self-discovery!"

"*Ahhhh,*" said Ralph, nodding with satisfaction as he signed his name. "So you got my spiritual message."

Teresa shook her head. "No, we went to all the bars. They were great!"

Next, a book critic from Miami.

"Oh, hi, Connie," said Ralph, opening her book and writing. "Don't you think you were a little hard on me in your last review?"

"It was more than fair. That one character you have who can never seem to score—he's overstayed his welcome."

Ralph finished signing and handed the hardcover back to her. "How'd you like me to pair you up with him in a book?"

"Ha, ha. Very funny."

Next, Eugene Tibbs. He pumped Ralph's hand. "I've been wanting to meet you for a long time. Your writing has completely changed my life."

Ralph began signing his name. "Maybe that's a stretch."

"No, it's true," said Eugene. "I've patterned my entire existence after your last book. I took every one of your lessons and put them into daily practice."

Ralph looked up, confused.

Eugene patted his chest. "I'm the urinal guy."

"Ohhhh, that's great! Thank you!" said Ralph, looking back down to finish his autograph. "You got my spiritual message."

"No," said Eugene. "I made a bundle in tips."

Serge was next.

"Great book."

"Thanks."

"Especially the spiritual message."

Ralph looked up. "What?"

"Your spiritual message."

"You actually got it?"

"Are you kidding?" said Serge. "The imagery was so vivid I could practically reach out and touch it. Screaming souls burning in a lake of fire. Drooling beasts ripping bowels out of the righteous, then avenging angels of the Lord chopping their heads off with big swords. A horrible blackness descending over the land. People running naked in terror, falling off cliffs and onto tall spikes. Manic little horned trolls scurrying about, slashing tires and sodomizing family pets . . ."

Tanner gently grabbed Serge by the arm. "Would you mind stepping aside? We need to keep the line moving."

"Oh, sure. Sorry."

Tibbs had retaken his seat at the back table, enjoying dessert and admiring the inscription in his book. Serge sat up front, keeping tabs on Tibbs in his peripheral vision.

Shouting broke out up front. Notebooks opened.

Spider bounced around in the aisle, throwing left hooks in the air.

"I know what you're thinking—'Just because he only has one arm, I'll bet he can't play the banjo!'"

"Who said anything about a banjo?" asked Preston.

"Okay, well maybe I *can't* play the banjo, but I can still kick your ass! . . ."

One of the passengers pointed with a pencil at Spider's right arm tucked behind his back. "Now *that's* acting!"

"*Hic,*" said Preston. "Dammit, now you gave me the hiccups . . . *hic* . . ."

"Breathe in a paper bag," said Andy.

"Drink water upside down," said Dee Dee.

"Pull your earlobes and swallow," said Spider.

"Boo!" said Steppenwolf.

Hic.

"I can cure hiccups," offered Serge.

"Who are you?"

"Just a passenger. But I've studied this phenomenon for years, purely on an avocational basis, of course. All the cures you've mentioned are simply power of suggestion. The actual mechanics have nothing to do with it. It's what you believe. So, Preston, do you want to get rid of your hiccups?"

"It's worth—*hic*—a try."

"Okay, focus on my voice. I want you to relax. Your muscles are getting loose. That's better . . ."

"*Hic.*"

"Don't worry about that last hiccup. The sound was a mile away. There will be a few more, but they don't concern you. Each hiccup is one less until they end. Picture each hiccup being typed on a piece of paper as it comes out of your mouth, then mentally wad up the sheet and throw it away . . ."

When Preston was completely relaxed, Serge leaned forward and whispered in his ear. Then he sat back and clapped his hands sharply, startling Preston.

"*Hic* . . . I still have the *hic* hiccups."

"Not for long," Serge said with a grin.

In the back of the car, Eugene Tibbs finished his dessert and got up to head back to the sleeping compartment. This was the moment Serge had been waiting for—getting Tibbs alone, away from the herd.

"Good luck with those hiccups," said Serge, standing and heading down the aisle after Tibbs.

"Everybody, look!" a passenger yelled in the middle of the car. They all turned to the window on the west side of the train.

"Unbelievable!"

Mild pandemonium as a crowd jammed the center of the car for a better view of the spectacle, blocking the aisle and Serge's only path to Tibbs. Fifty disposable cameras pointed out the window.

"What a mystery train!"

.   .   .

Zigzag and Ivan slowly but surely gained on the train. They had ditched their Charger in Ocala, even though Ivan told Zigzag his plan would never work. Now it was looking like they just might pull it off.

"There she is!" yelled Ivan, spotting a train emerging from around a distant bend in a palm hammock.

"Giddy-up!" yelled Zigzag, snapping his reins.

"How'd you know Ocala raises some of the fastest thoroughbreds in the country?" asked Ivan.

"Made a killing on one in the Derby."

It was a beautiful picture, the two horses—a brown-and-white filly and a pure black stallion—striding majestically, hooves thundering across the hot Florida scrubland, gaining on *The Silver Stingray*.

"They shoot horse thieves, don't they?"

"Not anymore," said Zigzag. "Come on, we're nearly there."

More passengers rushed to the middle windows of the dining car, pouring in from the sleeper and coach, lifting children up and pointing.

"Have to admit, this was a great idea," said Ivan.

"The beauty of it is stealth," said Zigzag. "There's no way in the world anyone will detect our approach."

The horses finally caught *The Silver Stingray*, and Ivan and Zigzag put the crop to their steeds. They gradually moved up the side of the train toward the break between the dining car and the first sleeper, passing a giant window filled with faces stacked three high, taking pictures and filming home videos.

Zigzag was in front. He reached with his left hand for the railing, two feet away, closing slowly. "Almost there." One foot, six inches. "Allllllll-most . . . Got it!" He grabbed the rail firmly and leaped from the horse to the tiny platform, the filly peeling off to the side and stopping. Ivan came up next. Zigzag reached out. "Give me your hand!"

Ivan strained, their fingertips inches apart. Zigzag saw the Russian's eyes grow large. "What is it?"

Several passengers looked sideways out the window and pointed ahead in horror.

"Tunnel!"

"Grab my hand!" said Zigzag.

"I can't!"

"You have to!"

Ivan whipped the reins a last time. Their fingertips touched, then parted, then touched again. Zigzag snatched Ivan's hand and jerked him out of the saddle. The stallion hit the brakes. They were in the tunnel.

Zigzag felt around in the dark. He unhooked an emergency entrance in the side of the connector between the cars, and they climbed through.

"Now if we can just slip inside without anyone noticing," said Ivan.

The tunnel still provided cover of darkness as they opened the back door of the dining car and quietly crept inside. They came out of the tunnel, light again. A carful of people was staring at them. Cheering erupted.

"This is definitely the best mystery train I've ever been on!"

"How can it possibly get any better?"

A woman let loose a bone-chilling scream.

Everyone turned. The screaming woman was up front, standing over a body in the middle of the aisle.

Preston.

"Someone must have killed him in the tunnel!"

"But who?"

*T*wo *crooked lines of cocaine* wound across the instrument panel, just above the pressure gauges in the red zone. They were vacuumed up by the empty fuselage of a ballpoint pen.

The engineer stood straight again and wiggled his nose, then pinched it closed to get membrane action. "We're not going fast enough . . . must go faster." He pushed a lever forward.

A crowd had gathered around the body in the dining car.

"I don't think he's acting."

"Of course he is."

"It's been five minutes."

"I've seen human statues in New York go for hours."

"He's really good."

Ivan and Zigzag wasted no time. The element of surprise was gone, but the train was still moving. They checked the schedule. Ten minutes until the Okeechobee depot. Ten minutes to find Tibbs or he could jump off with the briefcase. They worked quickly through the sleeping compartment, knocking on doors. "Tickets! . . ."

Serge tiptoed into the car behind them and peeked around the corner.

Eugene Tibbs heard a knock and opened his door. There was no nonsense. Zigzag tackled him and Ivan stuck a gun in his mouth. "The briefcase! Now!" Tibbs pointed up at the overhead rack. Zigzag pulled it down.

A voice from behind: "I'll take that, if you don't mind."

They turned around. Serge stood in the doorway with an even bigger gun. They handed him the briefcase.

"Thanks." Serge slammed the compartment door shut and took off.

Zigzag and Ivan ran out the door, and Serge took a shot at them from down the hall. They dove back in Tibbs's compartment.

Passengers in the dining car heard gunfire, took notes.

Ivan and Zigzag poked their heads back into the hallway. Clear. The Russian pointed to the back of the car. "You go that way!"

They checked everywhere, but no Serge. Zigzag tried to find his sleeping compartment. He knocked on doors and came to one that was locked with no answer. He gave it his shoulder. The door popped open. He tore through luggage. Nope. Belonged to a couple from Kalamazoo. Three more doors down, no answer, also locked. He gave it the shoulder again. The door popped easily. It swung open and hit a switch on a small control box on the floor. Zigzag heard a little train whistle as a toy locomotive began to chug around a small circle of track on the floor.

Zigzag smiled as the train stopped at the loading dock in front of his feet, the logging car automatically tipping out its load: several plastic logs and an unpinned grenade whose handle had been wedged in the car. The handle sprang off as the grenade wobbled a few inches and bumped into Zigzag's toes.

"Uh-oh."

The explosion rocked *The Silver Stingray* all the way to the dining car. Passengers wrote faster. Others were still timing how long Preston could remain motionless.

Ivan spotted Serge sneaking out the front door of the first sleeping compartment. He ran after him. As Ivan passed through the connector between the cars, he noticed the emergency door was unlatched. He stuck his head out the side of the train and looked up a ladder.

Back in the dining car: "How long has it been?"

"Ten minutes."

"Do you think we should poke him or something?"

They heard pounding and banging overhead and looked up through the clear skydome. Two men wrestled on the roof with a metal briefcase, rolling this way and that, legs swinging precariously over the edge of the train as it headed across the Indian River on an old steel-girder trestle. One man socked the other in the face; the other punched back. They rolled over again. Another punch. The briefcase went skidding away from both of them, sliding across the glass roof.

Ivan and Serge rolled over a couple more times until they came to the edge of the car. Ivan was on top, his hands around Serge's throat, Serge's head hanging back over the side of the roof and turning blue. Ivan reached his right hand back and slugged Serge in the face. Then he unsnapped his shoulder holster, pulled out a pistol and pressed it to Serge's forehead. Serge grabbed it by the barrel and pushed it up; a shot flew into the sky. It became a battle of arm strength, the barrel of the gun slowly moving back down toward Serge's face.

The train rumbled across the trestles, the vibrating briefcase sliding left and right across the roof. A hand reached down and grabbed it by the handle. The passengers pointed up through the glass at two new feet walking toward the pair of struggling combatants.

Ivan was winning the war of muscles, and the barrel of the gun reached Serge's face again. Ivan pressed it between his eyes. "You lose." He began squeezing the trigger.

Wham.

The briefcase slammed into the side of Ivan's head. He flew off Serge and rolled in disorientation and pain. The gun fell over the side of the train and clanged off bridge beams on the way down.

Suddenly, the air was full of green paper, countless hundred-dollar bills swirling into the sky. Serge and Ivan looked up at the money, then at Sam standing over them, holding the handle of the flapping, empty briefcase. The pair crawled to the side of the car and got down on their stomachs to look over the edge of the train's roof, watching in shock as the money gently fluttered down to the river and began floating toward the ocean.

They crawled back from the edge of the car and stood up. Serge pointed at the open case still in Sam's hand. "What'd you do that for?"

"He was going to kill you!"

Serge and Ivan looked at each other and shook their heads. "Women." They walked to the back of the roof and climbed down the ladder. Wild cheers erupted again as they entered the rear of the dining car. People shook their hands and slapped their backs. The drummer for —— walked up. "I couldn't come through." He handed Serge forty-three dollars.

The train approached the Okeechobee station. Teresa looked out the window. "We're not slowing down."

"What?" said Maria.

"We're supposed to stop at this depot. We won't be able to at this speed."

She was right. The train blew right past the depot and the confused people on the platform.

"Was that supposed to happen?" asked Maria. "Maybe because the mystery program's sold out?"

"Can't be," said Teresa. "They also handle parcels."

"Do you think something's wrong with the engineer?"

"We *are* going faster," said Teresa.

The women made their way forward. When they got to the back of the engine, they found the train's staff already on the case. They were trying to radio the engineer, but no answer.

"Why don't you force your way in?" asked Teresa.

"We can't," said one of the staff. "You can only get into the engine from the outside. Prevents interference."

"What about a backup guy?" said Rebecca. "In case of a heart attack or something?"

"That would be me," said the staffer.

"But then why aren't you up there? What are you doing back—"

"Look, I'm already in enough trouble."

. . .

A man and his young son crouched in the woods just before sunset, out where Palm Beach County meets the Everglades. Their eyes focused on the train tracks a few yards away, a tight bend just past the clearing where Pratt & Whitney tests its jet engines. A shiny new Lincoln penny sat on one of the rails.

"Why are we doing this, Daddy?"

"To get a flat penny."

"What for?"

"Because it's fun!"

A train whistle blew in the distance. "Here she comes! Get down!"

The pair crouched and waited, the train growing closer. It was in sight before they knew it, nothing but a blur as it entered the bend and hit the penny. There was a harsh grinding of metal. The father and son watched in astonishment as *The Silver Stingray* jumped the tracks and twenty cars jackknifed down the embankment toward the swamp.

"Daddy? Did we do that?"

"How'd you like some ice cream?"

A *half* *hour* *after* *sundown,* flashlights split the darkness, wisps of smoke. The crew worked its way through the train lying on its side halfway down the embankment to the swamp. They came to the dining car, but the door was jammed and blocked by twisted metal. The crew banged on it. "Is everyone all right in there?"

"We're fine," a passenger yelled back. "Just some scrapes."

"I think Preston's dead," yelled someone else. "But I think he was dead before. We're not sure."

"Everyone stay calm." An emergency generator came on, then backup lights. The car was a mess, but it could have been much worse.

"Yep, we're sure now," the passenger yelled again. "Preston's really dead."

"Did you poke him?" yelled the crew member.

"Twice."

"Stay put," he shouted. "We'll get you out, but it's going to take a while. We have to cut through some big pieces of metal out here, and we only have a hacksaw."

"What about the authorities? Won't they send someone when we don't show up?"

"Sure," yelled the crew member. "But the remoteness of our location and the trickiness of the terrain complicate it a little. Also, we don't really have an excellent on-time record, so they might not notice for a few more hours. But immediately after that, they'll be right here."

A naked, sobbing book critic from Miami wrapped herself in a towel and ran from the sleeping compartment to the dining car, followed by Johnny Vegas. "What's the matter, baby? It's just a little derailment."

The train lurched a few feet as soil gave way on the embankment; passengers fell over. It was still again. People uprighted chairs in the diner and sat down on the left wall, bracing for a long wait.

"Nobody leave this car!"

They looked up. Serge strolled through the wreckage in his burgundy smoking jacket. He stopped next to Preston's body.

"Someone murdered this man!" He turned around slowly. "And that someone is still in this room!"

The crew member banged on the door again. "I heard shouting. What's going on in there?"

"Someone's trying to solve a mystery," yelled a passenger.

"Jesus! We just derailed! Don't you people know when to quit!"

Serge paced and scanned faces. "Preston had accumulated quite an impressive list of enemies . . ."

"You!" he yelled, spinning and pointing at Dee Dee Lowenstein, holding a fruit hat in her lap. "Dozens of people heard you threaten Preston's life."

"I didn't mean it. It was just a stupid banana."

"You had motive and opportunity. People saw you near Preston when we went in the tunnel. . . . But you weren't the only one." Serge resumed pacing, looking people in the eye. He spun again.

"You're the one they call Spider! He humiliated you time and time again! . . . And you, Frankie Chan. He almost got you killed in Bridgeport!"

"But we didn't murder him!"

Serge nodded thoughtfully. He took a few more steps and stopped in front of the BBB.

"What are you looking at us for?" said Sam.

"You know why. You *all* know why," said Serge.

"What are you talking about?"

"The brochure for the mystery train that first got you interested in the trip—the name of one of the celebrity guests caught your attention."

Teresa nodded. "Ralph Krunkleton. We love his books."

"That's what you'd like us to believe," said Serge, then raised his voice dramatically: "But in fact the person you came to see was not Ralph Krunkleton at all, but Preston Lancaster!"

The women recoiled in their seats.

"Why would we want to see him?" said Maria.

"Because he got all of you pregnant at the University of Florida twenty-five years ago before fleeing to Nevada. *Isn't that true!*"

The women were speechless.

"That's how all of you got together in the first place!" said Serge. "It's the common factor that explains why a club would consist of such completely different—though unquestionably lovely—personalities."

"That's crazy!" scoffed Teresa.

"Is it?" said Serge.

"Where'd you get such a ridiculous idea?" said Rebecca.

"Sam talks in her sleep."

Four heads turned. "Sam!"

"I didn't know I talked in my sleep."

"We never intended to kill him!" said Rebecca. "We were just planning to confront him after all these years and embarrass him publicly. Sam wanted to kick him in the nuts, but that was it! I swear!"

"Maybe that was the plan, but when he picked you for hypnosis volunteers, everything went haywire," said Serge. "You never expected that, did you? But you had to go through with it or he'd get suspicious.

And guess what, Rebecca? He did it to you *again*! You were fit to be tied when you found out about Brad Pitt!"

"But not mad enough to commit murder!"

Serge walked away from the women, back to the center of the car. "So we have a whole roomful of people who had a bone to pick with Preston—all with ample opportunity. The question is, which one of you acted on that opportunity?"

A chorus of denials filled the overturned train car.

The train lurched another foot. Everyone shut up and grabbed something for balance. They waited a moment until they were sure it had stopped.

"All your protests will be moot in a few moments," said Serge. "I have irrefutable proof as to the identity of the killer."

Heads looked back and forth; suspicion everywhere. Serge walked to one of the passengers with a camcorder, the same one who had taped the hypnosis show with the BBB.

"May I?" asked Serge.

The man handed over the videocamera.

"You were filming when we went into the tunnel, is that not true?"

"Yes, but I wasn't filming Preston—I was shooting out the window at the two guys on horseback. Besides, it was completely dark in the tunnel."

"Doesn't matter," said Serge. "All we need is sound."

Serge rewound the tape, turned up the volume and hit *play*. Everyone crowded around and watched the tiny screen.

"Here they come," said Serge, the Russian and the Jamaican approaching the train on the monitor. "And here's where they jump to the train . . . and now the critical part . . ."

Serge turned the volume way up. "Listen carefully."

Nobody made a sound; the screen went black.

". . . *Hic* . . . *hic* . . . *hic* . . . (Thud)."

Serge turned off the camcorder. "And there you have it!"

Everyone looked puzzled. "There we have what?" said Spider.

"The identity of the killer," said Serge. "My guess is someone planted a hypnotic suggestion to get rid of his hiccups. He was probably given instructions for his soul to leave his body and take the hiccups with him. He had a heart attack, just like in 1894, when that hypnotist accidentally killed his assistant onstage the same way."

"That's right," said Frankie Chan. "Preston talked about that case all the time back in Reno. He swore it was true."

Serge addressed the whole car: "Find the person who hypnotized Preston to get rid of his hiccups, and you've got your killer."

"But that was you," said Frankie. "I heard you. I was sitting right there."

"I guess that settles it," said Serge. "It was me."

"Bullshit," said Andy. "You can't hypnotize someone to death!"

"I also sort of broke his neck, just to be careful," said Serge. "But I'm sure it was the hypnosis. I'm getting pretty good at it."

The BBB stared at him in disbelief. "But why?" asked Sam.

"Because of what he did to all of you. He was an embarrassment to my gender."

The train lurched a final time, sliding the last twenty feet into the shallow swamp, tumbling everyone and rupturing a hole in the side of the car. Serge went headfirst into the wall. The BBB ran to help him up.

"Serge, are you okay?" asked Sam.

"Who?"

"Serge. That's your name."

"I don't know any Serge."

They began to hear helicopters.

"Look at that knot on his forehead," said Teresa. "He really conked himself."

"Serge," said Sam. "Do you know who I am?"

Serge stood up and shook his head.

"We better get that looked at," said Maria.

"You must have the wrong person," said Serge.

The helicopters got louder and louder. Then thuds on the top of the car as a National Guard rescue team rappelled down.

Voices outside. "Hold on! We'll have you out in a second."

Rebecca touched Serge's arm. "You need to sit down."

"Really, you've got me mixed up with someone else," said Serge, warily backing away from the women. "It's been nice talking to you, but I have to be going." And with that, Serge jumped through the ruptured side of the dining car.

"Serge!"

But Serge kept going, deeper and deeper into the swamp.

Epilogue

A Greyhound bus cruised down the Florida Keys on a perfect cloudless day. The ride was comfortable on the Overseas Highway. The bus had plenty of air-conditioning, the tinted windows kept out the heat and bright light, and the insulated diesel provided a soothing, rhythmic amniotic hum.

The wino thought the passenger sitting next to him was nice enough, but he sure was different, even by wino standards.

Click, click, click, click.

The passenger lowered his camera from the window. "Excellent day for photography. The polarized filter is giving me killer stuff."

The wino offered a bottle. "Night Train?"

"No, thanks. . . . Hey! There's the Grassy Key Dairy Bar!" The passenger raised his camera again. Click, click, click, click, click. He lowered it. "The Overseas Railroad has been gone many a year, but the concrete arches remain. You can see them at Long Key and elsewhere, still going strong after a century of Florida hurricanes, outliving the critics and their worst predictions for Flagler's Folly. The trains only ran for twenty-three years, from 1912 to 1935, until an unnamed hurricane dropped a curtain on the works. Then they slapped roads down and built new spans to accommodate more lanes. And now, if you book Amtrak to Key West, you have to get off the train in Miami and take a bus the rest of the way. But imagine what it was like for just a brief period in history. You drive a car over the bridges today, and you sit low on wide bridges with tall railings. But back then, you sat high up in the train, perched naked on the narrow rails with nothing on the sides, just a wide-open view of the sea all around. How precarious and exciting it must have been! . . . Ooooo, there's the Brass Monkey Lounge!" Click, click, click.

The wino began to stand, but Serge grabbed him by the arm and pulled him back down. "You know, the closest you can get today to that Overseas Railroad experience is what we're doing right now: riding the Greyhound, way up high, the illusion of no guardrails." Click, click, click. "Did you know that?"

The wino indicated he hadn't considered it.

"It's true," said Serge. "The place we're in now is called Marathon. And that's the Seven-Mile Bridge coming up. The view is spectacular— better than any mind-altering drugs. I should know. They keep trying to get me to take them, but I just tell them, *no way José!* . . ."

The wino got up again before Serge could stop him and went up front and told the driver he would like to get off now.

"Hey, where are you going? I didn't tell you how it got the name Marathon yet! . . . It's because of how long it was taking them to build the . . . oh, well . . . *Alone again, naturally* . . ." Click, click, click.

Hydraulic brakes wheezed as a Greyhound bus pulled into Key West an hour before sunset, the fading orange light glancing off the silver frame. Passengers carried battered luggage and cardboard boxes into the station. The driver thought the bus was empty until he noticed one last passenger sitting in back, not moving.

The driver walked toward the rear of the bus and looked the man over with concern. The passenger's eyes were unfocused, staring.

"Hey, buddy. You okay?"

Serge nodded.

"We're here. We made it to Key West."

"I know," said Serge. *"I can hear the children, but I can't see them."*

"Will you get off my bus, already?"

Six months later.

A red Jaguar convertible pulled up the drive of the historic Biltmore Hotel in Coral Gables. A valet in white shorts ran around to the driver's side and opened the door for Samantha Bridges.

A red BMW convertible pulled up behind the Jag; Teresa Wellcraft got out. Then a red Mercedes convertible, a red Audi and a red 1962 Corvette. Rebecca Shoals, Maria Conchita and Paige Turner.

The women hugged on the steps of the Mediterranean resort before crossing the lobby for the courtyard.

They set five books on the table and pulled out chairs. Meeting time.

The waiter arrived.

"Strawberry coladas," said Sam. "Five."

"Diplomatico rum," said Maria.

The waiter nodded and left.

Sam patted the cover of her new hardcover. "Did everyone finish it?"

"Imagine that," said Teresa. "Sam's a Krunkleton fan."

"Of course I am. He put us all in the book."

"I think it's his best yet," said Maria.

So did the critics, and Ralph Krunkleton's career had rocketed into mediocrity with the release of *Blender Bender*. Ralph turned Sam's character into an undercover OSS agent, judo-chopping her way through a human jungle of deadly narco-criminals and ex-husbands. Paige became a plucky crusader against the bloody ivory trade in West Africa who is marked for death and overcomes the odds with an unwavering moral code and trusty machine gun. Maria and Teresa teamed up to run a prestigious New York fashion house until their top designer is snuffed by the mob, and they go on a merciless rampage of vengeance and cleavage. Rebecca became a nun with attitude, who finds no sin in hair that holds up under all conditions. Ralph even created cameos for Dee Dee Lowenstein and the other performers from the train, which Tanner Lebos was able to parlay into small but crucial roles in *Police Academy Eight* and *Nine*.

The five women all stopped for a long moment and looked at each other with knowing smiles, all sitting there in thousand-dollar sundresses.

"Has it sunk in yet?" asked Teresa.

"Not remotely," said Maria. "I'm still walking on air."

"It's like I'm permanently trapped in the moment I opened my suitcase," said Paige. "A million dollars takes up a lot less room than I would have thought."

"I remember every second, every detail," said Maria. "We're all standing there looking in Paige's suitcase, thinking, what the heck is going on? That can't be real money."

"Then Sam opened her suitcase . . ."

"No, Teresa opened hers next," corrected Maria. "I told you, I remember every single detail. The National Guard rescued us, Amtrak put us up in suites at the Hilton, and there we were in the room, Paige's open suitcase full of money, nobody breathing, so Teresa opened hers. When we saw the second million dollars, the rest of us literally dove for our own suitcases . . ."

". . . every one full of money," said Rebecca. "And then we all looked at each other and said it at the same time: *'Serge!'*"

"I still can't believe we're being allowed to keep it," said Paige.

"Believe it," said Sam. "We paid that lawyer enough. We paid *everyone* enough."

"What a country," said Rebecca. "You can buy anything."

"You sure we don't have anything to worry about?" said Maria. "I'm still expecting a knock at my door."

"I told you, it's all a matter of knowing which lawyers are wired in with the current administration," Sam explained. "Our attorney knows the Washington attorney who had lunch with the IRS attorney . . ."

"What on earth did he tell him?"

"The truth," said Sam. "That he was representing a Florida attorney who was representing an offshore corporation—remember? The company they set up for us?—and the attorney says the corporation tripped over five million dollars of drug money but had nothing to do with any of the crimes connected to it."

"And they gave us immunity just like that?"

"No, they turned it down," said Sam. "That's when the IRS started getting calls from the staff of congressmen sitting on their budget committee. The ones we contributed to."

"But what about those drug guys? Won't they come looking for it?"

"They think it floated away. Everyone on that train thinks it floated away."

"But if we have the money, what blew into the river?"

"We can thank Ralph Krunkleton for that."

"What do you mean?"

"You remember how everyone in *The Stingray Shuffle* was chasing five million bucks?"

"Yeah?"

"And you remember how Ralph's agent brought a briefcase on the train full of scripts and props to act out the book, toy guns and knives . . . and *play money* . . ."

"Play money blew into the river?"

"It's the only answer."

The drinks arrived, and Sam proposed a toast. "To Serge, wherever he is."

The women clinked glasses.

"To Serge . . ."

A twenty-eight-foot trimaran tacked across the Gulf Stream below the Bahia Honda Bridge in the Florida Keys.

"Hey, Johnny," said Sasha, an alternate Tampa Bay Buccaneers cheerleader and first-string dope date. "Let's go to Key Lois."

Johnny Vegas was a member of the all-virility team, wearing an

America's Cup rip-stop nylon yachting jacket, his black Vidal Sassoon mane snapping in the wind. He stood at the helm, turning the large chrome wheel with panache.

"But baby, Key Lois is off limits," he said. "It's federal law."

"I know," she purred. "It'll be deserted." She came up from behind, sliding her left hand up between his legs. Johnny reacted nonchalantly by losing sensation in both arms and letting go of the wheel. The main boom whipped over their heads and the sailboat momentarily pitched up on its port hull before Johnny grabbed the spinning helm and straightened her out.

"It's right over there," said Sasha, pointing at the low profile of a mangrove island on the horizon.

Johnny set his course for Key Lois, a mile south of Cudjoe Key and twenty miles east of Key West. He approached from the leeward side to make harbor and showcased his seamanship by gently rupturing the center hull on the rocky beach.

"Where's your coke?"

"Right here."

"Dump it out."

He did. She vacuumed.

"Weeeeeeee!" squealed Sasha, hopping over the side and running down the beach ripping off her bikini. "Let's go see the monkeys!"

Johnny was close behind but losing ground, trying to run with his trunks around his knees.

The monkeys Sasha had mentioned were the reason Key Lois was off limits. Charles River Laboratories of Massachusetts, a subsidiary of Bausch & Lomb, uses the island to breed rhesus monkeys for scientific experiments. And breed they do.

But Johnny didn't see a single monkey as he wiggled his swim trunks down to his ankles and flicked them aside with his left foot. He caught up with Sasha near the breakers.

"Where's your cocaine?"

Yes! She wants a little nitro to get her engine primed, then it's off to the races! Johnny ran back and got the swim trunks he had kicked off. He returned and pulled a watertight capsule from a Velcro pocket.

"Gimme that!" She snatched it out of his hands and stuck it up her nose until it was empty.

Her eyes glassed over, and her lower lip jutted and tremored with predatory sensuality. Show time, thought Johnny. But instead of making her amorous, it only made her want to look for monkeys.

"Here, monkey, monkey . . ."

Johnny followed her all the way around the island, four miles total, but no monkeys. They splashed out into a few inches of water to skirt the last outcropping of mangroves before returning to the sailboat. Johnny felt a hand on his thigh. The silly dust had kicked in. Sasha put her mouth to his ear and whispered in a husky voice: "I *love* seafaring men. Let's fuck in the boat . . . I feel a big blow's a-comin'."

Johnny developed a certain carefree spring in his step as they held hands and skipped merrily through the shallow water. They rounded the mangrove bend, and there was the boat.

Sasha screamed. Johnny gasped.

The trimaran—what was left of it—was covered with monkeys. Hundreds of chattering, swinging, shitting monkeys, ripping up the sails, tearing the stuffing out of life preservers, ransacking the galley. The monkeys cavorted across the stern and hung by their tails from the cabin railing. A dozen monkeys armed with marlinespikes and galley utensils jumped onto the beach and charged. Sasha screamed and took off in the opposite direction. The monkeys ran past Johnny and chased Sasha back around the bend. Johnny fell to his knees in the water. "Why me? . . ."

When he finally looked up again, he saw something he would never forget as long as he lived. It was a fleeting but searing image, like a Loch Ness sighting.

What he saw was a wiry man in a royal blue astronaut jumpsuit. The man stood atop the sailboat's cabin, arms akimbo, a monkey on each shoulder and more monkeys clustered around his feet in loyalty and affection. Then the man jumped down off the boat and disappeared into the mangrove thicket, and the hundreds of monkeys followed.

A   NOTE   ON   THE   TYPE

The text of this book was set in a face called Garibaldi Light, named after the influential Venetian typographer Pietro Garibaldi (1657–1708), who honed his craft at the royal mint under the master Von Blatt. The revivalist Pietro developed Garibaldi directly from recuttings of the original Sommevoire forgings using the Kronen-Leipzig method . . . Oh, what's the use? I can't believe I'm still stuck in this cubicle writing these fucking Notes on the Type in the backs of books by so-called talents, who get rich and famous while I'm left to squeeze drops of interest from the life of some dickless gnome with a Gutenberg press, like "the flamboyant Jöns Heikkenen, whose bold proposal to add three new letters between *M* and *N* was dismissed by the critics as 'sheer excess,'" or "the tortured brilliance of Otto Nijinsky, who conceived his most celebrated fonts during bouts of madness and spent his final years wandering the grounds of the sanitarium talking to his imaginary friend, Bobo the Alphabet Chimp." But nobody notices. Because nobody reads this shit. Then they bring people around on the office tour. "Who's in there?" "Oh, that's just the Notes on the Type guy." And then they laugh. Just like Nicole in accounting laughed when I asked her out. What does she see in that Roger? So I confronted her in the cafeteria: "Don't lie to me! It's because Roger writes About the Author, isn't it, you whore!"

F
DORSEY

Dorsey, Tim.

The stingray
shuffle.

DATE			